Also by Sage Webb

The Unremarkable Circumstances of Inmate 17656-090
Love & Other Misunderstandings

The Venturi Effect

The
Venturi Effect
a Novel

By Sage Webb

STONEMAN HOUSE PRESS, L.L.C.
HOUSTON

www.stonemanhouse.com

The Venturi Effect

Copyright © 2020 Sage Webb
All rights reserved, including the right of reproduction, in whole or in part, in any form.

Paperback ISBN 978-1-7337379-4-4
Ebook ISBN 978-1-7337379-5-1

Published in the United States of America
by Stoneman House Press, L.L.C. 2020

This story is a work of fiction. Names, characters, and incidents are the products of the author's imagination. In the case of real places, these locales are used in a fictitious manner. Any resemblance to actual people or events is unintended and completely coincidental.

Jacket author photo © Warren Talley
All rights reserved. Used with permission.

Jacket design © Stoneman House Press, L.L.C.
All rights reserved.

STONEMAN HOUSE PRESS, L.L.C.
Houston, TX
U.S.A.
www.stonemanhouse.com

To P. Laycock

For being there. . . .

Table of Contents

Chapter 1

Chapter 2

Chapter 3

Chapter 4

Chapter 5

Chapter 6

Chapter 7

Chapter 8

Chapter 9

Chapter 10

Chapter 11

Sneak Peek

Chapter 1
Carny

Red metal boxes lined the wood-railed tourist boardwalk, giving children access to fish food if the kids could finagle quarters from parents wilted and forlorn in the triple-digit Gulf Coast heat. With the food, kids could create great frenzies of red drum, snook, spotted sea trout, or whatever fish species gathered at the boardwalk's pilings in agitated silver vortices. Devlin Winters lifted her ballcap and wiped a sleeve across her brow. She favored long-sleeved t-shirts for just this reason—their mopping properties . . . and to protect her from the Galveston Bay sun in its unrelenting effort to grill her and the other boardwalk barkers. In the two years she'd been on the boardwalk, she'd never fed the fish.

A kid stopped beside one of the boxes.

"Can I have a quarter, mommy?" the boy asked.

He looked about eight or nine, though Devlin had little interest in guessing accurately the ages of the pint-sized patrons fueling her income stream.

"I'm not sure I have one," the mom replied.

She appeared a bit younger than Devlin, maybe late twenties.

Once upon a time, Devlin would have looked at a mother like that and made a snide remark about crib lizards and dead ends, but nine bucks an hour in the sun makes it awfully hard for a carny to judge others. Lacking a more interesting subject, Devlin watched the woman paw through a backpack-sized purse. The chick produced a quarter and handed it to the kid, who dropped it into the box's payment slot and ground the dial, catching in his miniature palm a limited portion of the fish food that spilled out of the machine when he lifted the metal flap. The majority of the pellets rained down onto the wooden boardwalk planks, bounced, and disappeared through the cracks between the planks.

Devlin fancied she could hear the tiny fish-food BBs hitting brown water: plink, plink, plink. Once upon another time, when she was still at Sondheim Baker, but toward the end, she would go outside in the middle of the day. Instead of sitting at her desk, drafting appellate briefs for the Seventh Circuit, she would ride the elevator down to La Salle, down seven hundred feet of glass and stainless steel and terribly expensive architecture. She would drop down those elevator cables at random times, at times rich, successful attorneys should have been at their desks. And she would turn left out of that great glass building the color of the sky and walk over to the river, that nothing-like-the-Styx river that mankind had turned back on itself, contrary to nature.

She would stand and look down into the water, which was sometimes emerald, sometimes the color of jeans before they are ever washed. Once or twice, she had reached into her purse (expensive purses, Magnificent Mile purses from Burberry and Gucci and Hermès) and she had dug around until she'd found a penny. She'd dropped the penny into the river and, even now, on the sauna-hot boardwalk with the whistle of the kid-sized train behind her and the pulses of unimpressive pop music overhead, she was sure she could hear those pennies hit the Chicago River, hit and sink down, down, and farther down.

Plink. Plink. Pli—

"You want to try this one?"

The fish-feeding entertainment had run its course and the mother stood in front of the water-gun game Devlin guarded. She gestured toward Devlin and the row of stools in front of their narrow-barreled water guns.

"Is it hard?" The kid looked up at his mom, and the mom turned to Devlin.

"He can do it, right?" she asked. "I mean, he can figure it out, right?"

"Sure, it's easy." Devlin lifted her cap for another mop across her hairline, and then wiped perspiration away from her eyes under her sunglasses. "It's fun, little dude," she said to the kid in his obviously secondhand clothes.

She wanted to care, wanted to be "affable" or whatever it is a carny should be toward summer's ice-cream-eating cash-crop flux of kids. But wanting alone, without effort, is never enough.

The mom held out a five-dollar bill.

"You both wanna do it? I gotta have more than one person to run it for a prize." Devlin rubbed the top of her right flip flop and foot against her left calf.

"Oh," the woman said, "I wasn't planning to play. I'm no good at these things."

"Um," Devlin stepped out of the shade of the game's nook and cast her eyes up and down the boardwalk, "we'll find some more kids." She took the woman's money without looking away from the walkway and the beggarly seabirds.

A young couple, likely playing hooky from jobs in Houston, held the hands of a girl sporting jet-black pigtails and lopsided glasses.

"Step right up, princess. You wanna win a unicorn, right?" Devlin reached back into her game nook and snatched a pink toy from the wall of unicorns, butterflies, bees, and unlicensed lookalikes of characters from movies Devlin had never heard of. She dangled the thing in the girl's direction.

"Would you like to play, *habibti?*" The mom jiggled the girl's arm.

"Tell ya what." Devlin turned to the mom. "The whole family can play for five bucks. We're just trying to get some games going, give away some prizes to these cuties." She turned back to the first mother. "And don't worry, I'll give him three games for the fiver."

"Hear that, Vince? You'll get to play a few times. Is that cool?"

Vince picked at his crotch. Devlin looked away.

"Yes, we'll all play," the second mother said. The dad pulled a twenty out of a pocket and Devlin started to make change while Vince's mom hefted Vince onto a stool.

"Just a five back," the father said. "We'll play a few times."

"Sure thing," Devlin replied. Then she raised her voice to run through the rules of the game, to explain how the water guns spraying and hitting the targets would raise plastic boats in a boat race to buzzers at the top of the game contraption. She offered some tired words of encouragement, got nods from everyone, and counted down. "Three, two, one."

She pushed the button and the game loosed a bell sound across the boardwalk.

A guy in waiter's livery hurried past, hustling toward one of the boardwalk's various restaurants, with their patios overlooking the channel and Galveston Bay. He'd be serving people margaritas and gimlets in just a few more steps and minutes. Devlin wanted a gimlet.

She drew a deep breath, turned back to her charges. "Close race here, friends."

An '80s-vintage Hunter sailboat slid past in the channel, leaving Galveston Bay and making its way to one of the marinas up the waterway on Clear Lake.

When Devlin again turned back to her marksmen, the girl's mother's boat had almost reached the buzzer.

"Looks like we've got a leader here. Come on, madam. You're almost there."

Devlin checked her watch. She'd be off in less than an hour. She'd be back on her own boat fifteen minutes after that, with an unopened bottle of Bombay Sapphire and a net full of limes rocking above the galley sink.

The buzzer blared.

"Looks like we have a winner. Congratulations, madam." Devlin clapped three times. "Now would you like a unicorn, a butterfly, or," Devlin pulled a four-inch-tall creature from the wall, not knowing how to describe it, "this little guy?" She held it out for the woman's inspection.

"*Habibti*, you pick." The mom patted her daughter's back. The kid didn't say anything, just pointed at the butterfly.

"Butterfly it is, beautiful." Devlin unclipped the toy from the wall of plush junk and handed it to the girl. "Well, we've got some competition for this next one, folks, now that you're all warmed up. Take a breather. We'll start the next game when you're ready."

"Can I try?" A boy pulled at a broad-shouldered man's hand, leading the guy toward the row of stools. It was hard to tell parentage with these kids and their mixed-up step- and half- and melded-in-other-ways families, and with this one, the kid's dark curls and earnest eyes contrasted with the dude's Nordic features and reminded Devlin of a roommate she'd had in undergrad, a girl from Haiti who'd taught Devlin about *pikliz*. Devlin hadn't thought about Haitian food in ages. She decided she would google it later and see what she could find in Houston. A drive to discover somewhere new to eat would do her good.

Any chance at plantains and *pikliz* would have to wait, though. The kid and the dude now stood in front of Devlin. Ultra-dark sunglasses hid the guy's eyes, and a ballcap with a local yacht brokerage's logo embroidered on it cast a shadow over his face. Devlin cocked her head. She narrowed her eyes and hoped her own sunglasses were doing as good a job of being barriers. He reminded her of—

"Still time to add another player?" The dude pulled out a wallet and handed Devlin a ten.

"Sure," she said. "Is this for both of you? You should give it a try, too. This'll get you both in on the next two games."

She didn't wait for confirmation. She shoved the money in the box beside her control board of buzzer buttons and waved the guy and his kid toward stools on the far side of the now-veteran players already seated.

"Uh, sure," the guy said, putting a hand on the kid's back and guiding him to a seat.

Running through the rules again, Devlin envisioned those gimlets awaiting her. With Bombay Sapphire dancing before her, she counted down and then pushed the button to blast the bell and launch the game. The buzzer over the newcomer father's boat's track rang moments later. What kind of scummy guy just trounces a kid like that? Devlin rolled her eyes behind the obscuring lenses.

"Looks like our new guy is the winner, ladies and gentlemen. Now, would you like a unicorn, a butterfly, or this little dude?" Devlin again proffered the hard-to-describe creature, walking it over for the fellow to examine.

"What is it?" the guy asked.

Devlin shrugged. "What do you get when you cross an elephant and a rhino?"

The guy's sunglasses gave away nothing. But something she couldn't articulate made her feel like he was studying her.

"An 'el-if-I-know," she said.

Still nothing . . . except that feeling of scrutiny.

"Dude, I've got no idea," she replied to her reflection in the lenses.

"Grant, which one do you want?" The guy turned away and handed the unnamed creature to the kid, and then gestured at the identifiable unicorns and butterflies hanging on the wall over Devlin's control station.

"Those are for girls," Grant said, waving at the recognizable plushes on the wall.

"So is this one okay?" The guy patted the thing in the kid's hand.

Grant wrinkled his nose. "Yeah, I guess so."

"All right, folks. You've all got another game coming here. Competition is fierce. Who's gonna take this last one?" Devlin strode back to her place at the control board.

"Deep inhale, everyone. Relax. All right, here we go. Three, two, one." She pushed the starting button.

Up shot the new guy's boat again. What a bastard. Poor Grant. This patriarchal showmanship would be worth about five or ten grand at the therapist's in twenty-five years.

Out in the channel, two jetskis purred past, headed toward the bay. The day's heat had cracked and the sky hinted at evening. Behind her, the victory whistle sounded. She turned. The dude with the sunglasses sat patting Grant's shoulder, with Grant's boat at the top of its track. So the guy wasn't a complete fool.

"A new winner here, ladies and gentlemen." She walked to Grant's stool. "Now, little man, because you've won two prizes today, you can trade that one you've got and this one you're going to get for one bigger one. You can pick from these if you want."

She pointed at a row with only-slightly-bigger caterpillars, ambiguous characters, and a dog in a purple vest.

"That one," Grant said, pointing at the dog.

"That one it is, good sir." Devlin retrieved the dog, taking back the first creature and returning it to the wall in the process.

As she retraced her steps to Grant, the dog in her hand, fuzzy pictures coalesced in a fog and mist of bygone memories.

Devlin handed the dog to Grant. "There you go."

She looked at the guy again, focusing on him for longer than she should have, feeling him perhaps doing the same to her. Yes, she had it right: it was him. She pushed a flyaway strand of bleached hair back into place beneath her cap and turned away.

"Thanks for playing this afternoon, folks," she called. "Enjoy your evening on the boardwalk."

The parents gathered their kids, and Devlin walked back toward her control board. Waiting for Grant and *him* to head off down the row of games and rides, she fussed with the cashbox and then lifted her water bottle to her lips. She could feel *him* and the kid lingering, feel them failing to move along, failing to leave her to forget what once was and to focus on thoughts of gimlets at sunset on the deck of a rotten old trawler.

"Um." His voice sounded low and halting behind her. A vacuum, all heat and silence, followed and then a masculine inhale . . . and then the awkward pause.

He cleared his throat.

"Sorry to interrupt, but are you from Chicago?"

Chapter 2
Death, or Detention, and Taxes

People said Xavier Charles didn't write well. He knew they said it behind his back: the paralegals, his secretary (if she was going to gossip about him, he certainly wasn't going to refer to her as an administrative assistant), his colleagues, the judges (the lowly magistrates and the vaunted Article IIIs), the Federal Bar Association president who'd declined his offer of a column in the monthly FBA newsletter . . . all of them. But Xavier didn't care. Uncle Sam didn't pay him to write; Uncle Sam paid Xavier Charles to indict and convict. So what if his indictments weren't page-turners?

An indictment serves to notify the soon-to-be-condemned that a passel of his (and sometimes her) peers thinks he (and sometimes she) qualifies as a brigand and must face justice. Once those sixteen to twenty-three people of the grand jury did their work and returned the inevitable indictment (Xavier Charles did not waste time presenting less than overwhelming evidence), Xavier did what his Creator had put him on earth to do: convict bad guys (and, less frequently, girls). Assistant United States Attorney Xavier Charles served his country by keeping it safe. Safe, wholesome, law abiding, clean.

Indicting Viggo Bryson continued this trajectory of patriotic service. Having Viggo arrested at Detroit

Metropolitan Airport as Viggo had stood in line to board that flight to Zurich with his kid had just been lagniappe before the unsealing—really, unveiling—of the indictment, a sort of bonus for the three years' toil Xavier had put into the "poorly-written" document (Xavier had heard that smug little prig Assistant Federal Public Defender in the stairwell at the courthouse). Given that arrest, the defendant's *petit* attempt at flight, Xavier had no worries about tomorrow's detention hearing. Viggo Bryson would not be getting bond.

Xavier pushed back from his desk. At the holiday open house at the Federal Public Defender's Office, he'd noticed that every office, even those of the support staff, held an Aeron chair. It didn't annoy him, such obscene decadence. But as a steward of the taxpayers' hard-earned dollars, he would never permit an Aeron chair at his desk. Let those public defenders, those alleged servants of the indigent, sit on their seven-hundred-dollar thrones. As a public servant, he took pride in humility.

On his way to the elevator bank, he noted, as he did each evening, that every office sat dark and empty. He couldn't remember the last time he'd left before his colleagues. In the elevator, he checked his phone—he avoided checking his personal phone while working. No texts. The building's lobby was dark, and he returned his phone to his pocket as he pushed open the door and walked out into the lingering summer twilight of the Midwest in July. At the bus stop, he pulled his phone out again and opened his ebook reader to continue the Winston Churchill book he'd started two weeks ago after the piece had received a decent review in the Grand Rapids Press. And he waited.

"Good evening," he mumbled to the overweight, bearded, liver-spotted driver when the bus finally arrived. God willing, the warm, dark, St. Kitts complexion he had inherited from his mother would save him from such splotchy aging.

The man nodded and the bus door gave a squeaky exhalation as it shut.

Four stops later, Xavier stepped off the bus in front of his building, an old furniture factory now housing trendy condos. Xavier didn't do trendy, but the condos were convenient, close to work and the courthouse, affordable, and friendly toward pets. People like Viggo Bryson might want penthouses with private hot tubs; Xavier Charles just wanted a comfortable place to call home with the boys.

"Menelaus! Agamemnon!" he shouted as he opened his condo door.

From the study, the boys emerged, great gray felines, as majestic as their Greek namesakes. Xavier hadn't weighed them recently, but at Menelaus' last visit to the vet, the cat had tipped the scale at seventeen pounds.

Xavier set his briefcase down and hung his suit coat on the valet.

"How are we tonight, boys?"

Agamemnon rubbed his leg.

In the kitchen, Xavier washed his hands and checked the cats' supply of food and water. He opened the refrigerator and retrieved a bowl of egg salad. He'd baked bread on Sunday, and now pulled the remainder of the loaf out of the plastic breadbox on the counter.

"So what shall we watch tonight, boys? We can't stay up too late. Big day tomorrow. Shall we finish *Jeremiah Johnson?*"

Xavier had a fondness for old movies and admired actors like Robert Redford, Paul Newman, Yul Brynner. Most nights, he and the cats would watch a few minutes of old films like *The Sting* and *Butch Cassidy and the Sundance Kid* with dinner atop TV tray tables.

"Maybe we should celebrate a little, though, huh? We've got Viggo Bryson behind bars and he's going to stay there. So maybe we should cut loose? How about *The Magnificent Seven?*" He paused. "And some of this?"

He pulled a plate of chocolate cake out of the refrigerator. He'd made it with applesauce instead of oil and it had turned out better than he'd expected.

Agamemnon rubbed against him again.

"Oh, you're right, Aggy. We need to finish what we start. We'll watch the rest of *Jeremiah Johnson.*"

He pulled back the plastic wrap over the cake and sliced into the pastry, arranging a fat piece of it on a tea-cup-thin, robin-egg-blue dessert plate. Once in front of the television with his repast, and the cats on pillows on the couch, he allowed himself one bite of the cake to start the meal. How good it tasted. How good everything tasted with Viggo Bryson finally put away.

***

"These allegations just relate to business transactions, correct, counsel?"

U.S. Magistrate Judge Robyn Morgan raised her eyebrows and peered over the top of her glasses' gold frames.

Xavier Charles didn't flinch.

"Your Honor, when agents took Mr. Bryson into custody, he and his son were standing at the gate at Detroit Metropolitan Airport, about to board a flight to Zurich. Your Honor, I don't think any set of circumstances could better indicate the flight risk Mr. Bryson presents here. Section 3142's enumerated factors militate in favor of detention here: we have a person with extensive resources, who was arrested at the airport awaiting a flight to Switzerland. The offense, as charged in the indictment, involves a byzantine web of fraudulent transactions with a loss amount reaching over $25,000,000. While each count carries a five-year maximum sentence, the advisory sentencing guidelines start with a base offense level of twenty-eight. Even without any enhancements or criminal history, that level alone produces a potential sentence of seventy-eight to ninety-seven months of custody. The government would advocate for stacking the multiple five-year-max counts to achieve at least a ninety-seven-month sentence if these proceedings result in Mr. Bryson's conviction. An eight-year sentence likely appears quite lengthy to Mr. Bryson, who seems to lack any prior criminal history."

"Mr. Charles, I'm not sure the potential sentence here is a factor for me to consider."

Judge Morgan's tone seemed short, but Xavier didn't mind. Some defense counsel called her Send 'Em Home Again Morgan behind her back, but the Zurich flight loomed too large here. Even Robyn Morgan wasn't going to release Viggo Bryson on bond.

"Your Honor, under section 3142(g)(1), courts consider the nature of the charged offense. That nature here includes a significant potential prison sentence. A sentence that could easily make Mr. Bryson—"

Xavier couldn't stop himself from using the name rather than his beloved label "defendant." This case warranted a personal touch. He shot a glance over his shoulder toward Viggo Bryson, whose own shoulders had rounded as he sat at the defense's table in his orange jumpsuit and tangerine-colored jail-issue shower sandals.

"Well," Xavier continued, "such a sentence could make Mr. Bryson consider another attempt to flee to a country like Switzerland, one that may or may not aid us in returning him to this country to answer these charges."

"I'm going to stop you there a minute, Mr. Charles." Magistrate Judge Morgan tapped her pen on the wooden ledge in front of her bench. "Ms. Stockton, what kind of community ties are we looking at here?"

Xavier pressed his lips together and stepped away from the podium. He set his file on the prosecution's table and took his seat, looking forward as defense counsel Irene Stockton stepped to the lectern.

"Your Honor, Mr. Bryson owns a home in East Grand Rapids. He also has a large home on the lake in Grand Haven. He has hunting camps near Traverse City and in the Upper Peninsula. My understanding is he has a large sailboat in Grand Haven. While he doesn't have much family in the area, he has sole custody of his son, and these extensive assets in the district. He has lived in Grand Rapids for almost four years and his business is now based here. He has no criminal history, not even a traffic ticket. And, Your Honor, I just want to return to the basics for a moment. This is a tax charge based on business transactions. This is not a violent offense or one involving drugs or guns. Honestly, I think the government may be overreacting a little here."

Xavier put his left elbow on the table in front of him and dropped his head into that arm's hand, resting it there to look up at Stockton. Despite her pithy "overreacting" remark, she looked nervous, her hair sagging loose from the sticks trying to hold it in a bun, a bun that had failed to stay centered. People talked about her at Federal Bar Association events like she was some up-and-coming star, but she didn't impress Xavier. She seemed gullible, like she believed her clients. Foolish.

"Now, I do have to ask you, Ms. Stockton," Judge Morgan broke in. "Can you explain this arrest at DTW?"

"Your Honor, the government is making much of Mr. Bryson and his son traveling to Switzerland, but Mr. Bryson has nothing to hide on this point. He has a small ski chalet on Lake Zurich, just like he has a home in Split, Croatia, and a condo in Rome. I don't know the details of these residences, whether he owns them or has some other arrangement for their use, but he travels to Europe regularly to stay at these properties. His son Grant is homeschooled and enjoys traveling with his father, and it's my understanding that Grant's favorite destination is the Zurich home and Mr. Bryson was taking Grant there for Grant's birthday."

Xavier sat up and smoothed his tie as Stockton paused. Stockton picked up her legal pad and straightened, telegraphing to Xavier that it would be his turn at the podium again in a breath or two.

"The timing," Irene Stockton continued, "was coincidence here. Mr. Bryson did not know of the sealed indictment. He was taking his son to Switzerland for the boy's birthday. That's all, Your Honor."

"Mr. Charles? Anything to add?" Judge Morgan looked over the spectacles again.

It was time. Xavier stood and stepped to the lectern.

"Your Honor, the government struggles to see a trip to a non-extradition nation, two weeks—well, thirteen days— before the boy's birthday, as coincidence."

Judge Morgan sat back in her chair. She was listening.

And Stockton was giving her client a look. How could she not know her client's whelp's birthday?

It all felt so warm and right.

"Nor does the government consider it a coincidence," Xavier continued, "when agents spoke with Mr. Bryson's business partner just thirty hours before the arrest at the airport, and Mr. Bryson moved $18 million dollars from a Chase Bank account to an offshore account just six hours before the arrest."

He paused. Inhaled.

"To the government," he said, "these circumstances aren't coincidence. They represent a flight risk."

He closed his file.

"That's all, Your Honor."

He sat down.

Judge Morgan shut her eyes, removed her glasses, and pinched at the bridge of her nose. Her case manager, a young-ish fellow named Mark Hopkins, clicked at a keyboard behind his imperceptible wall, a demarcation of disinterest. The marshal behind the defense table sighed. Xavier waited.

"Counsel," Judge Morgan opened her eyes, shook her forearms to free the sleeves of her robe, and sat forward, "I recognize that this is a close question. Mr. Bryson has no criminal history and significant ties to the community. On the other hand, agents arrested him at Detroit Metropolitan Airport, at the gate, while he and his son were waiting to board a plane for a trip to a non-extradition country. The government's proffer of evidence seems to suggest he moved a significant sum of money to an offshore account shortly before arriving at the airport, and it also suggests that he may have been aware of the sealed indictment and/or the imminent arrest through a business associate who had contact with agents the day before the attempted trip. While there is a potential benign explanation for this trip in the form of his son's birthday, it also appears that Mr. Bryson may have been attempting to leave the country, possibly to avoid arrest. I have the power to craft conditions of release to address the circumstances here, conditions such as barring travel beyond Grand Rapids, and while the probation office has confirmed in its report to me that Mr. Bryson surrendered his passport upon booking, I'm afraid, given Mr. Bryson's not inconsiderable resources, that detention presents the only option to ensure his presence for these proceedings."

Xavier didn't smile. He heard Irene Stockton exhale at the table to his right. He would share a bottle of Martinelli's sparkling apple cider with the boys tonight. Or at least he would enjoy the cider and he'd give the boys a scoop of tuna-in-oil atop their kibble for dinner.

Judge Morgan ran through some perfunctory remarks about remanding Viggo Bryson to the marshals' custody and about discovery and deadlines. Xavier handed a notebook of discs in sleeves to Irene Stockton. Her bun had sagged farther toward her collar. When squirrely case manager Mark Hopkins adjourned the court and called for all to rise, Xavier shot a look at Viggo Bryson. Orange suited him.

Chapter 3
Voodoo Priestess

Devlin didn't want to turn around. She didn't want to talk to this fellow with the kid named Grant. She didn't want to remember that she was from Chicago. And she didn't want to be right about who this guy was. But she couldn't stand here staring at cheap stuffed junk toys until the dude and the kid moved on.

"Yeah," she turned from her boardwalk-game control panel to face the man, "I'm from Chicago, Nils."

"Devlin Winters."

Devlin couldn't tell if Nils Bryson sounded surprised or horrified. She hadn't seen him in seven years, thirty pounds, and innumerable gimlets. Back then, she'd been sporting a couple hundred bucks' worth of Balayage highlights and a size-four frame that had invited viperous epithets from the insecure. Gone were the days.

She lifted her cap and smoothed her hair. After re-situating the cap, she glanced down at Grant, who had hold of Nils Bryson's hand.

"Small world," she said.

"I didn't know you were in Texas." Nils sounded like he was fumbling. "I thought you were doing the Big Law thing. Someone had said you'd become Sondheim Baker's youngest partner in history."

"I was." Devlin didn't offer anything else. She slipped her foot out of its flip flop and rubbed its calloused sole against the opposite ankle.

Nils shifted his weight. "Oh," he said, glancing down at the kid, "Grant, this is Miss Devlin Winters. She and I grew up together."

He seemed to wait for the kid to react.

Grant fixed dark eyes on Devlin's face, held out a miniature hand. "Miss Winters, I'm Grant Bryson. How do you do?"

Devlin swallowed a smirk. "How'd you do, little man? You can call me Devlin." She shook the kid's hand. It was warm and clammy, but the kid had a better grip than she'd expected from a mini-human.

"So, um, how long you been down on the Gulf Coast?" Nils asked.

Why didn't he wrap up this little walk down memory lane? What was the point of all this?

From the sun's declining angle, Devlin figured she would be off the clock in less than an hour. That almost-hour was going to seem like ten if Nils didn't move on and instead insisted on discussing a world long dead and obliterated to Devlin.

"I got down here about two years ago."

Maybe Nils felt the unresponsiveness. He glanced up the boardwalk, hesitated, removed his sunglasses and turned them around to rest, looking out, against the back of his neck, with their cotton keeper hanging down the middle of his chest.

"I've been down here since just after the last time I saw you, I think. Wow. How long has it been? Seven years. Wow." He paused again. "We should catch up."

Why?

Nils glanced at his watch. It was some cheap Casio with an after-market nylon band. Devlin rubbed her right hand up and down the cotton sleeve over her left forearm.

"When are you done here? You should let Grant and me buy you dinner. I'd love to hear what brought you down here and what you've been up to."

Seriously? To what purpose?

"I'm off at four." Devlin didn't know why she said it.

"Great. We'll wander back over around then and get you. You can tell Grant that once upon a time I was cool—that I haven't always been a stick-in-the-mud uncle with no sense of humor."

Whatever.

It would be a dinner she didn't have to pay for. And she would order cocktails with gin better than Bombay Sapphire.

***

"So where shall we go?" Nils sounded cheerful, upbeat, an hour later. "We can stay on the boardwalk and do tourist fare, or just stay here in Kemah but not on the boardwalk, or go across the bridge and find something over there, or head south toward Galveston. What about going to the island? Get something on the beach or down around the Strand? Grant hasn't been down there yet."

Devlin looked at the kid and at her once-friend, shrugged.

"I'm easy," she said. "If you're paying, I'm eating."

Nils's look in response came across crooked, curious.

"Let's do the island then," she said. "If you haven't been to the island yet, buddy, we should do that." She felt like she should try to include Grant. "You like the beach?"

"Yeah! We have a big house on the beach in Michigan! And a boat!" Grant's little-kid grin revealed a missing tooth Devlin hadn't noticed before. "I'll bet the beach here isn't as good as home, though."

Devlin arched an eyebrow at Nils. "Kid's done okay for himself, it sounds like."

"Grant is Viggo's son," Nils answered the eyebrow. "He's staying with me down here for a bit while Viggo gets some business affairs in order. Viggo lives in Michigan now—Grand Rapids."

"Viggo's a dad?" Devlin gave Nils a disbelieving look.

Viggo Bryson was two years older than Nils, if she remembered correctly, and he'd been the hell-raiser of the two brothers. She couldn't imagine Viggo Bryson married with a litter of pups, though Viggo and Nils likely wouldn't have imagined Devlin Winters as an alcoholic, too-heavy-in-her-eyes-but-probably-not-fat carny on a Gulf Coast boardwalk.

"Yeah, Viggo and Grant's mom met in St. Kitts nine or ten years ago." Nils broke off and Devlin figured, knowing Viggo, there was some story here.

"I miss my dad," Grant volunteered.

Nils shot Devlin what she figured was a request over Grant's head: help me. Devlin couldn't fathom what he wanted her to do. Or why. They were all standing beside the boardwalk's entryway arch. She turned toward the parking lot. Nils knelt in front of the kid.

"Your dad just needs to fix some stuff, so you and he can go to Switzerland again, okay? He just has to work some stuff out for his job, okay?" His tone led Devlin to believe Viggo Bryson was still in the hot water that had been the hallmark of Viggo's life when she'd known him.

"Switzerland, huh? You like going to Switzerland?" She didn't know why she'd decided to go down this road.

Grant leaned against his uncle's chest and turned deep eyes up to Devlin. He nodded, slowly—like he was confirming the existence of a Natural Law.

"Well, you'll like Galveston, too," she said. "Come on." She cocked her head toward the parking lot. "You're uncle's driving."

No one needed to see the dented and rusted, more than a decade old, Suzuki Reno she called her car. How the mighty had fallen. Nils stood back up, keeping hold of Grant's hand.

"Come on, buddy, this'll be fun. Here," he reached for Devlin's upper arm and gave it a we-were-teenagers-together nudge, "grab his other arm. Here we go."

Nils started to swing Grant's arm and seemed to want Devlin to do the same. Devlin debated rolling her eyes. Instead, she picked up the kid's free hand and followed Nils's lead, swinging the kid's arm.

"One, two, three!" Nils lifted and Devlin copied his effort, and Grant took a stride and sailed a few feet forward on the swing of arms.

"Again!" He giggled.

Devlin humored her new companions until they reached a beat-up Wrangler.

"This is me," Nils said, releasing Grant's hand and digging in a pocket.

He unlocked the Jeep and folded his seat forward to let Grant shinny into the back seat. Then he walked around the front of the car and opened the passenger door.

"Here we go." He grinned at Devlin as he held the door open.

She shook her head. When they'd been in high school, he'd stripped naked one summer night and gone for a swim in a fountain off Michigan Avenue. She'd shouted a warning when she'd spotted the cops, and he'd taken off like lightning, a grin the breadth of the Chicago River on his face. She fancied she was seeing that grin again, and she couldn't explain why her scalp felt tingly.

In the Jeep, Nils turned to her. "So what do you like on the island? What sounds good? You ever go to Gaido's? Technically, Viggo is treating, so we might as well enjoy ourselves. He wants to make sure Grant has a good visit, so I've got some funding for adventure."

"Well, if that's the case, Gaido's it is," Devlin said. A couple nice peach bellinis, some red fish or salmon, a slice of key-lime cheesecake: that sounded like a decent dinner, one worth putting up with a playboy's crib lizard for.

"You feeling seafood, bud?" Nils glanced in the rearview mirror at Grant.

"Salmon, maybe," Grant replied, all profundity and contemplation.

"So what brought you down here?" Nils checked his blind spot as he changed lanes.

"Needed a change." Devlin liked that answer. She had tried out a couple others, but that one suited her the best, and it had proved more social than some of the others.

Nils took his eyes off the road long enough to offer a skeptical cock of the chin. "D. Winters, we've known each other a long time."

"I needed a change." Maybe this dinner wasn't going to be worth it.

"Okay." The traffic light in front of them turned green, and Nils shifted the Jeep into second and then third. "Where you living?"

Fourth gear, fifth. Devlin watched Highway 146 unspool. "In Kemah there." *Devil take this interrogation.* Another red light. "I'm at the marina there. On a trawler."

"You're living on a boat?"

"Yep." The light changed and the local strip club and adult-novelties shop whipped past.

"What are you on?" Nils shifted.

"An old Grand Banks."

Devlin could at least claim residency on one of the finest trawler brands out there, a distinguished boat with classic lines. A thirty-six-footer of style and pedigree. Something that would make a dude she'd grown up with at Chicago Yacht Club realize she was still "of that world." God save the mechanic's lien and reprobates at boatyards who valued cash on the barrelhead sufficiently to part with old trawlers for a song.

"Nice," Nils affirmed. "I'm on a 1980 Chris Craft Commander. A forty-one-footer. Her name is *Mambo.*"

He paused, like he wanted Devlin to volunteer something about her boat. But what was there to say about an old wooden boat one bought because it was cheap, and it was cheap because the former owner had died before he could pay his repair bill at the boatyard?

"Her stern had a hailing port of New Orleans painted on it when I bought her," Nils cranked back up, "so I wonder if she was named for the word for voodoo priestesses rather than the Latin dance. Maybe. Anyway, I'm not one for changing boat names."

They crossed the bridge over Dickinson Bayou, and Devlin stared out at the shrimp boats moored in the bayou, watched the old workboats slide past.

"You believe in voodoo, Uncle Nils?" Grant asked from the back seat.

"No, bud, not really." Nils glanced in the rearview mirror. "But it's still a thing in Louisiana, and my boat was from over there. So maybe the people who owned my boat before me had a thing about it. About voodoo."

"I don't believe in that rubbish," the kid stated.

Devlin leaned an elbow on the tiny lip of the Jeep's passenger window and dropped her head into the hand attached to that arm. She'd earned an appetizer, too, at this point. Some sort of shrimp cocktail.

"How about you, Ms. Winters? What's the old Grand Banks' name?" Nils sounded like some middle-management dad at a PTA meeting.

Devlin didn't lift her head. "*A`uku.* It's the name she had when I bought her. I googled it. It means swordfish in Hawaiian."

"I went to Hawai`i last fall," Grant called from his back-seat sanctuary. "My dad took me to see the volcano. We walked on hot lava. My feet got *so* hot."

"It probably wasn't lava still when you walked on it," Nils said. "It was probably rock by then."

"No, it was basically lava, Uncle Nils. And very hot. My dad carried me at the end because it was too hot. He had really expensive boots on, so his feet didn't get so hot."

"Your dad always liked really expensive stuff." Devlin shifted, sat up.

"You know my dad?"

Devlin flipped the sun visor down and flipped up the cover over the mirror. She removed her ballcap and pulled the rubber band out of her hair, freeing her ponytail, letting it disintegrate.

"Yeah, little man, I grew up with your dad and uncle and a couple other kids. We all lived in the same building on Lake Michigan, in Chicago. I've known your dad since I was younger than you are."

"That's a really long time to know someone." The kid was a true sage.

"Time flies when you're having fun." Devlin thought about it. It had been close to thirty years. She was thirty-four. The Brysons had moved into Lake Point Tower when she was in kindergarten.

"I'd like to have some fun." Grant sounded like a very old man when he sighed.

Devlin gave in and turned to Nils, rolling her eyes.

"What do you do for fun, little man?" she asked, even turning farther in her seat to look at the kid sitting behind her.

He rattled off a list of movies, games, and books he enjoyed. Nils asked him his favorite parts in some of the movies and books. Devlin watched the island come into sight. She asked if the kid liked sports, and Grant volunteered an array of watersports he and his dad did together, including fishing in Cabo and sailing on the boat in Michigan, which apparently bore the name *Camilla*.

"It's for the warrior princess who fought near Rome in Virgil's *Aeneid*," Grant explained. "My dad and I like to go to Rome together. I like gelato."

"Good to know, little man," Devlin said, glad the Galveston seawall lay just ahead. They'd park and be in the restaurant soon and she'd have a bellini in her hand not long after that.

Then, because she'd always been a bitch and wanted to maintain her bona fides, she added, "About the gelato. That's good to know about the gelato. I already knew the whole Camilla story."

Chapter 4

Blue Tide

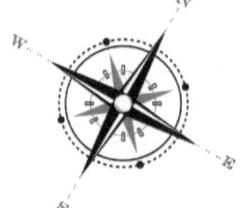

Viggo Bryson was an idiot. But then, Xavier had known that for a decade. Viggo's plan had been just plain stupid: banal, facile, cretinous. Xavier Charles shuffled copies into taxonomic piles on the conference-room table. Even if Irene Stockton arrived punctually, he still had thirty-eight minutes to prepare for this meeting. Xavier prided himself on liberal discovery. He had nothing to hide from defense counsel. He didn't need to ambush those weak, undernourished mercenaries (some might say whores). He would gladly share his entire file with defense counsel, and still he'd string up their clients from the highest tree. The clients, in the end, hanged themselves— with their deplorable life choices.

So of course, he would welcome Irene Stockton, Esquire, into the U.S. Attorney's Office, into this conference room, to review the evidence against her client. Once Brittney finished making the copies, he'd also have party favors to send home with Ms. Stockton: great, bursting files of tax returns and insurance policies and statements from offshore bank accounts and contracts related to "investments" in St. Kitts and Nevis. Irene Stockton wouldn't have to worry about reading material for months.

"Xavier, here are the Blue Tide, L.L.C., contracts." Brittney walked into the room with an armful of copies, oversized binder clips stacked in a formidable column on the left corners of the collated packets.

"Here, put them over there by the 2015 tax returns." Xavier swept a hand toward the upper left corner of the conference table.

He glanced at the clock over the wall-length whiteboard.

"Let's get on those insurance contracts next." He raised his fingers to make air-quotes when he said insurance.

"They're done. I just have to go get them. It was too much to carry them in here with the Blue Tide stuff."

Xavier raised his tea mug to his lips. His chrysanthemum tea had cooled.

"Brittney, after you bring those contracts in, would you mind popping this in the microwave for me?" He saluted the secretary with the mug. "I'm going to go check on Kurt. He should be in here setting up the projector."

"Sure, Mr. Charles."

Xavier didn't care that he thought he heard a hint of rebellion in her voice. He wasn't here to coddle underperforming termagants.

In the hallway, Xavier saw Kurt, the IT flunky, approaching with the outdated projector, its cable hanging and the VGA connector slapping the kid's knees as he shuffled down the carpet squares. Xavier turned and retraced his steps back to the conference room. Brittney, and his tea mug, had disappeared.

"Here," he said to Kurt when the kid made it into the room, "you can set it up here. We're going to be sitting at the table." Xavier removed files from a small, rolling cart, and Kurt set the projector onto the cart.

"Xav, here's your tea." Brittney walked into the room, holding out his mug. "And Irene Stockton just arrived. She's in the foyer. Do you want me to bring her down? She has a paralegal with her. I don't know him. And she has that investigator with her. Mya Reynolds. The one you don't like."

No, Xavier did not like Mya Reynolds and her single volume: loud. Nor did he like Brittney's occasional use of Xav to address him. Where she'd picked up that monstrousness was beyond him. He'd tried to stop it, suggesting (tactfully) that Xav did not equate to Xavier. (His closest friends might call him X, but Xav belonged in no one's lexicon.) In the four years of her tenure, Brittney Wagner had not gotten the Xavier clue, or many other clues for that matter.

"Leave them out there a few more minutes." Xavier tried the tea. At least she'd gotten the temperature right.

"Does that look good to you, Xavier?" Kurt waved at the screen and the projection on to it of Xavier's laptop's desktop.

"That will work. Thank you, Kurt."

"You know where to find me if you need anything." The kid didn't look at Xavier as he ambled out of the conference room.

Xavier checked the piles Brittney had finished arranging. Everything seemed neat and complete.

"Could you bring me a couple legal pads and pens, Brittney?" he asked. She was just sitting there staring at the screen. He might as well put her to use. "And a couple more markers for the whiteboard?"

"Sure." She got up and left the room again.

He really did love these events, their thoroughness. Caesar likely had similar feelings surveying his legions: row upon row of honed, armored men. Xavier had row upon row of damning evidence. It was lovely.

"All right, why don't you go get Ms. Stockton and her minions?" He nodded toward the door when Brittney returned with the office supplies.

As she went to collect the opposing force, he buttoned his suit coat and smoothed his tie, bumping the top knuckle of his pinky against his tie tack, with its Stanford "S" and coast redwood. He removed his glasses and pulled a polishing cloth from a pocket. As he replaced the glasses on his nose, the doomed came into sight.

"Irene, Mya, and . . . I'm afraid I don't know you." Xavier extended a hand to his professional colleague first and then greeted the investigator and paralegal.

"Taylor. It's Taylor Bradford." The kid had a flimsy handshake and weak eyes.

"Taylor's my new paralegal," Irene Stockton butted in.

"Well, I'm glad we could all meet today." Xavier pulled out a chair for himself at the head of the paper-heavy conference table. "Make yourselves comfortable. I have extra legal pads if anyone needs one. Pens. Coffee anyone? Brittney can get you coffee, and we may have some Danishes as well. Brittney, do we have any Danishes?"

"I'll take coffee, Brittney, thank you," Irene responded. "But we don't need Danishes. Unless these guys want them." She gestured with a pen at her staff. "And just black. I don't need anything in my joe."

"Anything for either of you?" Brittney looked at the foot soldiers.

The guy—Taylor—shook his head no. Mya Reynolds said, of course quite loudly, that she'd like some black coffee as well and that she'd take a Danish if there were any. If Xavier remembered correctly, the harpy had grown up in Atlanta. At least she had the accent to go with such a heritage. Or he figured it was the South he heard. He avoided going past South Bend and didn't need the details of a backward region's elocution.

"Shall we get started while Brittney gets refreshments?" Xavier slipped a DVD out of a sleeve. "Perhaps we should start with a movie. I have video of your client's business partners, Mr. Roberts and Mr. Giannakopoulos, making some statements to my agents. Mr. Roberts met with agents yesterday. Mr. Giannakopoulos, of course, made his statement the day before we arrested your client."

Irene Stockton didn't say anything. She looked up from her legal pad and focused on the screen.

"Here we go." Xavier clicked and the video began to play. His tea had cooled again, but he enjoyed a long sip anyway as Mr. Giannakopoulos walked into an interview room ahead of two IRS agents and began singing like a canary—to the tune of Viggo Bryson having concocted this entire scheme.

More videos followed: Mr. Roberts's statement and the statement of two business owners who had purchased "insurance" products from Viggo Bryson and his cronies. And then it was time. Xavier stood up and passed a large packet of "insurance" contracts to Irene Stockton.

"Irene, if your client insists on a trial in this matter, the government is prepared to prove that your client formed several L.L.C.s, including Blue Tide, L.L.C., and Gray Hill, L.L.C., for the purpose of defrauding the IRS out of millions of dollars. He sold these 'insurance' products to the owners of modest S corporations and L.L.C.s as insurance against 'lost income.'" Air-quotes emphasized Xavier's points.

The boy paralegal was taking notes. Mya Reynolds was sitting back in her chair with her arms crossed over her chest.

Xavier continued, content he had his audience's attention. "Premiums on these 'loss-of-income' policies were, shall we say, exorbitant, some rising into the millions. Once a company paid its premiums, that company reported the premium amount as a tax-deductible business expense. Your client then funneled a majority of the total premium amount through offshore accounts to his partner at SK and N, Inc., who, in turn, returned it to the company that had purchased the insurance policy in the first place. SK and N, Inc., labeled the money as repayment of business loans. Your client laid out this return in what he called a return-of-premium rider on the alleged insurance policy. Along the way, your client kept a not-insignificant share of the premium payments. As I just said, only a *majority* of the premium amount went back to the purchaser. Your client was keeping a few hundred thousand or more on each policy as his fee for arranging this 'insurance' and these 'tax benefits' for the purchasers. I'd rather call them fraudulent tax shelters."

"Xavier, I'm gonna stop you right there." Irene Stockton sat up, and Taylor Whoever and Mya Reynolds mirrored their leader. "Your discovery materials that you gave me at the detention hearing include an attorney letter with an opinion on the legality of these insurance products. Xavier, you know I'm subpoenaing Ms. Benedict for trial. We've got the advice of counsel supporting my client. That's worth something here."

"It could be, except it seems very clear that your client explicitly told Ms. Benedict not to consider the return-of-premium rider when Ms. Benedict was researching the legality of the insurance product. Ms. Benedict's attorney letter does not address funneling the premium payments back to the purchasing company. I'd say that omission is worth something too."

Irene Stockton leaned back in her chair and tented her fingers.

"Another aspect of this case that may be 'worth something—'" Xavier couldn't resist putting air-quotes around "worth something." Sure, it was obnoxious, but it tasted so good. "Another point is the failure of Blue Tide, L.L.C., to maintain the return-of-premium riders with the insurance policies themselves. For some strange reason, and I think a jury will have difficulty understanding the logic behind this choice, your client transferred all paperwork related to the return-of-premium riders to SK and N, Inc., and maintained those riders with loan notes to SK and N for which we haven't found records of loan monies."

Mya Reynolds looked chalky under the fluorescent lights. All that warm, blue, tanning-time July outside, yet

Mya looked almost pale, the mahogany luster of her complexion washed away. Irene Stockton's freckles had blanched. Xavier hoped the lights didn't have the same effect on him. He'd leave a little early today and walk beside the river and let a bit of late sunshine restore his own healthy, crepuscular lambency.

"Perhaps we should move on to some 302s," Xavier suggested when his pause didn't elicit a response from Irene or Mya. He lifted from the table a stack of FBI reports related to witness interviews. "Agents interviewed Miles Bakker in May. Mr. Bakker is the sole member of the Bakker Group, L.L.C., a commercial-real-estate firm with holdings across the state. He purchased a loss-of-income policy from Jocelyn Kennedy, an agent at Blue Tide, L.L.C., last year with a return-of-premium rider. The Bakker Group paid an initial premium of $2.5 million. The group received a return of monies from SK and N, Incorporated, operating out of St. Kitts and Nevis, this past September. That return of funds amounted to," he glanced at the FBI 302 form, "$2,210,000.00. In April, Bakker Group's taxes reflected a business expense of $2.5 million in insurance premiums. We are currently auditing the group's financial records, but we have seen no report of income from SK and N, Inc., in any amount. Mr. Bakker has produced a return-of-premium rider from Blue Tide, L.L.C., and he has produced the policy contract, which we've attached to the 302 form for your convenience. The rider clearly refers to returning premium payments to the purchaser."

Xavier rose in his chair and reached over the stacks of paper to pass a copy of the 302 and its attachments to Irene.

"You have all these records, of course, on the discs we supplied at the initial pretrial conference and detention hearing," he confirmed, "but we've made copies for your convenience today."

Irene took the 302 form, glanced at it, and handed it to Mya. Mya set it on the table, but turned her eyes to Xavier rather than glance at it. He didn't like that woman. He looked toward the corner of the room where he believed Brittney might be sitting. She was.

"Brittney, would you mind refreshing everyone's beverages. I could use some more tea. There's a box of masala-chai tea bags on my desk if you wouldn't mind." Xavier did not respect the use of tea bags. He preferred loose leaves in a mesh strainer, but he couldn't trust Brittney that far.

Was Stockton rolling her eyes? Strumpet.

"I'm fine, Brittney, but thank you," she said to the secretary.

"I'm good," Mya seconded.

The paralegal-boy didn't look up from his notes. He was still writing.

"Okay, so hypothetically, what's your offer here?" Irene asked as Brittney left the room. "Mr. Bryson has made it abundantly clear to me that we are going to trial on these charges, and I have to agree with him. This looks like business as usual. The good old American Dream: come up with a good product, sell it, make money. But let's say he is willing to consider a plea. What are we talking about?"

Xavier got up and walked around the table. He lifted a small stack of papers and handed packets off the stack to the two defense soubrettes and their scaramouch.

"As charged now, of course, we have twenty-two counts. I've considered superseding with a new indictment with additional counts based on additional transactions my agents have uncovered since the filing of the original indictment. I don't need to supersede if your client is willing to save everyone a trial. And I'd allow him to plead to five counts from the original indictment: the conspiracy, the first three fraud counts, and a tax-evasion count of his own. The government will not oppose acceptance-of-responsibility credit toward his sentencing guidelines, but we will seek a sentence at the high end of the final advisory guideline range. And we will advocate for stacking the counts, with the five-year maximum sentences, as needed to achieve a guideline sentence. We have already begun the forfeiture proceedings, with my agents seizing assets and freezing accounts. That process will continue."

Xavier snuck a glance at Viggo Bryson's three toadies. Each one stared at their copy of the proposed plea agreement.

"That's your best offer?" Irene Stockton raised her eyes from the plea agreement and set it aside.

"That's not only my best offer—it's a very generous offer and it's the only one Mr. Bryson will receive."

"With the relevant-conduct guidelines being what they are for sentencing, the judge is going to consider the dropped counts anyway for sentencing purposes, so I guess I fail to see how this is such a generous offer. I think I'd understand better if you dropped all but one count and we had a five-year sentencing cap, but that's not what I'm hearing." Irene Stockton smoothed her too-short skirt.

"Ms. Stockton, I can't offer a five-year cap." Xavier tried to sound earnest.

A five-year cap? For Viggo Bryson? If he wanted to laugh, he would subscribe to Netflix and watch one of those shows people talked about in the breakroom at lunch. He didn't need Irene Stockton to tickle his funny bone. With the loss amount Xavier had his agents preparing, Viggo would be begging for eight years by the end of this thing.

"Well, I'll present it to my client, but I think we're going to trial." Irene rose and her underlings followed suit.

Xavier noticed Brittney had returned and his tea mug sat steaming near his legal pad.

"Brittney, would you help Ms. Stockton gather her copies of these materials?" He waved at the piles of contracts, policies, witness statements, and spreadsheets.

Brittney got up and started sorting papers into a stack.

"If you have any questions," Xavier said, "you know where to find me. We'll keep the plea deal open for the next four weeks, but after that, I'll be shifting into trial mode, and I can't be as generous once we've committed resources to full trial preparation."

He paused, then continued. "If I remember correctly, your client has sole custody of his son. Mother overseas or something? Mental-health issues? If placement becomes an issue, you know, you can call Brittney. She can help you get in touch with a contact at Health and Human Services who can assist with information on putting him into foster care."

Chapter 5
Tramadol

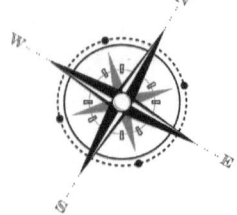

With the kid at the table, Devlin had not found herself forced to consider a lot of uncomfortable questions at the Gaido's dinner three nights ago. The conversation simply hadn't gone there. Instead, it had focused on the allegedly fun things Uncle Nils would do with Grant Bryson while Grant was "visiting" from Michigan. Devlin had gathered there was more to the visit than a little extended-family bonding, but she wasn't going to interrupt the cavalcade of bellinis, shrimp, red fish, and cheesecake to invite any sort of potentially substantive conversation.

Now, as she lay in her berth in the aft cabin of the old mahogany trawler that she called home, she didn't know how to respond to the text sitting there in its bloated gray bubble on the screen of her phone. She briefly wondered why she'd agreed to give Nils Bryson her phone number, but the past being the past, she didn't dwell there. She had done it, and he had texted her, and now she could choose to ignore him, delete and block, or respond.

The sun had been up for a while and the air in the trawler seemed golden and summer-hopeful. Was it past ten already?

"You said you're off today, right? Want to grab dinner and catch up properly? Grant's going to be with a tutor this evening." Nils's text sounded so casual, like he wasn't just a random dude from some long-lost world on the other side of everything.

Devlin stretched as best she could in the just-long-enough berth, reaching the phone over her head. She was off today and didn't have anything on the agenda except laundry and provisioning at the liquor store across Highway 146. Perhaps something decent was playing at the two-dollar-a-ticket movie theater over by Interstate 45. She brought the phone down and closed out of the text interface, opening the internet icon and bringing up the movie theater's page.

No luck with movies: crap, romantic crap, car-chase crap. Not her thing.

Her mind wandered back to Nils's text, just a tap away on the phone. At least he hadn't used some stupid emoji in it.

She closed out the internet and set the phone on the cabin sole. The marine air conditioning kicked on. Outside, someone shouted and an engine coughed to life. It rumbled and throbbed. Devlin guessed a broker was warming up the big Trojan powerboat that was for sale down the dock.

Nils had texted her a couple times since the Gaido's dinner: a note to say he was glad he'd bumped into her; another note to ask if she'd be up to going out again. That one had kicked off the problems. She wasn't going to turn down another nice dinner she didn't have to pay for, so she'd said she'd do it again. He'd asked when, and she'd told him her days off for the next two weeks.

She pushed herself out of the berth, slipping into her shower sandals, which sat at the ready beside the bed. What would it hurt to get another free meal? She stooped and retrieved the phone.

"I'm game for dinner. Lemme know where u wanna meet. & when." She tapped the send arrow.

In the boat's head, she brushed her teeth, and then she returned to the berth to pull the covers up into place. She gathered her shower supplies and towel and opened the aft companionway. Sunlight somersaulted through the wooden doors and spilled all over her. She squinted and turned away, blinking. Back in the head, she found an Excedrin, and in the galley, she retrieved a bottle of water. An empty gin bottle stood guard over the sink. It could wait—she'd clean herself up and then tidy old *A`uku*. One thing about being broke and living on an old boat: the lifestyle required minimal housekeeping. She clambered out through the companionway into the pain of daylight.

"Devlin! You're looking good, girl."

Yep, the Trojan must be going out for a pre-sale sea trial today. The formidable shadow of Sean Tofilau, yacht broker extraordinaire, preceded the big man down the dock.

"You're a blighted liar, Sean," she said, hearing the gravel in her throat.

"I mean it, beautiful. No one wears a hangover as well as you do. What you up to?"

"I'm going to shower. You selling that Trojan today?" Devlin hopped from the trawler onto the dock.

"If all goes well, I am. When we going over to T-Bone Tom's for some dinner and music again?" Sean was born in Apia, but his parents had left Samoa when he was a kid and he'd grown up in San Diego.

"Never, Sean, my love. I'm marrying money in front of the justice of the peace today and I'm going to live happily ever after and never have to sit with the likes of you again."

"Sure, Milady Devlin. *Mazel tov.* If you want to hang later, though, Joey and Kevin and I are going to be over there after work tonight."

"Maybe," Devlin mumbled, squinting and shuffling up the dock. The bathhouse seemed so far away when the sun got all bright like this and her head made these sounds.

Before jumping in the shower stall in the bathhouse, Devlin pulled her phone out.

Another text from Nils. "You up for Opus tonight? I can pick you up. 1800?" He must have thought military time made him more nautical. He'd always been like that.

Neither of the Bryson brothers had avoided putting on airs at times. Was he putting on airs now? Opus wasn't cheap. He didn't think this was some sort of date, did he? Maybe he was just eager to spend more of Viggo's money.

"Sure. Text me when u get to marina. I'll come up & meet u at gate." Devlin sent the text and then dropped her phone into her toiletries case.

The hot water felt good. It always did. Generally, she had the misfortune of not suffering from hangovers—a misfortune because it made drinking a little too much a little too easy. But if a hangover did slip past her, a hot shower always took care of it.

She finished in the bathhouse, slung her towel over a shoulder, and stepped out into the now far more welcome sunshine . . . and the humidity.

"Hey, beautiful." There was Sean Tofilau again, standing beside A`uku.

Devlin ambled up to her boat. "Shouldn't you be making that sale?" She wiped her upper lip with a corner of her towel and then dragged the towel across the back of her neck. A hundred yards in this stickiness and she was soaking wet.

"Yep," Sean answered, "so you wanna make a hundred bucks?"

Devlin narrowed her eyes. "Maybe."

"The captain I booked is a no-show. I've called and texted. Nothing. And the boat's owner insisted on a captain. He thinks it's better for liability reasons. He doesn't want me driving for the sea trial. He said he didn't want any brokers driving the boat—captains only." Sean shrugged.

Devlin knew where this was going. She didn't have a captain's license, but no one needed to know that. She and Sean had worked together before—in ways that made her a couple bucks and that saved Sean some of his commission.

"Sure," she said. "Gimme a minute and I'll meet you over there. Is the buyer here yet?"

"No, we got time," Sean replied.

"You got anything to drink on that boat?"

"Devlin, you gotta give your liver a break, sister."

"Don't lecture me, *hamo*." Devlin stepped onto her trawler and slid the aft companionway hatch back. "I'll be over there in a minute." She had to have some vodka on the boat somewhere. Something that would go undetected. She knew she still had some juice in the fridge.

A too-small screwdriver later, she stood on the bridge of the forty-foot Trojan.

"Are we fueled up?" she asked.

"Owner said he put a hundred gallons in last weekend. He texted me a picture of the receipt. He's a decent guy, so I think we are good to go." Sean flipped a switch on the breaker panel to power up the navigation instruments. "These are my buyers," he said in response to his phone's vibration. "I'll go collect them from the parking lot."

He patted Devlin's shoulder as he passed her.

"I have a real knack for making bad choices," he said.

"That makes two of us," she replied.

"No, really. I mean, if something did happen, I'd be in a world of hurt. I've got a random woman driving the boat, no licensed captain, and you've been drinking." He laughed, shook his head. "But the thing is, it works." He shrugged his beefy shoulders and stepped toward the ladder off the bridge. "We'll be fine."

"Plus, Sean, sweetheart, they suspended my bar license. They didn't wipe my brain clean of how to play the game. Anything happens, there'll be cross-claims and counter-claims from here to sundown. And anyway, I'm already a carny and you're a yacht broker. Doesn't get much more rock bottom. Worst case scenario, we end up together in Apia, huh?"

Sean turned to descend the ladder to land on the aft deck. "If we end up in Apia, you should marry me. We could live happily ever after."

Devlin snorted. "*Hamo*, there's no happily ever after for me."

While Sean headed to the marina's parking lot to find his clients, Devlin flopped onto the bench behind the helm station and pulled out her phone.

"Looking forward to it," Nils's text read, sitting beneath her confirmation of that night's dinner plans.

***

Despite what Devlin, deep down inside, recognized as her and Sean's less-than-adult decision making, the sea trial progressed swimmingly. Sean's clients loved the boat, and Devlin showcased perfectly its maneuverability and ease of handling.

"That went well," Sean said after he'd sent his clients on their way with a promise that he'd send a final sales contract to them that evening. "Thanks. You did me a solid."

He pulled five twenty-dollar bills out of his wallet and handed them to Devlin as they stood on the dock beside the motor yacht.

"And thank you, good sir." She pocketed the money.

"So you want to meet us for drinks later?" he asked.

Devlin glanced up the docks. An old man was making his way toward the parking lot with a large sail stuffed in a dockcart.

"Can't." She watched the dude turn to haul the cart up the gangway. He walked backward, facing the cart and its load of Dacron on the steep ramp.

She could feel curiosity thrumming off the big Samoan. A gull landed on the dock and began beating a shell against the dock's wooden boards, struggling to extricate dinner.

Sean didn't start walking.

"Okay, thanks for the gig." She lifted her backpack of foul-weather and emergency gear off the dock and slung it over a shoulder.

"What you got goin' on, Ms. Devlin?" Sean put a massive arm around her. His wrist sported a black, geometric tattoo, which he squeezed into Devlin's neck, pulling her head into his side. "You're awful quiet for someone who's usually up for anything."

"Yeah, well, I need to do some stuff." Devlin wrestled her head up, but Sean's arm stayed put.

They began walking up the dock. The sailboats' halyards slapped a marching rhythm in the hot afternoon breeze.

"Anything you want to talk about?" Sean retrieved his arm from Devlin's shoulders and stuffed his hand in his pocket.

"Not really, but . . . ." Devlin shrugged. "It's weird. This dude I grew up with brought his nephew down to the boardwalk the other night. He recognized me and asked me out to dinner. I went. I mean, free Gaido's. I wasn't going to turn that down." She turned to look up at Sean.

"No. 'Course not."

"So, he asked if I wanted to go to Opus tonight."

"Nice." Sean nodded. "You going? 'Cause if you're not, I'll go."

"Dude." Devlin rolled her eyes and shook her head. She inhaled. "Yeah, I'm going."

"So who's this guy?"

"Just this guy whose family lived in my building when I was a kid. He and his brother and I and another chick all hung out together for like my entire childhood. We sailed together at Chicago Yacht Club. We went to Lab together."

Sean cocked his head.

"The University of Chicago Laboratory Schools. It's a prep school. Ghastly expensive." She brushed her cotton sleeve over her eyes to wipe away perspiration. "Anyway, these peeps and I skied together in Wisconsin and

Michigan. Camped in Michigan. We were close. Then we grew up and went our separate ways. I haven't seen this guy for like seven years, and let's just say I wasn't at my best when I saw him that last time."

"Dancing on tables again, huh, you minx?"

"You guessed it." Devlin grinned. "You wanna drink?" She stopped in front of *A'uku*. The trawler's dock lines groaned as the boat rolled on the remnants of a wake from a sportfisherman heading out to the channel.

"Sure. I'll prep that contract for those people later." Sean followed Devlin onto the boat and in the main door to the saloon.

Inside, the boat felt refreshing. The air conditioning was doing well keeping up with the weight of summer outside. Devlin leaned over and opened the fridge.

"I gotta go to Spec's. I'm running low on everything. All I've got is tonic water. I finished off the juice, water, and vodka this morning. Sorry." She looked up over the top of the fridge. "I do have some chocolate almond milk."

"Tonic's fine." Sean dropped onto the settee, rested his elbows on the teak table. "So let's get back to you dancing on tables."

Devlin filled two glasses with ice and poured tonic water over the cubes. She dropped coasters in front of Sean and set the glasses on them.

"Yeah, so the last time I saw this guy—his name is Nils—I was on track to become Sondheim Baker's youngest partner in history." She took a sip of tonic. "One of the country's largest, most lucrative law firms." Another sip. "Long story short: I was burning out. It's hard to get to that level and it's really hard to maintain once you're there. I was . . . paying an emotional toll." She wanted to sound sardonic, hoped Sean heard the cynicism.

On the side of her glass, she drew circles in the condensation. Then she closed her eyes and placed her cool, moist fingers against her eyelids.

"So it's Commodore's Ball at the Chicago Yacht Club. One of the club's nicest events of the year. Nils Bryson is in town visiting his family. He's still a member of the club, so he stops by the ball to visit with his old sailing buddies. And there I am hammered on gimlets and my dog's tramadol."

"Wait. What?"

"Yep." Devlin sat back, stared up at the boat's torn headliner. The fabric had stains, and threads poked out from the tears. "I'd started crashing. I got this puppy because I thought it would help. It didn't. Dogs are a lot of work. My secretary took him in the end. But I got him and I took him to the vet for shots and to get fixed. They gave me a bottle of tramadol for him. He got half a pill. I took the rest. Just kind of curious, you know." She rolled her head against the bulkhead over the settee's vinyl back-support cushion, looked over at Sean. "I still feel bad I took all that dog's meds."

"I can't say as I quite relate, but I get it. We all get burned out sometimes."

"I know it's hard to believe now, but I was pretty clean-cut back then. Didn't drink. Didn't smoke. Didn't take tramadol." She pressed her lips together, wry and something else. Regretful? "But I was billing 3,900 hours a year. Set a firm record one year. And here was this bottle of pills and here were these nice drinks and these nice people drinking. And those people seemed happy. So I jumped in. I'd put on this little black dress and I'd gotten in a cab for the yacht club. And I was feeling pretty fancy when I walked in. And the party was nice, and the drinks were flowing, and I was good. Life was good. But then Nils Bryson walked in. The love of my life. So suddenly it seemed like a really good idea to jump on a table and 'Walk Like an Egyptian.'"

She sighed. She heard the ice in Sean's cup click as he lifted the glass to his lips.

"Well, my faithful Jimmy Choos failed me and I capsized. Nils came over and he's the one who called a cab and took me home. Got my keys out of my purse, put me in pajamas, tucked me in, and left. That was the last I saw of him. I limped along a few more years at the firm and finally fell apart completely and ended up down here." She sat up and finished off her tonic water. Then she leaned her elbows on the table and tried not to remember what she must have looked like that night, lousy with prestige and ruined all at once.

"Wait, wait, wait." Sean set his glass on the coaster. "Did I just hear Devlin Winters say 'love of my life'?" He leaned into her, his nose almost touching hers.

"You did. And I think that's enough storytime. You've got a sales contract to prepare." She pushed herself away from the table and rose.

"No, no, no, Ms. Winters. So this mystery man that has reappeared in your life is the one who got away?"

"The only things that got away from me, *hamo*, are my dignity and self-respect. Now, you're either going back to your office or you're taking me to Spec's for a liquor run. You pick."

"I better get to the office. But wait one more second. Did you say this guy's name is Nils Bryson?"

"Yeah, you probably know him. The other night, he said he brokers for Sunset Yachts. I don't know how I haven't run into him before."

"Well, you are a bit of a hermit, sister."

"Yeah, and when I do go out, I got no taste in friends. Come on. I'll walk to the parking lot with you. I'm going to Spec's."

"Nils Bryson, huh?" Sean rubbed his short black hair.

"Nils Bryson."

Chapter 6
Parental Rights

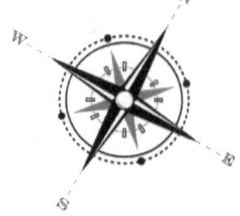

Xavier picked up the phone and dialed IRS Special Agent Lillian Carter's direct number. A ring, a second ring, and . . . .

"Good afternoon, this is Lillian Carter speaking."

"Agent Carter, how are you today? It's Xavier Charles."

"Xavier, good to hear from you. Let me guess: you're looking for some updates on the Viggo Bryson matter."

"Agent Carter, you're a mind reader. Tell me you've got something good from the hunt for Monique Arthurton and SK and N, Inc."

Xavier waited, listening to Lillian Carter inhale and shuffle papers. Then there were a couple clicks on a keyboard.

"Xavier, I know how bad you want a report on Arthurton, but there isn't much. The problem is simply geography. Obviously, we know SK and N is a St. Kitts corporation, but it seems to operate only on the island. It doesn't show up anywhere else, even around the Caribbean. I'm guessing SK and N stands for St. Kitts and Nevis. Someone wasn't into fancy business names, I'm thinking. I've found no ties to the U.S. other than through Bryson. I just don't have anything on the company other than what you've already got. It looks like a shell corporation that likely exists simply to serve Bryson."

"Except, of course, for the wholly independent ownership and management of the corporation and for its involvement in its underwater-environment preservation and conservation missions." Xavier sighed. These agents never got it, never understood the potential for jurors to glom onto irrelevant details, drink the defense Kool-Aid, and lose sight of the forest for the trees.

"But, Xavier, I think everyone agrees that the company's alleged diving and environmental efforts are just a cover for the fraudulent financial transactions. I kinda doubt the company's investors are really dumping millions of bucks into cleaning up plastic from coral reefs."

"Agent Carter, you and I may know that, but I need to prove that to a jury—beyond a reasonable doubt. If legitimate investment occurred, or if SK and N really was working to preserve the underwater environment, Mr. Bryson will argue those points, and he'll argue that the return of the premium payments to the companies allegedly buying insurance from him was simply a return of loan funds those companies provided to SK and N to further its mission. And then we don't have fraud. We have companies saving the whales . . . or sea turtles . . . or whatever. And then we don't have a conviction."

Now, Lillian Carter sighed.

"I get it, Xavier, but I just don't have anything for you. The company's incorporated in St. Kitts. It has no real online presence. The paperwork we've gotten a hold of shows inexplicable returns of money to alleged investors. We have no paper trail on income to the company—actual investment or loan income. Just the repayments. We've got some memos about financing plastic clean-up projects and lobbying efforts to preserve reefs and underwater habitat. That's it. I just don't have anything else."

"All right, moving on." Xavier didn't have time for people willing to come up empty handed. "I know you must have found records on Monique Arthurton. I was right about the Chicago connection, correct?"

"Correct. Monique lived in Chicago and I have records on her. She's a St. Kitts citizen and the sole shareholder of SK and N, Inc. But about nine years ago, she had an Illinois driver's license and an address in the 5500 block of South Kimbark Avenue, down near the University of Chicago. I checked the records at the school. She was not a student. But I do have a paternity and custody case out of Cook County. And bingo: initially, she shared custody of a son with Viggo Bryson. The kid's name is Grant Arthur Bryson. Currently eight years old. He'll be nine in a couple days. I have the birth certificate. It lists Monique Arthurton and Viggo Bryson as the parents. The kid was born at Mercy Hospital."

None of this was news to Xavier, but he favored the Socratic method: let the agents discover things for themselves. It made them feel like they were part of the team.

"So," Lillian Carter continued, "I think right there you have your answer to the SK and N problem. Viggo set up this foreign shell corporation, put his baby-momma on the paperwork, and funneled money through it."

"Yes, but isn't there a problem with that theory?" Agents suffered when it came to big-picture thinking. Xavier waited for Lillian Carter to see the hole, to remember what else she'd found. If she hadn't found it, he'd have to say something to her supervisor.

"What problem?" Lillian sounded surprised at Xavier's reluctance to buy into her simple explanation.

"Did you find anything else in the Cook County case related to the child?" Xavier pushed the button at the top of his pen in and out, extending the ballpoint and retracting it a few times.

"The case got reviewed when the kid was about three years old." Lillian sounded like she couldn't decide if she was making a statement or asking a question.

"What was that about?" *Wait for it, wait for it.* Xavier's impatience wrestled with his pedagogic impulses. On the other side of the phone, more papers shuffled.

"Well, the dad—Viggo Bryson—petitioned for termination of Monique's parental rights. He cited mental-health issues. He, I think, he claimed she'd been hospitalized. Maybe there was a suicide attempt. Or some sort of self-harm. I can't find the records in what's in front of me. But anyway, the court terminated Monique's rights. And right after that, we lose her again. I'm guessing she returned to the island. There's no more Chicago connection."

Xavier sighed once more.

Lillian must have heard the exhale and understood its meaning. "Well, I've got an address for a Monique Arthurton in the 1400 block of West Sherwin on the north side of Chicago a little over four years later. But it's a six-month blip. No driver's license, no vehicle registration, nothing else. I'm not even sure it's the same woman."

At least she had found the second apartment. Her efforts spared Xavier the need to talk to anyone about performance issues.

"All right. Send me what you have." He clicked the pen twice more. "But we need more on SK and N. What we have doesn't help us. The company's owned by Viggo's baby-momma—who lost her child because Viggo called her unfit. Hardly the foundation for a flourishing business relationship and fraud conspiracy. If anything, it seems like an explanation for why the company would not be in Viggo's pocket."

"Do you want the West Sherwin address and info, too?" Lillian asked. "Again, I'm not even sure it's her."

"Send me everything," Xavier replied.

"If it was her, why would she come back?"

Xavier examined the mineral-fiber ceiling tiles over his desk. Maybe Saint Thomas Aquinas would ask God to give him an extra dose of patience today.

"What's the timing on these addresses compared to SK and N?" He pushed the agent's reasoning forward.

"That's a good question." Lillian paused. "So I believe SK and N formed the same year Monique's parental rights were terminated." Another pause. "Do you think Viggo negotiated with her to sort of buy her parental rights? Like he offered to set her up with this company and money in exchange for her not fighting him getting custody of the kid?"

"It's one possible explanation," Xavier said.

"And what, she came back to Chicago a couple years later to see the kid? Or to check in with Viggo? Stayed a few months and then went home?"

"Perhaps. What do we have on SK and N from that time period?"

More pausing.

"Well, I don't have much on SK and N from that period. Xavier, like I said, I just don't have much on the company at all, but when you look at my spreadsheet on Blue Tide, L.L.C., and Viggo's insurance sales, business was booming."

Xavier listened to the keyboard clicks.

"Yeah, so this would have been over four years ago," Lillian continued. "From my records, it looks like it was the peak of Blue Tide's insurance sales."

Xavier sat back in his chair, leaving the pen on his desk so he wouldn't attack it with clicks.

"Wait," Lillian said, "if Viggo did buy Monique off to get the kid, and SK and N became an integral part of Viggo's scheme, did Monique come back to extort the kid away from Viggo? Like all of a sudden she realizes that the company he set her up with is integral to his operations, so now she has some leverage to get time with her kid?"

"That sounds interesting," Xavier said. "Why don't you send me what you've got. I'll look through it all. Then keep digging on SK and N. And how about calling over to ICE and getting the A-file immigration records on Ms. Arthurton?"

"Done," Lillian replied. "I just hit send on an email to you with a bunch of PDFs. And I put a call in to ICE yesterday. I'm sure I'll have everything by tomorrow. And I'll let you know if I can dig up anything else on SK and N."

"Lovely," Xavier said. "Lillian, thanks for your work."

It always helped to stay upbeat and appreciative with the agents. Even when he already had the facts, Xavier still needed someone to chase paper. And the wrinkle right now was he didn't have all the facts: Niqi's SK and N, Inc., still presented a wild card.

Chapter 7
Complicated

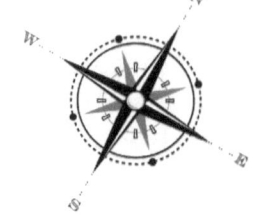

Nils looked like he wanted to hug Devlin when she approached him in the marina parking lot to go to dinner. She hesitated, debating whether hugging should make it onto the night's agenda. Deciding it couldn't hurt, she stepped into her old friend's arms, but then she felt him against her, felt the cotton of his yacht brokerage's polo shirt, felt the muscled torso beneath the blue material, felt the memory of a hot summer day in the cabin of a sailboat in a Chicago harbor when she was nineteen.

"D. Winters," Nils said into her ponytail.

"Hey, man, how you be?" She didn't want to remember that first time. She didn't want to remember anything.

"Better now. It's good to see you." He released her, but kept an arm around her shoulders. Did her shoulders have a sign on them today? Please use me as an armrest?

But she didn't pull away.

"So Opus sounds good?" He looked down at her. He'd always had a good smile . . . a great smile. And he had the same brown hair falling into his eyes he'd had back then, hair she'd once pushed away from his face and tucked behind his ear, back away from his sunglasses.

"Sure," she said, hearing a yoga teacher from long ago admonishing her to "be here now" and not dwell in the past.

"You're awfully quiet, D. Winters. What's up?" Nils asked, opening the passenger door of the Jeep for her.

"Just tired," she lied, as Nils climbed into the driver's seat. "I captained an old Trojan for a sea trial today. A broker I know asked me to cover for a no-show captain."

Nils turned from the windshield as he pulled the vehicle out of the parking lot, giving her a surprised look. "I didn't know you were a captain."

"I'm not. I just play one on TV occasionally."

"Devlin, you captained the boat for a pre-sale sea trial, but you're not a captain? What are you doing, girl? You know that's a huge liability issue." He made the left turn to pull onto Highway 146, then an immediate right.

"I know." She studied the fatigued and faded storefronts scooting past. "But we didn't have any problems. The boat performed well. And I still know how to litigate if need be." She adjusted her seatbelt, pushed it away from her and then reset it against her chest. "I'd represent myself."

The Jeep got quiet. The elementary school slid by and Nils kept the car's acceleration in check through the local speed trap.

"Which broker? I mean, who'd you captain for?" he asked after too long.

"Sean Tofilau."

"I know Sean," Nils said.

Devlin wondered if a question lurked in his tone. Was he prying?

"He's a good broker," Nils continued. "Ethical. He's a straight shooter."

He made a right, and they drove past the foliage of another marina, red, white, and blue flowers bobbing in the wake of air pushed aside by traffic. Devlin felt him studying the back of her head. The restaurant came into view and she was grateful for the distraction of parking and exiting the car.

"So you know Sean well?" Nils finally asked, setting the parking break.

Devlin was already out of the Jeep.

"He's one of the first people I met when I moved down here." She slammed her door shut. "Nils Bryson, are you asking me if I'm dating Sean?"

Nils held her eyes. "Nope," he said after she blinked. "I've got my answer." He caught hold of her hand and started leading her into the restaurant. "You're single, Devlin Winters." For a split second, it didn't feel like fifteen years had passed since an earlier summer and another hand holding.

At the maître d' podium, Nils stopped.

"Is that live music, I hear?" he asked the hostess.

"We have live piano upstairs tonight," she replied.

"What luck. Would you have a table for two up there?"

The woman led them past the bar, bathed in trendy blue light, and up a staircase to a table near a piano, the stool of which held a tall woman with long black hair and full lips singing about moondancing.

"Perfect," Nils declared, pulling out a chair for Devlin.

"If you say so." But Devlin grinned. "Are we spending Viggo's money tonight?" she asked, picking up the wine list.

"Yeah, about that." Nils seemed to study his napkin before unfolding it and laying it across his lap. "Well, first, yes, tonight is on Viggo. But, um, Viggo's situation is a little," he seemed to be casting for the right word, "complicated."

"Isn't Viggo's situation always complicated?" Devlin set the wine list aside and opened her menu, scanning prices, searching for the highest.

"Yeah, I know what people think, but he really is a good guy. He's a great dad. He and Grant are really tight."

Devlin slipped her eyes over the top of her menu. "It sounds like Grant has a pretty good gig with his dad." She didn't even want to curb herself: "But what about Mrs. Bryson?"

Nils narrowed his eyes. "I'm sure it comes as no surprise to you to hear that there is no Mrs. Bryson."

"No, really?" Devlin smiled at the young man who set a basket of rolls in front of her. She plucked one from its blue-napkin blanket. "I'm shocked." She paused to chew warm, buttery gluten. "Did Viggo pay her for her parental rights or do they share the kid?"

"That's complicated, too," Nils said. "And I don't know the details. Grant's mom is from St. Kitts. Eastern Caribbean. She lived with Viggo in Chicago for a couple years, but she wasn't happy and went home to the island. She left Grant with Viggo." Nils sliced into the butter. "Father and son have been thick as thieves ever since. That kid adores his dad. Viggo has a tutor for his homeschooling and a nanny for general childcare."

"Must be nice," Devlin said, very content to do so with her mouth full.

A waiter arrived and wrote on his pad an order of crab legs and filet mignon, lobster Thermidor and oysters Rockefeller—and a $98 bottle of merlot. Devlin didn't particularly favor merlot, but it was the most expensive bottle on the menu.

"So let's go back to the Viggo's-life-is-complicated thing," she said, settling down and smoothing her blouse, one of three non-t-shirts she had now. While it had been a long time since she'd cared, she still knew magenta did nice things for her skin, and the cut of the neck did nice things for her cleavage. She leaned forward. Before leaving the boat, she'd applied lipstick. She pursed her lips and figured from the feel of them some of the color had withstood the assault of rolls and butter.

Nils sighed and seemed to deflate. "Viggo's in jail," he said. "There's no delicate way to explain the whole thing. He's been indicted for tax fraud. He's in jail in Michigan." He rubbed his brow. "That's why I have Grant. Apparently, they were on their way to Switzerland when the feds arrested him at the Detroit airport. He asked the agents to let him put Grant on a plane to Houston and they did, so he just plunked Grant on a flight to IAH and texted me, pleading with me to take care of the kid. He sent a check for ninety grand in Grant's pocket with a note to cash it immediately in case the feds froze his account." Nils stuck both hands in his unruly hair and seemed to squeeze his skull.

"Aw, jeez, Nils, I'm sorry," Devlin whispered. "I know how devastating that is. I mean, once the feds have you, you might as well be in a meat grinder."

"You did criminal work, right?" Nils looked up, hands still tangled in his hair.

"Um hmm," she mumbled. "Federal criminal defense. District court and appellate."

"Yeah," Nils's eyes brightened and he unthreaded his fingers, "because I remember you represented the governor . . . or ex-governor . . . whatever . . . when he was charged with all that contracting fraud. I remember it was all over the news."

"Yeah," Devlin said to the tablecloth. "That was my last win." She fumbled with her water glass. "I got the jury's verdict reversed and the case was remanded for a new trial. And . . . ." She rubbed the denim of her jeans and looked toward the piano. "This is a good song," she whispered.

"And?" Nils pushed the breadbasket aside, fixed his eyes on her.

"And my career ended," Devlin said, biting off the tail end of the words. The woman at the piano had beautiful, smooth, dark skin and her dress glittered under the low lights. Her voice sounded deep and rich, molten and thick.

Nils didn't sit back, didn't look away.

"I punched him. I punched the governor—former governor. In the face. In front of the jury." Devlin hadn't meant to sound that loud. She could hear herself over the music . . . strident, emphatic. Did that couple at the table by the window turn and stare?

Nils's head jerked back in surprise.

"Yep, at the retrial, things got heated during a government witness's testimony, and he—the former governor—was all up in my ear about objecting and I told him to pipe down, and he called me a whore, and I stood up and punched him. It was that easy." She wound her napkin around her hands.

"Wow." Nils flipped his fork over on the tablecloth and pushed it back and forth. "I knew you'd been unhappy." He looked up. "Like that last time I saw you. And then a few years later someone said you'd left Sondheim Baker. But I didn't realize it was like that."

"Yep. The bar suspended my license for two years, and if I ever want to get it back, I have to do all this continuing ed and provide proof of counseling and so on, but whatever. I'm never going back."

The waiter appeared with crab legs and oysters, and Devlin thanked the seafood gods.

Nils lifted an oyster from the serving plate.

"It's good," he affirmed after finishing a bite.

Devlin began hacking at crab legs.

"So did you get some help? I mean like, did you take a break, maybe see a counselor?"

Crack—a crab leg yielded. "I spent a couple weeks 'in the hospital,' if you know what I mean. And then I packed up and moved here because it doesn't snow, no one knows me, and I can watch the boats in the channel every day." She bit into the crab, wiped her lips and fingers. "I like that: watching the boats. I used to like to sneak out at lunch and watch the tour boats on the river when I was at Sondheim. It was soothing."

The singer struck into "Chicago" and Devlin groaned.

"What happened to the governor?" Nils refilled his wine glass. He held the bottle up toward Devlin and she nodded, and he reached over and refilled hers as well.

"He came out almost smelling like a rose. Obviously getting punched by your attorney in front of the jury will get you a mistrial. The government didn't want to try the case a third time, so the U.S. Attorney's Office ponied up a sweet plea offer, the governor took it, did two years, and is now some sort of consultant or something."

"Gotta love America," Nils said. "Hey, maybe that's the ticket. You could get your license back, punch Viggo during the trial, and get him a sweet plea deal."

"I wouldn't mind punching Viggo."

"You never really liked Viggo, did you?"

Devlin shrugged. Beyond the windows, the sun had finished setting, and warm, murky, Gulf Coast night was settling in. "Maybe we were too alike. All full of ourselves." She lifted her wine glass, swirled the merlot in crimson waves. "Sounds like we've both come down a peg or two."

"Do you remember how to dance?" Nils set an emptied oyster shell onto his plate.

"Are you serious?"

"As a heart attack."

Devlin shook her head. "You're too old-school for me, Nils Bryson." The last notes of "Chicago" drifted away. Nils's frame filled his seat across the table from Devlin in just the right mix of imposing and toned, and the candlelight flickered across his face, his blue shirt making his eyes look navy in the dim dinner light. What the hell. "Yeah, I remember how to dance." She set her napkin on the table. "All those lessons our parents paid for?" She snorted. "We better remember."

Nils pushed his chair back. He stepped to Devlin's seat and extended a hand. Next thing she knew, she was two beats into a rhumba and she could smell lime aftershave and a hint of merlot.

"And the carny thing?" he asked, as he sent her into a turn.

"It's zero stress, and like I said: I get to watch the boats." She flourished her wrist and fingertips, walking in a lazy, flamboyant arc away from him, and then she returned to his arms, the music driving her steps. "Plus,

I've got my savings. I don't need to worry about retiring if I live within my means, and I like my lean lifestyle."

Another turn, and Nils's hand was pulling her into him and somehow his lips brushed her ear. The singer's voice crescendoed and then the piano's notes began dying away, and Nils dipped her very, very low, and she seemed to remember her mother once telling her she was striking, if not exactly beautiful.

At the table, the waiter had taken away the appetizer plates and replaced them with the lobster and filet. Devlin cut into the steak and watched another couple approach the dance floor. She told herself they owned a boat in one of the neighboring marinas, they were doctors and had never been sued for malpractice, they had two children and three grandchildren, and they were happy. They *were happy*, right?

"So what about you?" She swept her thoughts away from the couple and mankind's capacity for happiness and returned them to Nils. "What are you hiding from down here?"

"So you know I'm hiding?"

"I know the founders of RCB Capital didn't rear their youngest to be a lousy yacht broker making a cool $50K a year."

Nils dunked a chunk of lobster into the butter ramekin. "No, that they did not." He stirred the butter, looping the chunk of meat in a counterclockwise trip around the dish.

After watching four full stirs of Nils's lobster meat, Devlin held up the almost empty wine bottle.

"No, I shouldn't have any more. I'm driving." Nils didn't look up from his stirring.

"Well, if Viggo's paying, I'll get Courvoisier." Devlin gave the waiter an expectant eye, and the kid bustled up to receive her drink order. The piano player announced she would be taking a short break. A large party to Devlin's right was all laughter and shouts.

"Whatever," she said. "No worries, man. We all have our shit. You don't have to explain anything to me. Sorry I asked."

"No," Nils said. "No, it was a fair question. You told me your stuff. So, I finished at Rollins with that classical-studies degree my folks were so excited about." He was all sarcasm, and Devlin understood perfectly. "I spent that year wandering Europe and Turkey and North Africa." He reached for the wine bottle and poured the last of the merlot into his glass. "We'll have dessert. It'll metabolize." His eyes had changed, and Devlin couldn't name what she saw, but she knew it from when she'd lain next to him one night before he'd gone back to Rollins to finish buying a worthless degree.

"Look," he said, his eyes on a window across the room, "I'll only say this once and I'm not bringing it up again, but I am going to say it. I was an asshole. I know it. I fucked up." He turned to face her and held her eyes as he drained the wine. "Anyway, I came home, tried to work for Mom and Dad. You know how that went over. Tried law school. And you know how that went, too. It didn't help that your mom raved to mine about how you were leading your class in Ann Arbor. I did some sailing and racing and ended up waiting tables in Waikiki and turning myself into some sort of surfer and 'waterman.' I loved it. Mom and Dad and Viggo—not so much. They weren't terribly impressed. Dad funneled me some money to pay for some regattas. . . . Viggo gave me some cash for surfing. But after a while, I just kind of dropped out. When money got tight, I went back to Chicago for a second to stay with a friend and to get my shit together. That's when I saw you at the yacht club."

Devlin flushed. "Yeah, not my best performance."

"You don't have to explain anything, D. Winters. It's cool." He set his elbows on the table. "I poked around online and saw the cost of living down here and packed up the car. I started brokering for Gulf Coast Yachts and struggled for about a year. Again, Viggo kicked in some cash. It's a tough industry. But I hit my stride, made a couple big sales, and got an offer to join the team at Sunset Yachts. Now, I'm stable. I race and sail with some clients. I've got the Chris Craft and I'm living how I want to live. I surf down on Galveston and paddle and dive the wrecks off Corpus." He lifted his still-full water glass. "To the bad choices we savor."

Devlin lifted her cognac. "*Cin cin.*"

"So after this, you want to walk the docks a little? Maybe see *Mambo?*" Nils grinned. "I really am just asking if you want to see my boat. No strings."

Devlin held the snifter and drew loops in the air over the table. "Sure," she said after a breath or two, "I'd like to see your girl."

Nils smiled again. "Good. I'd like you to see her. And hell, if you're curious, maybe you'd like to look at the paperwork on Viggo's case. Give me your thoughts. I downloaded a bunch of stuff off the court's website."

Chapter 8

Handcuffs

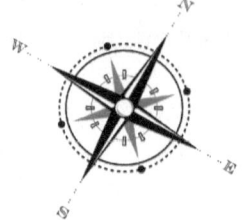

I've got a disc of jail calls I'm sending over to you right now. Our intern here will walk them over." Special Agent Lillian Carter hadn't found much of anything new on SK and N, Inc., but she'd delivered Monique Arthurton's immigration A-file to Xavier two weeks ago, and now she had called to report finding a charitable L.L.C. in Florida registered with the initials SK and N, and receiving audio files of recordings of calls Viggo Bryson had received while at the jail.

"I called up to the jail last week," Lillian continued, "and asked them to collect Bryson's calls for me. I got the disc two days ago and asked the intern to listen to the recordings and let me know if he found anything interesting. He gave me a memo on the calls yesterday. There are only three of any significance at all. I've listened to them and I think you might want to hear them. The intern's name is Hector. He's already on his way. Just walked out the door."

"Thanks, Lillian. I'll let Brittney know to look for him." Xavier hung up the phone. There was no use in asking the agent for details. It was better to review materials directly than rely on someone else's interpretations.

Xavier kidded himself he wasn't curious about Viggo Bryson's personal calls. He turned back to his computer and a spreadsheet of deposits and withdrawals out of Kalamazoo banks in an email-fraud scheme that he knew would result in a guilty plea. One of those you've-won-the-lottery schemes that affirmed Xavier's belief in the general stupidity of America. Reviewing the records served only to prevent him from getting too worked up over Bryson.

He opened his office email interface.

"Brittney," he typed, "please alert me when Hector, one of Lillian Carter's interns, arrives with a disc of materials in the Bryson matter. Thank you. X."

Maybe that was the problem: he liked to sign his emails with that capital X. Maybe that was where Brittney got off thinking Xav was an acceptable way to address him. He might have to rethink his email demeanor. He turned back to the rows of fraudulently obtained deposits. The numbers wouldn't stay put. The deposit amounts jumped up and down the spreadsheet, leaping into the cells with the withdrawal amounts, then leaping out again. The whole cursed thing swam in front of him on the screen. . . . His head swam.

Who had called Viggo?

Had she called Viggo?

The phone rang.

"Xav, that intern, Hector, is here," Brittney said through the receiver. "Do you want me to send him in?"

"No, I don't need to talk to him. Just get whatever he has and bring it to me. Thank you, Britt."

Perhaps she'd enjoy being Britt until she figured out his name had four syllables.

"Come in," Xavier responded to the two knocks on his door minutes later.

"Here we go." Brittney held out a large buckskin-colored interoffice envelope. "This is what Hector gave me for you."

"Thanks, Britt." Xavier took the envelope and turned to his desk, trusting the secretary to shut the door behind her on her way out. He removed the silver disc and slipped it into his computer.

"This is a call from the Newaygo County Jail," began the first recording. Xavier had a friend at the U.S. Attorney's Office in Houston. Down there, defendants awaited trial at an actual Bureau of Prisons facility within walking distance of the office. Those Texas practitioners didn't have to slog an hour and a half north on snowy rural roads in winter, or get stuck behind apple-orchard machinery on the same roads in summer, traveling to a county jail that housed federal prisoners under contract. They got to walk over to an actual federal facility to interview the condemned. Xavier didn't much care about the situation. He seldom went to the jail. If he wanted to conduct a proffer interview with a prisoner, he had the marshals bring the snitch down to the lockup at the courthouse. But he did see fiscal irresponsibility in paying all the public defenders to sit in their cars and listen to books-on-tape while they drove through Western Michigan.

The jail's recording unspooled, warning the parties to the call that the call would be recorded. Then a voice faltered. People unused to calling custodial facilities tended to falter at first.

"Vi— Viggo? Um, Viggo? It's Nils."

The brother. Xavier sighed. Was Lillian wasting his time?

"Nils," Viggo Bryson's pompous, still-overconfident voice responded. On the screen in front of him, Xavier examined the outlines of his reflection in the black space that filled most of the laptop's monitor as the recording played. He adjusted his glasses, smoothed his hair. He'd walk over to the barbershop after work today.

"Viggo, bro, it's good to hear your voice."

"Man, you have no idea."

During the obligatory awkward pause, Xavier checked the time stamp. This first call had originated two days after Viggo's arrest.

"How's Grant?" Viggo broke the silence.

"He's good. I mean, I think he's really confused and maybe even a little scared or uncomfortable, but he's good. He's got everything he needs. I cash—"

"Everything's being recorded," Viggo broke in.

No criminal history, and he'd been in custody all of two days, and he was already a pro. Xavier reseated his glasses again. With that kind of savvy, these calls might not be as helpful as Lillian Carter had implied.

"Oh. Well, yeah. Um, Grant's good," Nils Bryson continued. "We had a nice dinner last night. You'll never believe with whom. We went to Galveston with Devlin Winters."

"Are you serious?" Viggo laughed and he sounded natural to Xavier; the laugh sounded real and uninhibited, unmarred by a federal indictment and residence in a jail pod.

"Yeah, apparently she moved down here a couple years ago. Lives on a boat now."

"Is she still practicing law?" Xavier hated that Viggo's voice sounded self-possessed, even what women might consider attractive.

The brother hesitated. Xavier wrote the name on his legal pad and the time it occurred in the call: "Devlin Winters @ 1:08." He'd find out who this perhaps-attorney was.

"Uh, no, I don't think so." Nils Bryson fumbled around with his words. "We didn't talk much about ourselves. We mostly talked to Grant. He got to tell her all about *Camilla* and sailing with you. She kind of bonded with him over that. She told him how we all grew up sailing together at Chicago Yacht Club."

How endearing: the kid got to talk about the forty-two-foot yacht against which Xavier had initiated forfeiture proceedings.

"Devlin still got a nice ass?" Viggo sounded like he was smirking.

"I didn't notice her ass, but she's still pretty fuckin' hot, Viggo." The brother sounded as though he wouldn't pass a polygraph test on the ass issue—he'd noticed the posterior.

Xavier sighed. Listening to these calls took up time, but one couldn't skim an audio recording, and the best parts tended to lie hidden in the dross.

"To each his own, my brother. You've always liked 'em bitchy." Viggo's voice was losing its buoyancy. "In other news, can you stay in touch with my attorney? Her name is Irene Stockton. You can sign up for a PACER account to access federal court records. Google it. It's easy to get an account. Then go to the website for the U.S. District Court for the Western District of Michigan and look up my case. You can look it up with just my name. Her info—Irene Stockton's info—is on the docket. Call her. Introduce yourself. I'll make sure she knows she can talk to you. Stay in touch with her, would you?"

"Sure, Viggo, of course. Um, do you need me to like send you money or anything?"

"No, I'm fine," Viggo replied. Xavier scowled. He had not been able to freeze all Viggo's assets—right to counsel and all that. Viggo got to access certain funds to retain an attorney, and Xavier was guessing that some of those attorney funds had found their way into Viggo's commissary account.

"Well, don't worry about Grant at all," the brother said. "I'll get him into school in the fall or with a tutor. I . . . I know you want him homeschooled, but I'm not sure I can manage all that right now. I work a lot of hours, Viggo. I live off commission. Having a kid wasn't really in my plan. But I'll get him squared away and as comfortable as possible. I think he likes staying on the boat. Kid says he's sleeping well."

"Thanks, man. I know it's an imposition. I really do. And don't worry about the homeschooling. If he's gotta go to school, it's fine. I just would rather have him with you than with Mom and Dad. A little human contact is better than none. He's a sensitive kid."

"No worries, bro. We're good."

Was the brother some sort of "surfer dude"? Xavier realized he knew chapter and verse on Viggo's life but not enough on the family. He made another note: "Nils Bryson. Texas? Galveston?"

"Thanks, man." Viggo now sounded tired. "Oh, and hey, don't dip your wick in Devlin Winters again, man. That chick was never good for you."

"Fuck you, Viggo," the brother said. "Stay safe. I'll call you again soon."

"Hey, call my attorney more than me. Everything here is recorded. It's not much good talking on here."

"Okay, man. Hey, I, um, I love ya, Viggo."

"Thanks." Viggo paused. "Tell Grant I love him."

"Will do."

The call ended.

Xavier shook his head. Fools. He clicked on the next file. The jail recording preface repeated into his office. He checked the time stamp. This call had occurred only three days ago.

"Viggo, it's Nils. How are you holding up, man? You all right?" The brother sounded harried.

"I'm doing as well as can be expected on a diet of nacho chips, colored sugar water, and miniature hot dogs."

"I've been in touch with Irene, but I guess I just wanted to call myself and see how you're doing. Does she let you know that we talk? That she and I talk?"

"Yeah," Viggo replied, "she tells me she talks to you. I think things are about as good as they can be right now."

"Good. Hey, remember how I mentioned Devlin Winters?"

"Yeah." Viggo sighed. "Tell me you did not hit that."

"Fuck you, Viggo. Really. But anyway, no, I am not dating Devlin Winters."

"Who said anything about dating? I said hit that." Viggo snorted.

The licentious cretins. Xavier tapped his pen on his pad.

"Whatever," the brother continued. "Anyway, you know she was a partner at Sondheim Baker, right? And you know she did federal criminal defense?"

"Yeah, I know," Viggo said, "and she punched the former governor of Illinois in the face in front of a jury during his trial for all that contracting fraud he got caught up in."

"Okay, so you knew all that?" Nils Bryson paused.

"The whole state of Illinois knows it," Viggo said. "It was all over the news. Everywhere. I know it and I was already in Michigan by then. Everyone knows it."

"Well, anyway, I showed her some stuff and she had some ideas—"

"We're being recorded," Viggo cut in.

"Yeah, but this isn't anything—"

"Talk to Irene about it. She may be crazy, but Devlin was always smart. Have her call Irene. Fuck, have Irene hire her as a consultant or whatever. I don't care. If she has something to say, I'll listen. She's a bitch, but she's a smart bitch."

"Okay, I'll have her call Irene."

As the call wrapped up, Xavier scribbled on his pad: "Devlin Winters—disbarred attorney from ABA article. Gov of IL case." He remembered that debacle, had even included a discussion of it in an ethics seminar he'd taught.

He closed the audio file and clicked on the icon for the final call. While the jail message again warned parties they were being recorded, he made a couple notes, and then his stomach clenched:

"Viggo?" It was her.

He dropped his pen.

"Viggo?" Her voice sounded taut.

"Niqi."

Fuck Viggo Bryson. Fuck him. Xavier hit pause and stood up. He walked across his office. He didn't have any windows to stare out. Nothing on his walls except his law-school diploma and bar-admission certificates. He picked up his tea mug: empty save for a few errant leaves stuck to the bottom and sides.

Fuck. Viggo. Bryson.

He flung the mug across the room. It bounced off the bookcase and fell onto the carpet, a chip off its lip landing beside it and providing the only evidence of abuse. Xavier stared at the chip, hoped the carpet had shrouded the thudding sounds of his indiscretion.

"God forgive me for thinking in such language," he whispered, crossing himself.

He inhaled, felt his lungs expand.

He needed to go get some tea. Or go to the breakroom to refill his water bottle. Or . . . .

He sat back down at his desk and clicked play.

"Viggo, what are you doing? What have you done?" Monique Arthurton was hissing.

"Niqi, it's going to be all right."

"Viggo, it is not all right. You are going to ruin me. Again."

"Niqi, please, everything we say is being recorded. Please don't say—"

"Viggo, I do not care if I am being recorded. I do not care what happens to you. I do not care about any of this—this mess you've gotten yourself into . . . like you always do. You deserve whatever happens to you."

"Niqi." Viggo tried to speak.

Monique cut him off, making the recording somewhat difficult to understand for a few beats. When Viggo stopped trying to talk over Monique, the recording smoothed out, and Xavier heard Monique shout, "Want my son back. I will get my son back, Viggo. If you rot in prison, all the better."

"Niqi, enough," Viggo shouted back.

"No, Viggo, I want my son and I want my business to be safe. I've worked so hard. I've come so far. I'm not going to lose it."

"Then give my attorney the records to prove that none of this is fraud. That everything was above board. Niqi, send the paperwork on the loans you got from my clients to my attorney. The loans," Viggo sounded harsh, raspy, "my brother's ocean-loving fucking friends secured for you with my clients. My brother and his stupid fucking surfer buddies got my clients on board with your save-the-whales shit. I did that for you, Monique. So send the records to my attorney so I can get the fuck out of here."

"So you can keep me away from my son? No, Viggo, no, no, no. I'm getting my son back. I finally have a chance to get my son." Monique's voice cracked.

Xavier hit pause again.

He rose and walked to the bookshelf, knelt and retrieved the chipped mug. He left on the carpet the porcelain slice of its lip the impact of hitting the shelf had torn from it. At his desk, he slammed the mug on his legal pad. Once, twice, three times. Noise be damned.

Damn you to hell, Viggo Bryson.

He hurled the mug for a second trip across his office, then dropped into his chair and hit play yet again.

"Niqi, my brother will get Grant. I'm no more giving him to you than I would give him to Medusa." Viggo snorted. "You are not getting Grant. No matter what."

The progress bar at the base of the screen showed the recording advancing, but only silence streamed from the computer.

"Niqi, you can fix this," Viggo finally whispered. "Just come up here and testify and give my attorney the records. Explain to everyone how Nils got those investors for you, how those companies loaned you money, how my clients wanted to support your mission of cleaning up the waters of the Caribbean. Tell the jury how much you've done for your country's dive industry, how much you've helped promote tourism. Niqi, do the right thing here."

"I'm not testifying for you, Viggo Bryson. I'm not helping you get out so you can rob me of my own son again."

"My attorney will subpoena you."

Monique laughed, but it wasn't the laugh Xavier knew. It wasn't the laugh of sharing cheeseburgers and french fries at a wooden table at a seafood shack on Frigate Bay with boats anchored in calm water that recalled the glitter of pyrite as the sun disappeared behind clouds and the western horizon.

"Yes, Viggo, subpoena me. Send your henchmen to St. Kitts with their subpoenas. Tell them to bring guns and handcuffs, too. You always liked handcuffs."

There was a click and then silence, and Xavier couldn't get to the men's room fast enough. As he leaned over the commode and wretched, nothing came up, nothing truly released except the tears he thought he'd finished with years ago.

Chapter 9
And Even a Magician

Who would be knocking on *A`uku*'s hull at this hour? Devlin extricated her left arm from the blanket and looked at her watch. How could it be past nine already?

"One minute!" she shouted, untangling from the bedding and struggling to sit up. She slipped into her shower sandals and pulled her t-shirt down, making sure it reached past the waistband of the basketball shorts that comprised her usual sleep attire. Since Nils had been hanging around, she hadn't been drinking as much, so she opened the companionway with an unhealthy amount of vigor for having just crawled out of bed. Sunshine, Gulf Coast humidity, and a "good morning" in Nils's voice streamed in.

"Damn, Nils, what are you thinking, pounding on my boat in the wee hours?" Devlin shaded her eyes.

"D. Winters, it's hardly early. Hey, I'm showing two Beneteaus on this dock this morning, so I thought I'd stop by. I, uh, think I've committed a cardinal sin. And I'm hoping you might be up to helping me out. You're off today, right?"

"Yeah, I'm off. Come aboard." Devlin slipped back down into the cabin and sat on her berth, waiting for Nils to climb aboard the trawler and down the hatch.

"Did I wake you?" Nils asked, the stateroom's unmade berth greeting him as he stepped down the ladder.

"Yup." Devlin nodded. "So I guess you've committed two sins this morning."

"Sorry, D." Nils dropped onto the pilot berth across from Devlin's bed. "So did I tell you I've been working with Viggo's attorney, Irene, up north? And she recommended I get legal-guardian status over Grant for the duration of Viggo's custody."

"Yeah, you said something about it the other night at dinner at San Lorenzo's."

"Well, Irene set me up with an attorney down here to help me with all that stuff. And that guy just sent me a bunch of paperwork this morning, and I noticed Grant's birthday. I don't know how I forgot or didn't think about it, but I missed the kid's ninth birthday. Like what is wrong with me? The kid's going through all this turmoil, he's away from his dad, he's in a new environment, and I go and forget his birthday."

Nils rubbed a palm against his brow.

"Yeah, that's going to win you Uncle of the Year. You want something to eat?" Devlin pushed herself off her bunk and took the two steps up to the saloon and galley.

"Sure, what do you have?"

"Cereal," she said, already opening the fridge and pulling out chocolate almond milk. "I've still got pizza from the other night at Pomodoro's, too." She stared at the leftovers in the fridge, all of them from meals with Nils. What was she doing? Spending all her dinners with him, and often Grant?

"I'll take pizza." Nils joined her in the saloon, dropped onto the settee behind the table. "So, I'm wondering—hoping—maybe pleading—that you'd perhaps like to spend some time on your day off planning some sort of amazing surprise party for the kid tonight. I'll hire your services as an event planner. Viggo will pay for everything, of course. Could you?" he trailed off.

"You want me to plan a kid's birthday party? Nils, I don't even like kids. I don't know what to do for something like that." She pulled the pizza out of the microwave and set it in front of Nils.

The boat's saloon had navy curtains, but she seldom pulled them shut. Now, morning streamed into the varnished interior and lit up the inside steering station, which she almost never used, preferring the bridge on the upper deck outside when she infrequently took *A'uku* for a ride.

"Please, Devlin? I'll be with these people all day, showing boats. And I want to do it tonight. I mean, you're working tomorrow night, right? If we don't do it tonight, we'll have to wait till next week when you're off, and I've already missed the actual birthday by like a couple weeks."

"You're right there: can't have a party till I walk in." Devlin set her cereal on the table and slid onto the settee by Nils. He really wasn't going to celebrate this kid's birthday without her participation? Huh.

Nils twisted on the bench seat and dug in his back pocket. "Here. Seriously. Here's a thousand bucks. Put together a great party for this kid. Keep what you don't use. I mean, don't go absolutely nuts. It's for one kid—he still doesn't know anyone down here. But maybe a nice cake, some sort of cool venue, whatever toys or books you think he might like." Nils held out the cash.

Devlin stared at the ten one-hundred-dollar bills. She used to drop that much on dinner and drinks, but now, Nils holding out the money made her uncomfortable. "Nils, I don't know anything about this stuff. I really don't. I—"

His eyes held hers until she dropped her gaze to examine her chocolate-something cereal bathing in the chocolate almond milk. "I keep what's leftover?" she asked the cereal.

"Yeah, sure."

"Okay." She took the bills and stuffed them in the pocket of her shorts. "I'll put something together. It'll be mediocre, so I can cut corners and keep more of the money." She laughed.

"I know you too well." Nils took a bite of pizza. "The over-achiever in you still lives. And she won't let that happen."

"You obviously don't know me now," Devlin mumbled. She tried to sneak a glance at Nils, but he caught her eyes, and the cabin of the boat suddenly felt very small and her t-shirt very thin.

***

"Sean?" Devlin was on the bridge of the trawler, under the sunshade, trying to reach Sean Tofilau on the phone an hour later.

"Devlin, my love, what are you up to?"

"Well, my Samoan brother, I need your help."

"No, no, no, my love. Not without a little payment up front. We haven't talked in how long? Let's start with how you're doing. You and Mr. Bryson. Hey, my clients bought a Hatteras he had listed three days ago, so he's got some coin in his jeans to take you out somewhere nice. Just FYI."

"Oh, Sean," Devlin set her elbows on her knees and dropped her head into her hands, keeping the phone pressed to her ear, "that's a conversation for another day."

Beyond the canvas bimini top, a couple seagulls screamed at each other. For the briefest moment, Devlin wondered if she should pick up some gin after she finished the call, but somehow, she knew it wouldn't help.

"Well, just give me the Twitter version. Are you dating the guy?"

"No, Sean. I'm serious when I say that I'm not up for dating anyone. But I am planning his nephew's birthday party. He's taking care of the kid for a while and he forgot the kid's birthday, so now he wants me to put together some sort of blow-out party for the kid tonight."

"Devlin Winters is planning a child's birthday? Lemme just go pack my emergency supplies for the Apocalypse."

"Yeah, I know." She sighed. "But that's why I'm calling. You know that open house your brokerage did last fall that you told me you did most of the planning for? Can you get me the contact info for those Polynesian dancers and that magician you had on the docks for the kids?"

"Devlin, you are brilliant. The kid'll love that." Sean's side of the call went quiet, and Devlin waited while he ostensibly searched for the contact info.

On the dock below the trawler's lofty bridge, the marina manager walked past with a heavyset, Hispanic-looking fellow with a crewcut and a yellow polo-shirt. As she waited for Sean's return to the line, Devlin watched the manager point and gesture. She didn't know him well, had never really wanted to know the marina staff or her neighbors, though Southern hospitality, or general nosiness, had made some of the local personalities hard to avoid. The number of vacant slips, however, probably told the whole story here: the manager needed to rent boat stalls.

"Okay, I got the numbers." Sean came back on the phone. "I'll text them to you."

"You are a rock star."

"Any time, princess."

She ended the call, felt the vibration of Sean's text with the numbers, and climbed down to the trawler's deck. The marina manager and Mr. Yellow Shirt had turned and were heading back up the dock toward the parking lot. Devlin grabbed the garbage bags that needed disposal from the trawler's galley and head, and found herself following the two men past the slips of boats and up the gangplank to the parking lot.

That's it! Jumping World.

Devlin couldn't explain the inspiration's arrival at that exact moment, but with the idea's descent, she hurried to the dumpster, flung her trash into the receptacle, and walked to the shade of the bathhouse roof's overhang to pause and look up the phone number for a local trampoline place. She'd often overheard parents on the boardwalk comparing the value of the boardwalk attractions to an evening at Jumping World. When she looked up from her phone, a blur of excess yellowness caught her eye.

What are you doing, Mr. Sunshine? Are you taking pictures of Nils's Jeep?

Devlin watched the man stop and pull out his phone. The marina manager had, Devlin assumed, returned to his office, and now this visitor-cum-citrus-fruit stood to the side of Nils's vehicle and fiddled with his device. The show lasted only a few seconds and then the guy continued down the parking lot and opened the door to a blue Camry. Devlin watched the Toyota pull up to the marina gate, watched the gate slide open, and waited until the car had pulled out and disappeared around the corner, blocked by the topiary of the marina's shrub fence.

Devlin, hun, what was that? She shook her head and walked back toward *A`uku*. On the boat's bridge, once again beneath the sunshade, she tapped the phone number on the Jumping World website.

"Yeah, hi," she said into the phone three rings later, "I'm guessing you have like birthday packages. For kids. Like for a nine-year-old. Um hmm."

***

From her seat on the bridge with a paperback in front of her and the sun starting to set behind her, Devlin watched Nils walk up the dock hours-of-too-much-planning later. "How'd the boat showings go, Mr. Bryson?"

"I think I'll have a sale within the week," he replied as he stepped aboard. "More important: how's the party planning?"

"Well, $250 gets us a private room, pizza, soda, and all the jumping we could want for up to ten kids at Jumping

World. It's a trampoline place by I-45. $300 got me a magician, even on this short notice. And $400 got me a troupe of Polynesian dancers. But I kind of screwed the pooch on this one because I went to a bakery and spent $40 on a cake. Maggie has it in the fridge in the marina office. It wouldn't fit in my fridge. I stopped at a bookstore and got a Tolkien book on the way home. I hope Grant hasn't got *The Hobbit* yet. So all in all, I netted nothing for my day's work."

"You are magnificent." Nils sprang up the ladder to the bridge. "I'll make it up to you. I'll give you some cash tonight. You really are—" He faltered, stepped in too close to Devlin, and leaned over, putting his hand on the back of her pilot's seat. "You're—" Again, the pause. Devlin inhaled his day of schlepping over hot docks and into un-air-conditioned boats, and then she didn't stop herself: she reached up and pushed the lock of brown hair back away from the sunglasses.

Nils seemed to freeze.

"Sorry." She turned toward the boat's teak steering wheel, with its brass hub and eight spokes and desperate need for varnish. "I just haven't done that in a long time. Wanted to see what it would be like now."

"And?" Nils spoke after three full breaths, three inhales and three exhales Devlin heard as she examined a hairline crack in the wheel's felloe.

"And I'll go get that cake from Maggie's fridge." She pushed up abruptly and hopped down to the main deck. "Here, I'll grab the book—I wrapped it in pages from an old *Sailing World* Maggie gave me—and lock up and we'll grab the cake and get out of here. Our reservation is at six. With traffic, we should get on the road now if we're going to pick up the kid and get to this trampoline wonderland in a timely manner."

Nils swung down the steps from the bridge to land on the deck beside Devlin and grab her arm as she pulled the door to the saloon open.

"Just answer the question, counselor." His sunglasses reflected her distorted face into the too-close space between them.

She watched herself in the lenses, the brim of her cap and her cheeks, distended by the curve of the glasses. The boat creaked. Up the dock, a woman shouted something. Laughter and then another shout followed.

"It was like I remember it."

She turned from her distorted reflection and jumped over the step at the base of the door into the trawler's saloon to grab the book, in its wrapping of sailboat ads and serif fonts, off the table.

Chapter 10

Gone Bad a Marnin

After closing out of the jail calls, Xavier forgot all about going to the barber shop. He left a message on Lillian Carter's voicemail about having the jail send recordings of all Viggo's calls to the U.S. Attorney's Office each week. He would be listening closely from here on out. Then he redoubled his efforts to care about the email-fraud spreadsheets. When five o'clock arrived, leaving the office empty, he slipped his laptop into his briefcase and headed to the bus stop. Now, with the boys flanking him on the couch, he let himself breathe.

"What do you want to watch, boys?" he asked.

He was hungry, and he had the fixings for beef stroganoff in the kitchen, but he lacked the will to get up and make it. Instead, he grabbed the remote control and hit the button to open the DVD player.

"How about some Butch Cassidy?" As he pushed himself up, he thought of having to sit through the whole Katherine Ross love-interest subplot, but he pulled the movie's plastic case off the shelf by the TV anyway.

The DVD player sucked in the disc, and Xavier watched the screen light up, but he couldn't focus. Perhaps his blood sugar had dropped. He tended to get light headed when he was very hungry. In the kitchen, he pulled a coconut cream pie out of the fridge. As the Hole in the Wall Gang contemplated mutiny in the living room, he sliced into the pie, scrutinizing the staying power of the crust. He'd tried a new recipe for it, and it looked like it had held up. He carried a plate of pie and a bag of cat treats back to the couch.

Before sitting down, he adjusted the thermostat. The condo felt drafty despite the affable summer evening beyond the windows. In the bedroom, he dug out an afghan. The thing was hideous, with screaming stripes and an ugly wave pattern, but his sister had made it years ago, had given it to him one Christmas when he was in law school. With its unprepossessing aesthetics, he didn't feel bad when the boys clawed it.

Menelaus had hopped on the side table and was sniffing at the pie when Xavier returned with the blanket. Xavier set the throw on the couch's armrest and picked up the cat. Paul Newman filled the screen. Menelaus purred.

"Here, boys." Xavier set Menny down and pulled two cat treats out of the bag.

The couch grew cramped. The boys draped themselves over Xavier's lap. With some thirty-five pounds of cat on him, Xavier fidgeted, felt a bit suffocated.

"Keep watching, boys. I'll be right back."

He freed himself from the blanket and the cats and returned to the bedroom. He generally kept the shades drawn for privacy, and he'd chosen a nutmeg color for the walls, so the room always felt subdued. Tonight, it felt dark, even—

He caught himself. Xavier had never been lonely. Independent, self-driven, separate—yes. But never lonely. On the bureau, the Holy Mother reassured him from Her triptych. And then, without considering the action, he stepped to the bureau and pulled open the top drawer. He pushed aside a stack of CDs and removed a shoebox from the depths. Dropping to the floor, he lifted the lid . . . and there she was.

Desert-night eyes stared up at him, holding a smile, a joke only the two of them could understand, a laugh only he had heard. He grinned.

"Hey, Niqi," he whispered to a teenaged Monique Arthurton.

But then he could hear her shouting. *Handcuffs, handcuffs, handcuffs.*

Her voice rose. *Handcuffs, handcuffs, handcuffs.*

The TV in the living room spilled noise over the shouts in his head. Xavier shut his eyes, dug his fingernails into his scalp. He rolled onto his side. Above him, the Holy Mother cradled Christ.

He would pray for her. He would pray. He would pray—

"Ave Maria, gratia plena, Dominus tecum. Benedicta Tu in mulieribus, et beneductus fructus ventris Tui, Jesus."

Agamemnon pushed against his face, pushed his glasses into the bridge of his nose. The cat was purring. It bumped at him. He opened his eyes, reached out and stroked the husky creature, felt moisture on the fur. He hadn't realized he'd been, that he'd—

He pushed himself up to seated and pulled the great cat into his lap. *It's just weakness leaving the body. The tears are just weakness. I'm just shedding weakness.*

In the living room, Paul Newman said something . . . loudly.

Enough of this. Xavier managed to gather his legs under him and wrestle himself to standing while still cradling Aggie. He strode back into the living room, setting the cat beside its brother on the afghan, and pulled his laptop out of his briefcase, flipping open the screen. After satisfying the security criteria, he clicked on his work email.

Lillian Carter's address appeared on an unread note. Agent Carter? Actually working late? He clicked on the message.

X, I did some more digging on Monique Arthurton. I was able to track down the two landlords for the Chicago addresses, and they are the same people who rented to her. They still own the buildings. The first one, from the building on the south side, remembers her. It took him a minute, but he's an old guy and I got him talking and he says he remembers her because of a string of domestic-violence incidents. Apparently, Viggo's a wife beater. Or at least Monique and the guy she was shacked up with used to make a lot of noise and the neighbors would call the cops. The landlord said at least twice a neighbor called him as well. He used to live in the building, so he could respond to disturbances right away. He said more than once he went upstairs to find Monique and the guy in the hall pushing and shoving, and he said he saw bruises on both of them, including on their faces. He said he can't recall officers ever making an arrest, though.

Xavier was sitting on the carpet, with his shoulders resting against the back of the couch, the computer in his lap. His throat had tightened, dried out. He swallowed. Niqi, in her nightgown, in a shabby south-side tenement. Bruised. He shook his head, set the computer aside, rested his face in his hands. Someone should have castrated Viggo Bryson long ago, but then again, Niqi had chosen Viggo. She had had other opportunities. Helen had sailed off to Troy with Paris, only to discover his propensity for sniveling. Hector got dragged behind a chariot, and Menelaus . . . well . . . Menelaus had ended up with Helen in the end. It had simply taken a long, long war.

He rubbed his eyes.

What else did you find, Agent Carter?

He retrieved the computer.

The second landlord was an older lady. I'm guessing she's from somewhere in the islands given her accent. She was very cagey. It was clear she remembered Monique, even more so than the other guy, but she asked me to repeat who I was and where I was calling from. When I explained who I was again, she told me she couldn't talk to me. But she said she would take down my info. She said she has a son who's a lawyer and that she will talk to him and that he might call me. She said she wouldn't talk to me without talking to her son first. That's all I got.

Oh, Muma, *I've taught you well.*

Agent Carter went on to say she would continue digging and confirmed she would be getting recordings of Viggo's jail calls weekly. "And now we know the renter of the Rogers Park apartment was our Monique. So she did go back to Chicago. Looking for Viggo or her kid?"

Xavier rubbed his head. He hadn't expected Lillian Carter to be quite this motivated. He'd have to be a little wary from here on out. It wouldn't look good to get pulled off the prosecution and dumped on the witness stand. He shut the laptop and got up to find his phone.

"*Muma,*" he sang into it moments later.

"Xavier!" His mother's voice loosened his shoulders.

"*Muma,* how are you?"

"Eh, cookin' on gas." She laughed.

"That's good to hear, mum." He paused. "*Muma,* did a woman from the IRS call you today?"

"Eh, yeah. Some woman saying she was an agent with the government. She was looking for Niqi Arthurton." Xavier's mother paused. "Xavier?"

"I'm here, mum. Did you tell her anything? Tell the agent anything?"

"Never. I told her my boy is an attorney and I told her I'd talk to you about it. I told her you'd call her if you wanted to."

"That was good, mum. I'm glad you didn't talk to her. I don't think it would help anyone if you talked to her—or anyone from the government. You did the right thing. If someone contacts you again, just get their information and then tell me, all right?"

"Sure thing. I won't say anything to 'em." She fell silent for a breath. "Xavier, Niqi Arthurton—she was never good to you. Or for you."

"Did you say anything else to the agent?" Xavier held his breath. "Did you tell her my name?"

"No, no, Xavier. I didn't tell her anything." *Muma* paused, waited. "You all good, boy? Anything the matter?"

Xavier dug his toes into the carpet. "No, everything's fine, mum. It just looks like Niqi got into some trouble, and I don't want to be associated with it."

Muma clucked her tongue. "That girl." Xavier could just see his mum wagging her gray head.

"I'll pray for her," his mother said. "I'm going for adoration tomorrow. I'll light a candle for her, too." Xavier's mother lit a lot of candles.

He asked his mother about some elderly neighbors and listened to her recount her shopping exploits with Mrs. Kucharski. She admonished him to eat well, and then she asked about the boys.

"They're great, mum. Thriving. In fact, Menny is rubbing on my leg right now. I think he's jealous the attention's not all on him." Xavier tried to laugh.

"You be good then," *Muma* said as the conversation waned. "And, Xavier, don't you think much about Niqi Arthurton. That girl was never any good. *Wha gone bad a marnin cyarn come good a evenin.*"

The call ended and Xavier became aware of Robert Redford's voice and the sound of gunfire in the living room. Aggie was intent on the movie when Xavier walked in and grabbed his laptop from the floor.

"You're a good cat," Xavier mumbled, rubbing Aggie's head as he flopped on the couch.

"Irene," he typed into an email.

Our plea deadline is upon us. I'll assume from your client's silence that we are proceeding to trial unless I hear otherwise from you within three days. I will be sending you a disc of recordings of your client's calls at the jail. I do not believe they are exculpatory, and I will object to their admission at trial as they constitute inadmissible hearsay. But I will forward you copies via courier tomorrow.
Yours, Xavier Charles.

Sent. He laid the laptop aside.

He'd waited a long, long time to bring Viggo Bryson to justice. This was going to be fun.

Menelaus jumped onto the couch and walked across Xavier's lap toward the end table.

"Oh, yes. Thank you for reminding me." Xavier turned to the table and lifted the plate of pie, took a bite. Yes, the crust had held up well. He chewed as he turned back to the computer.

Agent Carter, thank you for your work tracking down Monique Arthurton. Some thoughts come to mind given the jail calls we've heard. First, I have my doubts that Ms. Arthurton truly runs and operates SK and N, Incorporated. All of the Blue Tide, L.L.C., records (and everything from Gray Hill) suggest Viggo Bryson is the puppet master for all of these entities.

Second, even if the company has some legitimate purpose, even if it engaged in certain legitimate transactions, the company cannot possibly account for the volume of revenue flowing from it to Bryson's clients. So even if records, or even Ms. Arthurton herself, appear for trial, I think we can still establish for the jury that these transactions were designed to circumvent the tax laws. Honestly, it seems dubious to me that a small, single-operator environmental-mission entity was legitimately handling the dollar amounts involved here. If that was the case, however, we have a duty to do justice. We certainly wouldn't want to convict someone wrongly.

But if in fact the defense can muster evidence that Ms. Arthurton was legitimately procuring and handling all these monies—to clean up coral reefs or whathaveyou—I would imagine jurors are going to be asking themselves some questions, again namely about the volume of funds here. It seems doubtful they would believe SK and N had tens of millions of dollars flowing through it as investments and loans. The attempt at proving legitimacy might actually serve to underscore Bryson's fraud here, help demonstrate it was all a cover.

Regardless, let's continue searching for information on SK and N. Also, let's look into Bryson's brother, this Nils Bryson. It sounds as though he may have been involved with bringing alleged investors to SK and N.

Thank you for your efforts,

X

P.S. Of course, you have probably already launched a search of social media, but I want to make sure we cover that avenue. I have no social-media accounts, so could you, or someone there (perhaps that intern), see if you can find anything on any of our players through any of the popular accounts? Many thanks. X

P.P.S. Let's also look into the disbarred attorney Nils Bryson mentioned in one of those calls. I believe the name is Devlin Winters. I remember some press on her from a few years ago. I believe she punched the former governor of Illinois while defending him before a jury. If she's helping Irene, I'd just like to know. Yours, X

P.P.S. Have you searched for that Florida SK and N, L.L.C., in the records we have? Does it show up anywhere? I'll start looking myself tomorrow. Is there a link? X

He chewed his lip. "There, that's enough, Menny." He lifted the plate away from the cat and hit "send."

It was Viggo's fraud. Niqi didn't concoct this scheme. She just got into the middle of it, in typical Niqi style.

He closed out of his email and brought up the internet. Nils Bryson . . . .

Sunset Yachts, L.L.C.

Meet the Team.

A smiling face in a ballcap with a Sunset Yachts logo on it beamed at Xavier.

Nils Bryson brings to the Sunset team a stellar racing resume and the true spirit of a waterman. Nils grew up sailing on the Great Lakes, bringing trophies and prestige to Chicago Yacht Club. He became the club's second junior sailing skipper to win both the Bemis and Smythe Trophies of the U.S. Sailing Junior Championships (and he was crewing for his Bemis Cup team member Devlin Winters when she became the first Chicago Yacht Club skipper to win both awards). He has won three Chicago-to-Mackinac races and four Key West Race Weeks (in J-70s and Melges 24s) and he ran an Olympic campaign in 49ers. His cruising accomplishments include passages from Los Angeles to the Big Island of Hawai'i and around the Farrallon Islands (often referred to as the Devil's Teeth) and over a dozen Gulf crossings. When not sailing, he enjoys scuba diving and surfing, and he spent several seasons as a tow-in surfer on Oahu's north shore before moving to Texas.

His goal at Sunset is to get every client into the boat that fits their needs and presents a good value. Everyone should experience the joy of life on the water and Nils is ready to get you there! Let's chase that Sunset!

Let's chase that Sunset? Pathetic. And they say I can't write.

Xavier stared at the screen. He'd heard of the Chicago-to-Mackinac Race. It seemed safe to say that most people who grew up in Chicago heard about the race at some point. He typed in "Chicago-to-Mackinac Race" and found himself staring at a picture of a sailboat passing a lighthouse. An expensive-looking boat. He brought up his email.

Agent Carter, I know we've discussed Bryson's parents' venture-capital firm and their access to funding and potential clients for Bryson's exploits, but it appears his brother may also have ties to potential investors (as Viggo hinted at in the call with Arthurton). It seems the brother is some sort of sailboat racer and may have access to investors through his ties to the yachting community. It may be worth investigating some of the alleged SK and N investors to see if they sail or if they have purchased boats from Sunset Yachts, L.L.C., in Kemah, Texas. I still think SK and N is nothing but a cover for Bryson, but I do not want to get ambushed.

I may also consider some sort of immunity agreement for Monique Arthurton if we can arrange a meeting. I don't want to go to trial without all the information.

Depending on who and what we find, I may supersede on the indictment. We may be adding co-defendants. Perhaps even the brother.

We will just have to see.
X

The Bryson boys might like bonding in a cell together. As soon as Xavier hit send, the computer chimed.

Xavier, you are correct. We are on our way to trial. Thank you for checking in. I'll stay in touch regarding the government's proposed witness list, exhibits, and jury instructions.
Irene

And then another chime.

X, don't you ever go off the clock? ;) I'm looking at Facebook again now. Hector and I have been on and off several social platforms over the past few months. Let's get lunch tomorrow and catch up.
Lillian

Lillian had used smiley faces before. They sustained Xavier's doubts regarding her professionalism. But he had never conducted a lunch meeting with an agent.
A third chime.

P.S. X, the jail just emailed this to me. Viggo received a JPay note today. Worth a look. Looking forward to seeing you tomorrow! ☺

A PDF sat at the bottom of Lillian's email. Xavier clicked on it. The document bore the logo of the inmates' JPay email system and then lines of text.

Viggo,

I'm getting Grant back. I've hired someone to help me and he discovered that you sent Grant to your brother. I'm willing to be fair. If Nils puts Grant on a plane to the island, I will send all the loan documents to your attorney. Then just leave us alone. You'll be free and we will be here. Stay away from us.

Monique

Chapter II
Trampolines

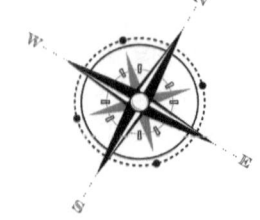

Grant passed Devlin the cake box. His smile *was* his face.

"You sure you didn't peek?" She accepted the box.

"No, Miss Devlin, I really didn't," the little boy assured her.

She set the cake on the Jeep's hood and helped the kid climb out of the back seat.

"Where are we?" Grant sounded something like breathless.

Pulling a canvas bag holding the wrapped book and some party tchotchkes from the dollar store over her shoulder, Devlin slammed the Jeep's door shut and hefted the cake.

"Jumping World, buddy. It's trampoline wonderland."

Or so I'm told. Heaven help me.

She started toward the beige stucco maw of the modern Cerberus. From the corner of her eye, she noticed a blue Camry pull into a parking spot a row over.

"Huh," she muttered.

"What's wrong, Miss Devlin?"

"Nothing, bud. You ready for some birthday fun?"

When Devlin and Nils had retrieved Grant from the tutor's place and explained they had a surprise planned, and Nils had fallen on the sword and begged forgiveness for forgetting the kid's birthday, Grant had responded with less of his usual adult aplomb and more of a nine-year-old's antsy excitement. The kid's fidgeting in the car on the drive had comforted Devlin in some way—maybe the kid was just a kid and not merely the annoying spawn of a grandstanding father.

At the check-in desk, a high-school girl pulled up the reservation Devlin had made and then led them to their private party room. She introduced them to Tasha, another high schooler, who would be their personal party liaison and guard their belongings in the party room when they went forth to bounce.

"Are you serious?" Devlin set the cake on the long, blue-plastic-covering draped table with its weighted bunches of balloons dropped upon it at uneven intervals.

"Of course," Tasha replied. "I'll be in here the whole time, so you can enjoy all the trampolines and attractions without worrying about your things."

Devlin peered out of the room at the rows of trampolines and the cage in which kids were throwing large foam-looking balls at each other.

"I wasn't planning to go out there," she said.

"It's included in the price of the room," Tasha replied. "You should enjoy yourself."

"Come on, D. Winters. We have to try it." Nils dropped his arm over her shoulders.

"Your pizza won't be served until 6:45, so you should enjoy yourself on the attractions." Tasha kept referring to "attractions."

"I take my shoes off, right?" Grant had already pulled off both of his loafers.

His continued eagerness surprised Devlin. The kid hadn't struck her as someone who'd rush to remove his shoes and rush to throw himself up and down on a trampoline.

"Yes," Tasha turned to Grant, "you are all set there, birthday boy."

Outside the party room, kids soared and plunged, flipped, and rebounded. Devlin couldn't decide if she regretted not bringing a water bottle of something adult to drink.

"Wow," Grant whispered, his awkward little-kid urbanity gone.

Devlin watched him as he reached up and slipped his hand into Nils's. A kid ran past, bumping Grant. Grant stepped into Nils and stood there. He reminded Devlin of a cousin of a senior colleague who had visited Chicago from Maquoketa, Iowa, when Devlin was a young associate at Sondheim. Devlin had pulled the unenviable duty of tour guide for this cousin and had witnessed the woman spend a full seven minutes in front of Seurat's *A Sunday Afternoon on the Island of La Grande Jatte* at the Art Institute. The woman's mouth had actually hung open.

Except this wasn't pointillism, this was—

Weird.

A ball of too much yellow walked in the front door and approached the registration desk. The dude was carrying a large cardboard box.

"You guys go do your jumping thing," she said to Nils. "I'll be back in a minute."

"Hey," Nils whispered, "when, uh, when's the rest of the surprise—"

"At 6:45 and then eight o'clock," Devlin replied, with the times she'd booked for Polynesian dancers and a magician. She patted Nils's arm and then walked away toward the Jumping World desk.

The guy had set the box down in front of the registration counter and was leaning over the desk talking to the high-school girl.

"Excuse me," Devlin broke in. "Sorry to interrupt, but I think we may be ships crossing in the night, so I wanted to go ahead and introduce myself." She extended her hand to the yellow shirt.

The high-school girl set her hands on the counter and looked at Devlin.

Devlin ignored her, focusing on the man. "I'm Devlin Winters. And I can tell you the marina by the boardwalk offers great amenities for people looking to rent boat slips. What kind of boat do you have?"

The dude in the yellow shirt cocked his head.

"I'm getting too old," he said.

"You a PI?" Devlin asked.

"Yeah, I work for Lonestar Private Investigators. I'm Frank Obregon." The guy had a firm handshake. "I'm not a process server," he added.

Devlin stuck her hand in the pocket of her shorts. "I used to like process, so no worries on that score, and if you want more pictures of the Jeep, I can arrange it. Otherwise, I don't think I can help you unless you explain some things to me." She nodded at the Jumping World kid. "He can come back to our party room for a minute." Then she turned back to Frank. "Well, you can come back and we can chat if you show me what's in the box."

"It's cool," Frank replied. "Incidentally, it's birthday stuff for the boy." With a foot, he pushed the cardboard box between him and Devlin, and then leaned over to lift the flaps and reveal a slightly smaller box inside, one sporting Star Wars wrapping paper and a yellow bow.

"You did a better wrapping job than me," Devlin said. "What kind of presents?"

"Legos and a set of books. Stuff wasn't cheap." The guy fumbled in a pocket. "Here's a receipt. It really is Legos and books." He held a length of narrow point-of-sale paper out to Devlin.

She took it from him. It was dated that day with a timestamp of 4:59 p.m.

"I believe you. Here, we've got a party room over here."

The guy picked up the box and began following her past the arcade crane game and a knot of squealing preteens to the party room. Devlin scanned for Nils and saw him watching her from a trampoline. She gave him a thumbs up. At the doorway to the party room, she asked Tasha if the girl would mind waiting outside the room for a few minutes. The room didn't have an actual door—just an open archway. But the din of Jumping World's soundtrack and patrons provided some privacy.

Devlin dropped onto the bench attached to the party table. "Okay, so let's break this thing down: you're a private investigator who enjoys buying expensive Legos for kids. What else?"

Frank set the box on the table and slipped onto the bench across from her.

"There are no secrets here," he said. "Someone asked me to locate this boy, Grant Bryson. They asked me to locate his current guardian, Nils Bryson. And they asked me to deliver this envelope to the guardian. I found Grant a couple days ago. Not a hard case at all, really. I confirmed everyone's identities over the last couple days. At the marina today, I confirmed Mr. Bryson's role as a yacht broker. I tried to make contact with him today, but apparently, he was with customers and showing boats. I returned to the marina later this afternoon to try to find him, but a woman at the office said she hadn't seen him recently. She showed me a sign-in sheet they maintain for yacht brokers and it showed that he'd signed out earlier. This chick told me to try back later, though, because his friend had asked her to hold onto a birthday cake."

Frank pulled his wallet out again.

"Here's my card." He handed it across the table to Devlin. "Again, I've got no secrets on this one. My client wants to make contact with Mr. Bryson and the boy."

Devlin examined the business card and then set it in front of her on the blue plastic table covering. "And then you went out and bought a bunch of Legos?"

"I emailed my client to let her know I'd located everyone, and I mentioned the circumstances and that I'd be returning to the marina to try to make contact. She told me the cake probably related to a belated birthday party and asked me to buy some birthday stuff for the kid. She gave me a generous budget. After that, I just returned to the marina, but I saw you all in the parking lot, so I didn't pull in the gate. I just waited and followed you here."

"Lovely." Devlin snorted.

"My client has in no way sought anonymity. She has instructed me to be open with everyone. Again, we've got nothing to hide."

Tasha peeked in the doorway. "Ms. Winters? Your food is ready. I could begin setting up dinner if you'd like."

Devlin patted the tabletop. "All right, Mr. Obregon. I get it. You're just doing your job. You want a slice of pizza? We've got enough coming to feed hordes." She turned to the doorway. "Sure, Tasha, come on in."

The girl led in two boys bearing pizza boxes and liters of 7UP and Dr. Pepper.

"Frank, if you don't mind waiting outside for a moment, I'll go get Nils, and you can introduce yourself and make your deliveries. Tasha," Devlin stood up, "would you mind keeping the room secure while Mr. Obregon waits outside? I'll be right back."

Tasha glanced at Frank, who'd risen from the table, and nodded.

Leaving Frank just outside the room, Devlin walked toward the entry area for the trampolines. Would-be jumpers had to enter the trampoline spaces from designated areas because netting encased the trampolines, ostensibly for safety reasons. She scanned the expanse of bouncing bodies.

"Hey," Nils came up behind her and touched her shoulder, "who's the dude?"

Devlin stopped and turned into Nils. "Private investigator. His name is Frank Obregon. Long story about a client trying to track you and Grant down. He was following you around the marina this morning. I saw him in the marina parking lot, so that's why I got a little weirded out when he walked in here."

She glanced around. "Where's Grant?"

"Throwing himself in a pool of foam." Nils shook his head. "This is the first time I've seen him being a kid."

"Well, let's let him continue doing that, and you can come back and talk to Frank for a minute. He's got some stuff to give you."

Devlin led the way back to the party room.

"Frank, this is Nils Bryson. Nils, Frank Obregon, of Lonestar Private Investigators." Devlin made the introductions at the doorway. "If you'd like to make your deliveries to Nils, Mr. Obregon, we'd like to return to our birthday arrangements. I've got a bevy of Polynesian dancers showing up any minute to entertain us as we eat our pizza. Again, you're welcome to a slice. You're welcome to enjoy the dance show, too, but I would ask you to offer the entertainers a tip afterward if you stay." Devlin tried not to smirk.

"No, I'm fine. Thanks. May I?" Frank waved at the doorway.

"By all means." Devlin stepped into the room and Frank returned to the table, retrieving a large brown envelope from the shipping box.

"My client hired me to locate you, Mr. Bryson, and to deliver these materials to you." He handed Nils the packet. "She also asked me to deliver these to Grant." Frank reached into the box and pulled out the wrapped presents, four total.

"Okay," Nils said. He shot a glance at Devlin.

"Mr. Obregon, it was a pleasure." Devlin stuck her hand out. "But if you're not interested in pizza, I'm going to have to adjourn this meeting."

Frank shook her hand. "Much obliged." He passed Tasha, and Devlin stepped to the doorway to watch him pass the registration desk and exit the facility.

"That was weird," Nils said.

"Not really," Devlin replied. "You've got Viggo's kid. Viggo's in custody. Who knows what's going on. Why don't you take a look at what he gave you, and I'll slice into one of the presents to see if it's legit."

Devlin grabbed her purse from the far end of the table and dug until she found her pocketknife.

"Ms. Winters?" Tasha approached. "I think your dancers are here."

Devlin glanced up to see intricately adorned heads over aloha-print robes in the doorway.

"Oh, great." She set the knife down. "Come in!" She held out her hand to each of the five dancers—two men and three women. "Thank you for making this happen on such short notice. You come highly recommended by Sean Tofilau and his brokerage."

"It's our pleasure." A petite woman, with a crest of yellow and red feathers on her head, grinned. "And our guest of honor is . . . ?"

"Grant Bryson. This is his ninth birthday. He's new in town and doesn't know anyone yet, and we wanted to give him something a little bit different, special, as a surprise. He's still in trampoline world out there." Devlin gestured at the doorway. "But we'll bring him in when you're ready."

"Perfect. And I'm Haunani." The woman turned and surveyed the space.

"I'll leave you to set up." Devlin returned to her knife and her attempt to slit open one of the presents, with as unnoticeable a mark as possible, while the dancers arranged a compact amp and iPod and some large, painted gourds.

Once she had slit through the wrapping paper and into the box of the largest present, Devlin poked a finger into the knife opening and shook the box. She pulled the paper aside carefully and peered into the slit.

"Yeah, Nils, I think this is just Legos. I think we're okay here."

"It's Grant's mom," Nils whispered, walking up to Devlin. He held out a business card.

"Well, that's awkward."

"Yeah, as far as I know, he doesn't know anything about her. I think he was like three when the court terminated her parental rights. She went back to St. Kitts, and that was that." His hand with the card in it dropped to his side. "Maybe she came back to Chicago a couple years later. Viggo told me there was an issue when Grant was around five, but I'm not sure what was involved in that. I don't know if Grant even saw her then. She's never been a part of his life."

"Well," Devlin folded the knife up and dropped it into her purse, "let's do this: let's put the paperwork aside for now. Let's do this party. And let's worry about the mom-thing later."

"What about the presents?" Nils lifted the business card and slipped it back into the thick envelope.

"I think they're fine. And Frank showed me the receipt. I think it's fine to let Grant have them. We'll tell him . . . we can say they're from . . . I don't know. They were part of the party package."

"And if there's something weird in them?" Nils dropped the envelope on the table by Devlin's purse.

"We'll worry about that only if it becomes an issue." Devlin refocused. "Haunani, how are you all doing?"

"We're ready when you are." The woman smiled. The dancers had shed their robes and stood in long, red-and-yellow, faux-grass skirts.

"Let's do this then," Devlin said. "Nils, you go get Grant. Haunani, I'll stand at the door and give you a sign to start the music when Nils and Grant are about to enter the room, so you'll all be dancing as they come in. That'll be cool."

"Wonderful." Haunani clasped her hands together.

Tasha stood watching the dancers and grinned. "This will be neat," she said.

Devlin figured most Jumping World parties didn't include Polynesian dancers and personal magicians. She stepped outside the room, as Nils went in search of the birthday boy, and leaned against the wall beside the doorway.

Are you actually enjoying yourself? What is wrong with you? At a kid's trampoline party?

She shoved her hands in her pockets. Maybe it had been busting the investigator's balls a little. She hadn't done that in a long time. Or maybe it was the prospect of the dance show. In Chicago, she'd enjoyed lush dinners and shows at places like the Alhambra Palace and at Kan Zaman before it closed. On the once-in-a-blue-moon nights she wasn't in her office, she had sometimes wandered over to Kan Zaman to treat herself to moussaka and watch the lavishly costumed women dance their Middle Eastern and North African dances to exotic soundtracks. Those nights had let her forget her golden handcuffs, her addiction to the footlights of Big Law . . . let her believe she could leave it all and disappear over the eastern horizon.

Tonight, though, something felt different. It had to do with the way the kid had looked when he'd stepped out and really taken in the mythic expanse of jumping equipage. His happiness had made her feel a little—

Oh, come the fuck on, girl. You need a drink.

Nils appeared from around a net-covered corner, holding Grant's hand. Grant was laughing and grabbing Nils's arm with his free hand. Devlin ducked into the party room and gave Haunani a thumbs up. Unbridled drumming filled the room. The dancers turned into yellow and red blurs. Grant stepped in with Nils on his heels, and the kid's mouth dropped open. Devlin tried to watch the dancers, with their hips and knees making visible the primal drive of the drums. But she couldn't resist coming back to the kid's look of unselfconscious absorption. Then he started to stomp his half-sized sock-clad feet into the floor in time with the drums. Devlin caught Nils's eye. Nils winked.

After the first song faded, Haunani called out, "Happy birthday, Grant! You want to dance?"

The little dude blushed and his head dropped.

"Come on, *keiki*. Come up here and dance with us!" Haunani beckoned Grant to step away from his spot by the room's entrance where he'd frozen.

"May I, Uncle Nils?" He looked over at Nils, who'd dropped onto a bench at the table.

"Of course, little man. You don't have to ask me. Go show us what ya got."

The kid ran up to the dancers and Haunani arranged him behind one of the men, a vantage point that let the kid mimic the fast knees and driving feet that started with the next song. Devlin walked over to the table and slipped onto the bench beside Nils.

"Seems like he's getting to enjoy something new, something Viggo hasn't beat us to the punch on."

Nils shook his head. "Always competing, D. Winters. You always had to beat Viggo."

"No, I just wanted to give the kid an evening that would bust him out of his blasé take on things."

Nils elbowed her. "You done good." He rubbed the blue plastic on the table with the palm of his hand. "He loved the trampolines and stuff. I've never seen him so *abandoned*."

"Abandoned?" Devlin turned back to the dancers, Grant pounding out the rhythm with those nine-year-old feet.

"You know what I mean." Nils patted Devlin's back.

The final drum beat of the song popped, and Haunani paused the action.

"Shall we take a short break, so everyone can grab some pizza? You can eat while we do the next number, Grant." She gestured at the side table with its boxes of pizza and bottles of soda.

Grant just nodded, his head tilted back as he watched her headdress.

"Great idea, Haunani. Thank you." Devlin stood up. "Tasha, you're welcome to grab whatever you'd like, too." She waved toward the food table. The teenager looked as captivated as the nine-year-old, her eyes wide and stuck on Haunani's feathers.

Devlin grabbed two slices of pepperoni and a plastic cup of 7UP and plunked herself back at the table, breaking her resolve to ignore Obregon's envelope package. She reached over and slid the thing toward herself before biting into the pizza.

"Mind if I?" She tapped the envelope as she caught Nils's eye.

"Nope. Be my guest. I was getting pretty curious myself." Nils slipped in beside her at the table.

Devlin didn't look up as she rustled the business card back out of the envelope and pulled a sheaf of papers after it.

"The only good thing about getting chunky is it takes the pressure off," she said, waving at the paper plate of dough and cheese and grease.

"You're not chunky, D. Winters. You just finally have curves."

"Whatever. I know what I am, and I'm okay with it."

Eyes on the top page, she lifted her slice of pizza. The sheet bore a letterhead: SK and N, Incorporated, St. Kitts and Nevis, The Ocean's Champion in Paradise. A sea turtle hovered over the words "Ocean's Champion."

Dear Nils Bryson,

I hope this letter finds you well. I know it's been a long time. I am writing because I hope you will help me, your brother, and your nephew. Obviously, Viggo is in trouble. I can help him. I can prove he is innocent. I have the documents his lawyer can use to prove the legitimacy of all of his business transactions. Enclosed are sample copies. But I want my son back. Perhaps you are not aware of the things Viggo said and did to steal Grant from me. As we both know, what Viggo wants, Viggo gets—hurdles, and others, be damned. He got Grant. But I am Grant's mother and I am now in a position to stand up to Viggo and demand that he let me be the mother he should have allowed me to be from the start.

Everything Viggo has done regarding business has been legitimate. Perhaps ill advised. But still legitimate. Viggo sold insurance products. Where he went wrong was using his financial influence to control me and keep me away from Grant.

When Grant was three years old, Viggo and I finally decided our relationship could not continue. Things had been, shall we say, stormy, and I was done with Chicago and the U.S.A. and Viggo. I wanted to take Grant home and raise him on the island with my parents. Viggo asked me not to. Then Viggo told me I couldn't. I had a personal crisis and I went away for a while to get help. When I returned to get my son, Viggo initiated court proceedings to terminate my parental rights. He told me that, if I did not contest the matter, he would help me start and fund a business back home. But I had to agree to go away and leave him Grant.

I was young, and Viggo was "persuasive." I knew I could not afford to fight him. So I made the ultimate mistake of relinquishing my son. I regret this decision every day. It is a shameful stain on my soul. But now I have the chance to make things right. For six years now, Viggo has encouraged his clients to invest in my business: SK and N, Incorporated. We do vital work in St. Kitts and Nevis, enhancing the health of our ocean environment. In exchange for supporting us, Viggo's clients have received certain modest financial benefits in their dealings with Viggo's insurance companies. I have all the paperwork to substantiate these clients' transactions with my company, the loans and investments they have made. Likewise, I have an affidavit as the records' custodian that these materials are business documents kept in the course of business transactions by SK and N, Incorporated. I have researched the issue and spoken with an attorney, and I believe everything should be admissible in an American court.

If you will put Grant on a plane for St. Kitts, I will send all of the files to Viggo's attorney. I have them packaged up and addressed to Irene Stockton, Esquire, of Crandell, Stockton, & VanderLugt, in the Waters Building in Grand Rapids, Michigan. I will pick up Grant from the airport and we will go directly to the post office and mail the box. God willing, the government will drop the charges against Viggo or a jury will acquit him, and he can return to his life.

Grant and I will live our lives, and I will make amends to my son for leaving him all those years ago. Please, please help a mother be with her son.

Below the closing's "Yours in the faith that you will do the right thing" sat a neat, legible signature: Monique Arthurton.

Devlin set the letter aside and studied the pages beneath it. They appeared to be non-sequential pages from contracts between SK and N and investors extending loans to the company, and Devlin could tell that Monique Arthurton had given her proposal more than minimal planning. Ms. Arthurton had included samples to prove she had the goods but not enough paperwork to be of any real use for anything—like evidence in court. The pages bore swaths of black across sections, like someone had redacted them with a permanent marker. Even flipping the sheets over and holding them to the light, Devlin couldn't discern the words hidden under the black. Setting the contract excerpts aside, Devlin lifted a pale-blue envelope with "Grant" printed in neat handwriting across it.

She turned toward Nils. He seemed to be struggling to pay polite attention to the dancers, enjoy Grant's rapt happiness with the performance, and study Devlin and the envelope all at the same time. His eyes flicked toward her the minute she turned.

"Yep, it's the mom," she whispered, holding out the blue envelope. "She wants the kid back." Devlin dropped the envelope on the stack of papers and slid everything toward Nils. "She wants to trade exculpatory evidence for the kid."

"What?" Nils stared at the letter on top of the copies.

"She says she'll send Viggo's attorney the contracts to prove his insurance products were legit—if you put Grant on a plane to St. Kitts." When she'd read through Viggo's indictment with Nils a couple weeks ago, Devlin had said evidence like these supposed contracts could perhaps clear Viggo . . . maybe.

Nils finished reading and paged through the sampling of contracts. He sniffed. Devlin plucked a pepperoni from her pizza and put it in her mouth.

"Would these do what she says?" Nils ran a hand through his hair.

"Probably. Maybe. If they're what they seem to be and she includes the certification as the records custodian." Devlin picked at another pepperoni.

"So this stuff could clear Viggo?"

"If a jury bought it, which they might. But they might not." Devlin shifted her eyes to the dancers.

The drumbeats wound into throbbing tension . . . and then released. The dancers' hips moved impossibly fast and then froze. The Jumping World soundtrack filled in lightly where the Polynesian song had ended.

"I can't give her Grant." Nils's voice came out too loud in the vacuum left by the end of the song.

"Nope." Devlin turned from him briefly to clap and hoot for the dancers.

"Well," Nils said, dropping his head into his hands. "I've got to talk to Viggo, but I don't know how. Everything's recorded at the jail. I— I guess I can call his attorney. I don't know what to do."

Devlin shrugged. "You should call his attorney." She grinned. The kid looked so happy. Somehow it was like his little-kid happiness was catchable.

"Let's get a picture," she said, nudging Nils. She rose from the table and tapped her phone. "Grant, would you mind if I took a picture of you with Haunani and everyone?"

Grant ran over to stand in front of the performers. She snapped the shot.

"Okay, back to jumping, kiddo. But come back in here for another surprise at eight o'clock, little man." She patted the kid's back, and he bounded out of the party room.

"Thanks," she said to the dancers, holding a hundred-dollar bill out to Haunani as a tip. "That was perfect."

The dancers shuffled out with their amplifier and gourds. Tasha set to clearing pizza boxes.

"Viggo owes me a hundred bucks for that tip." Devlin refilled her cup with soda and gave Nils a half-smile.

"Devlin, seriously, what am I supposed to do with this stuff?" Nils hadn't moved from the table. He had the papers spread out in front of him.

"I'd start by slicing open the card and seeing if it's something you want to give the kid." Devlin retrieved her knife from her purse and handed it across the table to Nils. "Then I'd call Irene Stockton in the morning and see what she says. And then I'd see about finding someone to watch Grant for a few weeks because it looks like it's time for a trip to St. Kitts."

Chapter 12
Immunity

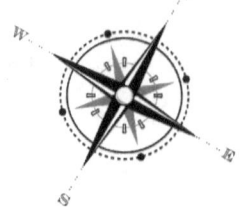

Lillian Carter's skirt didn't reach her knees. Xavier stood up from the marble-topped table to greet his agent. As he extended his hand, he tried to resist running a scenario in his head in which he told the agent to return when she'd found proper attire. He understood how these things worked: one couldn't dictate hemlines. Still, he would expect an agent of the United States government to have better taste and manners than to arrive at a working lunch dressed like some trollop off South Division. If he'd had need of an undercover sex worker, he would have rung up one of those girls over at Secret Service.

"X!" Lillian smiled as she took his hand, turning the handshake into some sort of half hug.

Xavier's spine stiffened. "Good afternoon, Agent Carter."

He tried not to draw away from the warmth of her hand on his back—he didn't want to seem awkward. But he did release the handshake and take a step backward, dropping into his seat.

"I'm glad we can actually meet and chat," Agent Carter said. "I love the Bull's Head. They have a stellar veggie burger." She pulled out the chair across from Xavier and sat, her skirt hiking up her thighs.

Xavier took a sip of water.

She leaned forward, her brow and chin and shoulders and too-big eyes crossing the center of the table, coming into Xavier's space. "Want to start with some hummus? And," the eyes flicked conspiratorially toward the tavern's door, "what if we had something to drink? I won't tell if you won't."

Xavier leaned back, drew his chin back. "Agent Carter, I don't think drinking lunches are professional." He picked up his menu and scanned for something with meat. Veggie burger? Preposterous.

The agent sat back, unfolded her napkin and put it in her lap. A waitress arrived and smiled with too-big teeth. She asked about drinks and appetizers. Agent Carter wisely said she'd be fine with water.

"Same for me," Xavier said, tapping his already present water glass.

He glanced at Agent Carter. She looked so terribly small for a federal agent, skinny, but she was working hard on this case.

"How's the hummus?" he asked the waitress, trying to sound affable.

"Oh, it's delicious. It comes with fresh vegetables and the pita is toasted perfectly." The waitress's big teeth bobbed with her words.

"Well, I think you've convinced us." Xavier mustered a smile. "We'll start there."

The waitress bustled off and Agent Carter grinned at Xavier.

"I like hummus," Xavier faltered.

"I do, too." Agent Carter put her elbows on the table. Xavier tried to tell himself it didn't matter, that it was somehow okay for a grown woman to be sprawled all over a café table.

It's how things are now. It's casual.

But he settled back away from her.

"I'm glad you could do lunch," the agent continued. "Brittney says you don't usually go out to lunch. She says she thinks you just eat at your desk." Agent Carter fidgeted with her fork. "You should get out more. Especially when it's so nice out."

Brittney felt free to speak on my lunch preferences? What sort of permissive office has the department devolved into?

Xavier cleared his throat.

"Did you find anything regarding Nils Bryson on social media?" He took a sip of water.

"Better than that." Agent Carter sounded too young, too excitable. Xavier valued competence, not enthusiasm. "Miles Bakker, Blue Tide, L.L.C., client extraordinaire, likes to sail." The agent ducked her chin and raised her shoulders slightly, like a pleased little girl.

Xavier fought the urge to rise, step to her chair, and straighten her spine.

"I looked into his assets and discovered that, about a year and a half ago, he purchased an eighty-foot Hatteras Cockpit Motor Yacht for $475,000 out of Fort Lauderdale." She sounded like she was reciting a script she'd prepared. "And guess who brokered the sale for him? Yep, Mr. Nils Bryson of Sunset Yachts, out of Kemah, Texas." She smiled and bit her lower lip. "And guess who captained the boat across the Gulf to Corpus Christi, where Mr. Bakker kept it for six months? Yep, again: Mr. Nils Bryson."

Xavier raised a hand to his chin. He wanted to support Agent Carter and he appreciated her new-found diligence, but this excitement bordered on an unacceptable self-satisfaction.

Or is she trying to impress me?

Xavier shifted his hand from his chin to rub his temple. "Well, isn't that convenient for Mr. Bakker," he said, putting the agent's odd behavior on the back burner.

"Bakker purchased the loss-of-income policy from Blue Tide agent Jocelyn Kennedy four months after he bought the boat. Its name is *Bad Investment*, by the way—the boat's name is."

The waitress and her teeth bounced up to the table before Xavier could respond.

"Have we decided?" She clasped her hands behind her back.

Xavier gestured toward Agent Carter. "Are you still favoring the veggie burger, Agent Carter?"

Did she blush?

"Yes, I'll take the garden burger," Agent Carter said to the server, but her eyes darted toward Xavier.

"And I'll do the french dip." Xavier reached out for Agent Carter's menu and then handed both menus to the waitress.

"I'll get this order right in and your hummus should be right out." The girl showcased her teeth a final time before turning and heading toward the kitchen.

Agent Carter fiddled with her straw, stirring her water. Xavier adjusted his cuffs.

"Bakker had Nils Bryson move the boat from Corpus Christi to Galveston Island last summer. That's where it is now, at a marina called Pelican Rest." The agent had stopped stirring and had tented her fingers. "And Bakker's not the only Blue Tide client who seems to like boats. I've got," she leaned around to rummage in the oversized purse she'd hung from the back of the chair, "a list of over a dozen Blue Tide customers who have bought boats from Nils Bryson."

She untwisted with a brown portfolio and opened it to hand a memo to Xavier. "Nick Giannakopoulos, our favorite Blue Tide partner, also seems to be an avid fisherman."

Xavier glanced at the memo. The first page included a picture of a glowing white fishing boat bobbing in obnoxiously blue waves.

"That's Nick's boat," Agent Carter explained, "which he bought from Nils Bryson when Nils was at another brokerage, called Gulf Coast Yachts, about six years ago. Nick keeps it, you guessed it, at Pelican Rest Marina on Galveston Island. Apparently, he 'winters' down there."

The waitress popped up at Xavier's elbow and set a plate of hummus, colorful veggies, and pita triangles between Xavier and his agent.

Agent Carter put her elbows back on the table. "Remember how he told us he'd met Viggo through the 'financial network'?" She used air-quotes around financial network. "Well, I'm meeting with Mr. Giannakopoulos to clarify that network tomorrow. I'm starting to think that that network means Nils Bryson, and now I'm starting to wonder if it means RCB Capital and the parents, though I don't really think the parents are involved. I've got absolutely nothing to show any link to them."

She reached for a carrot stick and whirled it through the hummus. When she'd finished pushing it along its loopy course, she put the tip of it between her lips and smiled at Xavier. He sniffed, adjusted a Stanford cufflink. Then he sat up and reached for a pita triangle and leaned forward to dip it into the hummus. The woman's hand lingered over her side of the dip too long as she trifled with another carrot, and her pinky brushed the back of his hand.

Is this woman flirting with me?

"I think you're right," Agent Carter said, her eyes feeling intrusive now. "Nils Bryson has been funneling potential partners and clients to Viggo. I think he's involved."

The hummus lacked garlic. Xavier made much better hummus, often spicing it with a touch, or more, of jalapeño.

"Perhaps it's time for me to draw up that immunity agreement I've mentioned." He took a sip of water and studied a table of four diners across the room.

"Immunity?" Agent Carter crunched yet another carrot. She ate loudly, too loudly.

"I want to know what was going on here. I want someone to explain all the details to a jury. And I think that 'someone' should be Ms. Monique Arthurton."

"Monique?" Agent Carter's eyes didn't reveal enough understanding.

Xavier sighed. Other than the tomfoolery with the skirt and the carrot and hand brushing, she'd been doing well enough.

"If I offer Ms. Arthurton immunity, I think I can persuade her to come forward and testify." Xavier lifted another pita triangle of bland hummus to his lips. He felt stuck finishing the subpar stuff since he'd be paying for it, or at least half of it. He would think about the etiquette of handling the check later.

"How will you find her?" Agent Carter's eyes continued to reflect confusion.

"I'll go to St. Kitts and inquire after her." Xavier wiped his lips.

"You'll go to St. Kitts?"

The waitress appeared with the sandwiches.

"Thank you, madam," Xavier said. "You can take away the appetizer plates."

He gestured at the hummus-splotched flatware.

"Oh, you are finished, aren't you?" He looked at Agent Carter.

She nodded.

"You might," Xavier addressed the waitress, "tell the kitchen the hummus could benefit from a more generous infusion of garlic." He sat back as the woman lifted the remnants of the spread.

"I'll let them know."

Did she sound skeptical? Xavier scrutinized his french dip as the server nodded and strode off.

"You're from St. Kitts, aren't you?" Agent Carter sounded like a teenager again. "Brittney told me you were from an island. I guess it slipped my mind. You know, no more shop talk. Not while we eat. Tell me about St. Kitts. And your cats. Brittney told me you have two giant cats."

What sort of indiscreet strumpet was he harboring in his office? Xavier blanched. He cut into the sandwich and popped a slice of it into his mouth to avoid responding and thus dignifying this fishwife gossip.

As he chewed, his agent filled the space between them with nonsense. "I love cats," she assured him. "I have a tabby named Pixie. I got her two years ago from Rosa . . . from Agent Vasquez. Did you know Agent Vasquez does a bunch of cat rescue? She's really involved with rescuing cats and fostering and finding forever homes for the little guys. It's pretty cool. Anyway, I got Pixie from her and I've been debating about getting another kitten now that I know I can be a cat-mom. I'm just not sure how Pixie would take it. She's quite social, though. She might like a sidekick. What are your cats' names?"

Oh, St. Thomas Aquinas, pray for me, for patience for me, that I may have some . . . he searched his mind for the right virtue . . . *generosity of spirit with this silly poppet.*

"Menelaus and Agamemnon." He lifted his napkin from his lap and blotted his lips.

"Don't tell me—let me guess. I know what those names mean. It's on the tip of my tongue." Her eyes rolled upward. "I know I've heard those names."

She bit into the veggie burger and commenced another round of audible mastication. After a few more smacking sounds, she lifted an index finger. "Like from Troy!"

Nodding and trying to smile with that sought-after generosity of spirit, Xavier sliced off another bite of french dip.

"I loved that movie. I've never been a huge Brad Pitt fan, but that's a good movie. I haven't seen it in forever, though."

Xavier fought the reflex to choke on the juicy sandwich.

"What else do you like? Movie-wise?" The woman grinned over her burger.

"I haven't seen that movie. With Brad Pitt. I'm more of a fan of classic cinema." Xavier violated his own rule and offered this small fact about himself (and, obliquely, his opinion of John Ford's work . . . because it truly was the best, but he wouldn't ever say that to one of his agents). "The boys are named for the Greek kings of the *Iliad*. The movie, I'm sure, did not do the story justice."

"Don't prejudge, Mr. Charles." Agent Carter, chewing, gestured at him with the garden burger. "It was a pretty good movie. If you like the Greek stuff, I'll bet you'd like it."

"Perhaps," Xavier fibbed, hoping to end the vapid exchange.

"But tell me about the island. About growing up there."

"I didn't really grow up there. I was born in Chicago, but I have dual citizenship through my mother. She's Kittitian. I spent summers with her family down there, even after I started college."

"That's pretty cool, X."

Xavier shrugged.

"It will be helpful now," he said.

"So you want to go find her? Find Monique Arthurton? Down there?"

"I don't think I have a choice," he said. "We need to know what was really going on. I mean, we know what was going on—the paper couldn't be clearer. But I want a live witness. I want a full explanation for the jury. And I know I can get it with an immunity agreement."

He lifted his water glass and swirled the ice cubes.

"And I don't want to get caught off guard. I'm going to win this case. I'm going to put Viggo Bryson behind bars and seize his assets for the defrauded citizens of this country. That means I need to know all the evidence, everything that could arise."

"But, X," Agent Carter got serious, "why would Monique Arthurton agree to testify, even under an immunity agreement? We can't reach her down there. She's safe. She doesn't need our immunity, right?"

"She does if she wants to come here and get her son back, doesn't she?"

Agent Carter's eyes flickered. "The email. The JPay message she sent to Viggo."

Xavier inhaled. "We know she's trying to get in touch with Nils Bryson and trade evidence for the boy, correct?"

Agent Carter nodded.

"And we know Nils Bryson is involved and might want that evidence, correct? But we also know he's Viggo's brother, and since he's involved, his livelihood depends on Viggo, correct? What are the chances of Nils Bryson betraying his brother—and meal ticket—by sending the kid to Monique Arthurton?"

"He won't?"

"I don't think so," Xavier said, again wiping his fingers on his napkin, even though he'd used his knife and fork on the french dip and kept his hands clean. "So she'll have to come to the States if she wants her son, and if she does that, we'll know and we'll arrest her."

"So she needs immunity if she hopes to get her son back?"

Xavier blinked, let the woman absorb everything.

"So if you go down there and find her, she'll take the immunity deal and testify, and then we'll have a witness to testify to everything." Agent Carter leaned over her plate.

A nod, slowly.

"But what if she testifies that it was all legit? What if she really does have investment and loan agreements?"

Now, Xavier sniffed. "She doesn't. Or if she does, they're fake, like everything else, and I can blow them out of the water. Regardless, though, I want to know. And that's what she can do for me: give me information, things to be prepared for at trial."

"Do you think you can find her?"

"I know I can find her."

"Xavier?" Agent Carter had poured herself across the table, her fingers curled in excitement, her blouse too loose.

Xavier waited for whatever it was she wanted to ask. She just looked at him.

"What is it, Agent Carter?" he finally responded.

"Xavier, you need an agent to question her with you. Xavier," she paused, "let me go down there with you."

Chapter 13

The Story of Viggo Bryson

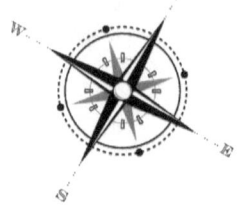

Devlin hunched over her laptop at *A`uku*'s saloon table.

"From Galveston, it's 2,184 miles to St. Kitts," she said.

Nils sat on the settee across from her with a pad of paper. "So what are you thinking?"

"I'm thinking we're not flying. First, you can't fly. That prosecutor? Xavier Charles? I know him. He was just starting out at the U.S. Attorney's Office for the Northern District of Illinois when I was at Sondheim. He did appellate work, so I argued against him at the Seventh Circuit a couple times. Dude's almost as neurotic as I was. He'll know the minute your passport's scanned, I'm sure. Same for Grant."

"Well, neither *A`uku* nor *Mambo* are going to get us over there." Nils reached up and patted a teak galley cupboard. "Sorry, old girl, but you just aren't up to it right now."

"They won't," Devlin said, "but Sean Tofilau's Cal 40 will make the trip. He takes great care of her and still races her offshore. He sailed her in the *Regata del Sol* last year to Isla Mujeres. Won his division."

"Did you sail with him?" Nils looked slightly surprised. "I guess I can't believe I didn't know you were down here if you were sailing and racing."

"I didn't race." Devlin snorted. "That's ancient history."

"Not if we have to sail to St. Kitts. We'll be sailing together again. Imagine that: Team Bry-Sin together again." Nils threw out the name competitors had used to describe Nils and Devlin when they'd raced together as teenagers.

"Fuck that." Devlin picked up her phone. It rang twice. "Sean Tofilau," she crowed into it. "You with clients? . . . I've got a bit of a favor to ask. . . . Yeah, it's not sexual. . . . To you to, buddy. . . . Just wondering if you might be up to chartering *Manuia* for a trip to St. Kitts. . . . Yeah, I'll pay in a bottle of Bombay Sapphire and my eternal gratitude. And I won't mention herpes next time I see you out with a chick. . . . Yeah? You sure? . . . Uh, like six weeks? . . . Yeah, of course. . . . Dude, plenty *mahalo*s. Yeah, we'll come over there tonight and hash it all out with you. . . . You can have your pick: stay in my posh digs or on an authentic Chris Craft Commander. . . . Yeah, that's not what your momma said about it last night. . . . Okay, cool. . . . See ya in a few hours."

She tapped the screen to end the call. "We've got a ride to the island. Gotta love the brotherhood of the sea." On the laptop, she typed in a search for "Sailing to St. Kitts."

"Okay, then." Nils bounced the legal pad on his knee.

"So," Devlin turned from the computer screen and tapped the calculator on her phone, "let's say seventeen days over, seventeen days back. Couple days on the island. Let's plan for a six-week excursion."

"You think Viggo and the attorney can wait that long?"

"Viggo's not going anywhere. His trial's four months away. It's fine. Plus," Devlin got up from the table and walked to the refrigerator, "you said you told Viggo I checked out his case, right? You told me that you talked to him about me, right?"

"Yeah." Nils looked at her . . . looked confused.

"That means my passport's probably flagged now, too. The recordings of all your jail calls with him are going straight to the U.S. Attorney's Office, and like I said, Xavier Charles is an OCD sonofabitch. He may not remember me as a colleague, but he'll flag a passport on someone helping Viggo Bryson."

Devlin straightened up after reaching into the fridge for a ginger ale. She held a green can out to Nils, condensation already gathering on it. "You want one?"

"Sure." Nils reached toward her.

She handed him the can, grabbed another for herself, and returned to the table.

"What do I do with Grant for six weeks?" Nils cracked the soda open with a hiss.

"Bring him. The little man said he likes to sail." Devlin savored the bubbles, the cold. Something in her also noted that she wasn't craving anything more "serious" or "enjoyable." For now, the soda was enough.

"You think?"

"Yeah, I thought about it. I think it'd be fine—a good adventure for the kid. Plus, the little dude's growing on me. I'd never admit this publicly, but it was cool seeing him so happy at Jumping World. Little man's actually a neat kid when he settles down."

Nils grinned. "Devlin Winters likes the crib lizard."

"Yeah, I do. I'm woman enough to admit the kid's all right." She dropped back down at the table and punched the laptop's keys. "Okay, so I think we'll clear in at Basseterre. Looks nice. Here, make some notes there." She waved at the pad on Nils's lap. "We'll want to make sure Sean has extra Racors on board—I'd say at least two extra fuel filters. And a spare water pump and impeller. We'll want to check his ground tackle. I've got a Rocna on here plus a CQR and two Danforths if Sean isn't hooked up. Old dude who had *A`uku* before me liked his anchors."

Nils jotted notes.

"We'll check the sail inventory," Devlin continued. "Like I said, Sean races his boat, so I'm sure she's kitted out. We'll want a sea anchor and we need to check the safety gear: flares and signaling devices. I'll go through the electronics with Sean, but he's a gearhead. I'm sure he's lousy with gadgets. I've got a handheld VHF for backup if he doesn't have one."

"Dinghy?" Nils asked.

"Nah," Devlin replied. "Too much hassle for a quick trip with a known marina destination. If you want, Viggo can buy us an inflatable stand-up paddle board. We can take that in case we find ourselves in need of transportation to shore."

"Whatever you say, skipper." Nils chuckled.

"Oh, it's gonna be like that, is it?"

"Hey, it just sounds like you want to be skipper."

Devlin glowered. "Stuff it, Bryson. You've done a lot more sailing than I have lately. You can drive the damn boat all you want. Knock yourself out."

Nils didn't reply, but he raised his eyebrows and Devlin looked away. She slid out of the settee again and dropped into the aft cabin.

"What're you doing?" Nils called.

"I've got a couple cruising guides back here. They've got tips for making passages around the islands, reviews of marinas, details on anchorages, that kind of stuff." She pulled two books off a shelf over her berth, a wooden appendage far more varnished than the rest of the boat.

"Hey, Winters?"

"Yeah?" She stepped back into the saloon and set the books on the table beside her computer.

Nils put his pad aside and rose from his seat. He stepped across the saloon and leaned into her. "It'll be nice to sail with you again. It's been a long time."

Devlin slipped onto the settee, away from him and away from the confrontation she'd contemplated for the last week or so. She shook her head and pulled a corner of navy-blue curtain aside from the window over the settee. The boat in the slip beside *A`uku* needed washing. Its owner only came around every couple months, and the deck of the boat wore the marks of too much attention from the gulls and pelicans and egrets that fished in the marina.

"Nils?" How could a window she never touched have fingerprints on it?

"What's wrong, Dev?" He sounded concerned, and his hand on her shoulder put her back on a small boat in the middle of Lake Michigan with a hot summer sun overhead and a silly idea about love, or some idiocy like that, addling a young brain.

A tall, white bird made its way down the finger pier between *A`uku* and the dirty neighbor.

"Nothing's really wrong, Nils," she said, the bird walking stiff-legged but somehow making the movements elegant. "I'm just not up for anything, okay? And this trip and me helping you with Viggo's shit and with the kid and all that—none of that changes anything. You know? I'm not gonna lie, Nils. I've thought about things, about us, in the last month or whatever, but that ship sailed a long, long time ago. Okay?"

He put his arm around her shoulders and, standing beside her seated frame, pulled her head into the outside of his leg, away from the window and her view of the goose-stepping bird.

"I know," he said. "Hey, I know I fucked up. And I know I can't fix anything there." He lifted his arm from around her and stroked her head. "I'd go back and change all that if I could. But I can't."

She let her head rest against his leg, let herself lean on his solidity.

He didn't say anything for a while, and Devlin wished she could pull away and walk outside to the stern of the trawler and sit in the sunlight and watch the white bird and the boats, the old girls rocking in their slips and the ones underway out in the channel passing into the bay and back.

"I'm just grateful for what you're doing for me and Grant and Viggo." Nils's hand ran from her hairline to the nape of her neck. "And I really am looking forward to sailing with you again." He paused. Perhaps the sound he made was a chuckle or some sort of sigh. "You were the best."

The little girl that still lived somewhere dark and cloistered within Devlin, who'd survived the crash at Sondheim Baker and "resting" at the psych facility and banishment to a shit-stop boardwalk in backward-ass Texas, reached out and wrapped an arm around Nils's leg. Devlin pulled her cheek into the only friend she'd ever had in whom she'd confided a true piece of herself, even if all that—the telling and confiding and trusting—had happened a long, long time ago.

He leaned down and drew her head back.

The kiss stretched across a gulf of a decade and a half, of triumph and failure and disappointment, reached all the way back to all that—the telling and confiding and trusting. It didn't fix anything or promise anything or go anywhere. It just settled into the warm, wooden interior of an old boat tied to a creaking pier with the sound of the harbor murmuring against mahogany planks and the scent of salt and hot summer on a muddy bay. When it was over, Devlin returned her head to the outside of Nils's thigh, and somewhere up the dock, someone turned on a hose and the sound of boat washing trickled into the vacuum.

"For old times," Nils whispered.

***

"Devlin, girl, lemme come with you. It'll be plenty easier with three helmsmen rather than two." Sean took a sip of Shiner Bock, his back against the coaming of *Manuia*'s cockpit a few hours later.

"Are you serious?" Devlin nursed a condensation-sweaty bottle of water.

"Sure." Sean crossed his legs, resting his left ankle atop his right knee. "I got nothing going on. Ask this fool." He pointed the beer bottle at Nils. "Summer's our slow time for boat sales. People don't want to march around marinas looking at boats when they could go cool off in a sauna. I've got no sales in the hopper, no potential boat-moving gigs, nothing. A trip over to the islands'll break things up a little."

Beside Devlin, Nils pushed his ballcap back and pressed his beer to his forehead, swiping the condensation back and forth across his brow. "Makes sense to me. It is deader 'an doornails here right now. I haven't sold anything in a couple weeks. And if Sean's willing to take watches, it'll make the crossing a hell of a lot more relaxing, especially with Grant on board. Kinda frees us up a little to help the kid if he needs anything."

Devlin swiveled on the cockpit bench and pulled her feet up under her, knees to her chest. She wrapped her arms around her shins and looked from Nils to Sean, stripes of shadow from the cockpit's bimini sunshade shifting over her. "Sounds like it'll be four of us then. With the kid. And I say we give him an official watch. He can stand a watch."

Sean took another sip of Shiner. "Sweet. When do we leave?"

"Next week?" Devlin rubbed the back of her neck. "You think she can be ready to go in a week?"

"All we need are provisions," Sean said. "She's ready to go. I've got more spares in that lazarette under you than we'll ever need. I'll grab storm sails and the emergency tiller out of my storage space. The big question is what we want to eat and drink."

"Okay, then," Devlin said, "let's plan to pull out of here on Monday." She grinned, clapped a hand against her leg. "We'll pick up an inflatable paddle board in case we need to anchor out and get to shore. And I'll bring over my foulies and harness and stuff tomorrow. I'll start in at Aldi's tonight. I'm thinking lots of muesli and powdered milk, and I'll grease up a mess of eggs we can pack up tight in one of the cabinets. I'll get a bunch of mac 'n cheese and ramen. Do you guys like Nutella? And what do you want to drink?"

"Devlin, girl, you know me. I'm not picky when it comes to eats." Sean sat up. "You want some paper for a list?"

"Sure." She unwound her legs and stretched her arms upward, toward the blue canvas blocking the sun. She glanced at Nils as Sean dropped into the cabin. "I can't believe I'm doing this."

Nils leaned back, his red aloha shirt aglow against *Manuia*'s clean white fiberglass. "I can. It's in your blood. Oh, you'll deny it. Claim you just want to be left alone, but Devlin Winters doesn't back down from a challenge."

Devlin clicked her tongue. "Yeah, no. Devlin Winters likes to get drunk and take naps."

Sean returned and held out a spiral-bound notebook, and Devlin settled into list making, marking "Provisions" across the top of a page.

"Put me in for a bunch of Hopadillo and some Goose Island," Nils said. "What beers do you favor, Sean?"

"I'm more a rum man," Sean answered. "I mean, I do my Shiner Bock occasionally, like now, but I'm not much for beer. And I know Ms. Winters will want her gin."

Devlin focused on the college-ruled sheet. "I'm thinking not for this trip. I think I'm gonna make this excursion some sort of a cleanse." She tapped the back of the pen against her cheek, eyes on her handwriting on the page. "Like a juice cleanse, but without a lot of juice because I know your galley is small, Sean, and the reefer's limited."

"Devlin Winters on a juice cleanse?" Sean slapped the ankle he'd re-crossed after resuming his seat. "Get out your coats, boys and girls, because it sounds like hell's freezing over."

Devlin lifted her eyes and glared at the big man across the cockpit from her.

"You're serious?" Sean grinned into the scowl. "Wow. Good for you, girl. That puts some pressure on me, though. Maybe I should do something." He rubbed a hand down his own ample aloha-print shirt, the black, yellow, and orange pattern even louder than the flowery red of Nils's shirt. "So, I just gotta ask. Where's all this coming from? A juice cleanse . . . a sudden burning desire to sail off to the islands?"

"The juice cleanse I just need. My liver's tired." Devlin sat up and put the notebook aside, stretching her long legs across the cockpit sole. "The sailing? Well, that's a bit more complicated." She glanced at Nils.

Nils shifted, lifted his ballcap again and ran a hand through his hair. "My, uh, brother's in a bit of trouble with the law." He reset his hat and picked up his bottle, scratched at the label, swirled the beer in its amber cage. "My brother's a couple years older than I am, and he's always been a little . . . reckless."

"He's an asshole," Devlin interrupted. She looked across at Sean. "Always has been."

Nils sighed. "Viggo and Devlin never really got along. We all grew up in the same building in Chicago and we all sailed together, and Viggo and Devlin were both hyper-competitive, so they butted heads a lot."

"Viggo's a lying cheat," Devlin broke in.

"Dev, sweetheart, tell me how you really feel." Sean smiled a toothy, lopsided smile.

Nils shook his head. "Anyway, Viggo got indicted a couple months ago for tax fraud. The government's accusing him of selling bogus corporate insurance policies. They're alleging he and his partners and clients pocketed millions in unpaid taxes. They want to put him in prison for years, and he's got a kid—this kid Grant I'm taking care of and who's coming with us to St. Kitts. I'm watching him while Viggo's in jail."

"Grant's grown on me," Devlin offered. "He has. He's an okay kid. I think he's just never really had a chance to be a kid."

"Sounds familiar," Sean replied, and Devlin flashed uncomfortably back to a drunken night of cards on *A`uku* when she'd told Sean some nonsense about never having had a chance to be a kid or make mistakes or lose.

Nils shot Devlin and then Sean a curious look, and Devlin thought back to the kiss earlier that day and wondered if Nils was sizing Sean up.

"There's a woman on St. Kitts," Nils said, "she's actually Grant's mom, who may have a bunch of business records that we hope could help Viggo's case. She runs an environmental charity down there, does a bunch of stuff to clean up and preserve coral reefs. Viggo used to send investors her way. We think her records will demonstrate that Viggo's insurance business was legit, so we need to find her and talk her into giving us copies of what she's got."

"And we don't need anyone scanning our passports and letting the government know we're heading to St. Kitts." Devlin smoothed her shorts. "Once upon a time, back up in Chicago, I knew this prosecutor, and he's pretty," she paused, "tenacious. He'll be looking for airline and passport alerts on Nils and Grant, and we think, because of some things that got said, he may even have an eye on me—as someone involved in the defense now."

Sean raised an eyebrow. "Are you practicing again?"

"No, oh, fuck no." Devlin shook her head. "No way. I'm never practicing again. But Nils told Viggo, on a recorded jail call, that I was looking at the case. I'm not involved. I just pulled the docket from the court's website—it's all public record. Just helping Nils make sense of things and giving him some ideas to pass on. That's all."

Sean uncrossed his legs, sat forward, and rested his elbows on his knees. His eyes made Devlin's shoot away to the stern of the boat, to the stainless barbeque hanging off the rail there. It felt like Nils had vanished and that Devlin faced the Samoan's next question alone.

"Why are you so involved, Devlin I-Never-Give-a-Damn Winters?"

Fuck you, Sean I-Ask-Too-Many-Questions Tofilau.

"Bored, I guess." She shrugged. "And maybe I like the kid. Seems kinda a shame to see him end up without any parents. I mean, the mom left him to Viggo when he was a toddler and Viggo could end up in prison till the kid's an adult. That'd be pretty sad, you know? For the kid to get orphaned like that." She shot a glance at Nils. "I mean, I know the family would look after him, but it's still sad."

Sean didn't sit back. "I'm not convinced, Ms. Winters. I think there's something else here."

What is this fool fishing for?

"Nope," she said, "that's it. Boredom and the kid." She fixed her eyes on Sean. "And a free trip to St. Kitts." She jerked a thumb at Nils. "Viggo gave him a bunch of money to take care of Grant and everything. Viggo's paying for this boondoggle."

Still, Sean leaned into the cockpit, filled up the space in front of the boat's wheel. "Devlin Winters, I think you want to defend this guy. I think you want to come out of retirement."

"Nope." Devlin slipped a foot out of its flip flop and rubbed her toes on the boat's rough, nonskid fiberglass. "Like I said, Viggo's an asshole. I got no dog in this fight. I don't care." She jerked her chin up.

Finally, Sean sat back. "Maybe." He shrugged. "Maybe not. Either way, I'm in. A front-row seat to the return of The Great Devlin Winters will only make it more fun."

"Sean," Devlin cocked her head, "how do you even know? I'm a fuck up. For as long as we've known each other, I've been a fuck up. Why do you think there's something else here?"

She held his eyes. He didn't look away, just raised his beer bottle to his lips.

"No reason," he said, after a long draft.

Nils's voice sounded odd when it broke in, too low and too real. "Devlin, you've never been a fuck up. *Fucked up*, perhaps, but not a *fuck up*."

She felt his hand on her back.

"Whatever," she said. "Regardless, it'll be a good adventure, even if it is for Viggo Bryson, who is, unequivocally, a giant fuck up."

"He's changed a lot," Nils said after a long inhale. "You'd be surprised. Did you know he gives a ton of money to the Chicago Atlantic Grove Mission on Canal there, south of Roosevelt Road and Maxwell Street? The shelter? And in Grand Rapids, he donates to a place called Dégagé. Another shelter. It offers a bunch of services to the homeless."

Devlin turned toward him, toward the warm hand still resting on her shoulder blade. "Seriously? Viggo gave money to a cause? I mean, besides his baby-momma's supposed save-the-turtles deal?"

"Yeah. Like $500K a year for the last five years or something." Nils's hand slid up toward her neck.

"You're kidding me?" She lifted her water bottle to her lips.

"Nope. And he gave a huge chunk of change to this adult literacy program in Grand Rapids. A couple years ago, he became a tutor for them. He was teaching people to read in his free time. You can ask Grant. He told me about his dad telling him about how much his dad enjoyed helping people learn to read stories."

Devlin swallowed, lowered her water bottle, and studied Nils's face. "For real? Viggo Bryson? The Viggo who cut every line on my Laser the morning of the second day of Junior Olympics, so I almost couldn't race and had to scramble to re-rig the boat before the first start? That Viggo? The one who loved quoting Nietzsche for the idea that 'women are dangerous playthings'? That Viggo? Viggo, who—"

Nils dropped his hand from her back and placed it on her knee. "No one ever found out who really vandalized your boat at Junior Olympics, and Viggo—"

"For real?" she repeated. "You're still pretending we don't know who did that? Well, we know who put forty pounds of weights in the inspection ports of our 420 at Midwinters to slow that boat down. And we definitely know who 'hit it and quit it' with Maureen." Devlin shot a sad look at Sean. "Maureen Clark was the fourth member of our little group growing up and probably Viggo's biggest fan. So he took advantage of her and then dropped her like a bad habit. She was messed up for a couple years over it."

"Well," Nils hesitated, "I guess I'm still not convinced Viggo was the one who messed with our boat at Midwinters, and I'm not sure what was involved in the whole Maureen thing. I do feel bad about her, though. That was kind of messed up." He took a breath. "But anyway, Viggo has grown up. He's been really involved in helping people in his community."

Devlin rolled her eyes. "Sean, Nils's brother is a cheating asshole, even if Nils feels the need to protect him. But cheating asshole or not, he's in trouble and his situation gives us an excuse to have a little adventure. So that's the story of Viggo Bryson and this Gulf crossing we're about to make."

Chapter 14

Heat Lightning

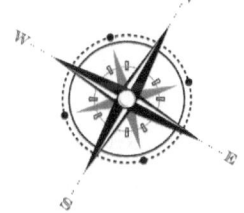

Grand Juror Number Fourteen had stopped yawning. The old man had his fingers tented in front of his lips and could have passed for a post-*Wrath of Khan* Ricardo Montalbán in an ill-considered sweater vest.

Xavier lifted a sheet of paper from the table to his left, pretended to read something from it. "Agent Carter," he began, "now you've discussed for us the financial arrangements you've seen laid out in the Blue Tide, L.L.C., insurance contracts and the unaccounted-for returns of capital to Blue Tide insurance clients. Could you back up a little for us and explain the evidence you have related to Viggo Bryson's younger brother and his role in recruiting Blue Tide investors and clients?"

He stepped toward his agent, who sat on the witness stand before the twenty-three grand jurors, and then turned to those jurors with the subtlest flourish, presenting his prima ballerina to them for her solo.

"Of course," Agent Carter said. "I'll start with some background. Nils Bryson is Viggo Bryson's younger brother. They were both born in Chicago and both spent some time working in the family business, a venture-capital firm known as RCB Capital, an Illinois corporation. Mr. Charles, I have, for submission to the grand jury, copies of the articles of incorporation for RCB Capital and the company's corporate tax returns for the last three years. I also have screen captures of the RCB website, listing Richard and Catherine Bryson as managing directors of the firm. I have copies of Viggo Bryson's and Nils Bryson's birth certificates, listing Richard and Catherine Bryson as the boys' parents."

"Agent Carter, are you implying RCB Capital was somehow involved in Blue Tide, L.L.C.,'s insurance sales, the transactions we are scrutinizing here?" Xavier liked to stand as someone even-handed—objective—before his grand jurors. He slipped his glasses off and tapped an earpiece pensively against his lips.

"No, Mr. Charles, not at all," Agent Carter clarified. "I offer this evidence merely as background. Nils Bryson's involvement with Blue Tide, L.L.C., appears to have begun approximately eight years ago. I have for the jury a copy of the sailboat racing results from a regatta in Key West, Florida, that occurred eight years ago. The first-place boat in the Melges 24 division of this sailing competition was named *Heat Lightning* and was owned by a man named Lloyd Roberts."

Xavier replaced his glasses and strode to the table at the front of the room and hit a key on his laptop. A chart of boat names and racing placements flashed onto the screen to Agent Carter's left.

Agent Carter lifted a laser pointer from the wooden lip of her witness box. "This is the boat here." She wrapped the red-light dot in a swirl around the name *Heat Lightning* on the screen. "Now," she continued, glancing at Xavier, "the crew of this boat *Heat Lightning* included, in the position of tactician, Nils Bryson."

At the computer, Xavier flashed a logo-laden press release onto the screen. "Is this a press release from Solace Sails announcing *Heat Lightning*'s win at that sailboat-racing event?" He smiled at his agent. Her zeal in the last several weeks had surprised him. He wouldn't say yet that it had impressed him, but certainly, it had pleased him.

"Yes, Mr. Charles, this press release was issued by the company that manufactured the sails used on *Heat Lightning* to win this racing event."

"And does this press release list the names and positions of all crewmembers?" Xavier planned to treat himself and the boys to salmon in just a few hours to celebrate the grand jury returning a superseding indictment, one that would include NILS BRYSON in big, bold, capital letters beneath the VIGGO BRYSON entry.

"Down here," Agent Carter pointed the red dot at a paragraph on the screen, "we have the names of the owner of the boat, Mr. Lloyd Roberts, as I mentioned a few minutes ago, and the racing tactician, Mr. Nils Bryson."

One day, he'd get through to Agent Carter, get her to understand that these scofflaws did not merit the respect of a title, even a simple one like "mister."

"All right, Agent Carter, we have Lloyd Roberts racing on a sailboat with Viggo Bryson's younger brother. What does this mean to us?" Xavier closed out of the press release and let a dark desktop replace it on the screen.

"Less than three months after this sailing event, this regatta, Mr. Roberts invested approximately $750,000 with Viggo Bryson, who used that money, and other monies I'll touch on shortly, to build Blue Tide, L.L.C. Mr. Roberts became Viggo Bryson's first business partner in Blue Tide."

Xavier inhaled, opened his mouth, and then bit his tongue. He realized he was listening to a proactive agent who'd anticipated his next question. While he couldn't consider it appropriate to smile at that moment, he told himself to remember to say something encouraging to Agent Carter once they'd dismissed the jury.

"Nils Bryson," Agent Carter was saying, "brought Lloyd Roberts to his brother as a potential investor. Two months before this sailing regatta in Key West, Viggo Bryson filed to organize Blue Tide, L.L.C., with the State of Illinois. He listed himself as the sole member of the L.L.C. Immediately after organizing the L.L.C. and obtaining a bank account for it at Chase Bank, he issued two checks to his brother. Mr. Charles, if you'd bring up those checks for me."

Lillian Carter was doing so well Xavier believed he could even forgive her once-again-tawdry hemline. He brought to the screen a set of check images.

"Here," she said, pointer working, "we have the first check. It's signed by Viggo Bryson, and as you can see, it was for $1,500.00. In the memo line, if you can make that out, it reads 'Race Week: Investor Recruiting Expenses.' Then we have the second check, dated just four days later. It is for $1,000.00 and the memo line reads 'Draw Against Commission.'"

Agent Carter paused and lifted the clear plastic water cup in front of her. When she replaced the cup empty, Xavier reached for a gray carafe that had been standing guard over a stack of papers. He gave the agent a nod as he refilled the cup.

"Essentially," Agent Carter continued, "Viggo Bryson gave his brother $2,500.00 leading up to this sailing event. Nils Bryson deposited both of these checks into his own Chase Bank account and then attended the racing event and sailed with Lloyd Roberts. Immediately after winning this sailing regatta with Nils Bryson, Lloyd Roberts invested $750,000 in Viggo Bryson's fledgling Blue Tide, L.L.C., and," the agent paused perfectly, "Viggo Bryson issued a third check to his brother—this one for $5,000.00 and marked 'Commission' on the memo line. Mr. Charles, if you would."

The third check glowed on the screen.

"Now," Agent Carter said, "the total payment to Nils Bryson was $7,500.00, or 1% of Lloyd Roberts's investment in Blue Tide, L.L.C. Ladies and gentlemen, if you'll remember that 1% number, it will come up again shortly."

You're beautiful, Lillian Carter.

Xavier's gut jolted as the words burst into the sphere of his thoughts.

Just a few feet from him, Lillian Carter continued her monologue, explaining the 1% commissions Nils Bryson received for recruiting Nick Giannakopoulos (as Blue Tide's second investor), Miles Bakker (as an insurance purchaser over the course of several years and several transactions), and numerous other avid sailors and boat owners. But Xavier couldn't keep the agent's voice on its track. Her words jumped around between his ears, hung up on that thigh-high hemline, and spilled into a sticky pool at his feet. As he tapped the laptop's keys to continue the display of exhibit documents, his body grew heavier and heavier until he could barely stand—and her lips seemed to glow redder and plumper as she spoke.

"I'll back up a minute, ladies and gentlemen." Agent Carter wrapped those red lips over the rim of the plastic water cup again, but now the action made Xavier feel something like dizzy. "And I hope you'll forgive me jumping around like this. It's just extremely difficult to make all this data neat and linear." She smiled at the jurors. "But let's go back to that sailing competition in Key West eight years ago."

Xavier closed his eyes and pinched the bridge of his nose.

"Just over two weeks after Nils Bryson sailed in that regatta and then introduced Lloyd Roberts to Viggo Bryson, Blue Tide, L.L.C., purchased a ticket for a United flight from Chicago O'Hare to Daniel K. Inouye International, Honolulu's airport—Hawaii. The name on the ticket was Nils Bryson. The total cost for the ticket was $867 with all taxes and fees. Would you mind, X?"

As soon as she said it, as soon as she slipped and said X instead of Mr. Charles, her eyes widened. Xavier stopped reaching for the laptop's keyboard. He looked at her, his hand hovering in space near the computer. She lowered her gaze, and the room of more than two dozen people grew very quiet and seemed very empty. Xavier could hear the hum of the HVAC system, could smell faint traces of cleaning products, and then he could feel his viscera all tight within him.

"Pardon me, Mr. Charles." Her voice cracked, but probably not enough for anyone save him to notice. "Would you mind displaying that flight record for me?"

"Of course," he replied, his voice far lower than he intended. And then it happened. "There you are, Lillian."

Lillian?!

He rested his fingertips on the tabletop beside the computer and steadied himself.

"Here is a copy of the flight record for this trip to Hawaii," he heard her saying. "Nils Bryson arrived on the island of Oahu on the first of February. Three weeks after this arrival, he placed third in the Quiksilver surf competition known for being," she glanced at her notes, "in memory of Eddie Aikau." She paused and Xavier noticed something flitter across her eyes. "Excuse me, ladies and gentlemen, I don't surf, so I feel, pardon the pun, a bit like a fish out of water here. But yes, that's it, the Quiksilver in Memory of Eddie Aikau. I've got that right."

"And, Agent Carter, can you point us toward the significance of this surfing competition?" Xavier would put a stop to all this nonsense balling up in his stomach.

"Yes, Mr. Charles. Could you project the Quiksilver competition video, please?"

Xavier tapped the keyboard and up popped a still frame showing a mountain of turquoise water with men clad in bright red and blue and green clinging to it on tiny yellow and white boards.

"Thank you, Mr. Charles. If you'd press play, I'll holler when I need you to stop it." Agent Carter fiddled with the laser pointer.

A deep, Australian-accented voice filled the room with a spiel about men riding mountains and the spirit of the islands and some other fluff.

"There we go." Agent Carter cut into the narrative. "Could you pause it there, Mr. Charles? Oh, back up just a little. There, right there."

She stabbed the red beam into the screen and waved the light around in a circle. "This, ladies and gentlemen, is Nils Bryson paddling on his surfboard, and if you'll look at the sleeve of this blue lycra shirt-thing he's wearing, you'll see the Blue Tide, L.L.C., logo. I'll be showing additional depictions of the logo momentarily, just so you can assure yourselves that this is indeed the logo here on Mr. Bryson's surfing shirt." She glanced at Xavier. "Mr. Charles, would you mind advancing the video just a bit?"

He hit play.

"There, there we go," she said, and he paused the movie. "Here we've got Mr. Bryson standing on the board, and from this angle, you have an even better shot of the Blue Tide, L.L.C., logo. Now you can see it on the sleeve of the shirt and on the chest. And," she swung the pointer, "take a look here at the surfboard. Can you see the logo on the nose of the board?"

A few jurors murmured, implying they could indeed see the garish wave pattern of the logo.

"Now, Agent Carter," Xavier picked up, "couldn't Mr. Bryson have simply been an athlete sponsored by his brother's company? A sort of billboard for insurance products?"

"No," Agent Carter replied, focusing on the jurors. "First of all, at least to me, it makes no sense to advertise a company that sells corporate insurance at a surfing competition. So that just seems like a stretch."

Xavier cringed ever so slightly at the agent's conjecture, but she was back on track almost immediately, and he knew they were on the homestretch.

"Regardless," Agent Carter was saying, "even if Viggo Bryson just felt like sponsoring his brother and decided to throw his company's logo all over his brother for good measure, Nils Bryson wasn't simply wearing Blue Tide's blue lycra." She grinned. "Sorry, ladies and gentlemen, that sounded silly. Anyway, Mr. Bryson wasn't simply wearing the Blue Tide logo while he surfed. Just four days after he won this surfing competition, Viggo Bryson, Nick Giannakopoulos, and Lloyd Roberts met together at the Halekulani Hotel, beside Waikiki Beach. Mr. Charles, would you mind putting the hotel records on the screen for me?"

Another tap, and a hotel bill danced in front of the jurors, at the top of which rested the name Nils Bryson.

"At this time," Agent Carter continued, "I cannot confirm that Nils Bryson participated in financial or business discussions or planning with his brother and his brother's partners in Blue Tide, L.L.C., but the hotel records show that Blue Tide, L.L.C., purchased a hotel room for Mr. Bryson—for Nils Bryson—at the Halekulani for three nights for $520 a night. And I can confirm, with the evidence I'll ask Mr. Charles to put on the screen shortly, that seventeen days after the Brysons checked out of the Halekulani, Viggo Bryson obtained an initial memorandum from an attorney named Veronica Benedict advising, essentially, that the sale of the Blue Tide loss-of-income policies was legal. Four days after that, Blue Tide sold its first policy. And two days after that, Nils Bryson deposited a check from Blue Tide, L.L.C., for $5,000.00 into his Chase account. The memo line said," she waited, and Xavier flashed the check onto the screen, "'thank you.' It said 'thank you.'"

Thank you, Lillian Carter.

Agent Carter continued, explaining how the attorney Veronica Benedict had not had all the facts when she'd issued that initial memorandum condoning the insurance products, that Viggo had not told the attorney he would be refunding buyers' premiums, save for his skim of the cream. But none of that mattered. Xavier knew he had what he needed: probable cause. He'd heard all the rhetoric. A grand jury would indict a ham sandwich, as the vapid, unoriginal pseudo-intellectuals would taunt—fools who didn't respect the hard-working, sincere members of the community who sat on Xavier's grand juries and who wanted to see justice done.

It didn't take long. Amanda Ralph had a tight, neat signature that looked very nice sitting beneath the words "A True Bill" and over the title "Grand Jury Foreperson." Her signature floated just above Xavier's on the superseding indictment that charged Nils Bryson with one count of conspiracy to defraud the United States. The new indictment appeared on the docket of Viggo Bryson's case the following day as record entry number seventy-one. As Xavier saw it, the return of the arrest warrant for Nils Bryson, marking the warrant as executed, would appear as record entry seventy-two.

Chapter 15

He's in the Middle of the Gulf of Mexico

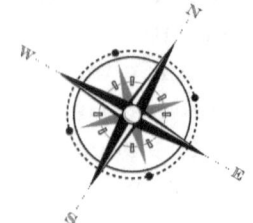

"Does my dad know where we're going?" Grant wore that earnest, old-man expression Devlin no longer found surprising on the kid.

In the boat slip to the right, *Manuia* seemed like she was straining at her dock lines, ready to set out, as Nils and Sean loaded the last boxes of groceries and emergency gear.

"Kinda, kiddo." Devlin didn't want to lie to the kid, but trying to explain federal custody, recorded jail calls, attorney-client privilege, and the prosecutorial reach of the world's leading superpower seemed counterproductive. "He's been really tied up, little man. I'm sorry. But a friend of his is keeping tabs on everything, and she let him know we're all going sailing."

When she'd been in practice, Devlin hadn't considered herself a friend to her clients, but calling Irene Stockton a friend to Viggo seemed like the easiest way to explain the situation to a nine-year-old.

"So, you're going to be wearing this while we sail, okay, little man?" Devlin pulled a strap on the boy's new lifejacket, tightening the bright-yellow floatation device around him. "Even when you sleep, okay?" She gave the kid a playful punch on the foam. "Even if you're knocked unconscious, this thing'll float you. You've got a knife in here." She unzipped a mesh pocket on the jacket and pulled out a stainless rigging knife with a lanyard attaching it to the lifejacket. "And you've got a whistle in here." From another pocket, she withdrew a neon-orange ball-less whistle. "Here, try it."

Grant popped the whistle in his mouth and blew.

"Good job, dude." Devlin grabbed another strap of the lifejacket and pulled on the kid, lifting him slightly onto his toes. "Anything happens and you go in the water, you blow and blow and blow till we come pick you up. You got it?"

Grant gave his slow, contemplative nod.

As Devlin started to set a straw hat on the kid's head and explain sun protection, Grant ducked his chin and whispered, "I miss my dad."

Ah, fuck. This is so above my pay grade.

Devlin glanced from the dock to *Manuia*'s companionway. The boys must have been conveniently occupied in the cabin.

"Hey, man, I know it's rough," she said, adjusting the hat on the kid's head.

She dropped down to sit cross-legged on the dock in front of Grant. "So when I was your age, I didn't see my folks much. They paid a nanny to look after me and do chores around the house and stuff. I'd get up in the morning and they'd be gone—already at work. The nanny would make me breakfast and take me to school on the train. She'd come get me in the afternoon, and when we'd walk home from the train station, we'd go through these parks in the city. You know Chicago, right?"

Grant again offered that solemn nod.

"You know Millennium Park?"

"Of course I know Millennium Park." The kid rolled his eyes.

Yeah, you're still Viggo's son.

"Well, when I was your age, Millennium Park wasn't there, but we'd go to Buckingham Fountain and stuff."

"You must be really old."

"Thanks, buddy. Anyway, after we'd walked around the city awhile, the nanny would take me home, give me a snack, and watch TV while I did homework. The drill varied because I had several nannies over the years, sometimes multiple nannies at the same time. The daytime nanny might leave and another would come in for the dinner and evening shift. That one would be more like a tutor. She'd make dinner and answer my questions about my homework. She might play dolls or a board game with me. And then we'd read together and she'd put me to bed. And that was that. I guess she'd watch TV or whatever till my folks got home. The next day, it was wash, rinse, and repeat."

She put her hands on the dock behind her and leaned back on them, looking up at Grant. "So I know how it feels to be parent-less in a way."

"Not the same," Grant whispered.

"I know, little buddy."

"I haven't talked to my dad in *ages*."

Ah, fuck. Is he crying?

Nils had told Devlin that Viggo didn't want Grant knowing anything about the case or his custody, so Grant hadn't been on any jail calls with his dad. It seemed that Viggo was worried one of the intermittent recorded announcements, reminding callers that the call involved an inmate, would pop on while Grant was on the phone. Nils had asked Devlin to keep things light, telling the kid that Viggo was traveling for work and couldn't make international calls where he was. As savvy a world traveler as the little man fancied himself, the story was a stretch for all of them.

"I know it's rough, kid," Devlin mustered. "I'm not going to try to make you forget how you're feeling. You're allowed to be sad. That's okay."

Grant turned teary eyes on her.

"But," she continued, "we are going to have a lot of fun on this trip. You're going to love sailing all far out there, and Sean is a cool guy. You'll get to know him. And his boat's really cool. And we'll play card games and do some fishing."

"His boat's not as cool as *Camilla*." Grant waved the back of a hand at *Manuia*. "*Camilla* is way nicer."

"I'm sure your dad's boat is beautiful." Devlin swallowed the rest of her thoughts on the subject of Viggo's boat and lifestyle.

Grant flopped onto the dock, dropping flat on his back in front of Devlin, hands tucked into the armholes of the lifejacket, straw hat brim squished under his head. "My dad's in trouble, isn't he, Ms. Winters?"

The kid still fell back on "Ms. Winters" occasionally, leaving Devlin to ponder what he meant when he did.

"He's really caught up in some heavy work stuff."

"No, he's in trouble. Bad trouble."

"What makes you say that, kiddo?" Devlin shot another look at *Manuia*'s companionway, hoping one of the boys would emerge and relieve her.

Grant rolled on his side, away from Devlin, and Devlin saw his shoulders shudder. A sniffle followed.

Without turning back, the kid began mumbling, and Devlin leaned in to listen.

"When I was little, one night, my dad was reading to me. He used to read to me a lot. The last thing we read was *The Last of the Mohicans*. That was a good book. My dad's a really good reader. He has voices for every character and he stops to talk to me about geography and history and stuff. But there was this one time. We were reading *The Deerslayer*. And he told me that, if anyone ever took me or if we were ever separated or if he were ever taken away, somewhere somehow, he'd find me. He said he'd come back and get me. He said nothing could keep him away from me. My dad loves me. He should come get me."

Devlin could barely hear the kid. She wanted to stand and walk up the dock and hide in the bathhouse. He was truly crying now, sniffles, hiccups, and all. She knew that if she rolled him over and took a look there'd be snot and tears all over him and the new lifejacket.

And then she did just that. It felt clumsy, awkward, even intrusive, but she scooted into him and rolled Grant toward her, gathering him into her lap and arms as well as she could.

"No, I want my daddy." Rolling him over seemed to have released something, and he wailed for a moment, but then he snuggled into her shoulder and took a few short gasps and started calming down.

"I know," she whispered, "I know."

"Everything all right?" Nils's head popped up in the companionway of *Manuia*.

"Yeah, we're fine." Devlin nodded toward him. "We'll be down in a minute to help you guys."

Grant kept his head pressed into her shoulder and cried just a little longer.

***

In the relative cool of the shadowy, air-conditioned cabin, Devlin handed Nutella jars to a cleaned-up, snot-free, tear-free Grant. The boy nestled the jars into a cabinet in *Manuia*'s saloon.

"Are we going to eat before we leave?" Grant shoved the last of the hazelnut spread into the cubbyhole.

"Sure, kiddo. We'll go grab lunch before we push off." Devlin bent to retrieve bags of smoked almonds to hand to the kid next for stowing.

To her right, Sean was shoving foul-weather gear and safety harnesses into a hanging locker. Nils loaded limes, bananas, and oranges into a net above the galley sink. Devlin's phone vibrated and she straightened to dig it out of a pocket.

"Good morning, this is Devlin Winters speaking." She didn't recognize the 616 area-code number.

"Ms. Winters, hello, this is Irene Stockton. I'm an attorney in Grand Rapids, Michigan. I represent Mr. Viggo Bryson in a case in the U.S. district court up here."

Devlin glanced at Grant and then made her way to the forward cabin of the boat, wrestling the cabin's door shut behind her.

"Sure, Irene, I'm familiar with Mr. Bryson's case. I'm a friend of his brother, Nils Bryson." Devlin kept her voice low as she went through the preliminaries. Neither she nor Irene Stockton needed these introductions.

"So I understand," Irene replied.

For poops and giggles, Devlin had googled the attorney one night with Nils, seen her frank-looking face, red hair, and freckles. She'd reviewed Irene's record: magna cum laude from a mid-grade law school, law review, clerkship with a state supreme-court justice. Devlin had then pulled up Irene's recent bar-journal article on proposed amendments to the federal sentencing guidelines. After twenty-five minutes, she'd declared Viggo in good hands.

"I wanted to reach out to you," Irene continued, "because I understand from Nils that you're assisting him with retrieving some documents related to Viggo's case, and Viggo has asked me a few times to get in touch with you. I apologize I didn't reach out sooner. As you can imagine, discovery in this case is extensive and has been eating through my time like crazy."

"No problem."

"Ms. Winters, Mr. Bryson has expressed a strong interest in bringing you onto the defense team as a 'litigation-support specialist,' if you will. He has explained some of your expertise and the assistance you're lending his brother, and he hopes you'll agree to join the defense team. We see some advantages to that arrangement related to attorney-client privilege, work product, and the like."

Devlin fidgeted with the hem of her t-shirt.

"Ms. Stockton, I understand the concerns here and the need for confidences. Regardless of a formal arrangement, I'm in no hurry to go tell Viggo Bryson's deep, dark secrets to everyone. Plus I'm guessing the government already knows most of them, given their zeal for recording jail calls and reading JPay emails."

Irene chuckled. "Unfortunately."

She offered that Viggo's defense fund would pay a generous rate for Devlin's time in tracking down and reviewing business records in St. Kitts and said she would email a contract immediately.

"That'd be great," Devlin said. "I'll be on the road shortly and it will be a little more difficult to sign and return a contract while I'm traveling."

"I'll have my paralegal send it to you immediately. Oh, here, one moment please."

Devlin could hear papers shuffling on Irene Stockton's side of the phone call. There were a few indistinct murmurs and the sound of keyboard clicks. Devlin slid open the cabin door and peeked out.

Nils was gathering empty grocery boxes and wrestling them out the companionway. Devlin watched him climb from the cabin into the cockpit behind the cardboard. The murmuring on Irene's side of the line continued. It would take Nils a few minutes to get the boxes and other trash up to the dumpster. After that, the boat would be about ready. They could feed Grant and then—

"Sorry," Irene said into the phone. "I apologize."

"No worries," Devlin replied, pulling the cabin door closed again.

"We, um, we seem to have had a bit of a development here." Irene faltered.

Devlin waited.

"My paralegal just came into my office with a superseding indictment in Viggo's case."

"Xavier Charles superseded, huh?" Devlin shook her head. She remembered the "persecutor" as bloodthirsty.

"You know Charles?"

"Once upon a time," Devlin said. She dug her fingers into her hair.

I don't give a fuck that I'm essentially disbarred.

"Yeah, a long time ago," she restarted, "he and I met up a couple times at the Seventh Circuit."

"Oh," Irene said. "Well, yes, apparently, he just filed a superseding indictment. It hasn't added any counts against Viggo, but it has named a new co-defendant."

The attorney sounded uncomfortable. Devlin shifted the phone to her other ear. Maybe it was a bad connection.

"He's added one defendant to the count of conspiracy to defraud the United States," Irene continued. "He's," she sighed, "he's charged Nils Bryson in that count."

Devlin froze. Outside the tiny cabin, in the main part of the boat, Sean's voice rose and Grant's answered. Then it sounded like Grant laughed.

Devlin swallowed. "Well, that's disconcerting." She bit her lip. "But I'm not sure it has any real impact at this point."

Irene didn't reply. Anticipation expanded through the phone connection.

"I'm not completely sure what his plans are or what his work involves right now," Devlin said into the anticipation. She knew Irene knew—knew the need not to know. "But I do know he's on a boat in the middle of the Gulf of Mexico. I don't have any other information like GPS coordinates or anything, so I don't think anyone's going to be getting a hold of him too soon."

"All right." Irene sounded steadier.

"Let's do this," Devlin said. "You have your paralegal send me that contract. I'll review it and reply with my agreement to the terms, which I'm sure will look fine. And I'll get in touch as soon as I can. But give me a couple weeks because, like I said, I'm going to be on the road for a little while in the very near future."

"I'll have Taylor email you right now. Thank you for your time today, Ms. Winters." Irene signed off.

Devlin rose and shoved her phone into a pocket. Returning to the main cabin, she stepped up to Grant and put a hand on his shoulder. "Sorry to do this, little man, but we're going to have to skip getting lunch right now." She glanced at Sean. "Are we set to go?"

"We are all set. Ready when you are." Sean gave her a confused look.

"Then we are pulling up tent stakes. We've got a date with the middle of the Gulf of Mexico we've gotta get to." Devlin hopped up the companionway ladder to the cockpit. "Let's get her running. I'll go grab Nils, and we'll be right back, and then we'll get the you-know-what out of Dodge."

"Aye aye." Sean followed her into the cockpit.

Devlin jumped off the boat and headed up the dock.

On the dumpster's pad, Nils was breaking down cardboard grocery boxes and throwing them into the garbage.

"Nils," Devlin called as she jogged up to the waste-area's enclosure, "time to go. Let's get this road on the show."

Nils looked puzzled. "Um, sure. But what's the rush there, skipper? What about lunch, and I'd like to check the supply of spare lines Sean has—"

"Yeah, I think we gotta consider everything checked and good to go." Devlin grabbed the last box and threw it into the dumpster. She took Nils's arm. "We'll talk about it on the boat."

She pulled him out of the trash receptacle's gated space and glanced toward the parking lot. As she hurried him toward the gangway to Sean's dock, she checked for dark-clad, arrest-warrant-toting agents in tacky, aviator sunglasses.

Nils broke into a trot beside her. "Devlin, what's wrong?"

She didn't reply, just looked at him with wide eyes. Neither said anything while they untied the boat and gathered up dock lines. They stayed quiet while Sean took *Manuia* through the channel, under the bridge that held Highway 146 seventy-some feet above Galveston Bay's inlet to Clear Lake, and past the boardwalk.

As the sloop nosed into the bay, Devlin asked Grant if he wanted to watch a movie in the forward cabin. She took him below and opened his laptop to the first *Lord of the Rings*. Galveston Bay's muddy wavelets slapped *Manuia*'s hull as Devlin reemerged into the cockpit a few minutes later.

She inhaled the steady ten knots of breeze tinged with diesel fumes and broke the silence between her and Nils. "The U.S. Attorney's Office indicted you for conspiring with Viggo to defraud the IRS."

Chapter 16

Mr. and Mrs. Cane

Xavier made the very difficult decision to arrive late to lunch with Agent Carter. Appearing less than punctual wounded him, but arriving early and waiting for her and dealing with the unrighteous fay barnstorming through his body would have caused greater distress. When he walked into the teal-walled Thai restaurant off Grand Rapids' central downtown park, he spotted Agent Carter in a booth at the back of the narrow dining room and sniffed in relief to notice she wore a pantsuit.

"Good afternoon, Agent Carter," he said as he slipped onto the booth's bench across from her.

"X, don't do that."

Why on God's most majestic earth would an agent of the United States government feign a pout?

"I thought we'd reached like a new level when you called me Lillian in the grand jury." She narrowed her eyes at him, and he paid close attention to his hands as he tucked his napkin into his lap.

"I apologize for that." He looked up from the napkin. "I didn't mean to be so unprofessional. But," he shocked himself with a stammer, "but thank you for all your hard work. You did an excellent job with everything."

"Thanks, X." Now, it was her turn to look down.

At least she has some sense of decorum.

She flipped open her menu, but Xavier had the uncomfortable feeling she was watching him read his own.

"What about this, X? You want to go family style? Split a couple entrees? I love the *masaman* curry, but I'd also love to try something new."

Are we swine bound to feed from the same trough?

But then he heard himself saying, "Sounds like a brilliant idea. A little sampling. How about the *masaman* and the *pad see ewew?*"

"Sounds great." Agent Carter sat back and grinned at him, forcing him to take a long sip of water. "I've got some good news . . . and another idea."

Holy Mother, save me from sloth and indecency.

"What would that be, Agent Carter?"

"Seriously, X. Lillian's enough. I promise I won't tell anyone you're human and not a legal super-bot." She reached across the table and touched the back of his hand.

And he didn't pull away.

His tailbone throbbed and the sound of the other diners grew terrifically loud.

"I got the powers-that-be to approve my request to go to Houston to arrest Nils Bryson myself," she was saying. "I want to be the first one to talk to him. I'm not letting anyone else question him till I've had a crack at him. And," her hand wrapped around his, "I think you should come."

Xavier tried to inhale, but the restaurant's air was too thick or something.

"You should go down there with me," she said. "I'll arrest Bryson. We'll see if he'll talk. And then from there, we can fly over to St. Kitts and find Arthurton and get her to agree to testify under your immunity agreement. It's perfect—efficient and effective."

A short girl with thick glasses arrived at the table, and Xavier heard himself ordering curry and noodles for himself and 'his companion,' and then he heard himself asking, "Lillian, would you like some tea? I know it's warm out, but hot tea is always lovely." And she agreed and the bespectacled girl bustled away and the agent's hand was still on his and he still couldn't get the overly thick air into his lungs.

"The only thing is," Agent Carter removed her hand from his and swiveled in the booth to dig in an oversized beige bag, "I don't have a home address. For Nils Bryson. So we'll have to improvise a little." She squared herself to Xavier, holding her familiar brown portfolio, which she'd excavated from the bag. "This is a copy of Nils Bryson's driver's license."

She handed a photocopy from the portfolio across the table.

"I looked up the address," she continued, "and it's the street address of the local post office. It's essentially a post-office box. And I checked: Texas doesn't allow using a P.O. box on your driver's license. But Mr. Bryson has seen fit to ignore that prohibition."

She pulled more copies from her supply.

"So I decided I'm in the market for a boat, a," she glanced at the top copy, "a forty-two-foot Vagabond cutter, and," another glance down, thumbing to the next page, "if the Vagabond doesn't fit my needs, a Morgan 41. There are a couple of those to choose from and they're cheaper than the Vagabond."

She handed this new set of copies to Xavier. He looked down at black-and-white pictures of sailboats sitting in a marina.

"They're boats Nils Bryson is brokering for sale," Agent Carter explained. "I have an appointment to meet with him next week at Sunset Yachts."

The tea arrived and Xavier drew back, giving the waitress ample room to place the service between him and Lillian Carter.

"I'm not sure, though," Agent Carter continued once the petite woman had left them with the silver kettle, "that he'll be there when I go in. That Nils will be there at the

Sunset Yachts office. The fellow I talked to on the phone this morning was a total used-car salesman." She snorted. "I should say used-boat salesman."

Xavier poured tea into two ivory porcelain cups and passed one across the table to Lillian Carter. He had thought the air had finally started to thin and become breathable, but her smile as she accepted the cup made everything grow viscous again.

"I think," she said, "they would have told me anything to get me to book an appointment to come in. The guy gave me this line about the brokers working as a team and how they could all help me. I tried to nail him down that Bryson would be there. He was a little vague, but I'll see when I get down there. If Bryson doesn't meet me for the appointment, I'll just wait."

She took a sip of tea, and Xavier wondered at the delicacy of her fingers wrapped 'round the cup.

"I should say *we* will wait. Because you should come. We should do this together. We'll pose as a couple looking for a boat to sail off into the sunset. It'll be fun."

Tea and bile backed up in Xavier's throat. "Pardon me, Agent Carter. I've got to step into the little lawyers' room."

Xavier dropped his napkin on the table and beelined for the men's room.

In the single, unisex restroom, Xavier stared into the mirror. Go to Houston? With this . . . was she . . . should he say . . . call her . . . Lillian? Slattern or dryad or . . . ? Xavier knew he wouldn't be able to eat. He would feign a stomach bug and return to the office.

He splashed water on his face.

Xavier, you need to shake up your routine.

His face did look pale.

You could go to Texas with this woman, interrogate another Bryson, head over and see all your folks on the island, and secure Niqi's testimony. That's all it'll be. It's your job. The boys can stay with that woman on the fourth floor who watched them when you had to go to that seminar in Phoenix. She loves them. They can enjoy a little break from the routine as well. You can leave her with a bag of catnip for them. A little perk.

He stared into the mirror. Then he took a deep breath.

Back at the booth, the curry and noodles had arrived.

"All right, Agent Carter," Xavier slid into his seat, "I'll tell Brittney to get the travel arrangements in order. Let's go to Texas and St. Kitts."

Lillian Carter shook her head, grinned. "X, from here on out, it'll be Mr. and Mrs. Cane. Let's be the Canes. Looking to retire early on a sailboat."

***

Kemah, Texas, didn't impress Xavier. Behind the wheel of the rental car, Lillian Carter beside him in the passenger seat, he crested a steep bridge over a channel between an inlet and Galveston Bay, and took in the sprawl of tourist boardwalk and marinas and box stores unrolling below him.

Tawdry.

"X, we probably want to see about getting in the right lane." Lillian Carter stared into her phone, into a navigation app she'd opened as soon as they'd gotten into the rental car. "We're going to turn right in like two lights."

She wore a floppy, multi-colored hat and oversized, bug-eyed sunglasses. Early that morning, when they'd met at Gerald R. Ford International Airport in Grand Rapids for their 6:45 flight, her apparel had felt assaultive to Xavier's eyes. Now, these several hours later, he still hadn't reconciled himself to the sailboat-print shirt she'd chosen or her bulky necklace of green and blue marble-sized beads. The ensemble had made a long morning even longer.

"We're getting close, X." Agent Carter looked up from the phone. "What do you think about stopping for a bite to eat? We've got plenty of time. And I'm getting kind of hangry."

Hangry?

Xavier could feel St. Bede cringe.

And then he glanced at her smile. She'd put on lipstick when they'd gotten in the rental. In front of him. Like she'd wanted him to see her do it. But she hadn't put on too much and it was a nice, neutral color, and it made her look—

"If you're hungry, Agent Carter, we can stop." Xavier squared his eyes away from the lips, checked his mirrors.

"What do you feel like? Let's see. . . ." She was back in the phone. "There's a bunch of stuff at the boardwalk over there to the left." She pointed toward a large roller coaster and amusement-ride tower looking over rows of sailboat masts. "Or there's a Chili's or an IHOP. Up on the right."

A Chili's?

"We've come this far. We might as well go all the way. Let's visit the boardwalk."

Who is talking through me? Who am I?

Xavier activated his blinker and pulled into a left-turn lane.

"In that case," Agent Carter said, "let's go to the aquarium restaurant they've got. We're getting per diem, right? Might as well have a little fun. Plus, it'll help us get into character for our attack on Sunset Yachts. We can warm up to being the Canes."

She pulled her too-large, too-colorful, too-cheap canvas bag, with its picture of a cruise ship spread across it, from the space at her feet and began rummaging. Through the course of waiting at the gate at the airport in Grand Rapids, the flight to Houston, and the almost-hour in the rental car to get from Houston's George Bush Intercontinental to this misbegotten tourist trap, Xavier had come to realize his agent spent an inordinate amount of time rummaging.

She emerged from the canvas depths with a plastic cube.

"Gum, Mr. Cane?" She shook the container, rattling the chewing-gum pieces within it as though to make them more appealing to him.

But you know what? I do feel like a breath freshener. Huh.

He removed a hand from the wheel and Agent Carter shook a single cube of white gum into his palm without saying anything, which surprised him because he'd also found on the trip that his agent felt compelled to remark on every turn of circumstances.

"All right, left here." She pointed past him as he pulled to a stop sign moments later. "And we can look for parking when we get to the end of this lane." She tapped out of whatever app she'd been studying on her phone and darkened the screen, dropping the device into the abyss of the cruise-ship bag. "So do we have kids, Mr. Cane? And if so, how old are they? And how'd we make our money? Because we are retiring awfully young, you know?" She peered at him from beneath her sagging hat brim.

***

The aquarium dining room had boasted a massive fish tank holding a massive grouper. The fish had qualified as the first noteworthy aspect of the trip. The gray monster had given Lillian Carter something else to comment on, and when she'd implored Xavier to join her for a "selfie" in front of the creature, he'd . . . well, he hadn't just acquiesced. When she'd shown him the image on her phone afterward, his smile had looked . . . sincere.

Nor had the food been bad. Overpriced, but he'd enjoyed his tempura shrimp and scallops. Perhaps he did need this trip, this change in his routine, this—

"Right here, X." She touched his arm. "We'll turn right at this light and that should put us in the Waterford Harbor Marina and then we should find Sunset Yachts up here on the left. Yep, right there."

A bright yellow sign announced the Sunset Yachts, L.L.C., office, an unprepossessing modular on a concrete pad overlooking row upon row of docks and boats and obnoxious flags with the Sunset Yachts logo emblazoned on them. Xavier pulled the rental into a parking spot crowned with a sign that reserved the spot for Sunset Yachts Sailors and threatened to tow anyone not looking to be recruited to the crew. Xavier readied himself to confront the self-indulgent rubbish of salesmen and turned to Agent Carter.

"Are you ready to effect an arrest, Mrs. Cane?"

She grinned, patted her cruise-ship bag. "All set. I've got cuffs in here. I even brought a bellychain. Just for fun."

"That's my little missus."

Have I turned complete fool? What is this woman doing to me?

Xavier opened the car door and pushed through a-hundred-something-degree heat and humidity, as thick as molten amber, to stand up. Instantly, his glasses fogged and his upper lip beaded with perspiration. He addressed both issues with a handkerchief, blotting his brow for good measure.

He turned. Lillian looked . . . fresh. Light.

He followed her up three steps and onto a covered porch and then stepped past her to open the brokerage's door. Air conditioning crashed into them and a bell chimed.

"Welcome to Sunset Yachts, y'all!" A stocky woman in heavy makeup sat at a cheap wood-veneer desk in a screaming-pink Hawaiian-print shirt.

"Hello," Lillian started, "we've got an appointment with a broker named Nils Bryson to take a look at a few sailboats he has listed for sale. A forty-two-foot Vagabond and two Morgan 41s—"

"So you're here to see *The Other Woman, Must Be Nice,* and *Sea Mistress.* I know them well." A blaze of yellow polyester Hawaiian print, and khaki shorts, swept into the reception space. "I'm Captain Norm Vance. Welcome to Sunset Yachts. We can't wait to get you onto the water in the boat of your dreams." His toothy smile revealed an inability to afford braces.

Agent Carter accepted his outstretched hand. "Thank you, Captain Vance, but I think we're supposed to be meeting with Nils Bryson. I believe he's the listing agent on the boats we're interested in."

"No worries, mon." Norm Vance feigned, poorly, a Jamaican accent. "We work as a team here at Sunset. Our goal isn't to make the sale. It's to get you sailing!"

Xavier considered excusing himself and finding a private corner in which to regurgitate the aquarium's tempura shrimp.

"And you're?" Captain Vance waited for Agent Carter to make the introductions.

"I'm Lillian Cane," she responded. "And this is my husband Xavier Cane. We're from Saugatuck, Michigan, but we're looking to retire and cruise the islands, so we're in the market for a coastal cruiser. Something rugged enough to make island passages, but we're not looking to do the Southern Ocean or anything."

Well, there you go again, Lillian Carter. Doing your homework.

Xavier stepped up to Vance. "Norm, Xavier Cane. A real pleasure." He added a few extra pounds per square inch to the handshake.

"We've got a Hunter 340 now in Michigan," Lillian said. "But we'll be listing her for sale shortly. So, um, is Mr. Bryson available to show the Vagabond and Morgans?"

"Good old Nils is in the middle of the Gulf right now, as far as I know." Norm Vance crossed hairy, freckled arms over his chest. "He's making a delivery of a Pearson to Nevis. But again: never fear! Captain Vance is here. I'll go get the keys to those girls, and we'll have you aboard in just a couple minutes. They're all right out here on our broker docks. Delilah, honey, would you get the Canes a couple bottles of water while I go get keys and spec sheets?" He assured Lillian and Xavier he would return momentarily and left them with the receptionist, ostensibly Delilah, who rose from her desk and disappeared, ostensibly in search of water bottles.

Lillian touched Xavier's sleeve. Her eyes told him she'd had the same thought he had had: Nevis? *Badwud.* So Nils Bryson was sailing to St. Kitts.

Touché, *Nils Bryson. But you won't score again.*

"Sweetheart," Lillian said, "this still works. We'll check out the boats, get a feel for the layouts, get all the details. And then we can hash it over tonight at the hotel and see if anything's worth making an offer on."

Xavier studied her. Her eyes told him she would get her man and that this setback simply presented an opportunity to gather information. And then she . . . winked. Lillian Carter winked at him and he had an unholy desire to lean over her and—

"Here we go, Lillian, Xavier." Norm Vance trotted in with a sheaf of papers and a jangle of keys on oversized plastic keyrings. "Here are spec sheets on all three vessels, and I gotta tell you: you're gonna flip for that little Vagabond. She's sweet. Owner's a mechanical engineer with one of the chemical plants up the road. Takes really good care of her. Repowered her in 2010. New main and head sails in 2015. New marine air conditioning last year. She's a real doll."

They followed him out of the office and into that oppression of unrelenting sunshine. This time, Xavier had his handkerchief at the ready. The docks felt like they might melt and ooze into the water underfoot under the solar assault. A few ducks floated in a slip, and Xavier envied them their aquatic berth.

"So, Mr. Vance," Lillian said as she clambered aboard a large, off-white boat with *The Other Woman* painted across her stern. "X and I haven't done any long-distance cruising. So we've got some learning curve in front of us. And the first thing we're wondering about is kids. We have a seven-year-old son and we're wondering if he's too young for this adventure."

"No, not at all," Norm boomed. "They're never too young to fall in love with boats. I myself don't have kids, but I've had several clients who decided to take a few years off and go cruising. They homeschooled the kids on board. It worked great, they said. But you know, that is something I'll tell Nils to get with you on. I can handle the sales paperwork for you if you see something you like, but I'll make sure he follows up with you when he gets back because I believe he took his nephew with him on this delivery. So that's something. He can tell you a little about how the kid fared."

"Oh," Lillian continued, and something stirred in Xavier as he watched the woman in her bright tourist garb work the fat captain brilliantly. "That would be perfect. Because we just want to make sure it's something Caleb will enjoy. We don't want to force it on him."

"No, kids love it. Love being on the water." Norm had gotten the boat open and led the way down into her dark, cooler interior. "Air conditioning's on. You can see how well it cools down the boat." He gestured around the cabin. "Well, look around all you like. I'll give you some space. Check 'er out."

Xavier pulled his prescription sunglasses off and blinked, inhaled the damp scent of an unvisited maritime space. He dropped the sunglasses in a pocket and pulled, from a different pocket, the slim case with his regular glasses. After adjusting his eyewear, he followed Lillian to the rear of the cabin and into the main stateroom, trying to poke around and look interested in the boat's accommodations.

"Oh, X, look at all this room!" Lillian clapped her hands together, even convincing Xavier that the boat impressed her. "This would be perfect for us. Can't you just see us sailing through the islands together?"

***

Xavier pulled his blue polo shirt away from his back as he folded himself into the rental car's driver's seat, perspiration having soaked through his undershirt to the polo shirt to glue both layers to his back. He removed his prescription sunglasses and adjusted an air-conditioning vent to blast his face.

"Let's go check into the hotel," he said, "and then I'll call Brittney at the office and see about getting our stay in St. Kitts extended." He replaced his glasses and dropped the car into gear, turning over his shoulder to begin backing the vehicle out of the Sunset Yachts parking spot.

"Extended? You want to try to intercept Nils on the island?" Lillian had flipped the sun visor down and was reapplying that lipstick in the mirror.

Xavier pulled out of the marina, leaving Captain Norm Vance, Delilah, and the three cruising boats in his wake. Their work on the water was done. "I don't just want to intercept him. I want to take him into custody."

Lillian turned away from the mirror, holding the lipstick canister beside her cheek as she watched him, her eyes asking the question: what about jurisdiction?

"Lillian," he was becoming more . . . accustomed . . . yes, accustomed . . . to using her first name, "I spent all my summers there as a kid. My family's there. This isn't about jurisdiction."

She waited, the lipstick still at attention.

"Sounds like Nils let it slip to his coworkers he was taking the kid on his little escapade, right?" Xavier continued. "We know he's going over there for the same reasons we are, correct? To find Monique Arthurton. I'm sure he thinks he can get some sort of exculpatory evidence to clear Viggo's good," he snorted, "name. But for whatever ill-advised reason, he took the kid with him."

The lipstick didn't move.

"It's easy. We wait till he sails into town and then we give him a choice. He can come back with us to face the superseding indictment or he can face my uncle, who practices family law on the island, and who, I'm sure, would be more than happy to file for reinstatement of Monique Arthurton's parental rights pro bono, so an island mother can be reunited with her son and little Grant Bryson can stay with her."

"Xavier." Lillian dropped the hand holding the lipstick into her lap, glanced down to cap the cosmetic, and threw the tube into her bag. "That's perfect. Honestly, it feels a little cold, but—"

"But? Lillian, he's charged with a federal felony and he thinks he can avoid arrest and finagle evidence for his thieving brother by sailing off to St. Kitts? And he takes a kid who isn't his along, and whose mother wants him back? Now, I don't know anything about the Hague Convention, but I am going to look into it because some of this sounds a bit like international child abduction to me, and I think the authorities on St. Kitts might be interested in it if Nils Bryson doesn't make good choices when we meet him. You see: it is quite easy. Either Nils Bryson comes back with us to answer the charges against him, or Viggo Bryson never sees his bastard son again."

He paused, slowing the car for a red light. Lillian Carter gazed at him.

"What's wrong, Lillian?"

"Nothing. Nothing at all. You're just a really smart guy, Xavier."

Warmth crept through Xavier, warmth and something else.

"Lillian, what would you say to joining me for dinner tonight? Something nice."

Chapter 17

Taking

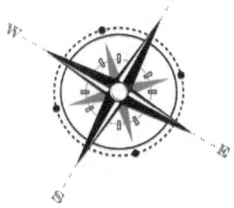

Manuia had started to bob and roll in the way boats do when their breeze dies but the seas under them persist. Galveston lay way off to the west in her wake and the Gulf spread before her the color of sangria. Devlin could hear Sean and Grant laughing in the boat's stern. She laid back on the hard fiberglass of the bow and studied the post-sunset weft of dirty, slightly frayed strato-something clouds strung overhead like the train of Ms. Havisham's wedding gown.

As soon as *Manuia* had cleared the channel and gotten settled on her southeast course down Galveston Bay, Devlin had opened her laptop, created a hotspot with her cell phone, and downloaded the superseding indictment in Viggo's case and the contract Irene Stockton's paralegal had sent. At some point early on, Sean had disappeared below to root for cheese and crackers in the galley, and Nils had asked about the indictment and Devlin had outlined the basics, told him he was charged with conspiring with Viggo and recruiting purchasers for Viggo's tax-evading insurance products, and helping these clients defraud the IRS. But mostly she'd ping-ponged internally, swinging between cursing Viggo and questioning Nils's integrity.

Sean had returned to the cockpit with a cutting board of Havarti and water biscuits, and then everyone had settled down and focused on getting past the Galveston jetties and into the Gulf, and dolphins had appeared off the bow, all gray and slick in the bay's muddy water, and a gull with a black head and orange beak had landed on the stern rail and ridden south as a crewmember for at least half an hour. And so for a few hours, she'd forgotten the purpose of the trip and it had felt like she was a kid again, racing the Chicago-to-Mackinac Race as she had with Nils for years. He hadn't been indicted and he hadn't bailed on her all those years ago and they weren't trying to outrun whatever it was they were now fleeing and couldn't quite explain.

But now the dolphins were long gone.

"What ya thinking up here all alone, D. Winters?"

Devlin opened her eyes to Nils's ankles and bare feet beside her head. She shut her eyes again.

"Honestly?" She kept her voice low. "Honestly, I'm wondering if you're a crook like your lying brother or just a complete dumbass."

"Is there an option C?" Nils dropped down next to her hip, so when she opened her eyes for the second time, his back in a long-sleeved red t-shirt with sponsor logos and a regatta name across it filled her view.

"Not from what that indictment says."

"You think Viggo's crooked and I'm in on it?"

She had to push herself up to seated to hear him over the creak of rigging and burble of wave action.

"I know Viggo's crooked." She wrapped her arms around her knees. "And frankly, Mr. Assistant U.S. Attorney Xavier Charles makes a strong argument that you were, indeed, in on it, as you say."

Nils sighed.

Manuia stabbed into a larger-than-its-brethren wave and spray left Devlin's legs and shorts damp.

"Look, Dev, I know you pretty much hate Viggo. There are days I think he's a scumbag. I get it. But he's my brother, and even though we aren't exactly Frodo and Samwise, I love the guy. And I trust him." He paused.

Another wave smacked the boat, catching her crosswise and pushing her port rail toward the water. "Most of the time."

Devlin rubbed her eyes. "You're an idiot."

"Devlin, look, I know we've got our junk. I know you and Viggo have had your junk. But I also know this: Viggo loves Grant. He was running a highly successful business. He's greedy, but he's not stupid. He wouldn't do anything that would jeopardize his relationship with that kid."

He shifted, turned to face Devlin squarely.

"I talked to Irene. She's got a letter from an attorney saying Viggo's insurance products were legal. He didn't cheat anyone."

"Are you serious, Nils? He's got some advice-of-counsel letter he paid some ham-and-egger to write up, and you think that puts him on the up and up? Are you that naïve? Your brother is a crook. Now the question is: are you?"

"Why do you care?"

Manuia banged into another cross-cut wave and the boom crashed against the port shrouds. Nils's question hung in the space left behind the impact, a rugged, annealed edge to it, cooling slowly in the advancing evening.

I don't. I don't care. I don't want to reach over and wrap my hands in your hair and find out if your lips still taste like amaretto stolen from the yacht-club bar.

"I just want to know if you're playing me again," she whispered.

"I never played you, Devlin."

"Are you kidding? Are you fucking kidding me? The playboy of the western world makes me a notch on his belt and dis-a-fucking-ppears after a set of sloppy 'I love yous' and 'let's run off to Vegas and get married because you're the love of my lifes,' but ho no—that's not playing me."

Dusk had turned sooty around the boat, and Sean must have kicked the navigation lights on because when Devlin tossed her head back the red and green masthead lights winked overhead, something like consoling. The lights cut arcs and zig zags out of the sky as *Manuia* rocked, and Nils stood up and went to the bow pulpit, riding the boat's pitching—up and up, and falling into the troughs.

"I loved you, Devlin Winters."

The rigging was shivering and aching and groaning, but she knew what she'd heard.

"I loved you. Those sloppy 'I love yous' as you call them: I meant that shit. I meant it and I fucked up." He turned away from the bow and dropped back down beside her. "I was a stupid twenty-something kid, ready to disappoint anyone dumb enough to trust me, and I wish to God it hadn't been you, but it was, and I've spent a lot of time regretting a lot of things—leaving, and never calling once I got back to school, and bragging to Viggo that Devlin Winters had finally put out and it was to me, and his dumb ass saying all the shit he said to you, and the party at the club where he came on to you and asked if he could have a taste since you'd given it up for me. I'm a dumbass and Viggo is a creep sometimes. And I fucked up. And for that I am ever—so—godawful—sorry."

The nonskid deck ground into Devlin's tailbone and the just-arrived night smelled of brine and garlic. Sean must have set the autopilot and gone below to start dinner.

"I let go of the only real teammate I've ever had," Nils whispered. His eyes hid in the dark. "And I look at her now and wish I hadn't."

The sea sounded like sorrow. No wonder stories of Flying Dutchmen and Davy Jones arose from it, with its relentless slamming and washing over. And then slapping, wet footsteps interrupted the sorrow, lightened it.

"Are you guys hungry?" Grant stood at the shrouds. "Sean says dinner's almost done."

The breadth of Nils's shoulders shifted in the dark. "Sure, big guy, we'll be right down. Give us one more minute."

Grant padded away, and it registered in Devlin's mind that the kid was wearing his lifejacket without complaint.

"I'll just say this." Nils's voice drifted beneath the green and red mast lights sparkling far, far overhead. "I cheated you. I know that. But you're the only one I cheated. After that, I was broke and drifting around in search of adrenaline and adventure, and I let Viggo give me some money for regattas and surfing and shit. But I didn't cheat or steal from anyone. The only person I've ever stolen from was you, and I would—"

And his mouth was on hers, hard and driving. He pushed her down onto the damp deck and he took from her again—took and took and took. He tasted just as he had all those years ago, and she dug her fingers into his hair. And then her tongue and teeth and cells and sinews pushed back, grasped, began their own relentless taking. The boat bucked beneath them, and the hard fiberglass dug into her back, and she pressed into him, and the night dissolved into saltwater and hot breath.

"I cheated you, Devlin," he whispered, pulling away. "But I never, ever lied to you. I loved you. Loved you hard."

She sat up in the darkness, the navigation lights pulling her to her feet. He was on his knees, and she could feel his chin tilted up toward her. She could feel him in the darkness breathing hard and his blood pumping through him and his heart in his chest, and she found the lifelines and the shrouds and slipped through the night back to the cockpit, toward the smell of dinner and the safety of company and noise and light, toward a cabin too crowded to make room for the past.

***

"The game is Skip Bo, little man. You ever play it?" Sean shot Grant a solemn look across *Manuia*'s saloon table.

The kid shook his head. "Uh uh."

"No worries. It's easy." Sean began dealing cards and explaining the game.

The cabin still smelled of Sean's risotto dinner. The warm, happy glow of the brass cabin lights made the scene feel all Norman Rockwell, but even Sean's ample stock of pillows and fleece blankets couldn't make the place comfortable for Devlin. She stole a glance at Nils's back as he stood at the galley sink washing dishes. The boat's water pump hummed.

"Nils, man, you almost done there?" Sean asked across the cabin. "The kid's ready to go."

Devlin considered options for dirtying more dishes and keeping Nils busy at the sink, but then he was drying his hands and crossing the cabin and settling in beside Grant. And the dinette got terribly cramped.

"Okay, here we go, so I've got a one." Sean laid a card down. "What's wrong, Milady Winters?"

"Nothing. I'm just tired." Devlin adjusted the blanket around her shoulders. The cabin was plenty warm, but the fleece felt cozy and provided something like a barrier.

Grant took his time with his cards, and *Manuia* rocked. The sound of the wave action against her hull shifted, changed.

"You sure you're okay?" Sean held Devlin's eyes. Then he cut a glance at Nils.

"Yeah, I'm fine. Maybe I'll get some chocolate." She pushed out of the settee.

Nils and Grant bantered behind her and she rifled in a cabinet for the truffles she knew she'd stowed.

Manuia rocked onto her side and then seemed to twist as she righted herself. Devlin turned over her shoulder. Nils and Sean met her eyes.

"Something doesn't feel right," Sean said.

Yeah, Nils Bryson is an incubus.

"There's something wrong with these waves." Devlin found the bag of truffles and walked over to the table. "Anyone?" She held out the bag.

"I'm gonna go take a look upstairs." Sean slid out of the settee and climbed out the companionway to the cockpit.

Devlin set the chocolates beside the cards and followed him outside.

"Something doesn't feel right at all, Sean," she said.

"Let's shorten sail," Sean said. "Just to be on the safe side." He started forward to the mast.

"Hey, man, I know it's weird, but let's put harnesses on," Devlin said. "I just have a feeling something is going to break loose soon."

"Sure," Sean said, returning to the cockpit.

Devlin ducked below and opened a locker full of foul-weather and safety gear, pulling out two safety harnesses. "Nils, you wanna see if you can get the weather report on the radio? Just see if we're still within range?"

"Sure." He walked to the VHF and switched it on to a bubble of static.

Devlin listened to him scan stations as she stepped back on deck.

"Here we go." She handed a safety harness to Sean and then wriggled into one herself.

As she and Sean dropped the mainsail part way down the mast and tied up the excess fabric into a neat storm reef, the Gulf grew more and more restless, the air heavier. She went forward with Sean to secure a storm jib in place, and waves washed over the deck, deep enough to reach past the ankles of her rubber boots and wash inside.

"Anything on the radio?" she asked as she and Sean dropped back into the cabin.

"Nothing." Nils had pulled out an iPad and loaded up the navigation charts. "I just wanted to check our position."

She nodded.

"Okay, buddy." She turned to Grant. "What say we call it a day? I'm thinking we're in for a storm, and the best way to weather it will be in snuggy pajamas tucked up in that v-berth, little man."

Behind her, Sean and Nils donned foul-weather gear. Grant went to the head to change and to brush his teeth, and Devlin started lining the berth with pillows for the kid, a little protection and comfort in the event the ride turned bumpier. In safety harnesses and inflatable lifevests, Nils and Sean climbed into the cockpit. Devlin pulled on waterproof coveralls, cinching the gaskets over her boots. She wriggled into a foul-weather jacket and pulled a traditional foam lifejacket over her head—she didn't trust the inflatables in an emergency. She re-situated her safety harness on top of everything.

"You ready to hit the hay, kiddo?" she asked as Grant stepped out of the head.

He nodded. "Can I read a little first?"

"Sure, buddy. But here." She pulled the lee cloth up to seal the kid into the v-berth, so he couldn't be thrown out of the bunk if the boat got truly wild.

"I'm like a dragon in its lair." Grant kneeled and smiled over the top of the lee cloth.

Devlin laughed. "Exactly like a dragon. All right, buddy, we'll be on deck. Don't stay up reading too long."

She reached to turn off the cabin light, and *Manuia* lurched like she'd been flung from a trebuchet. Devlin slammed to the floor and into a bulkhead. Dishes and provisions clattered and books hurled themselves off a shelf and onto the cabin sole. One of the men on deck shouted.

"WTF. You okay, little man?" Devlin got to her knees.

The boat crashed to its side again and Devlin went back down. A galley cabinet sprang open, and cans and bottles smashed across counters to the floor.

And then the world dissolved into a banshee scream of wind and the explosion of the boom smashing across the boat into the rigging and waves tearing at fiberglass . . . and Sean screaming.

"Devlin!"

She found her footing, grabbed hold of a rail and made her way aft toward the cockpit.

"Man overboard! Man overboard!"

Waves had filled the cockpit to mid-shin. The scuppers couldn't keep up with the water crashing in. *Manuia* hurtled through the night like she was harnessed to a demon. Sean was staring over the stern rail.

"I activated the man-overboard protocol on the GPS, but I can't see a goddamned thing," he shouted. "I'm not sure he's okay. He tried to clip in and then we gybed. . . ."

"He's not clipped in and dragging behind us?" Devlin shouted over the wind.

"No, I'm sure he didn't get his lifeline clipped." Sean tore at the man-overboard marker on the stern rail. He pulled it loose and cast it into the darkness. Its light activated, too-tiny blinks struggling against the storm.

"Fuck." Devlin wrestled with the wheel to bring the boat around.

"I'm not sure he's okay." Sean shouted again, turning from the stern to release the jib sheet as the boat came around.

"What?" Devlin adjusted the mainsheet.

"I think he hit himself pretty good on the stern rail when he went in."

"Shit. Did his lifejacket inflate?"

"Dev, I don't know. I couldn't see a damned thing. We were both underwater." Sean reached for the engine controls and the Yanmar roared to life.

Devlin snatched the emergency GPS transmitter from the helm station. She shoved it into a jacket pocket.

God be with me.

"Try to find us, man," she screamed over the wind. "And take care of that kid." She stepped to the lifelines and flung herself into the blackness.

Chapter 18
The Duke

Lillian.
* Lillian Carter. *
* Lillian Amelia Carter. *

She'd offered over steaks that her mother had named her Lillian Amelia for Amelia Earhart. And Xavier hadn't called her Agent Carter once this evening. They'd decided on something completely Texan for dinner—or as Texan as a tourist trap could provide—and returned to the boardwalk for steaks at a place with an old-timey-brick façade and a faux-roadhouse foyer. Now, in the still-hot, gold-streaked evening, he heard himself ask about ice cream.

"Lillian, what do you say? Shall we go all the way with this Cane-family tourist yarn and splurge with some ice cream?"

She reached out and rubbed Xavier's arm, plucked a tuft of cat hair from his sleeve with a grin. "That sounds perfect, X."

Past a carousel and kiddy train, and beyond a stretch of boardwalk carnival games, they found Sprinkles.

Sprinkles? You're about to enter an establishment named Sprinkles? And what's more, you're . . . giddy. Xavier Damien Charles, for the love of all that is good. . . .

"It feels like it's going to rain or something," Lillian was saying at his elbow as he pulled open the Sprinkles door for her. She glanced over her shoulder as she stepped into the confectioner. "Maybe there's a storm trying to build over the Gulf. Look at those clouds."

Sprinkles' ice-cream display stretched for yards, with local creations like Whiskey Tango Butterscotch and Armadillos and Grubs, which seemed to consist of graham crackers and gummy worms.

"What about splitting something?" Lillian squeezed his arm. "Like a banana split with everything on it? Wouldn't that be fun?"

And Xavier said yes. He said yes to sharing a trough of mismatched mess covered in something called marshmallow fluff. And . . . he put his arm around her and pulled her in—for just a moment. He could sense the surprise in her frame, and some other thing, some response that made his heart feel like he'd already skyrocketed his blood sugar to 260. He heard her order the ice-cream monstrosity and he heard her thank him when he paid for it and he heard her suggest sitting outside because it looked like a band was setting up and it was a beautiful night, even if a storm was brewing, . . . it was fine out now, . . . and then he followed her to a wrought-iron table of black metal curlicues and he sat across from her and almost thought it would be acceptable if the whole world paused like this for a while, a long time, a long, long time. Yes, this was nice. This was enough.

And then she said it.

"Okay, we're traveling like this together. Adventuring. Thrown together in some high-stakes venturi effect of crime fighting that's pushing us faster and faster toward St. Kitts and convicting the bad guys before we're released—boom—with a jury verdict of guilty at trial. Because that's gonna happen. Because you're the most dedicated lawyer I've ever met. So. I'll make a confession.

I'm a total nerd. You know who my favorite actor of all time is? Ever? John Wayne."

John. Wayne.

Time stopped.

Time stopped and an angel emerged from a tiny, star-spangled door in the heavens and strummed a lyre made of opal and stardust and cherubim began waltzing across the sky and Xavier decided he liked marshmallow fluff very, very much.

A glow hovered over her. "Can you believe me? Pretty bad, huh? But my dad was a total nut for old westerns. So I grew up on a diet of Sunday afternoons in front of *The Searchers, How the West Was Won, She Wore a Yellow Ribbon*, and all that." She lifted a pile of ice cream and fluff to her lips. "What about you? What deep, dark secrets do you have?"

I love you. Marry me, Agent Lillian Amelia Carter. God, thank you for denying me Niqi Arthurton. Please give me this woman. It's okay that she likes detestable desserts. She loves The Duke. Let her love me.

Didn't love depend on truth? Should he . . . ? They would be on the island together. Would she discover . . . ? Xavier returned to a debate he had been conducting with himself for days.

"John Wayne is the greatest actor in the history of moving pictures," he said. And then he added, "I know Niqi Arthurton. Personally. And well."

Chapter 19

Red and Green

The crash of water against Devlin's ears tore away the tail end of Sean's "shit!" as she threw herself into the teeth of the Gulf. The sea closed over her, black and unimaginably heavy, and the world turned vacuum. She sank. And sank. And then she started clawing, ripping apart the water overhead, tearing, grasping, pulling. When she broke the surface, the world screamed as she'd never heard and a concrete truck of water broke over her, burying her beneath its contents, sending her back to the utter darkness she'd just escaped.

If she could only get to the surface, if the Shades would defy all possibility and let her drift into Nils. The GPS transponder in her pocket would relay her position to the autopilot on *Manuia* and Sean could find her—find them—and pick them up.

God, please! Please! Please! Please, whoever listens in the dark! Please! Oh, shit, please!

She broke the surface again and saw the tiny blinks: the man-overboard pole Sean had deployed. So far away, so, so far. She struck out, kicking, clawing, pulling, gasping. The water weighed thousands and thousands of pounds, thousands, as she tore at it, as it crashed over her. Her eyes burned. No division between sea and sky existed.

The world was all black bowl: cold, cold, burning, strangling, seething wetness in a black bowl.

Another light. Lights. A strobe. A strobe. On-off-on-off-on-off. Teeny, tiny light-wave screams into the night beyond the higher blinks of the man-overboard pole.

Oh, please, please! God in Heaven, please!

Stroke, arm-tearing heavy stroke.

A screech: a whistle!

"Nils!" The storm backhanded her, tearing the word away from her.

Stroke, stroke.

She reached the man-overboard pole, caught hold of the lifering. The strobe light had grown larger, throwing itself into the night with an abandon only the condemned know, crying out with its pulses and then disappearing behind the mountains of Gulf.

Stroke, stroke, reach, kick.

The whistling grew louder.

"Nils!"

Louder, louder: blare after blare of whistle.

And she was there, she was so close, almost beside the strobe. But where? Where in this great mass of darkness? Where?

"Nils!"

She remembered her own light, tore at her lifejacket, freed the light and activated it. The world burst into white pulses.

The whistling became a steady shriek.

Then he was there, a darker black against the blackness.

"Nils!"

The whistling ceased, the sea roared, and—

"Dev! Devlin! Dev?"

"Nils!"

She had hold of something, of him, of nylon, a strap.

"Nils!"

"Devlin!"

She groped at the nylon, worked her fingers down the harness he still had on, found the carabiner and tether. She clipped it to her own harness.

"I have the GPS transponder," she screamed. "Sean can find us!"

"Oh, God, Devlin!" Nils coughed up water.

"We've just gotta wait—"

"I'm not going anywhere." Nils coughed again.

"Are you okay?" she shouted.

"My arm's busted up!" he yelled back. "Can't move my arm."

"Okay, okay." Devlin clipped Nils to the man-overboard pole's lifering and tried to situate it under Nils's chest to help his lifevest do its job and keep his head high.

A freight car of water pounded her downward, ripped her away from him and the pole. She felt her body hit the end of the tether, felt herself drag Nils and the pole downward.

"Shit." She surfaced and groped for the tether, groped to follow it back to Nils, clawed her eyes, clawed at the burning salt, blew water from her sinuses.

"I'm back!" She bumped into him.

"I can see that."

"Can you?" she shouted. "Because I can't see anything!"

And then she could: red and green! Red and green, red and green, red and green! Navigation lights! Bow lights. A darker darkness against the towers of waves . . . and the sparkle of red and green.

"Whistle!" she shouted, tearing to find her own.

She and Nils blasted their whistle screams into the night. And then even with the whistling and the *dybbuk* howls of the storm, she could hear it, hear the engine. *Manuia*'s Yanmar. That majestic diesel lullaby.

Sean came in textbook—just upwind of them and slow. He had a swim ladder out, and as he drew close, Devlin could hear him shouting.

"I gotcha. Right here!" he yelled.

Thank you, God, thank you, God, thank you, God!

"Which arm?" Devlin shouted at Nils. "Which arm is busted?"

"Right!" he yelled.

She floundered in her rock-heavy foul-weather gear and against the tethers, wrestling to get around to Nils's left side. She grabbed hold of his left biceps and kicked toward *Manuia.*

"We got it, we got it, we got it!" She caught hold of the swim ladder and pressed Nils's left hand into it.

"Got it!" he yelled.

"His right arm's broken!" she shouted up to Sean.

The hulking Samoan wriggled under the stern rail and took hold of Nils's torso. Devlin clung to the bottom rung of the swim ladder and unhooked from Nils's tether.

Let me get onto this boat. Please, God, just a little longer. Let me make it onto this boat.

She dragged beside *Manuia.* Nils's body rose from the water, and both men disappeared into the boat's cockpit. She hung from the ladder alone in roaring, howling black space.

And please let Sean have her in neutral. Please.

She imagined the propeller beneath the hull, imagined getting sucked into it.

"Your turn, beautiful!" Sean reappeared beneath the stern rail, an angelic Hercules.

Thank you, God!

Sean's hands caught her as she lurched up the ladder.

Then the three of them were sprawled in the cockpit, gasping, spluttering, and Devlin heard herself asking, "She's in neutral?"

"She's in neutral, honey. I wasn't going to grind you into ground round, sweetheart." Sean laughed, hard and long.

The cockpit melted into choking, salty, wet sobs and laughter. Coughing and more gasping. The hard fiberglass bucked and pitched and Devlin's head slammed into something, and nothing mattered except being in that plastic box, crammed against legs and arms and heads . . . and alive.

***

"It's dislocated, man." Sean sat braced on a settee with his first-aid-at-sea book in his lap.

In dry clothes and a fleece blanket, Devlin sat crammed against him. They'd strapped Nils into a berth across from them.

"You feel spasming?" Sean turned to Nils in the berth.

"Yeah." Nils's voice came from the bed, tight and strained.

"I got muscle relaxants in the head." Sean pulled himself up and struggled across the slant of the boat's floor. "You okay up here, little man?" he asked Grant, who they'd insisted stay bundled in the v-berth.

The storm had the boat pinned on her left side, and a wicked chorus of water rushing past the hull played on an endless loop.

Grant nodded, bug-eyed. Devlin tried to crane around the bulkhead and smile at the kid, but it took so much energy and she was so, so tired.

Sean returned from the head with three orange tablets. He stumbled as the boat pitched, and then he continued toward the galley, returning with a bottle of water.

"Here, man." He nestled the water bottle into the cavern of Nils's berth and handed him the tablets.

Devlin pulled her blanket tighter around her shoulders.

"We'll give it like forty-five minutes or an hour for those things to work, and then we'll put that arm back into place." Sean dropped down beside Devlin. She curled into him and he pulled her head into his chest.

"You doing okay, honey? You scared the ever-living shit out of me."

She buried her face in his shirt.

He patted her head. "I didn't know what you were thinking. I thought you'd lost it. But then I realized you'd grabbed the transponder."

She pulled her face away from his torso. "Yeah, I don't know. I figured I was in a win-win situation. Either I'd find this worthless lug and he'd owe me his worthless life, or I'd make some family in Haiti rich."

"Obviously, I was worth enough to make you want to jump in and have me owe you my life." Nils's voice floated up from the berth.

"I have bad taste," Devlin replied.

"You know people in Haiti?" Sean asked.

"Nah," she said, "but my boss at the boardwalk has my will, and in the event of my untimely demise, pretty much everything I've got, like my retirement accounts, all go to this charity that helps people in Central America and the Caribbean. So, someone would get something out of it."

"Your boss?" Sean's arm rested around her shoulders and he patted her.

"She's as good as anyone," Devlin mumbled. "Who do I know? Who would notice if I died on old *A`uku*? At least my boss would notice if I missed a shift."

"Damn." Sean pulled her in even tighter. "What about like your folks? I mean, I know you're not close with them, but?"

"Nope" was all Devlin could offer.

"Are we gonna survive?" Grant squeaked.

"We're gonna survive, kiddo," Sean said. "Heck, we're gonna have some story to tell. The worst is behind us now."

"I feel sick," Grant responded.

"I know, buddy. If you gotta throw up, use this." Sean hauled himself up again and steadied himself to make it to the galley and retrieve a large bowl. He handed the receptacle into the v-berth.

"You want me to just throw up in here?" Grant sounded so scared.

"Yep," Sean said. "Believe me. When the time comes, it'll be easy."

Devlin patted Sean's knee when he reseated himself. "This'll be over soon, buddy," she called toward Grant. Her head felt too heavy to raise, and getting up and checking on the kid loomed in the realm of superhuman. "Thanks," she whispered to Sean.

Sean lowered the lights, and they all dozed until he announced it was time to fix Nils's arm.

"Well, let's give this a try." Devlin struggled free from her tangle of blanket and pushed off Sean's lap. She grabbed one of the cabin ceiling's rails and pulled herself across the forty-five-degree slant of the floor to Nils's berth. Sean followed.

"How you feeling, man?" he asked Nils.

"Like a million bucks." Nils grinned weakly in his hole of pillows and blankets.

Devlin removed the pillows from around his head and straightened his torso and neck, and then she wrapped an arm under his left armpit. She stroked his cheek with her right hand.

"Got him?" Sean asked, and she nodded.

Sean took hold of Nils's right arm and tractioned it a bit and then pulled.

Pop.

Nils snorted.

"Shouldn't I have gotten a stick of wood to bite down on or something?" He looked up at Devlin.

Heat washed through her, heat and electricity and relief and something that howled like the night outside. She leaned over him and kissed him, drank his lips, drank and drank and drank. Greedy.

Chapter 20
Yes

Lillian's spoon stopped dead in its tracks, hovered just below her lips. The cherubim stopped waltzing and the angel dropped his lyre.

"You know Monique Arthurton? How? Xavier, I— I don't understand."

Xavier sighed, blotted his mouth with an undersized paper napkin. "I'm sorry Lillian. I should have explained the situation fully, but I didn't want any irrelevant personal considerations to color the investigation." He paused. "Forgive me."

"Xavier, it's fine. I'm sure you have your reasons. But what are they? Just, well, I'd like to know so I can rethink my approach to this investigation."

Xavier rubbed the back of his neck and looked toward the stage where the evening's musical entertainment had finished setting up and was just striking into "Sweet Home Alabama." A family opened the door to Sprinkles behind him and let the air conditioning escape and crawl into his black curls. He shivered, but he couldn't blame it on the errant chill.

"When I was a kid, I spent summers on the island, with my grandparents and aunts and uncles and cousins. My cousins and I would sit on the edge of the fountain in Independence Square and we'd watch Basseterre come and go for long, lazy, hot afternoons." He gazed past the bandstand to the boats in the channel from Galveston Bay. "It was one of those places. It's not home, but it is. It stays with you forever afterward because it's where you truly grew up. And you saw it grow up. Like when I was around ten or twelve, Hurricane Georges leveled the island, wasted half the sugar crop. I was back in Chicago when it hit, but we went down there that Christmas—my mom and sister and I did—and I saw the ruin. I remember the end of the sugar industry when I was a teenager, and the excitement and controversy over the remaking of Port Zante when I was in my twenties and the investment in the cruise-ship facility there. I saw the island shift from those lazy days on the edge of the fountain to chasing cruise-ship tourist dollars in folksy costumes and headdresses."

He blinked and turned back to Lillian. "The island meant my family, and then, as I got older, it meant the friends I'd wait all year to see. Kids I'd spend endless days with on the beach."

He searched Lillian's face, watched her dig absently through the syrupy waste of the banana split. Was she avoiding his look? "And one of those kids I'd swim with, and sit by the fountain with, and fish with was a girl named Monique Arthurton."

"You grew up with her?" Lillian whispered into the ice-cream dish.

"I did." Xavier shifted forward and put his elbows on the table and then shifted back again, leaning back in his chair.

"Xavier, you should have told me."

"I know."

"I don't know what to say now. I don't know how to react. I've worked so hard to find information on Monique Arthurton, and you probably know more about her than anyone. Why didn't you just tell me? Why would you hide that?"

His ear suddenly itched, and Xavier scratched behind it, lifted and reset his glasses. "I didn't want to compromise the investigation. Viggo Bryson is a liar and a thief, and my childhood ties to the island, my memories of it, my childish friendships should have no impact on this prosecution. It was simply luck or coincidence that the case arose in the Western District of Michigan, that I prosecute financial crimes, that the file ended up on my desk. Sheer dumb luck. And I didn't want some twenty-year-old, childhood relationship to interfere with anything."

"So you knew Monique when you were a kid."

"Yes."

"When was the last time you saw her? Or talked to her at all?"

"Oh—" Xavier honestly, truly did have to think. How long had it been? He'd proposed when she'd gotten pregnant almost ten years ago. Met her a few times after that. And they'd talked the last time she was in Chicago. "I think the last time I talked to her was a little over four years ago."

"Four years ago? Xavier, that's not some long-lost, I-knew-her-as-a-kid thing. Four years ago? Wait." Lillian shut her eyes for a moment, opened them again. "When Monique returned to Chicago. The second time she had an apartment in Chicago. When she rented a place from the elderly island lady who wouldn't talk to me, who has a son who's a lawyer— Wait, Xavier. What aren't you telling me?"

She leaned onto her elbows, holding his eyes across the table. "You know this woman. You've known her a long time. You knew her as a kid and when she was a mother in Chicago. You know the woman who was her landlord. Xavier," she stopped, cocked her head to the left, "Xavier, is your mother a landlord in Chicago?"

Her eyes contained this ember, this burning, curious, driving thing. They smoldered. Not angry, but alive.

"She is now," Xavier whispered. "My mother rented an apartment to Niqi so she could come back to Chicago and see her son and . . . do whatever it was she was doing with Viggo back then."

"Xavier." Lillian Carter pushed the ice cream out of the way and dropped her head into her arms on the table.

"I truly have no idea what she was doing." Xavier reached across the table and put a hand on Lillian's back. She didn't move. He left his hand on her, the warmth of her shoulder reaching through her shirt and into his skin.

Then he touched her head and electricity shot through his arm. "Niqi and I were kids together. She got pregnant when she was seventeen. She didn't want to tell her family. She didn't have anywhere to go. Viggo—"

"Wait." Lillian's head shot up. "You knew Monique Arthurton as some scared teenager pregnant with Viggo Bryson's kid?"

Xavier nodded, then let his eyes slide away to study the concrete's black pockmarks of ancient bubble-gum scars beneath the shadow of the table.

"And you didn't think you should tell me any of this? As I scoured God's green earth in search of anything on this woman and her dealings?"

"I didn't want it to be a problem. I didn't want it to affect the case."

"Xavier, it's affecting it now."

"I understand." He sighed.

"Go on," Lillian said.

"I don't know the whole story, but as I understand it, Viggo breezed into town on a cruise, met Monique at a local tourist shop, and seduced her. Took her to a hotel and . . . she got pregnant. I was in college at the time, and she called me when she found out, and I flew down there. And then—"

The truth. Only the truth can fix this. Only the truth can bring back that smile over John Wayne and ice cream.

You . . . want this woman. You want her to believe you. Tell her.

"I told her I'd marry her." Xavier's voice cracked. His throat was dry and his tongue too heavy.

"You. Proposed. To. Our. Witness."

"Yes."

"Because she was pregnant with our defendant's baby."

"Yes."

"And now we're flying to St. Kitt's tomorrow to find this woman and give her immunity to testify against that defendant."

"Yes."

"All right, Xavier Charles." Lillian's eyes had this radiance. "Here's the million-dollar question. Did you love her?"

The world's air evaporated away and Xavier was left in a place devoid of breath and sound and movement. "Yes."

Chapter 21

The Arena

I'm loving the black-and-blue look. The palette is mellowing nicely on you." Devlin sat with her legs hanging over *Manuia*'s side, her arms wrapped around the boat's lifelines.

Nils wore a sling Sean had fashioned after reading further in the first-aid book. He dropped to the deck, carefully favoring his right arm, and slid in beside Devlin, letting his legs hang overboard next to hers. With the Gulf glittering from horizon to horizon and the breeze cooling *Manuia*'s crew with a gentle ten to twelve knots, the storm had dissolved into ancient history and the morning sparkled, a nautical idyll.

"So what do we do when we get to St. Kitts?" Nils asked.

Devlin shrugged. "I don't think it will be hard to find Monique Arthurton. I figure you and Grant and Sean will hang out on the boat. We don't need Monique finding out her son is on the island and trying to make trouble. I'll check that address for SK and N from her fancy turtle letterhead, and if that doesn't pan out, I'll ask around the local dive shops. I'll say I'm an American interested in marine conservation and that I've heard about SK and N, Inc., and want to learn more. If the company is the least bit legit, or even just well formulated as a cover, there'll be some link between it and the dive and tourism communities it allegedly serves through its work."

Nils's eyes stayed on the horizon.

"If I can get any sort of a lead on Monique, I'll follow it. If I can track her down, I'll meet with her, introduce myself as Viggo's lawyer's litigation-support specialist, which apparently I am now." She let her head roll back, felt the sun on her face. "I haven't worked for so little in the law in a long, long time."

"Wait," Nils turned from the expanse of water, "you're on the defense team for real?"

"Yeah, Irene Stockton's paralegal sent me a contract before we pulled out of town."

"Good." Nils smiled.

"Maybe." Devlin crossed her arms over the top lifeline and set her chin on them. "It's really not me."

"Yes, it is, Devlin. It's you. I know you're good at this. Good? Rumor had it you were a god or titan or something."

"Nils," she whispered, her eyes lingering on the rollers flowing past, "that's all dead and buried and I have no desire to resurrect any of it."

"Why, Devlin? Why?" He paused, and when he spoke again, his voice was higher, brittle. "Why do you love to sabotage yourself and throw away your trophies just as you're sliding into home for your biggest win? Just answer me that."

She lifted her chin from her arms, but didn't turn her face away from the water. She lowered her voice, balanced it against Nils's higher volume. "Because it's not worth it. It was all too damn much work. Too much blood, sweat, and tears for what I got back."

"Bullshit." Nils didn't turn his head either. Out of the corner of her eye, she saw him adjust the sling without glancing at it. "You're a coward, Devlin Winters. You're afraid of your own potential. You're afraid to finish because you don't know what you'll do with yourself if you actually, truly finish a race and get the prize."

Now she did turn. She turned and she fixed her sunglasses on his profile. "Fuck you, Nils. You flunk out of everything, squander your parents' money, don't finish anything, and you're going to lecture me about failing? Seriously. Fuck you."

"You know what the difference is?" The violence with which he whipped around to face her surprised her, made her pull back. "You had it. I didn't. You had the talent. The God-given, natural, never-have-to-practice, always-perfect talent. I would have sacrificed babies to have the talent you had. But you didn't do jack crap with it. Sure, you won some shit, but what did you ever see through to the end? A national champion, but you wouldn't even register for the Olympic trials. A full ride to law school and you end up disbarred. All that talk all those years ago about wanting to get married and have kids, and now you're so alone on a fucked up old boat that your boss is the executor of your estate if you die? That's just fucking sad."

"No." Devlin gathered her legs under her and stood up. She stepped across the deck and took hold of *Manuia*'s mast to steady herself. "You do not get to talk. You do not get to judge on those accounts. I wanted a family, to get married and have kids—not go to the Olympics, not be a lawyer, not chase all the superficial bullshit that drove our parents. And you screwed that pooch for me. Law school was because I didn't know what the fuck else to do with my life after you burned those dreams down for me. So no, you don't get to talk."

Even with the breeze and the rush of the boat's movement through the water, she was shouting loudly enough for someone in the cockpit to hear. She pressed her lips together and stepped back to the gunwale and sat back down beside Nils.

"Look, Nils Bryson," she hissed. "Shove your fucking judgments up your ass. I'm here because I care about you, and now, damn it all, I care about that kid. And now I'm also here because Viggo's attorney is dumb enough to shell out $120 an hour for me to chase some paper, and $120 an hour buys a lot of gin. But I'm not here to rehash the past or let some bastard who never got past half-assed tell me about winning and losing. You want to tell me about throwing away talent? Get in the fucking arena first and try it. And I don't mean with your brother footing the bill and smoothing the way. I mean, really try it. Fight to win. Then you can talk to me about throwing shit away."

She rocked back, pulled her legs in, and jumped up, but as she stepped past Nils to move toward the cockpit, he grabbed her ankle with his good left hand.

"Devlin, why'd you jump in?"

"What?"

His sunglasses held hers in their reflection. "Why'd you jump in last night? We both know that was a dumbass thing to do. Suicidal. A violation of everything anyone is ever taught. No one leaves a boat voluntarily in that situation. For any reason."

"Fuck you, Nils. I'm not saying shit."

"You knew there was a 0% chance of finding me. You knew you would likely drown before Sean picked you up, even with the transponder in your pocket. You knew it was a fool's errand." He didn't release her leg.

"I didn't think about it," Devlin said. "I just jumped."

"You thought enough to grab the transponder."

"I'm not an idiot," she replied. "If I hadn't grabbed the transponder, it would have been a fool's errand."

"Why'd you jump, Devlin?"

The bill of his cap cast a shadow across his face. This stripe of shade danced and shifted as the boat plowed through the waves, the lunging and pulling of *Manuia*'s momentum making the morning light flow in shimmering rivers over everything it touched. Spray across the bow rainbowed, and the day smelled of salt and pole stars and tomorrows on the other side of the world.

"I didn't have a choice, Nils. I couldn't not jump."

***

Manuia's forty feet of fiberglass cramped Devlin. She helped Grant get the hang of steering and talked to him about standing watches. She read. She played solitaire. Around four in the afternoon, she went below, and Sean, who'd been shooting her pregnant, inquisitive looks all day, asked if she wanted to learn to cook Samoan banana fritters he called *panikeke*. The sea was flat calm and the galley flat peaceful and free of boat heeling and rocking, presenting a warm invitation to make something a bit more elaborate.

So Devlin dug in, clattering a stainless mixing bowl against the door of a galley cupboard as she wrestled it from the overstuffed space.

Sean pulled vegetable oil out of another cabinet and retrieved bananas from the net hanging over the sink. "This is probably a terrible idea while we're under way. Who fries anything in oil on a boat that could pitch? But desperate times call for desperate measures."

Devlin could hear Nils shuffling around on deck overhead. She glanced up through the companionway and saw Grant looking pensive at the helm.

"It's not exactly desperate around here." She elbowed Sean.

"Says you. I'm feeling tension I could cut with these bananas it's so thick." Sean waved the fruit and then pulled the first one's peel back and deposited it in the bowl. He pointed at a plastic tub of flour. "Three and a half cups, please."

"It's not that bad." Devlin measured out the first cup of flour.

"It's that bad." Sean dumped sugar into the bowl on top of the bananas. "What's going on?"

"I don't want to talk about it." Devlin measured out another cup of flour.

"Great, so Grant and I just get to chill out while you and Prince Charming up there grind whatever axes you all have between you. Lucky us." He reached into a cupboard and pulled out a plastic container of baking powder. "You guys seemed pretty tight last night after we fixed that arm. And you did, after all, jump into the Gulf of Mexico in a pretty much suicidal bid to save his life."

Devlin sealed the flour tub up and shoved it back into its cabinet. She rearranged cans of peaches and pears in front of it. "We should have some of this canned fruit tonight with these. I love canned pears."

"You serious?" Sean rolled his eyes. "Devlin, just tell me what's going on. Release the tension for me. This boat's about to explode."

"It's really nothing. What do you need next in that mess?" She pointed at the bowl.

"Gimme a tablespoon of vanilla." Sean's big hand brought a mixing spoon down on the bananas in the bowl, crushing the pale fruit beneath the flour. "And it's not nothing. The kid's asked me like four times if Uncle Nils and Miss Devlin are okay, if there's anything we should do, if he's done anything wrong on the boat." Sean looked up from the mashed bananas. "He's back to calling you Miss Devlin."

"WTF. Poor kid. He thinks this is about him? Something he's done?" Devlin dumped the vanilla in the bowl.

"He's still pretty shook up from the storm, and I think he's feeling really lonely. I mean, poor little dude's dumped out here in the middle of the ocean with three people he really barely knows. He misses his dad. He's been telling me all these stories about him and his dad. After sitting up there with him this morning, I know the kid's life history." The spoon made scraping sounds as Sean beat the mixture in the bowl smooth.

"Sorry, man," Devlin mumbled. "Sorry you're babysitting."

"Hey, I don't mind. I like the little dude. My sister's got three kids. I like 'em. It's all good." Sean put the bowl down and turned to the cabinet below the sink, digging into it for a high-sided saucepan.

Devlin slumped against the counter.

"So what's wrong?" Sean straightened up with the pan.

"It's too much family and closeness and too many memories and too much responsibility." She wiped her sleeve across her face. "And sunblock. It's too much sunblock in my eyes."

"Aw, sweetie." Sean put his arms around her.

And then she couldn't stop herself. She sobbed, sobbed out the storm and the fear and the past and the failures and the trepidation about what lay in wait on St. Kitts.

"I'm a fuck up, Sean. I can't take this responsibility. I don't want people trusting me, relying on me. And I'm supposed to hate kids, and hate Nils." She buried her face in the big man's chest. "And I don't. I don't hate them. I don't hate him. I want to, but I can't. At all."

Sean put his hand on the back of her head and she stood pressed into him for a long time as *Manuia* cut through the water, with the ceaseless whooshing of sea just beyond the hull, and the smell of mashed bananas and piña-colada sunscreen filling the cabin.

Chapter 22
Basseterre

Basseterre. As the warm, damp, vegetable scent of sunrise in the tropics simmered around the aquamarine motel patio, with its Formica-topped tables and weary wicker, Xavier's thoughts drifted toward the idea of home. Something in him felt so settled, subdued. Like he'd set a heavy, shoulder-rounding backpack down when he'd stepped out of the terminal at Golden Rock, or Robert L. Bradshaw International, or whatever they wanted to call the airport now. He remembered that feeling from his childhood, how his mom would hug him at O'Hare and give him a Milky Way bar and tell him to enjoy *limin* down there, and he'd be in the air and then changing planes in Miami and then standing in the Golden Rock terminal, and his uncle would be taking his bag from him and patting his back and telling him he'd grown.

He would step out into the sun with his uncle, and the world would feel very soft, very bright, and kind. It would feel kind. He wouldn't worry about the things that made him worry in Chicago. Things like his mother and how sometimes it seemed like she struggled, like the time in the Co-Op when the woman behind them paid the last $2.36 because *muma* came up short. Or about Mrs. Walls at Bret Harte Elementary and her willful ignorance when it came to understanding the symbolism in Kipling, how she'd tried to get him to read *Charlie and the Chocolate Factory* instead of *The Scarlet Letter*. On the island, after a couple nights of getting comfortable on the broken-down mattress of the bed in his cousin's room, it was easier to sleep, and the popsicles from the old man with the ice-cream bicycle cart tasted better than anything in Hyde Park.

He felt like that now. Like it would be easier to sleep here and maybe he'd be able to find an ice-cream cart and the ice cream would taste better than anything at that lamentable Sprinkles. Agent Carter's stream of commentary had ceased after Sprinkles, and the silence Xavier had thought he craved now felt sodden and musty. It had been a long flight over from Houston.

On the street below, three women passed, laughing and carrying on. Xavier figured they were on their way to work at the shops of the cruise-ship terminal just across Bay Road and past, poetically, an ice-cream shop called Scoops. Scoops, Sprinkles, Lillian Carter, Niqi. . . . Xavier rose from the table.

At the check-in desk in the wood-veneered lobby, an older woman pulled a piece of paper from a Clinton-era printer in response to Xavier's "good morning" and inquiry of whether he might trouble her for a pen and paper.

"Eh, you local, *maas*?" the woman asked.

"I have family who live up past the Circus," he answered, "and out in Old Road Town. But I live in the States. Michigan."

"Ah, but so you home now."

Home. . . .

Xavier bid the woman good morning once again, wrote out a note to Agent Carter, which he slipped under her door to let her know he would be finding his family, and turned left out of the motel. With Nils Bryson in the middle of the Gulf or the Caribbean or some other God-forsaken sea, and Niqi oblivious to everyone's movements, there was no need to hurry.

Bay Road this early was quiet. A cruise ship sat docked at the terminal, but Xavier knew disembarkation wouldn't start for another hour or two. A few people bustled by, ostensibly on their way to work, like the women he'd seen earlier. Two men wore the folksy red, ribbon-festooned costumes of performers for the ship's tourists. In the roundabout locals called the Circus, Xavier stopped at the green and gold clock tower of the Berkeley Memorial. When he was a teenager, he'd spent a certain full summer night running through Basseterre with Niqi. Now, as he fiddled with the spigot of the water fountain, felt the tap-water-temperature water run over his hand, he blushed at the memory of buying beer and . . . engaging in . . . well . . . heavy petting in the UK-style ruby-red telephone kiosk across the circle from the tower. When he'd returned Niqi to her home in Old Road Town the next morning, he'd been drunk, and certainly too ashamed to walk her to her door and return her to her *muma* and *pupa*. He'd skulked home to a battery of aunts who'd smelled his smoky, beery breath and hauled him off to St. Joseph's, where an older cousin, who'd recently been ordained, heard his confession and sent him away to say a rosary focused on the sorrowful mysteries.

Oh, Niqi.

He sighed.

In college, he'd wondered if he'd helped push Niqi toward the life of bad choices that led to . . . what she had now. But as he'd grown up, he'd realized the truth of people's very free will . . . free will to make terrible, terrible choices on their own. Free will for which, in Niqi's case at least, he was not responsible. No. Even that night so long ago, she had suggested the Carib Lager, the BAT cigarettes, the . . . unwholesome . . . behavior in the phone booth. She'd put his hands—

He shook his head.

It was going to be hard to talk to her. He admitted that. And it was going to be even harder if Agent Carter continued to pull away from him and the investigation. He could hardly blame Lillian Carter for her reaction to what he knew was his unprofessional withholding of details, but what choice had he had? If he had explained to the First Assistant at the office that he knew a witness in the case on a personal level, the case would likely have ended up reassigned and, very likely, bungled. He'd made a choice in the interests of justice.

**

"Did you have a good day?" Lillian Carter wore her odd bug-eyed sunglasses and floppy hat with a teal halter top and ghastly khaki trousers—pedal pushers, or something, weren't they called? She sat on the motel patio overlooking Bay Road, and she'd offered Xavier a seemingly weak, half-hearted wave as he'd approached the inn.

He'd entered the motel and climbed the stairs to the second floor and the patio, and when he'd stepped out into the space of white lattice and festoons of greenery around those outdated tables, she'd set her paperback down and studied him, as though expecting something.

And then she'd broken the silence.

"I guess I did," he answered. "I went to my oldest uncle's law office and surprised him."

He grinned. It *had* been a good day. "We had lunch, he and I and three cousins. Then I caught a van out to Old Road Town and surprised two of my aunts." He patted his stomach. "They fed me some more."

Lillian chuckled and Xavier felt a tentative sense of relief. If she was willing to laugh, perhaps. . . .

"So does this mean you're not up for dinner with me tonight?"

He couldn't see her eyes behind the glasses, but he felt in his gut that this entrée into the idea of a dinner together was another good sign. He took a chance and pulled out the chair opposite her at the table.

"No, no, not at all. Dinner would be lovely." He leaned forward across the table, focused on the chai-colored lenses. "Dinner with you would be lovely."

She smiled.

"We'll take a cab down to Frigate Bay and go to Marshall's." He heard his words rush out—too loud and too fast. "It'll be lovely." And too repetitive. How many times was he going to say "lovely"?

Agent Carter slid the sunglasses off with a sly glare. "Someplace you liked taking Niqi?"

You minx. You know you have me over a barrel.

"No, no, we never went there together. I—" And then he plunged, threw himself, into a sticky pool of soul-bearing earnestness that shocked him. "I've never been there. I've never been to Marshall's. It's just a thing. For me. It's just an idea I've had in my head for a long time. You know, when you're a kid and you think things, and you build them up, and then one day, maybe, you do them? As an adult? And you just hope they won't disappoint you, but usually they do? But I don't think I'll be disappointed tonight. I've just always wanted to— to— to take— to take someone to Marshall's. It's supposed to be quite lovely." There it was again: "lovely."

She didn't interrupt or even shift.

"It's just got this reputation. And when I was young, it was the kind of place you took someone special to, and as I got a little older, I thought it would be nice to take someone there. But I've never had the chance. But tonight, I will take you there. And I'm sure it will be lovely."

Lovely.

Then her eyes flicked away. She looked down at the Formica. "It sounds nice. I'd like that."

***

The maître d' sat them in yellow chairs at a table with matching yellow napkins rolled into flower shapes and stuck in the soon-to-be-filled water glasses. The window beside them was thrown open and they could look out over palm leaves below the sill, look out at boats bobbing at anchor on water that the gold of the sunset had turned the color of the champagne Xavier suddenly decided he would order.

"Enjoy your dinner," the man admonished after handing them menus.

"Xavier, this is lovely." Lillian Carter opened her menu. "Thank you for doing this."

No, Lillian, you *are lovely.*

She'd abandoned the offensive clamdiggers for a full-length floral-print dress with an appropriately modest neckline and real sleeves instead of trollop-y straps. Her hair was rolled up neatly with a pretty green clip holding it in place. The sunset lit her perfectly.

"Champagne," Xavier said, dragging his eyes from her to the wine list. "We should get a bottle of champagne. We're so close to putting this thing to bed and putting Viggo Bryson behind bars. And we're on the island. We should celebrate a little."

Lillian was pulling her napkin out of the water glass in front of her and spreading it on her lap. "All right," she said, "on one condition."

Xavier waited, slightly worried.

"If it's going to be a champagne night," she continued, "no 'Agent Carters,' all right? Just Lillian. Agent Carter shouldn't be drinking champagne with AUSA Charles, but she wouldn't mind sharing a bottle with X."

"Fair enough." Xavier smiled. "Any conditions on starting with conch fritters?"

"None at all." She grinned back.

A waiter greeted them and recited some specials or something, and made some banal recommendations, and finally left with the drink and appetizer order, and Xavier gazed out the window and thought of nothing, simply enjoyed the view. He was at Marshall's. With a beautiful woman.

"Penny for your thoughts." Lillian took a sip of water and Xavier realized he hadn't noticed anyone filling the glasses.

Focus, man. Where's your situational awareness?

"A penny for my thoughts? I'm not sure they're worth even that." He picked up the menu he'd set aside.

"I'll be the judge of that." She leaned forward, elbows on the table, and he didn't mind—at all.

"Well, then, I'm thinking I'm here. With you." He leaned back, resting his palms on the table.

She didn't respond immediately, and the sounds of other tables' dinner conversations and of palm fronds rustling in the evening breeze filled the space between them.

Then she drew something in the condensation of her water glass. "And I'm thinking I'm glad. That you're here. With me."

The waiter returned with the champagne, and they supplied him with an order for grilled lobster and curry shrimp.

"We can splurge a little, right?" Lillian fidgeted with her butter knife. "We're getting per diem money we can play with, right?"

"Lillian," Xavier reached across the table and patted her hand, "I'm going to cover it. You needn't worry."

You touched her. You *touched* her.

And she didn't draw back or away. Instead, she put her other hand over his. "You don't have to, X. It's fine. We should split it."

"I'm paying, Lillian."

His hand remained between hers.

Until the conch fritters arrived and they both drew back to allow the waiter to place the plate between them.

"Now," Lillian said after a few bites and a remark of praise for the dish, "let's talk about Monique Arthurton."

Monique?!

Xavier had decidedly *not* planned to discuss Monique Arthurton tonight. Here. With Lillian.

"All right." He breathed deeply, tried to put himself in a different place, a place he admitted he should have been in anyway—a professional place. But then the light caught that green hairclip, and Lillian's eyes sparkled, and he returned to not wanting to talk about Monique Arthurton, and (was it ironic?) Lillian's frankness and commitment to the investigation made him want to avoid the subject of Monique even more. How *lovely* Lillian looked in that dress and with that professional resolve.

"I know this thing is more complicated now than I'd realized," she was saying, "but I think we can salvage it. I'll meet with her. Alone. I'll interrogate her and offer her the immunity and get her to sign the agreement. I'll prepare her for trial. If you're not involved, I think we can make this thing work."

If I'm not involved? In my case? With my witness?

Xavier's gut clenched. But she was right: he couldn't end up on the witness stand himself. His relationship with Niqi couldn't jeopardize this case. He had to convict Viggo Bryson, and he couldn't let his past with Niqi interfere with that process.

He twisted the Stanford Law ring on his left pinky.

Is this the only way?

"All right," he repeated. "That makes sense, given the circumstances. You handle Niqi."

"Let's start there," Lillian jumped in. "Niqi. You call her Niqi?"

Saint Francis Xavier, pray for me.

"Yes, everyone calls her Niqi. Or called her Niqi, but I think they still do. My family does." Had he flushed?

He reached for his champagne glass. It would take the edge off, wouldn't it? His drinking, carousing colleagues all talked about how happy hour took the edge off.

"Did they talk to you about her today? When you saw them? Your family? Did you talk to them about her?" She had lifted her glass as well.

He nodded. "My aunts filled me in. We have all the information we need to find her, and really, she's not going to have any credible exculpatory evidence for Viggo Bryson."

Another sip of champagne and it all poured out: growing up with Niqi, her encounter with Viggo Bryson, her calls to Xavier when she had discovered she was pregnant, his proposal and efforts to save her, his efforts to get her to Chicago to allegedly fight for custody of her son after she'd lost the boy, her alleged marine conservation work, her office's location, and the disbelief of his family in her business's legitimacy.

"No one thinks she's just cleaning up coral reefs. People know her and they've met Viggo, and no one thinks the Porsche 911 she's apparently driving came from some sea-turtle charity. The island gossips, and apparently, the taxes alone on the car were like two hundred grand in Eastern Caribbean dollars. That's like $74,000 in U.S. dollars. For taxes."

"Wow." Lillian turned to the open window. "Seems kinda silly to buy a Porsche to drive around here. I'd rather have something small and cheap, and just enjoy the island pace." A beat passed. She turned back to him. "But so it won't be a problem finding her?"

"No." Xavier shook his head. "She was never missing."

Lillian gave him a wry look. "She was for me. If you'd told me earlier it would be this easy. . . ."

"I know. I'm sorry." When would the champagne start easing the discomfort?

"And your family knows Viggo?" Her question splashed across the table.

"He's been to the island a few times. People have seen him . . . encountered him." Xavier swished the wine around his glass, aureate waves lapping up the sides of the bowl.

Lillian poked at the last fritter on the appetizer platter, lifted it to her plate and pushed it around the white surface. She took a bite and then laid her fork down.

"So now the hard questions," she said, after finishing the fritter. "How do I get her to talk? I mean, immunity is good, but Monique doesn't need it if she stays here. We've talked about her son—"

Xavier fiddled with his law-school ring again. *All* of the questions, this whole conversation, had been . . . cumbersome . . . so far, but this one was hardly the worst.

"Grant Bryson," he replied, leaning in. "Yes, her son. It's easy. If she plays nice with you here, we may work something out with Nils Bryson to give her Grant when we take Nils into custody here. If she doesn't behave reasonably, or if Nils Bryson refuses to be reasonable, we take Grant Bryson back to the States with Nils and place him in foster care when his uncle-slash-guardian is ordered detained by the court. If Niqi wants to come to the States to try to get custody, we indict her. With the boy's father going to prison, she will want her son more than ever. With immunity, she can come to the States, testify, and apply to have her parental rights reinstated. Or whatever. I know nothing about family law, don't know the details, but we can, I'm sure, point her to someone who can help her. This is her shot at getting her son back."

The entire dining room seemed to have grown very quiet.

"You really would indict her?" Lillian said after several breaths.

Xavier studied her. He removed his glasses, pulled a handkerchief from his pocket and began polishing the lenses.

"Yes," he said, "of course."

"But you loved her."

"Lillian, I probably still do love her in some small way, somewhere in my heart. She was a part of my youth. She meant a great deal to me. But, Lillian, every choice has a consequence, and she and her," he groped for a delicate term, "paramour chose to break the law and steal millions of dollars. I can't turn my back on that."

Lillian seemed lost in scrutiny of the wine bottle.

"It's our jobs, Lillian," he said, after another moment. "It's what Uncle Sam pays us to do. We have a duty."

"I understand," she whispered, still focused on the bottle. "Is—" She broke off. Then she inhaled and looked around the room. "Is Grant Viggo's son?" Her eyes settled on him, bored into him.

Xavier's stomach flip flopped. "Yes," he said, "Grant Bryson is Viggo Bryson's son. I have no reason whatsoever to doubt that."

"Okay," she sat back, "I'm sorry. I just wanted to ask." She picked at the hem of the accent cloth adorning the table over the larger white tablecloth. "You . . . you and she weren't like . . . ?"

Were the saints and angels enjoying this humiliation? These wages of his youthful sins?

"Lillian, I committed," he sighed, casting about again for a discreet phrase, "mortal sins with Niqi, if that's what you mean, but I can say with complete confidence, that that boy is not mine. He's Viggo Bryson's son. And—" Something caught in his throat. "And if he were . . . of other parentage . . . , I might handle the situation somewhat differently, but still consistent with my duty as an officer of the court and an Assistant U.S. Attorney."

"I'm sorry." She had returned to picking the hem of the green accent cloth. She looked up from it. "Mortal sins, Xavier?"

Another sip of champagne. Xavier took his turn at studying the bottle. Its contents had dwindled.

"I don't believe in . . . carrying on . . . that way. Outside of marriage." He sniffed. "I think it's disordered and unhealthy. If two people love each other, they won't use each other. They will make a commitment to one another and care for one another. Within the structure of marriage."

Apparently, the saints had heard his pleas for relief. The lobster and shrimp arrived and the waiter set the plates down and asked if they'd like another bottle of "bubbly."

Xavier raised his eyebrows at Lillian. She nodded, and he fancied he saw rose creeping up her neck and cheeks. The man hustled off, assuring them he would return shortly with the wine. The food proved worthy of the expectations Xavier had carried, and they sat chewing in silence.

"Thanks for being so open." Lillian looked up several beats later. "It's gotta be kinda weird to be rehashing all this."

"Oh, you've no idea." Xavier laughed a small, champagne-y laugh.

"I just . . . I need to know, so I don't get ambushed by her. But I know I can make this work. I know I can get her to testify." Lillian placed her silverware across the top of her plate. "Dessert?"

"Anything you'd like." Xavier sat back. "And I know you can, too. You'll get her onto that witness stand. I've no doubt."

Over crème brûlée—shared—Lillian asked, "Could we walk on the beach after this? If you're tired, no problem. I just figure you'll know the best spots, and I'd love to see the water at night. It looks so perfect out there." She tipped her head to the window.

"Yes, of course, Lillian, I know the perfect spot for you to see how beautiful St. Kitts is at night."

The maître d' called them a cab for the short ride to South Friar's Bay. On the moonlit sand of the quiet stretch of oceanfront, Lillian tugged at her sandals, pulling them off. Xavier reached out to take the shoes.

"Oh, you don't have to carry them. I've got them." She held onto the sandals.

"I know, Lillian, but I want to. I want to carry them for you. And anything else you need carried." He took hold of the straps and she let go.

The moon drew glowing undulations on the calm water, and Xavier's head was positively buoyant with the evening's libations. He removed his own shoes and rolled up the cuffs of his slacks. With the straps and laces of the shoes in his left hand, he reached out for Lillian with his right, and she didn't hesitate, and he led her into the tiny lapping waves, and then they were ankle deep in the Caribbean Sea, and he was sure he could feel paradise spread overhead, with its heavenly host gazing down at the pearls of light floating all around them.

"It's beautiful," Lillian whispered.

He didn't reply. He simply pulled her to his chest and pressed his lips into hers and felt them both melt into the sea in exquisite silence.

Chapter 23

Good Afternoon

Sixty-eight. Port Zante Marina beside Basseterre's cruise-ship terminal monitored VHF-radio channel sixty-eight. As *Manuia* pulled nearer and nearer the island, a waterfront of a docked cruise ship, marina, and heat-hazy downtown rose before them. Devlin ducked below, and in the boat's cabin, lifted the radio's handheld microphone transmitter.

"Port Zante Marina, Port Zante Marina, this is the forty-foot sailing vessel *Manuia* out of Kemah, Texas, U.S.A. Over."

"Good morning, *Manuia*," a woman's voice responded, "this is Port Zante Marina. Over."

"Port Zante Marina, we are within sight of the marina and have a slip reserved. We estimate arrival within an hour or two. How should we proceed? Over." Devlin released the microphone's transmission button and waited.

"Welcome to St. Kitts, *Manuia*. We are looking forward to having you." The line went quiet for a few beats. "We have slip four available for you on pier one. You'll see the open slip to port as you come in the harbor. It's on the seawall dock, rather than the bulkhead. It's the fourth slip in, toward the far end away from the island. Tie up there and then proceed to the marina office for check-in. If you hail us again as you enter the harbor, we will have someone meet you at the slip and assist. Over."

Devlin pressed the transmit button. "Thank you, Port Zante Marina. That sounds easy. See you shortly. *Manuia* out."

"Port Zante Marina out."

It would be good to make land, to get off the boat, to walk, and to have a little space away from Nils. It had been a long couple weeks. Not unpleasant, but slightly awkward. After the storm, the weather had held, and sailing had been magnificent—blue seas and skies and *Manuia*'s efficient, sea-kindly gait. But everything with Nils had been off, out of step, artless. His arm had regained strength and, he said, ceased hurting, and he'd put away the sling, and Grant had grown into his role as a crewmember, and Sean had kept an eye on Devlin, checking in with her when she spent too long alone on the bow or in her berth. But something sticky and slightly overripe had stayed wrapped around Devlin or at least wedged between her and Nils, some quality of unease, even as the crew had played games and enjoyed dinners and fished together.

Devlin grabbed the sides of the companionway and sprang on deck. "All right, we are all set. The marina says to dock in slip four, pier one. The slip is toward the harbor, away from land, on the port side. They'll send someone out to meet us if we hail them when we enter the marina basin."

"Sounds good." Sean grinned. "Hey, what do you say, buddy? We're about to make land. You ready to stretch your legs?"

Grant sat up. The bimini top's shade covered him and he'd been sprawled with a book on the cockpit bench, his bare feet rubbing idly on the rough canvas of the cushion beneath him. He still had on his lifejacket.

"Yeah, I'm ready for a long walk!" He swiveled, pulled his legs under him, and wrapped his fingers around the stern lifelines, gazing toward the island.

"Me too," Devlin agreed. "Whatya reading, buddy?"

"*The Hobbit* you gave me." He didn't turn from the view of land.

"Nice." Devlin felt a tiny, strange thrill that the kid was enjoying the birthday gift she'd picked for him, and she noticed a substantial portion of new tooth filling the gap he'd been sticking his tongue through since she'd met him.

Nils shuffled back toward the cockpit from the bow, where he'd been sitting for most of the morning. "Another passage done." He seemed to watch his footing as he dropped onto a cockpit bench, and then he turned to follow Grant's gaze toward the buildings and hills and humanness of their destination. "It's always exciting, and sad at the same time. Something done, but something new to explore."

"I can't wait to go exploring," Grant said. "My dad took me to St. Kitts when I was little, but I haven't been back in a long time."

He sounded grave, and Devlin had to resist laughing. She did catch Sean's and Nils's eyes and grinned. She could still exchange that grin with Nils.

"What's the first thing you want to do on land, little man?" she asked.

"A cartwheel," he answered, "and get ice cream. I think I can do a cartwheel."

Now she allowed herself to laugh. "That sounds like a perfect plan. I'm in for a cartwheel and ice cream too."

As they drew into the sheltered hook of the Port Zante marina, the sun sat almost overhead. The smell of land, of a town, and vehicles and tropical lushness and human movement, reached over the water to them. Two young men in white polo shirts stood at the slip and caught the dock lines Devlin and Nils threw to them.

"Good afternoon!" they called. "Welcome to Port Zante."

The teenaged dockhands led *Manuia*'s crew to the marina office, and Sean checked the boat in as Devlin paged through local tourist magazines and brochures. She followed the men and Grant as they all proceeded through customs at the marina and then walked over to the immigration office and port authority at the cruise-ship terminal. Nils paid the fees for inbound clearances, and then they were through and the island unrolled at their feet.

"Well, what do you think so far, little man?" Devlin patted Grant's shoulder.

"This is cool!" He jogged ahead of her a few yards and stopped. He threw himself into a cartwheel, and a local man passing them grinned.

"Eh, boy, nice *bumflick!*" The man clapped.

Grant smiled, but with his eyes to the pavement, all shyness now.

Devlin kept walking, past the tourist shops of a cruise mecca and past the shops' patrons, people likely from places like Cleveland and Dallas, who wore unfashionable shorts and oversized hats.

"Look! That's perfect!" Grant shouted, pointing.

"What's perfect, buddy?" Nils asked while Devlin followed the kid's gesture.

Scoops. An ice-cream parlor dubbed Scoops sat ahead and to the right.

As Devlin took her first bite of chocolate and whipped cream and sprinkles, she acknowledged that very little, if anything, could taste quite as good as ice cream after more than two weeks at sea.

***

On the curb just outside the storefront at the address matching the number printed beneath the sea turtle on the SK and N letterhead, from Monique Arthurton's epistle that the investigator Frank Obregon had delivered to

Jumping World on Grant's birthday, sat a silver Porsche 911.

"Saving the oceans must be paying well," Devlin muttered as she stepped to the storefront's door.

She'd left the boys to explore Basseterre and had set to locating Monique Arthurton as soon as she'd finished her ice cream at Scoops and had a quick shower at the marina. She'd found the address from the letterhead just beyond the National Caribbean Insurance Company, in an island-natty pink building with faux pillars shaped into its concrete exterior, just a couple blocks due north of the marina. A bell tinkled as she pulled open the door.

After her eyes finished screaming for a chance to adjust to the dimness of the space, Devlin took in the simple interior: vinyl flooring, a cheap metal desk with a wood-veneer top, a shabby black rolling chair, a water cooler with a dispenser for conical paper cups, and a waist-high bookcase holding a few dog-eared volumes on its shelves and a ceramic turtle painted in vivid colors on its top. In a corner away from the door, a tired stand-up fan prodded the un-air-conditioned interior to move.

Guess the money goes toward the company car.

"Hello?" As soon as she called out, Devlin remembered the island etiquette she'd seen on a website before they'd cast off the dock in Texas. She corrected herself. "Good afternoon?"

No hellos. Just good morning, good afternoon, good evening.

She took another step into the space. A narrow hallway at the back of the room led somewhere into deeper dimness. The spines of the few books on the bookcase revealed *Cruising the Caribbean, Caribbean Dream Dives, All in a Day's Dive*, four romance novels, a 2009 Westlaw U.S. federal criminal code book, and *Representing the Audited Taxpayer Before the IRS.*

Huh.

"Good afternoon."

From somewhere down the dark hallway, she had simply appeared—Viggo Bryson's Monique Arthurton—a sort of high-voltage pulchritude obviating the need for a verbal introduction. Rows of glossy obsidian braids falling well past her shoulder blades, roseate lips, enviably plump cleavage over an impossibly trim waist. She wore long earrings of blue and green feathers with nails painted to match, a starched white blouse that mocked the wilting heat and had only a minimal number of buttons impressed into service, and tight gray slacks showcasing a voluptuous stern. Devlin estimated the heels at five inches, and for an instant, her thoughts darted to her unironed khakis, unimpressive knit shirt, flat black sneakers, and hair that had just tasted conditioner for the first time in three weeks.

My kingdom for a pair of Jimmy Choos. No, forget that. You don't need Jimmy Choos when you were first in your class at Michigan Law.

"Good afternoon. Monique Arthurton?" She strode toward Monique in her flat sneakers and extended a hand.

"I suppose so," Monique replied, accepting Devlin's hand and offering a weak, disinterested clasp, and no hint of surprise or curiosity. "Would you like some water?" She gestured at the jug over the cooler.

"No, but thank you. Ms. Arthurton, I'm Devlin Winters. I work with Viggo Bryson's attorney. I understand you're familiar with his current situation."

"Yes." Monique stepped toward the desk and pulled the chair around from behind it. "My investigator told me he'd met you. And that he delivered my packages to you." She arranged the chair in front of and facing the desk and then gestured to Devlin to sit in it, as she arranged herself half sitting, half leaning on the corner of the desk in front of it.

"Yes," Devlin replied, "I met Frank. Crack investigator, that one." She dropped into the chair and sat back, hands on the armrests.

"So what brings you to my island and my humble place of employment?" Monique crossed her arms over the straining blouse.

"I'm sure it's no surprise that I'm here. Simply, you'd indicated you have exculpatory evidence, and I have a client in need of exoneration. You said in your letter to Nils Bryson that you have a box of business records and a records-custodian affidavit, and that you'd be willing to ship these materials to Viggo's lawyer in exchange for Nils bringing your son Grant to the island and turning him over to you."

"I did say something like that." Monique examined the lustrous blues and greens of the nails on her right hand.

"Well, obviously, Monique, Nils Bryson isn't going to bring Grant here. He certainly doesn't have the authority to just give you the child. But Viggo's defense team has an array of resources at its disposal, and we're very willing to consider some sort of arrangement to review the records you claim to have and, if they are legitimate and exculpatory, obtain copies from you."

"I'm not interested in Viggo's resources." Monique fidgeted with the heart pendant that had been nestled between the two causes of the blouse's straining. She slid it back and forth on its gold chain.

Devlin waited.

The pendant moved right and left.

"I'm," Monique started after another breath, "exceedingly aware of Viggo's resources." She paused. "Exceedingly."

"And he's exceedingly ready to extend a share of them to you to obtain your records." Devlin couldn't resist.

"No." Monique pushed off the desk.

The heels clicked as she crossed to the understocked bookcase.

"No," she repeated, "I'm finished with Viggo and his self-assured presumptions and belief that his money can buy him out of anything, buy him whatever he wants, give him anything."

The heels clicked again as she returned to the desk.

"It can't." She shook the braids, used the motion to rearrange the rows that had slipped over her shoulders and return them to her back. "His money isn't going to buy him out of this."

"All right," Devlin didn't break stride, "if money isn't the answer, what about drawing up a custodial arrangement under which you could have partial custody of Grant? I haven't spoken with Viggo about such an arrangement yet, but I'm sure an agreement could be reached. Given the circumstances. Perhaps Grant could spend summers here on the island with you and then return to Michigan for the school year with his father."

"I'm not interested in sharing anything with Viggo ever again." Monique bit the words off, but Devlin caught something, caught the faintest hiccup . . . something.

What are you hiding, Monique Arthurton?

Devlin watched the woman's dark eyes, watched them lower to the vinyl, watched them try to hide behind their blue-and-green-hued lids and their perfect, almost-indiscernible-as-false eyelashes.

You loved him, didn't you? You loved Viggo Bryson, didn't you?

The fan across the room whirred. Outside on the street, a car passed and two men called out to one another in creole.

"Without your evidence," Devlin didn't look away from the eyelids, "Viggo stands a very good chance of getting convicted. He could face a sentence of seven, eight, nine years." She paused.

Devlin's eyes caught Monique's when the other woman looked up from the dirty plastic flooring. Devlin held her gaze.

"That would be a long time for Grant to be without a parent." Devlin didn't blink.

She waited.

The fan whirred on.

"If we were able to reach some sort of a custodial agreement, he could be with you at least part of the time. Part time is better than nothing, right?" Devlin shrugged. "And any sort of an arrangement would certainly be better than the child having to be without either parent should Viggo get convicted."

She paused.

Monique didn't move, didn't shift at all.

Devlin released her gaze, turned to look out the window. "If Viggo's convicted, Grant's going to grow up in the care of more distant relatives—his uncle or even his grandparents."

Another car passed beyond the window. Dust motes floated on the room-side of the glass.

"I know the grandparents," Devlin continued. "You wouldn't want that. They're not a happy lot."

Monique lifted her head, pushed off the desk again. "He couldn't be with his uncle. The government's indicted Nils. If Viggo gets convicted, Nils will get convicted."

How do you know Nils has been indicted? Someone's watching the court docket pretty closely.

"You saw the superseding indictment?" Devlin studied the wall on the far side of the desk, the chipped and dirty paint.

"I did." Monique paused. "After Xavier Charles told me he'd indicted Nils." She walked to the window.

Devlin made herself keep her eyes on the wall. She inhaled.

Xavier Charles told you?!

Another inhale. Devlin didn't let her hands or arms move from the chair's armrests. She sat forward and casually turned to face Monique. "Did Xavier Charles get in touch with you?"

"His agent visited me a week or two ago. Wanted to talk to me. She's a tenacious *ting*."

Fuck.

"Did you make a statement?" Devlin decided it was time to study her own nails.

"I talked to her." Monique seemed to be contemplating the lazy afternoon on the other side of the window.

Perspiration had collected across Devlin's back. She sat up and pulled her shirt away from her skin. When she sat back, the fabric simply re-adhered itself to her lumbar.

"But then I told this agent woman that I wanted to talk to Xavier Charles. He's from the island, you know?"

No, I didn't know that. But thanks for sharing, Monique. Good to know. And fuck me while we're at it.

"So you met with AUSA Charles?" Devlin tried again with the shirt . . . to give her hands something to do.

"I did." Monique hadn't turned from the window.

Care to share?

A half dozen school kids in uniforms giggled and shouted, passing the Porsche at the curb in a happy, shoving gaggle.

"He offered me immunity to testify against Viggo at the trial." Monique's head turned as her eyes followed the kids up the street.

Immunity? Really?! And did you take it?

The heat, the fan's futile whirring, the sparkle of the dust suspended in the slanted sunlight backlighting Monique, cracks in the dingy white wall all pressed in on Devlin.

"I accepted his offer," Monique said. "I signed an immunity agreement. I'm going to go to the States to testify against Viggo at his trial." She paused. "And to apply for reinstatement of my parental rights and custody of Grant."

Devlin stifled a groan. She held this mother's eyes, searching for an explanation for the thing she saw flicker over them again. "Monique," she murmured, "your son shouldn't be a pawn in all this."

Monique turned away. "Tell that to your government."

Chapter 24
Hailing Port

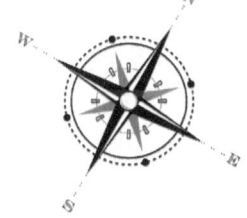

For something like two weeks, Xavier and Lillian had been walking the horseshoe-shaped Port Zante Marina in the evenings, taking in the sportfishing boats and catamarans, elegant sailboats with bright new-looking canvas sunshades and weather-beaten old girls with grimy hulls and sun-conquered ropes hanging every which way. Every few days, Xavier had ducked into the marina office to chat up an older woman about the boats' comings and goings. But they'd seen no sign of a Texas sailboat with a young boy aboard.

Until tonight.

They'd had a dinner of creole fish and garlic conch at El Fredo's down past the cruise-ship terminal, and now with the sun setting and clouds gathering around the hills overlooking the city, the evening had a certain magical quality, enhanced by Lillian stopping abruptly, pulling on his arm, and inhaling sharply.

And whispering, "Look. Look across the marina. Look at the back of that boat. That sailboat is from Kemah, Texas. And it wasn't here last night."

No, it hadn't been in the harbor the evening before.

"*Manuia*, it says." Lillian squeezed Xavier's hand and smiled up at him. "Let's get over there. Nonchalantly. We'll just stroll by." She winked. "Two lovers in the moonlight."

The moon hadn't risen yet, but Xavier didn't mind the mischaracterization.

Don't you flush, old boy!

Instead, he rubbed the back of his neck.

"Good catch, Lillian. You have magnificent eyes." He squeezed her hand back.

"When we get back to the hotel," she whispered, "I'll run the boat name and hailing port through the Coast Guard documentation interface. We'll get the owner's name and address, and the boat's ownership history. It'll take me two minutes." She pulled his hand and arm into her side.

They worked their way around the broad, concrete walkway that wrapped around the marina, chatting and maintaining a casual pace. A man hopped off a fishing boat, dragging a cooler after him.

"Isn't that a sweet boat, honey?" Lillian burbled, gesturing to a sailboat beside the fishing craft. "Could you see us buying something like that? You and me, sailing off into the sunset." She sounded light, easy. "No, I don't think I could give up the comforts of home. I am enjoying this cruise, though. I could go on like this for months. It's such a beautiful ship."

Her cover banter continued to impress Xavier. She had that focused, unselfconscious ability to adapt to circumstances and keep rolling regardless of setbacks and curve balls. When she'd returned to him after two tries at Niqi alone, she'd remained unfazed, saying simply that Monique Arthurton understood the circumstances but insisted on speaking with the prosecuting attorney. Niqi, of course, was just being Niqi, making things more complicated than they needed to be, but in the end, after he met with her twice, she signed the immunity agreement. It only made sense—her only chance at reuniting with this son she said she wanted to play mother to.

Perhaps the two meetings had been somewhat . . . ungraceful . . . initially. She'd asked to speak with him alone and then inquired into his life, whether he'd married, had children. Was he well? Asking in that way that makes "well" sound like something else altogether. But all that aside, he had a signed immunity agreement and a name to add to the witness list he would send to Viggo's Irene Stockton when he returned to the office. Niqi had agreed that trial preparations would have to proceed with Lillian's oversight, and Lillian had met with her multiple times in the past week to prepare her testimony and review documents. Viggo was as good as convicted. With her alluring attention to task, Lillian had even procured three family-law attorney names for Niqi, so Niqi could prepare to seek custody of the boy.

Now, Lillian was smiling and tilting her head to passing tourists and tugging his arm to draw him down the last leg of the port's docks, the one on which the Texas boat sat tied.

"Oh, look, that boat has a French flag." She was pointing at a vessel with teal canvas covers over its sails and two bikes lashed to its deck and stanchions. "There are boats here from all over."

As they strolled up to the Texas boat, she squeezed his hand again. They couldn't see the boat's stern, with its name and hailing port emblazoned on it, because the boat was pulled into the slip with its front toward the dock and its back toward the harbor, but it was the right one, the one they'd seen from the other side of the harbor. A woman in rumpled khakis walked past them toward an older boat down the way.

"Look at this charming one," Lillian said at just the right volume. "I'd love to have a boat like this, sweetie. Wouldn't you? Look how sleek she looks. I bet she's fast compared to that French boat. Look, honey, she must be from Texas."

Lillian pointed to a sort of lifesaving, floatable cushion device sitting on the front of the boat, with a rope tied to it and securing it to the metal pulpit on the boat's nose, so the cushion thing couldn't be blown into the water or somehow fall overboard, Xavier supposed. The printing on the cushion included a gaudy sailboat design with a red, orange, and yellow sunset behind it, and the words "Sunset Yachts, L.L.C.," and "Kemah, Texas."

Chapter 25

Real Showers

After Devlin had left Monique Arthurton's office, she'd made her way through Basseterre, looking for her favorite creature of the '90s and early '00s: an internet café. In the cruise-ship complex, she had found a place called CyberLink, offering internet, notices about Bollywood movies playing at the Caribbean Cinema SKB, and an array of products from India. She'd ordered *samosas* and those awfully sweet *gulab jamun*, and set to emailing Irene Stockton.

Irene, I made it to the island, and I've met with Monique Arthurton. I can confirm that her office address is the address on the letterhead on which she wrote to Nils Bryson. From the package she had delivered via the private investigator. (I believe Nils sent you copies of all those materials.)

The office is very unimpressive, though I did not see the entire space. I believe, however, that Ms. Arthurton is driving a late-model Porsche 911. At least such a car was parked directly in front of the office, with no other cars parked within several yards of the office. The office also had a bookcase with a few American legal treatises on it, namely an outdated Westlaw criminal-code book and a treatise on IRS audits. I found those selections interesting.

The long and the short of the meeting is that Ms. Arthurton refuses to testify for the defense. Nor would she share any materials when I pressed her at the end of our meeting. Apparently, the government has been in touch with her. In fact, Ms. Arthurton indicated that a case agent and AUSA Xavier Charles have met with her, implying the meeting happened here on St. Kitts. She also told me that AUSA Charles is from St. Kitts. She told me she has entered into an immunity agreement with the government and that she will testify against Viggo at trial.

She indicated that she accepted immunity so as to be able to travel to the U.S.A. She's hoping to travel to the States to obtain custody of her son, Grant Bryson.

Ms. Arthurton is aware that Nils Bryson has been indicted (I am still unaware of his exact location; I believe he may be in the Caribbean for an extended while for his boat-related work).

I would note that multiple times during my exchange with Ms. Arthurton I had a strange feeling that she was withholding information. This doesn't surprise me, but what I found odd was a feeling that she may have some sympathies for Viggo Bryson. I can't put my finger on anything specific she did or said, but her body language and the way she said things make me believe she actually feels some conflict about testifying against Viggo. Given what she told me, however, I have no reason to believe she will do anything but support the government's theory of the case.

I am still on St. Kitts. I plan to spend a few days here poking around and seeing what I can discover related to SK and N, Ms. Arthurton, and Viggo. I will be in touch.

Sincerely,
Devlin Winters

After she had hit send, she'd skimmed through her inbox and remembered that she needed to print out and sign Irene's contract to retain her in Viggo's case. After deciding to worry about it later, she'd closed out of the interface, left the shop, and wandered back toward the harbor, where she noticed a dive boat with a large PRO DIVERS banner adorning it. Two men were unloading air cylinders from the boat. On a whim, she'd wandered over and chatted them up, inquiring about local dive conditions and then steering the conversation toward ecology and the health of the local reefs. When she'd asked if either man knew of SK and N, Inc., and the company's preservation efforts, both men had chuckled.

"Yeah," one had volunteered, "I know the company. It's run by a local woman, but, honestly, and don't quote me on this, I think the thing's probably some sort of tax shelter or money-laundering scam. They throw around a couple grand occasionally, get some local press, but they don't really do anything with the dive community."

After a little more chat and some gentle, flirty probing, Devlin had headed off with the men's offer of discounted diving any time she'd like. With the sun starting to set, she'd turned back to the CyberLink and ducked in for another email to Irene.

Irene,

A quick P.S.

I talked to a couple guys from a local dive place. They'd heard of SK and N, but described it as a "tax shelter" or "money-laundering scam." Those were their words. They said the company spends a couple grand a year here and there and gets some local press but doesn't really do anything related to diving or real marine conservation.

They described the company as being run by a local woman. They did not mention any names.

I'll see what else I can find.
Devlin

From the CyberLink's multi-cultural shelves, she'd grabbed a few grocery items for the boat (toothpaste, soap, a couple pieces of fruit), paid, stuffed the things in her purse, and stepped into the gathering evening.

Now, she walked past the quiet shops toward the marina. The cruise ship seemed to have reabsorbed its tourists, and the area rested in the pink and violet of evening. She passed the marina office, continued past the closest row of docked boats, and turned down the far breakwall toward *Manuia*. The boys would be headed back to the boat soon to meet up for dinner. Having not asked about cell-service options on the island, despite two visits to the CyberLink, Devlin planned to chill at the boat until they arrived. Then they could all vote on dinner options.

A couple ahead of her seemed to be lost in conversation, hand in hand, engaged in the "boat dreaming" Devlin knew well from the marina back home. People would wander the waterfront and docks, looking at the boats and telling themselves that "one day. . . ." Yeah, one day.

The woman was petite, maybe five-foot-four-ish. The man was huskier, tall and broad, arguably slightly overweight. He wore a short-sleeved, red-white-and-green plaid shirt and khaki shorts and looked very comfortable in his skin, decidedly not touristy. The woman's sundress and floppy hat were sweet, perhaps perky was the word Devlin wanted. They stopped in front of *Manuia*, and Devlin's hackles went up.

"Look at this charming one," Ms. Sundress exclaimed. "I'd love to have a boat like this, sweetie. Wouldn't you? Look how sleek she looks. I bet she's fast compared to that French boat. Look, honey, she must be from Texas."

WTF. How would she know that?

Manuia's name and hailing port sat out of sight on her stern.

Devlin kept walking, passing behind the couple. She glanced over and noticed the throwable personal-flotation cushion on the bow. Nils had tied it to the bow pulpit and had been sitting on it for the ride into the harbor.

Okay, it's got the Sunset Yachts logo on it. Does it say Texas? And why would Ms. Flower-Print look that closely?

Devlin took another peek at the pair.

Oh. Shit.

She didn't break stride, didn't falter. She continued down the walkway to a seen-better-days '70s-era Morgan Out Island sloop at the end of the quay. Hopefully, no one was home. She hopped over the lifelines, her grocery-stuffed purse swinging on her shoulder. No response from the cabin. Good. She fussed with the companionway and made a show of checking her pockets and then digging through her bag, muttering.

"Oh, shoot. Paulie has the key. Darn it." She grabbed her purse again and hopped back over the lifelines to the dock.

Assistant United States Attorney Xavier Charles, or his doppelgänger, and Ms. Flower-Print remained in front of *Manuia*.

"Oh, sweetheart," Perky Print was saying, "they're American. We should hang out a little and meet them. See if they'd tell us about their sailing adventures. I bet they've got great stories."

Devlin stole another glance. She hadn't seen Xavier Charles in probably three years. He'd been opposite her for one of her last appellate arguments. But she was pretty sure this fellow on the dock was him. And it sounded like he and Ms. Sunshine were too interested in *Manuia*. As Devlin passed them and retreated up the dock, she fancied she could feel eyes on her back.

"Paulie, Paulie, Paulie," she muttered. "You and those keys."

At the marina office, she turned and caught her breath behind the building. Darkness had fallen in earnest and Basseterre glittered, all blue and red lights. She could smell meat grilling, and strains of Bob Marley floated up from a catamaran moored on the other side of the pocket-sized harbor, close to the marina parking lot.

Damn, now I really wish I had some Jimmy Choos.

She clutched the strap of her bag, strode across the pavement to the far dock, and approached the festive catamaran. Several men and two women were in the boat's cockpit and sitting in canvas folding chairs on the dock, surrounding two coolers.

"Good evening," she called out.

"*Guten abend!*" A tall man with blond curls and a shirt supporting some soccer team waved from the boat's cockpit.

"Welcome," shouted another man with a heavy German accent and a tin coffee mug of something in one hand.

"I was hoping you'd say that," Devlin said, stepping aboard the catamaran in response to the men's gestures to board. "I've lost my crewmates and they have the keys to the boat, and I've nowhere good to wait for them."

Sean had given her and Nils keys to *Manuia's* cockpit, and her set sat beneath the toiletries and bananas in her purse, but the catamaran provided the best point from which to watch the marina parking lot. From the party boat, Devlin would be able to see Xavier Charles and his partner leave the dock area, and she'd be able to see the boys return, whether they came down from Bay Road or walked over from the cruise-ship complex. Even in the dark. If she stayed alert.

"Would you like a drink?" the man in the soccer shirt asked. "We've got beers over here," he gestured toward yet another cooler, "and there's nice rum punch in the cabin."

"Thanks, I'd love a beer." Devlin hated beer, but she needed to be amiable. Mr. Soccer Shirt pulled a Spaten Oktoberfest out of the cooler, popped the top, and handed it to Devlin.

"*Danke,*" she offered, and the dude laughed.

"Are you on a boat in the harbor?" he asked.

She focused on the far side of the marina, trying to watch *Manuia* and that line of boats in the evening shadows. She believed she could see the prosecutor and the woman strolling very slowly back toward the parking lot.

"I am," she said absently to the German.

Yes, it looked like the prosecutor had reached the head of the dock. It was hard to see, but—

Was that Grant's laugh?

Devlin whipped her head toward the road leading to the cruise dock.

"I think I hear my friends," she said, pointing toward the road with the neck of the Spaten.

"Good!" the guy said. "Bring them over. Everyone is welcome!"

"Really? That'd be great." Devlin grabbed her purse and jumped from the catamaran to the dock.

With the beer in her hand and one eye on the far dock for any sign of the prosecution, she took long strides toward the road.

Sean, Nils, and Grant appeared in the darkness. She grabbed Sean's arm. "Hey, Tofilau, man. There's a party on this catamaran over here. Bunch of cool dudes. Let's check it out." She kept her voice low but forceful.

Sean stopped and gave her an odd look in the blue light of a dock lamppost.

"Come on. Seriously. It's a rocking party. We need to get over there." Devlin tugged at his beefy forearm.

"Dev's, Gra—" Nils started.

"No," Devlin broke in, "seriously. We cannot miss this. Come on."

Nils and Sean shook their heads, but they followed, Grant just behind Nils.

At the catamaran, Devlin introduced the guys as Tofilau, 'Sin, and Buddy (for Grant), announcing they were all about the rum punch and making a joke about the kid and the punch.

"Help yourself," her friend in the soccer jersey said, opening the door to the boat's cabin. "What kind of music do you like?"

"Anything," Devlin replied. "Surprise us."

"Okay." The dude started messing with a set of stereo controls beside the boat's steering wheel in the cockpit.

Alone with Grant, Sean, and Nils in the cabin, Devlin set down the bottle of Spaten she still had and ladled rum punch into one of the tin coffee mugs stacked haphazardly beside the rum basin, handing it to Sean. The Germans seemed to like their libations in tin mugs.

"I think I saw AUSA Xavier Charles on our dock," she said. "Looking at *Manuia*."

"Who's that?" Grant asked.

"A guy I know from Michigan," she replied, "and someone we don't really want to have to deal with right now."

"You saw him here?" Nils tapped his fingers on the boat's saloon table.

"Yep." Devlin handed him a cup of punch. "Now, I haven't seen the guy in years, but I'm pretty sure it was him, and he was with a chick in a flowered dress and big hat, and now I'm wondering if it was a case agent playing unobtrusive tourist."

"Wait, so?" Sean looked at her.

"So, we kill a little time here, and then we head for a hotel. We can't go back to the boat." Devlin retrieved the Spaten, took a sip of the sour liquid.

"Why?" Grant asked. "Why can't we go back to *Manuia*?"

"It just isn't a good idea tonight, buddy. But we'll get a nice dinner and then chill at a hotel with real showers. Sound good?" Devlin felt bad for the kid, for all the confusion he'd faced in the last several months.

"I don't mind *Manuia*'s shower," he said.

"I know, kiddo, but think how nice a real one will feel." She caught Nils's eye and he nodded.

"Another adventure, right, buddy?" Nils patted the kid's back.

They took their drinks out to the boat's spacious cockpit and Devlin asked the dude in the soccer jersey where they'd sailed in from. The guy launched into a story about making the Atlantic crossing from the Azores. Snoop Dogg now blared from the cockpit speakers.

Another fellow handed them plates of grilled-fish tacos. Devlin took a bite and gazed through the night at *Manuia*'s dock. She couldn't tell if anyone was still over there. She glanced at her watch. It had been almost an hour since she'd hopped on the Morgan and pretended to have lost her keys. Yeah, she must have been right about the prosecutor walking up the dock to the parking lot . . . and perhaps clearing out.

Even over Snoop Dogg, Devlin heard footstep up the wharf and muffled conversation. She pulled Grant to his feet from where he sat nibbling a taco. Then she grabbed Nils's hand, pulling him from a conversation about boats and one-design racing.

"Here, will you get some punch with me?" She tugged him and Grant into the catamaran's cabin.

"What's up?" Nils was studying her eyes.

Devlin sighed. "Someone's coming down the dock. It's you two Xavier Charles could potentially recognize. So let's just hang in here."

Grant flopped onto the boat's dinette bench, which wrapped around the cabin's central table. "I want to go home," he whimpered.

He hadn't expressed any homesickness while they'd been sailing. Devlin turned to the kid, then looked back at Nils.

Poor little dude.

The pulse of the music in the cockpit beat against the cabin door. Laughter and jeers in German crept in. The aroma of rum punch and the musty smell of a boat desperate to have its waste-water holding tank pumped out blended and filled the saloon. Devlin felt like she could smell herself. Suddenly, she craved that hotel shower. And a real bed. And some privacy.

"Okay, we should be clear," she said after several more beats. "Let's get out of here. We'll say our goodbyes and head into the cruise complex. Then we gotta figure out what to do about a hotel."

"Let's get out of downtown," Nils said. "We explored the island today. That's why we got back so late. Just got too far and it took a while to get one of the taxi vans and get back here. But there are a bunch of resorts on the other side of the island. Let's get a taxi and go over there. I'll bet we can find a taxi outside one of the bars. Like have you seen that Timo's place north of the cruise dock?"

"No, but you lead the way." Devlin looped the long strap of her purse over her head, so the bag hung on her hip with the strap running across her chest. "I'll keep my eyes open for Mr. Charles and his girl. If we see them, we split up. I take Grant." She leaned over and patted the kid's knee. "Is that cool, buddy? You stay with me."

He didn't look at her, just nodded.

"Hey," she whispered to Nils, "if we get stopped, you just get to the boat, okay? Who knows what kind of agreement, if any, they've got with the local cops. I didn't think St. Kitts extradited for tax fraud, but who knows, so just get to the boat and get out of here. You can lay low in the islands for a bit and then we'll figure it all out. Just don't get arrested. Promise?"

"Would you miss me if I did?" He put his hand on her waist.

She studied her sneakers and the teak floor of the boat, and then met his blue eyes. "Yeah. I would."

Chapter 26

The Honors

In the shadows past the marina parking lot, near Bay Road, Lillian paused. The hotel sat just to their left.

"Let's wait around here," she murmured to Xavier. "They've gotta be coming back tonight, right?"

"Perhaps. Or they may have checked into a hotel." Xavier turned and looked back at the dusky marina.

"I doubt it," Lillian said. "Our place is the most convenient to the marina, and if they'd checked in there, we would have noticed them this afternoon."

Opposite the Texas boat's dock, and closer to the parking lot, a larger, double-hulled boat rested in its berth, lit up and pouring out obnoxious American music. It sounded like some trashy sort of party. A few people came and went from it, with a man shouting something from it at one point.

Undignified.

Beside Xavier, Lillian paced. He admired her tenacity, the coiled energy seeking its outlet.

"Perhaps," he repeated. He scanned the concrete walkways around the harbor. "It's still relatively early, Lillian. Let's stroll a bit more."

The gesture felt odd yet . . . new . . . electric, but he picked up her hand.

"Eh, *guten abend, guten abend,*" a drunken fool shouted from the boat hosting the party.

"Good evening," Xavier hissed in reply. On the island, one couldn't afford to snub even a tosspot. He released Lillian's hand and wrapped his arm around her, shielding her.

They turned and wound toward the cruise terminal, now quiet and dark, ghostly, with only an occasional laugh or shout coming from the obscurity. They traced a lazy circuit through the terminal and wound back toward the marina. As they drew close to the docks, rap or some such atrocity throbbed from the maritime bacchanalia of the boat they'd passed earlier.

Lillian sniffed, pulled him up short. "There," she whispered, pointing toward the wharf.

Xavier looked past her dainty finger. A small figure clung to the seeming hand or arm extending off a feminine frame. Behind these two shadows floated two more, the latter two being broad, masculine forms.

"It's a kid," Lillian said. "He's about the right size for a nine-year-old. And we've got a couple decent-sized guys in the mix. One could be Bryson." She turned those glowing eyes up to him. "Shall we?"

He brushed her cheek. "You do the honors."

Chapter 27

Halt

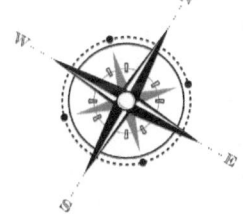

Devlin held Grant's warm mini-hand. The kid felt heavy, like he was slogging through knee-high banks of fatigue and sadness and wouldn't make it much farther.

"We'll be in a nice hotel room really soon, buddy." She jiggled his hand in hers. "Just a little longer."

Another step along the quay, and then, out of the shadows of a single-story building sitting on the path to the cruise-ship terminal, came a dark figure and a feminine shout.

"Stop! Halt! Law enforcement."

Aw, shit.

Devlin stopped, pulled Grant close to her side. She drew herself up to tower over the diminutive, elfin figure jogging toward her.

"Seriously? What're you talking about?" She debated bolting but instead waited as Ms. Flower-Print from earlier on the dock reached the circle of blue light from the pier's lamppost.

"I'm Special Agent Lillian Carter with the United States Internal Revenue Service. I have an arrest warrant for a Nils Bryson, and I have reason to believe that you sailed to the island with him."

Ms. Flower-Print's head jerked away from Devlin, ostensibly to survey Nils and Sean behind Devlin. "I'm going to need to see some ID," she said.

"So am I," Devlin replied, "especially because, last time I checked, you're out of your jurisdiction, Agent Carter." She took a step away from the pool of light, gripping Grant's hand even tighter.

"Halt," Special Agent Carter shouted again.

What are they doing back there?

Devlin prayed Nils was taking off in the opposite direction . . . or something.

"Agent Carter, I'm sorry to be rude, but unless you've got jurisdiction here, I've gotta be going."

The woman seized Grant's free hand. He made a little peeping sound and whipped his head back, turning to stare at Devlin with saucer-plate eyes.

"Let him go," Devlin demanded. "Seriously, if you don't have some ID for me, we're going to have a major problem."

"You already have a major problem." Agent Carter dropped to face Grant at his eye level. "What's your na—"

"Don't answer her, kiddo." Devlin stepped away from Agent Carter. "Special Agent Carter, we've established you're out of your jurisdiction. You've offered me no ID. Drop his arm."

She pulled Grant away from the agent, but the tacky wench wouldn't release the kid. Devlin dropped Grant's hand and reached for his opposite wrist and Agent Carter's hand, trying to pull the agent off the boy.

Shouts breaking through the din of Snoop Dogg, who was still blaring from the party catamaran, interrupted the confrontation with Special Agent Carter.

"Stop—"

"Halt—"

"*Scheisse! Kommen sie!*"

"Stop, Nils Bryson!"

"Don't—"

"Whoa! Check this out!"

"Run!"

That was Sean. Sean yelled "run."

Devlin grabbed Grant, whipped around.

Agent Carter shot up.

Nils sprinted down the dock, away from Devlin and the parking lot and land. Sprinted into the darkness, toward the dead end of the harbor. A large man—the man who'd been studying *Manuia* earlier, Xavier Charles— disappeared after him, swallowed in the shadows.

Sean jogged up to Devlin.

Snoop Dogg cried out about gin and juice.

The men's footsteps pounded on in the darkness.

And then a splash.

Chapter 28

Handcuffs Again—Or Restraints

The asinine buffoon had jumped off the dock.

St. Christopher be with me!

Xavier pulled off his shoes, dropped his glasses into one of them.

And jumped.

Wet, salty night.

The woman shouting.

Lillian shouting.

The worthless playboy krauts shouting.

Niqi's bastard son shouting, screaming.

People running down the dock.

Xavier struck out toward his suspect. The harbor was inky and warm and still, making it easy swimming, almost meditative. It smelled of salt and marina flora and diesel fuel.

"Stop, Nils Bryson," he shouted, pulling through the water, raising his head high from the surface. "What are you going to do? You're indicted. You think you'll swim away from that? Sail away? You'll never be able to return to the United States."

No reply.

Up ahead, the sound of water torn through by athletic hands and arms.

Then a "fuck you!" thrown backward from the night spread out before Xavier.

The swimming became less easy.

It pulled at Xavier. His arms and heart and legs and lungs grew heavy, heavier. Far away in the blackness, more screaming, more shouts, an incredulous German *"polizei."*

The sound of pounding, hands or limbs banging against a solid surface. Had Nils Bryson reached the other side of the harbor, reached the boats? Was he trying to climb aboard?

"Nils Bryson! If you flee, I will turn your nephew over to local authorities."

Snort, cough. Painful salt and water in his nose and throat.

His limbs felt even heavier still, and Xavier struggled to keep his head high.

"Monique Arthurton will have legal assistance to challenge this international child abduction under—"

Spluttering.

The salt burned his sinuses, made him smell iron.

He pulled himself high once again.

"Under the Hague Convention. She'll challenge this abduction under the Hague Convention. She'll get her son back. Your brother will never see his son again."

More salt, more gagging, more iron.

His eyes burning.

"Never!" he shrieked. "Viggo Fucking Bryson will never see his cur-dog son again!"

Xavier was at the boats. He banged against one of the vessels, felt metal.

A ladder. A metal ladder.

He pulled himself up, climbed up the back end of the boat on the ladder, on the metal ladder . . . in the dark, salty, iron-stinking night.

Without his shoes, the ladder ground into the soles of his feet. Water dripped down his arms, down his face, down his shins.

He broke.

"Fuck you, Nils Bryson! You're a common fucking thief, you fucking worthless coward!"

He tumbled into the cockpit of the boat, struggled and clawed to pull himself up. The rough surface of the boat's deck bit into his knees, his feet. He clawed along the wires enshrouding the cursed boat, squinted blindly, or at least quite fuzzily, into the shadows.

The dark to his right held the sound of scrambling, of footsteps pounding.

More footsteps pounding, lighter footsteps.

Lillian screaming. "Halt, Nils Bryson!"

The dock beneath his throbbing feet. The dripping.

"I've got him, Xavier! He's here! I've got him in the restraints. He's not resisting."

Chapter 29
Defense Counsel

Devlin marveled at the wire-mesh screen in front of her. It had been a long, long time since she'd sat in front of a screen like this one.

"How are you doing?" she whispered to Nils, who sat on the far side of the screen, on his side of the divide, in this visiting cell, in the U.S. Marshals lockup, on the fifth floor of the Gerald R. Ford Federal Building and U.S. Courthouse, in Grand Rapids, Michigan.

"It was a long, long trip from the island." He seemed to be half-smiling.

That was a good sign, right? The half-smile?

She drew in a deep breath. "An arraignment is a pretty fast, anti-climactic thing. The magistrate judge will review the charges against you and your rights, and we'll plead not guilty."

We'll plead. . . . The Illinois Supreme Court had said she could have her license back. It hadn't taken long at all. And the U.S. District Court for the Western District of Michigan had admitted her. And Nils had said he wanted her to represent him. And she'd never signed that contract to work for Irene Stockton on Viggo's defense team. And because she'd never been on Viggo's team, there was no conflict with her representing Nils. And if there had been a conflict and she shouldn't have taken Nils's case, what was the bar association going to do? Suspend her license?

She really, really needed a drink.

She hadn't had a drop since that beer on the German party catamaran.

"We'll plead not guilty," she repeated. "Then Xavier Fucking Charles will give me discovery discs, and then we'll fight about whether or not you should be detained pending trial. That's gonna be the fight here. Charles is gonna be a complete bitch about this, I know it. He'll accuse you of fleeing the country, of resisting arrest. And he won't mention he and his case agent were playing footsies on St. Kitts on the taxpayers' dime and were way beyond their jurisdiction."

A door banged outside the visiting cell.

"I'll explain you're a yacht broker," she continued, "and sailed to the island for professional purposes. I'll explain that neither Charles nor his agent produced identification when they tried to effect their illegal arrest."

She jotted a line on her yellow legal pad. "I'll bring up your ties to the Midwest, your lack of financial resources to flee. But," she paused, another long inhale, "if Viggo's in, I'm betting you'll be detained as well."

Nils echoed her inhale with a heavy sigh. "I'm betting you're right."

"I'm sorry," she whispered.

"I miss you." He touched the screen between them with the tips of his right fingers.

She saw the half-smile again. Touched her fingertips to his.

"You look good in a suit," he whispered.

***

Magistrate Judge Robyn Morgan's courtroom didn't have the vaulted ceilings and somber oil paintings of dead judges found in the Article III judges' courtrooms on the lower floors of the Gerald R. Ford Building. But it did have a nice set of windows overlooking the city, a quaint Midwestern urban scene that had escaped the fate of its eastern brother Detroit and somehow defied becoming Rust Belt-y.

Devlin had been to Grand Rapids a few times, but Michigan's place on her radar was relegated to that of being a cheap destination for summer getaway weekends for Illinois People. It showed up as beach venues like Saugatuck and Grand Haven. Not as mid-sized cities with federal courthouses.

The courtroom door swung open, and in walked Assistant United States Attorney Xavier Charles, followed by Special Agent Lillian Carter and a heavyset woman in a cheap, tacky, department-store skirt and knit top crowned by a shopping-channel gold necklace. Probably the probation officer. Back in Chicago, Devlin had known all the players, had known their drinking habits and paramours and their pet quips that made them harassment-suit liabilities in their offices. Here, she knew no one.

But she still knew the law.

That hadn't changed. At least, not much.

She ignored Charles and Carter, thumbed through a file, listened to the outdated clock tick from its place on the wall over the mini-jury-box.

The prisoner-entry door opened and two marshals ushered Nils into the courtroom. He wore a neon-orange inmate jumpsuit, white socks, and light-orange shower sandals. And shackles. Heavy, clanking chains.

His hair hung long and untrimmed, and stubble clouded his lower facial features. He smelled of starchy foods and ineffectual soap and a lack of Speed Stick. The younger marshal, a husky woman with close-cropped hair, unlocked his shackles, and Devlin extended her hand to him. The shake lasted longer than it would have with another client. And felt better.

The clock ticked again, and beyond the window Indian summer caressed the polis, lingering over its convention center and performance-arts center, and a bright-orange sculpture installation that couldn't rival the Picasso in Daley Plaza.

A young case manager broke the silence, entering the courtroom through the door to the judge's chambers.

"Is counsel ready?" He looked from Charles to Devlin.

"The government is ready to proceed," Xavier Charles said, standing from his chair at the prosecution's table. He held his tie to his belly to halt the neckwear's swing as he rose, buttoned his suit coat.

Beneath her own coat and pale, silk blouse, Devlin's stomach filled with acid. Why hadn't she begged, borrowed, or stolen her way to a clonazepam 'script?

This isn't me anymore. No, shhh. This is you.

"The defense is ready. Thank you." She rose from, and returned to, her seat in the customary bobbing up and down of an attorney poised for action.

And then she was on her feet again as the case manager returned and called "all rise."

She was responding to Judge Robyn Morgan's questions and directions, and she was standing beside the first man she'd ever loved as he responded "not guilty" to Judge Morgan's question of "how do you wish to plead today." She was saying something about section 3142 of title 18 of the U.S. Code in response to the judge asking if the defense wanted to be heard on the issue of bond. She was listening to Xavier Charles call down the wrath of God upon the head of "the defendant" who had—

"Fled the country in a sailboat," Charles was saying, rather too loudly for a courtroom this size. "My case agent and I secured permission to travel to Texas to effect the arrest of the defendant only to visit his alleged place of employment and discover that he had set sail to the island of St. Kitts in response to discovering that he had been indicted in the superseding indictment filed in this matter."

Charles paused.

"He sailed to St. Kitts," he continued, "which, I would point out to the court, is a significant site for the illicit banking and financial exchanges that occurred in this case. It is also a non-extraditing sovereign for purposes of the charges at hand. Viggo Bryson, the defendant's brother and co-conspirator in this matter, who is currently in custody at the Newaygo County Jail, used the island's processes to form a number of shell corporations for the purpose of hiding assets and financial exchanges from the Internal Revenue Service."

Charles glanced at Agent Carter.

"After discovering that the defendant had fled to the island, my case agent and I continued to St. Kitts to interview witnesses and investigate potential documentary evidence in the case. We secured volumes of evidence against both these defendants, and in a stroke of coincidence, happened upon this defendant in a marina on the island one evening. When Agent Carter approached the defendant and his companions, a group that included defense counsel here present, the defendant fled on foot, going so far as to dive into the harbor and attempt to swim to the sailboat on which he had arrived at the island. We believe he would have launched that boat and attempted to flee to sea again had we not been able to intercept and secure him."

"Mr. Charles, I'm going to interrupt you briefly," Judge Morgan said from her raised bench. "Has Mr. Bryson cooperated since you secured him?"

Xavier Charles cleared his throat. He kept his eyes fixed straight ahead. Devlin studied him as he refused to acknowledge her or Nils.

"Yes, Your Honor," he said. "Since he agreed to accompany me and my case agent back to the United

States, the defendant has not proved to be a management problem."

"Thank you, Mr. Charles," the judge said. "I'll hear from the defense and then follow up with you."

Judge Morgan nodded to Devlin.

"You Honor," Devlin rose and stepped to the podium, "I'd like to point out three things here. First, my client knew nothing of the superseding indictment when he set sail to St. Kitts, which he did for professional purposes, as a sailboat yacht broker. Second," she bounced over the lying speedbump without slowing down, "when Agent Carter approached my client, she refused to produce any identification to substantiate her claim that she was an agent with the IRS, and she refused to explain her authority, given she was operating outside of her jurisdiction. And third, my client has been completely compliant since voluntarily submitting to custody under Agent Carter and AUSA Charles in this matter. Again, they were operating outside their jurisdiction, in a non-extradition country, yet my client agreed to accompany them back to the United States."

She didn't mention Grant. Grant was far away from this mess, snuggled on *Manuia* with Sean for the time being. She wanted nothing interfering with that arrangement—no legal entanglements or posturing, no specter of foster care or state guardianship. Xavier Charles wouldn't broach the subject, given he'd basically tried to kidnap the kid.

"I'll also add this." She tapped the file she'd carried to the podium and placed in front of her, beating out some cryptic, something like Morse code, message with the pen that she'd likewise brought to the lectern. "My client, while hailing from a wealthy family, has very limited resources. He has little to no contact with his parents, and as a yacht broker, earns less than sixty thousand dollars a year. His savings are limited. He simply doesn't have the resources to flee the United States or even whatever district he's released to. And while he has only limited ties to Michigan, he does want to maintain regular contact with this district, not just for the proceedings against him, but to support his brother, his co-defendant, in this matter."

"Counsel, if your client has only limited resources and minimal ties to West Michigan—" Judge Morgan stopped, turned a page of a packet on the desk in front of her bench. "Your client is originally from Chicago?"

"Yes, Your Honor. He grew up in the City of Chicago." Devlin glanced over at Nils, checked on him.

He sat staring straight ahead.

"And he currently lives in," Judge Morgan hesitated, "Ka-meh? Kame? How do you say this town?"

"Kee-mah," Devlin answered. "It's pronounced Kee-mah. It's southeast of Houston, on Galveston Bay."

"All right. Kemah." The judge turned another page. "If your client is from Kemah, where will he stay for the duration of these proceedings?"

"Your Honor." Devlin glanced at Nils again. His eyes had awakened and he was watching her. "My client would, ideally, like to return to his home in Texas. He would report to the probation office in the Southern District of Texas and could travel to the Western District here for hearings as needed. If, however, the court considers that situation untenable, we could find Mr. Bryson an apartment and employment locally."

Judge Morgan clicked her tongue, read something in the papers before her. She adjusted the thin gold spectacles riding on her nose, looked up. "Mr. Charles, what would the government say to a combination of conditions that would include Mr. Bryson's return to Kemah, electronic monitoring, weekly meetings at the probation office in the Southern District of Texas, an employment condition, and assignment to the personal custody of a family member or friend who could report to this court any violations of the conditions of release?"

Xavier Charles rose, smoothed the jacket of his suit. "Your Honor, it is my understanding that the defendant does not have a standard home arrangement. He lives on a boat, a seagoing vessel, and frankly, given the history in this case, the government is skeptical that he will not flee. He's demonstrated flight on multiple occasions."

He sat down.

Well played, you little weasel. Don't oversell it. Nice.

Devlin focused on the legal pad in front of her, jotted meaningless notes to allow herself to ignore the prosecutor with dignity.

Grant would be without family for a long, long time if Nils didn't bond out.

Damn it. Think, Dev, think.

She'd researched the custodial facilities in both districts. . . .

"Your Honor." A seldom-cited subsection of section 3142 glowed in neon lights on the dark curtain of her mind. "It is my understanding that the Bureau of Prisons maintains a facility in downtown Houston." She laughed as lightly as she could. "It is Texas after all. They take their prisons seriously."

No one else cracked a smile, not even Nils.

"Unlike in this district," she continued, "which relies on contracts with the local jails, the Southern District of Texas has this federal facility. Thus I believe this court could take advantage of the option available under section 3142(c)(1)(B)(xiii) and order incarceration in that facility for evenings and weekends, leaving Mr. Bryson free to work during the day, without having to burden a local jail facility with these less standard arrangements."

Fingers crossed. So crossed.

Judge Morgan fiddled with her glasses again, paged through those papers. But when the judge raised her eyes, Devlin knew she'd lost.

"Counsel," Judge Morgan removed her glasses, "after reviewing the relevant factors under section 3142(g), it seems to me that, given the defendant's history, no combination of conditions will assure his appearance in this matter. I will enter an order of detention in this case. Now let's turn to the scheduling considerations here. . . ."

Devlin felt Nils cringe, felt him contract.

As the marshals stepped forward to shackle Nils after Judge Morgan ended the hearing, stepped off the bench, and returned to her chambers, Devlin reached for him. Again the handshake, the lingering, the desperation. The touch not nearly long enough.

Chapter 30

Happy Accident

The rear tires slipped on dirty, slushy April snow. Xavier eased up on the accelerator and drifted gently into a left turn onto Patterson Avenue, making his way toward Gerald R. Ford International Airport. He ran the windshield wipers, watched the wet snow smudge and streak the glass. The temperature was dropping, and he knew the roads would start icing up soon. Niqi was not going to like this. The wheels slipped again as he braked for a red light.

In the terminal at Gerald R. Ford, he waited near baggage carousel two, working the buttons open on his double-breasted wool coat and then on the sport coat beneath it. Given the terminal was akin to a public corridor, he decided he could leave his fedora on. He adjusted his cuffs, fidgeted with his watchband, rubbed a thumb into droplets of former snowflakes. Niqi had insisted he pick her up alone. He'd seen the dubious flicker in Lillian's eyes over Niqi's request, but nothing had grown out of that initial hesitation, so here he stood, awaiting Monique on this miserable spring evening. It was supposed to be spring, wasn't it?

A final pretrial conference before Judge Hadley Elizabeth Montgomery tomorrow, a week of trial prep, and they'd be off to the races in *United States v. Bryson*.

Perhaps bringing Niqi in a full week ahead of trial was a waste of hotel costs, but it would give Lillian plenty of time to prepare their star witness. Not that they needed much additional preparation. Lillian had done a magnificent job of preparing trial exhibits and slideshows, prepping the other witnesses, and organizing reams of documents. They'd provided that disgraceful slattern Devlin Winters with their final witness and exhibit lists this afternoon. He still couldn't believe Illinois had given her back her license.

"Good evening, *putus!*"

How could her voice still make him feel whatever it was that had just hit him down low, in that pit of his belly?

He turned.

"Good evening, Monique." For courtesy's sake, he touched the brim of the wool hat, tipped it ever so slightly.

Her jeans looked like Henri de Toulouse-Lautrec had painted them on her in an attempt to make his streetwalker works modern, or "relevant" as the pundits said.

"So here I am," she said. "All for you. And your victory over our beloved Viggo Bryson." She paused, adjusted the strap of a large, too-red bag hanging off her shoulder. "You look good. Really good. Have you been working out?" She stepped into him, ran a purple fingernail from his Windsor to his Stanford tie tack.

He sniffed, backed away.

Lillian did have him doing yoga. He'd only agreed to it after she'd consented to substituting recital of the Our Father for all the om-ing and namaste nonsense at the end. He conceded it made him feel good . . . limber.

"What does your bag look like?" He approached the luggage carousel.

"It's hard-sided. Silver." She was digging in the purse now. She looked up. "Don't be like that *putus*. We've known each other too long." Back to the excavation. She emerged from the depths with a tube of lipstick and a silver, handheld mirror.

"We have known each other too long, Monique. I know you well enough to tell you to stop acting like a trollop. If you need to paint yourself, by all means, go and do it in the ladies' room."

She uncapped the lipstick, swept color over her lower lip. "So you and this Agent Carter? She's your *choonkaloonks* now? A little skinny, that *ting*. Little bony."

She finished with the lipstick and dropped her painting supplies back into the red bag. Three black suitcases thunked onto the baggage-claim belt. A baby car seat wrapped in plastic followed.

"Enough. Your imagination has always been too vivid, Monique."

"Monique, Monique, Monique. So it's going to be like that?" She was back to rummaging. "But I'm not imagining nothing, Mr. Charles. I saw that girl on the island. I've been replaced by a skinny, pale Babylonian. But it's all right. It's been so long."

A massive silver case appeared on the conveyor.

"Is this one yours?" Xavier didn't make eye contact as he asked.

"That's mine, *putus*. Thanks."

He pulled the case from the belt, telescoped out the handle, and stepped toward the glass doors of the terminal, wheeling the bag after him.

"Do you want to get a coat out of here?" He held the case's towing handle out to Monique.

"I've got a sweater in here." She dove into the red-bag cavern yet again, coming back to the surface with a light-green cardigan knit from bulky yarn.

"Niqi." He sighed. "How long did you live in Chicago? You know that's not enough."

"It's April!" She shoved an arm into a sweater sleeve.

"Niqi, you'll never grow up." He stood the suitcase up and pulled his wool coat off. "Here." He held it out, and she accepted it, the purple nails shining against the dark fabric. "We can stop somewhere and you can buy something sensible on the way to the hotel." He began buttoning up his sport coat.

Then he couldn't stop himself. "Hopefully, you've saved enough of Viggo Bryson's pirated lucre to afford a proper coat."

"Tut-tut, *putus*. You shouldn't hate on Viggo so much. Bad for the stomach, you know?" She struggled into the coat, balancing the handbag every which way as she pulled the wool over the cardigan.

After waiting for her to button up, Xavier snugged his hat down and hunched his shoulders against the blast of blurry gray iciness, leading the way out of the terminal and over to the parking garage, dragging the ponderous silver case behind him. He loaded the bag into the trunk and got Niqi buckled into the passenger seat of the car. At the garage's payment booth, he held out a credit card, and once free of the airport, turned north toward 28th Street. He considered turning on the radio simply to put something between himself and her. Instead, he sliced into the space, pressed a blade into the air the heater hadn't yet warmed, into the upholstery he'd never liked and had only tolerated because the car was a good value, into the stereo he should probably have turned on rather than opening his mouth.

"Niqi, why did you insist I come pick you up? Alone? What do you want?"

She fussed with the coat's buttons. "*Putus*, we just didn't get any time together on the island to really talk." Fingers adjusting braids. Turning to the sun visor, lowering it, and flipping up the cover over the mirror. "You were all business, all let's-convict-Viggo. We never talked. I just want to talk. We need to catch up, have a little *ol talk*."

"Niqi, I've no need for *ol talk*. There's nothing to talk about." He drummed his fingers on the steering wheel, glanced at that radio knob. You should have let Agent Carter pick you up."

She snapped the mirror's cover down and the sun visor up, sat back in the seat. "Xavier, did you charge Viggo just to get some sort of revenge?"

He inhaled for several seconds, pressed his lips together. The windshield wipers pushed slush-flakes across the glass and the lane stripes on the pavement flashed past beneath a dirty, icy film.

"No," he murmured, "Viggo's case coming across my desk was nothing more than a happy accident."

Chapter 31

Worn-Out Laundry

The Newaygo County Jail rose in front of Devlin's bumper, a sullen picture of bricks behind a sad, unraveling doily of out-of-season snowflakes. She sat at the wheel of Irene Stockton's Jeep Grand Cherokee, staring through the windshield at the building looming before her front-row parking spot. Irene had turned out to be the sisters-in-arms type and had given Devlin her spare bedroom and a set of car keys, so Devlin could be comfortable while preparing for trial. She'd gotten a colleague to lend Devlin a spare office, including the use of a trendy, exuberant legal secretary named Tammy, who wore jeans to work every day. Irene had instructed her investigator, Mya Reynolds, to share her work, as Viggo and Nils had agreed they wanted their defense counsel working in tandem. A few nights a week, Devlin would have dinner with Irene at one of Grand Rapids' surprisingly upscale eateries, sharing a bottle of wine and thoughts about the defense.

Drinking with someone helped keep the drinking in check, but Devlin missed the boardwalk, missed the boats in the channel and the ability to sleep at night, the lack of ventricle knots and the absence of insomnia. Irene had talked her into a relationship with a massage therapist, and with Nils's parents paying generously for his defense, she'd visited the woman and was coming to appreciate the joys of hot stones. But they didn't fix the stress, the throb of anxiety.

"Come on, Winters, time to do this thing." She could see her breath as she climbed out of the car and dragged her briefcase from the back seat.

In the lobby of the jail, she signed in and waited for the heavy metal door at the back of the room to click, signaling that someone had unlocked it and would admit her. When the click came, she pulled the thing open, considering that criminal-defense attorneys are among the very few in mainstream American culture familiar with real live dungeons. In the space on the far side of the door, she stood, waiting for the next bunker door to click, and then she followed a young guard from the observation room down a beige hallway with a nonspecific offensive odor. The guard pulled open the door to a large space that served as a chapel and general meeting room. He flipped on the lights, and Devlin slipped out of her snow-damp coat, snapped open her briefcase, and laid out papers until another guard arrived with Nils.

The orange and dirty-white striped jail scrubs hung over his shoulders like worn-out laundry on a sagging clothesline, the garments a vision of the spirit Devlin was desperately worried about. As the door clanked behind him, he sank into one of the beige plastic chairs and dropped his head into his hands.

"D. Winters, tell me we're going to be okay." His voice seemed to rattle.

She took a long, long breath. "Nils, this isn't going to be good."

They'd been over the materials dozens of times: the insurance contracts, the financial records, Blue Tide, L.L.C.,'s generous sponsorship of Nils and his sailing and surfing. They'd looked at Xavier Charles's glossy pictures of Nils wearing Blue Tide's logo at surfing competitions, copies of a series of checks from Blue Tide, L.L.C., to Nils, checks with unhelpful memos. Blue Tide partners and clients had made statements, and Devlin and Nils had pored over FBI 302 memos that gave the government's version of these statements. Special Agent Lillian Carter had put together piles of spreadsheets, records summaries, and witness charts, complete with pictures of the witnesses and arrows pointing from their unsmiling faces to their corporate entities and to icons representing their financial transactions. Devlin had gone through it all with Nils.

And they had speculated about Monique Arthurton.

How bad it would be when she got on the stand.

It would be bad. Very bad.

Devlin glanced over her shoulder at the windows looking out on the charmless hallway. All clear. She reached a hand toward her client and buried her fingers in his hair . . . flat, greasy, . . . and paradisiacal. If they made it out of this mess, she would wash that hair.

She listened to herself review the procedure for the coming day's final pretrial conference. She explained how she expected copies of the witnesses' grand-jury testimony tomorrow. She'd be up reading through all of it till the wee hours. She'd be ready come trial. She already was. She had a list of objections and case law should Xavier Charles start playing fast and loose with testimony, which she fully expected him to do. She had motions in limine for the court to rule on tomorrow. She had as much as she could have.

"If Viggo goes down, I go down?" Nils didn't fit in the budget-sized chair. Even with the weight he'd lost, he dwarfed it.

"Not necessarily."

They'd been over this ground before, but Nils had waffled on the issue of whether or not to throw Viggo under the bus. One defense theory revolved around distancing Nils from Viggo, arguing that the brothers had no business dealings. Sure, Blue Tide, L.L.C., looked like a crooked scam, but Viggo's support of Nils was nothing more than brotherly love. Nils had known nothing of the scam, and given his brother's resources, had had no reason to doubt the cleanliness of the money he'd received.

The problem with that approach was the checks. And their cursed memos.

Nils could deny any understanding of why Blue Tide would have marked the checks as it did, but what juror would buy that? Especially in the face of luxury Hawaiian vacations and corporate meetings on Waikiki Beach.

They considered the fall-on-the-sword course: admit Nils's involvement with Blue Tide but deny any knowledge of fraud, any review or understanding of the insurance products and the return-of-premium riders. Nils didn't want to hang Viggo out to dry though. He believed that by mounting a strong defense, by discussing his willingness to recruit partners and clients for Viggo, he would reinforce for the jury the legitimacy of Viggo's operation. The problem with this approach was Monique Arthurton. If Monique took the stand and claimed that Viggo had set Blue Tide, L.L.C., up knowing the insurance products it would sell involved tax fraud, and if she testified to the company's fraudulent operations, no juror was going to be in a hurry to acquit the business owner's brother who'd recruited participants in the fraud scheme and profited from it. Nope, the jury wasn't going to jump on that train, no matter how duped, or dumb, Devlin tried to paint Nils.

The one thing they hadn't discussed at length was pleading guilty. Nils had remained adamant: no guilty plea. No matter what. But she had to raise the issue again . . . tonight.

"Nils," she smoothed the palms of her hands across her slacks, "we've gotta talk about this one last time. You could plead guilty tomorrow. You could go into that pretrial conference and plead guilty and save yourself a couple years off those sentencing guidelines. You know, with your background, minimal participation, and complete lack of criminal history, we stand a good shot at a sentence of time served. At least I could fight like hell for that." She faltered.

"You know what those sentencing guidelines look like if we go to trial and you get hit with being responsible for the full loss amount."

Nils had struggled with the concept of "relevant conduct" and the idea that he could be sentenced as though he'd caused the entire financial loss to the IRS, regardless of the actual scope of his alleged role in the offense. Her bones had ached explaining the potential for a six- or eight-year, or longer, sentence. She hadn't let herself pick at the decisions she would have to make if he were sentenced like that. They lurked in the shadows, but she refused to light them up.

"I can't. I won't." Nils swallowed. "I can't, Dev. I'm scared shitless of a trial, especially one with Viggo's jilted baby-momma accusing him of all sorts of things. But I can't plead guilty to stealing money I didn't steal. And I can't undermine Viggo's case by copping out and leaving him alone to face all this, with me basically sitting back and telling the court everything is true, that we did this, and that I deserve a break because I'm admitting it. I can't."

"I'm not sure Viggo would do the same for you," she said. "I'm not sure he'd hold out like that for you." She touched his hand.

She wasn't clear on the jail's policy related to co-defendants, didn't know if the jail even had a policy. But she suspected Viggo was communicating with Nils, and she didn't like that possibility.

"He would," Nils mumbled. "He's my brother."

Devlin bit back a response. The room closed in, its beige walls threatening to rob both of them of their color, their breath, and leave them frozen and transparent at the table until the end of time. Perhaps such a fate would be superior to having to march into court and witness the crushingly slow interment of your dreams of happily ever after. Again.

A few more papers passed between them. A few more notes on the legal pad. A few more touches of hair and hands. And then she was clicking back down the hall and out the multiple doors, to drive to a city she'd never called home, in weather she'd never wanted to see again, to try to sleep before an ordeal she thought she'd never have to endure again—a federal criminal trial.

Chapter 32

Toscanini Opens

Jurors. Lovely, hardworking, law-abiding jurors. Taxpaying jurors. Xavier watched the jury pool file into Judge Montgomery's courtroom, men and women dragging armfuls of wool and soft down and Walmart-bought synthetic coats, and scarves and hats and gloves, with them.

The first fourteen people in line took seats in the jury box while the rest arranged themselves on the gallery benches of the high-ceilinged, blue-carpeted courtroom. Nice West Michigan citizens: employees and business owners, students and retirees, people struggling to make ends meet and put their kids through Grand Rapids Community College, young people with stars in their eyes at Grand Valley State University, readers, craftsmen, hunters with cabins up north, vegans who refused to wear leather. The jury questionnaires Xavier had reviewed showed that a fine swath of Americana would be seated for voir dire this morning, seated to discuss biases and proclivities, beliefs and backgrounds.

Fourteen of these people would sit in that jury box for the trial of *United States v. Bryson*. Twelve would end up judging Viggo and Nils Bryson, while, if all went well, two would be shipped home without the fun of deliberation. Those two alternates would only be called to action if one of the first twelve came up sick or got in a car accident or suffered some other misfortune or circumstances that rendered them unable to continue with their civic duty.

More than half the jurors had the light hair and skin and eyes of Dutch Reformed West Michigan. Tall, blond people with names like Jansen, DeVries, and Visser. One or two looked Hispanic, three were African American, and Xavier had seen two Arabic names. Homemakers, clerks at the Khol's department stores on Alpine Avenue and over by Woodland Mall, an editor at a publishing house specializing in religious works, a few restaurant owners, a pediatrician, factory workers in plants supplying widgets to the auto industry, a physical therapist, a ballet teacher. No one seemed to have roots in the Caribbean Basin. He hadn't expected anyone from the islands, and it didn't matter. What mattered was the simple fact that virtually all these people paid taxes. They gave the IRS their hard-earned money in exchange for roads and public schools and Social Security and maintenance of B-52 bombers to keep the home hearths safe. April 15 meant something to these people.

These people didn't have summer homes on the Adriatic. (Xavier couldn't wait to flash Viggo's Croatian villa across the wall-sized projector screen set up on the far side of the courtroom, facing the jury box.) These people didn't take their kids to Switzerland for birthdays. If they were lucky, these local folks would go skiing once a year at Boyne Highlands. More likely, they just went tubing on the hill at the park at Pando for a winter adventure, and walked the pier in Grand Haven, wading in Lake Michigan, for summer fun. For a treat on those summer days, Mom and Dad might buy the kids corndogs at the Pronto Pup and ice cream at the Dairy Treat off the boardwalk.

These people weren't going to like the Brysons.

"All rise!" Judge Montgomery's case manager breezed into the courtroom from the judge's chambers, the judge on her heels, black robe billowing.

No one rose. Everyone was already on their feet. But they did fall quiet, turn, pay homage.

With Her Honor's "please, be seated," Xavier settled in. He smiled at his jury pool as Judge Montgomery introduced herself, welcoming these stalwart men and women and thanking them for their service. Beneath the courtroom's distant ceiling and wrapped within its wood paneling, with Judge Montgomery's predecessors looking down from their oil portraits and gilt frames, Xavier leaned over the prosecution's table and flicked the corner of his trial brief back and forth. The court reporter stared ahead. The blue-coated court security officer stood sentry at the courtroom door. United States Attorney Norah Smit sat near the security officer. Xavier had noticed his superior when she'd arrived to join the audience.

And Viggo and Nils Bryson sat in tailored Armani with which virtually none of these salt-of-the-earth Midwestern jurors could relate.

So, yes, Xavier was smiling, smiling and enjoying the tiny, almost inaudible scratch of Lillian's pen on her legal pad beside him.

***

"Ladies and gentlemen, while the evidence in this case may at times seem complicated, the issues are simple. These two defendants, these brothers Viggo and Nils Bryson, concocted a scheme to sell fake insurance products to owners of companies so that everyone involved could defraud the IRS and keep millions of dollars in monies they otherwise owed in taxes." Xavier paused, made eye contact with each juror.

He'd rehearsed his opening statement dozens of times over the past week, run it through his head hundreds, maybe thousands, of times over the past months. Lillian had heard it and offered her thoughts. Agamemnon and Menelaus had heard it while waiting for their Fancy Feast suppers. In front of these fourteen members of the jury, the story poured out easily, like a perfect béchamel flowing from the saucepan over fresh crêpes.

"The evidence the government will present—" No, it was the evidence *he* would present. He was the government. It was his evidence and they would be his convictions. For his government, of course, but *his* nonetheless. "This evidence will show a scheme involving Viggo Bryson organizing multiple business entities, including a company known as Blue Tide, L.L.C., and setting these entities up to sell what Viggo Bryson called loss-of-income insurance policies. It will show Viggo Bryson's brother receiving payments from Blue Tide, L.L.C., in exchange for recruiting people to invest in Blue Tide, L.L.C., and recruiting clients to purchase the insurance products Blue Tide was marketing."

He tapped the clicker in his right hand to advance the glowing PowerPoint slideshow Lillian and a paralegal had prepared. That lovely full-color picture of Nils Bryson riding a surfboard in that garish blue lycra surf shirt, with the Blue Tide logo, lit up the full width of the screen.

"The evidence will show that these defendants, these brothers, went to great lengths to try to cover their tracks, to try to avoid detection of their wrongdoing. The government will present evidence regarding the efforts these defendants took to try to hide their intent to knowingly defraud the IRS and, in some cases, their own clients. This evidence will show that these defendants did not act in good faith and did not act believing their actions were legal. For example, we will show that Viggo Bryson, through checks from Blue Tide, L.L.C., paid his brother to recruit investors and clients, and tried to disguise these payments as athletic sponsorship for his brother to compete in surfing competitions. The evidence, however, will show that the payments were not for Nils Bryson's athletic endeavors but were actually commissions Nils Bryson received for using his position in the yachting community," he'd chosen yachting over sailing, and he liked the effect, "to recruit wealthy clients looking for tax shelters."

A quick lick of the lips, a smoothing of his suit coat's placket. "The evidence will also show that Viggo Bryson made an act of consulting with an attorney to obtain advice as to the legality of the insurance products Blue Tide, L.L.C., was selling. As the documents you will see will show, however, Viggo Bryson did not provide his attorney with the full details of these insurance products. He withheld key information related to what we will call in this case the return-of-premium riders. These riders, which you will get to see, provide for the return of a majority of a client's premium payments, so the monies these clients deducted from their taxes as business expenses in the form of payments for insurance actually flowed back to those clients."

Standing in court like this always felt so good. So—

Righteous? May I be so bold as to refer to righteousness? St. Thomas More, guard and keep me.

Xavier advanced the slideshow to display some key phrases and terms with definitions and to flash up unimpressive pictures of documents. As he continued to assure these fourteen allies of what he would prove to them, he struggled to maintain a professional vigor without crossing the line to unseemly vaunting.

"Finally," he inhaled deeply, "you will hear from a woman who is the founder, owner, and CEO of SK and N, Incorporated, a corporation organized in the Federation of Saint Christopher and Nevis, or as you may have heard it called, St. Kitts and Nevis, an island nation in the Lesser Antilles. This woman's name is Monique Arthurton and she is the mother of defendant Viggo Bryson's nine-year-old son."

An elderly lady in a white sweater with a gaudy gold brooch, Mrs. Catherine Visser or Juror Number Ten, sniffed. Xavier would have wagered a week's salary, if the wagering had been morally licit, that Mrs. Visser was not one to be impressed by unwed mothers, and that the lack of the title "wife" had precipitated the sniff.

Xavier clicked and Niqi's smiling face filled the wall-sized screen.

"Ms. Arthurton will explain to you that defendant Viggo Bryson concocted a scheme to deprive her of her parental rights over her son and offered her a key participatory role in his financial fraud in exchange for her not challenging his efforts to obtain full custody of their son. She will tell you how she regrets her decision to, essentially, sell her parental rights. As she will testify, her participation in this scheme has made her quite wealthy, and she will explain that she knows defendant Viggo Bryson's insurance products were designed to defraud the IRS and, in some cases, Viggo Bryson's own clients. She will testify unequivocally that Viggo Bryson formulated the insurance products, designed the fraudulent offerings, and set up the commercial entities to handle sales, the returns of the premiums, and the movement of the monies."

To Xavier's right, Judge Montgomery sat at her raised bench, looking from the projector screen to the jurors and then to the parties. The fluorescent lights high overhead washed out her skin and hair, despite the better-quality light fixtures. When she nodded at his finish, Xavier couldn't help but fancy she approved of his presentation. He resumed his seat, smiled a tight, professional smile at the jurors, and inhaled the scent of cheap perfume, no doubt escaping off the ample frame of one of the fine matrons in the jury box, and of expensive carpet treated with some Febreze-like product. The show had begun and he was Toscanini in front of the New York Philharmonic.

Chapter 33
Happy

An island in a sea of paper. Devlin was that island. She adjusted her legs beneath her as she knelt in Irene Stockton's guest bedroom in the middle of a circle of copies and folders. One last review. One last check.

She'd made it through voir dire and Xavier Charles's vapid, imperious opening statement. She'd sat through Irene's able and succinct opening for Viggo. For Nils's defense, she'd reserved her opening statement. She'd mulled the decision over, turned it every which way in her head. Was she simply delaying? Giving into the fear, the gut-devouring anxiety? No, she knew, especially with Irene making an opening statement right after the government, that the best thing would be to reserve her opening and get a couple cuts in after the government rested and before she launched into her defense case.

It wasn't the nerves.

It was solid strategy.

And she didn't need a drink.

Or she did need a drink, but she wasn't going to allow herself one. She needed her wits sharp, her intuition uncompromised.

Irene had a charming, funky Victorian in what she referred to as Eastown, which was itself a charming, funky neighborhood on the eastern edge of downtown Grand

Rapids. Devlin had found a number of satisfying dining options within walking distance, and she could grab a bus into downtown if she didn't want to hassle with traffic and parking or if Irene had the Jeep. The hospitality and surroundings had left no room for complaints. It was just that the little spare room with its peaked ceiling and steeply falling eaves, its Amish-quilted bed and cute rocking chair, grew hollow at night, got bigger and emptier and fuller of doubts and second-guessing.

"Monique Arthurton wants you to believe that Viggo Bryson bought her off, gave her a stake in his company in exchange for full custody of her son," Devlin recited to her reflection in a floor mirror with a rustic, barn-wood-type frame. "But what do we know about Monique Arthurton? The evidence has shown, and will continue to show, that Ms. Arthurton has an axe to grind, a score to settle."

Devlin picked up an accordion file. Irene's investigator Mya Reynolds, brash, cheerful, and adept at obtaining unobtainable records, had produced a full copy of the file in the custody proceedings involving Grant Bryson. Mya had also procured a copy of an old Chicago P.D. report. The cops had been called to an apartment building on South Kimbark, near the University of Chicago. A neighbor had phoned with a complaint of a loud domestic disturbance that had spilled into a hallway of the building. When the cops arrived, the male was sitting on a couch in an apartment with the front door open and the female was in the hallway outside the apartment. The female identified herself as Monique Arthurton and explained that she was interested in rough, sexual role playing and that things had gotten out of hand. The male corroborated the story. Both individuals exhibited bruises, but neither wanted to press charges and neither offered any allegations of wrongdoing against the other. The officers departed without making any arrests.

To Devlin, it sounded like the dark side of Viggo, like manipulation and abuse and a weak cover story, but she'd have to see what kind of use she could make of the incident during cross-examination of Arthurton. It certainly could help paint the woman as angry and out for revenge. But it would be hard to attack a mother robbed of her child by a woman-beater without losing the jury's sympathies completely. Not that Devlin harbored any illusions of enjoying jury sympathy.

The records Mya had dug up on Monique Arthurton's stay at the Ecker Center for Mental Health in Elgin, Illinois, fleshed out this picture of a troubled, trapped young woman . . . and further complicated Devlin's preparations for cross-examination, preparations for the assault on Monique to keep Nils out of prison. (They had also awakened memories of Devlin's own stay at, coincidently, Ecker after her crash at Sondheim. She cringed upon seeing the name and tried to resist the urge to identify with the woman she would have to attack.)

On the records' sterile white pages lay the story of a teenaged mother, a young woman who had left her homeland and followed an older man to a new country, one in which she had enjoyed no support and had no resources. The copies described a pill-based suicide attempt and Viggo's discovery of an unconscious Monique in his Chicago condo, the woman found sprawled in front of a view of the city when Viggo arrived home slightly drunk one evening, as he described it in a statement in the Cook County Circuit Court, Domestic Relations Division.

Slightly drunk? Shitfaced, you asshole. You were shitfaced. Left her with the kid, so you could go out drinking and whoring around, you worthless piece of shit.

Devlin dropped the papers and pushed herself up from the carpet, shimmying a little in her pajama bottoms and t-shirt to jumpstart blood flow to her tingling legs. Irene had told her to help herself to anything in the fridge and the kitchen, and she even had her own stash of groceries tucked downstairs, but that stash didn't include anything to drink . . . intentionally.

But Irene had brought home a couple bottles of some sort of Michigan pinot grigio the other night and they were lined up on the granite countertop beside a box of Pim's cookies.

She wiggled her fingers and rolled stiff, achy shoulders. *Too many fucking questions!*

She was still wrestling with the idea of Nils testifying. He was insisting he wanted to take the stand. Irene said Viggo was being similarly stubborn.

Xavier Charles will rip Nils a new asshole. And bury him in those stupid checks. Fuck!

Texas was an hour behind Michigan. Only 9:15 p.m. down there. Not too late. Totally decent. A couple taps on her phone later and she was listening to ringing on Sean's side of the line.

"Hey, hey, beautiful, howzit in the frozen north?" Sean sounded like warmth and support and strong arms and things better than lonely guestrooms and Michigan pinot grigio.

"Sean, I'm done. I can't do this, man." And the tears simply let go and slid down Devlin's cheeks. She flopped onto the mismatched colors of the Amish quilt. "I can't fucking do this."

"Ah, sweetheart, I'm sorry. I'm so sorry you're going through this. I wish I could be there to support you." He kept talking, saying nothing important and yet everything important, saying soothing things, things Devlin didn't believe but which made her feel better, about her talent and her preparation and her ability to fight.

"He's going to prison," she whimpered.

"You don't know that, sweetheart. You've got a whole trial in front of you." But Sean wasn't convincing anyone.

"How's Grant?" Devlin reached out, unseeing, and groped across the top of the nightstand for the box of Kleenex she'd replaced yesterday because she seemed to be going through Kleenex like a teenaged boy with a full bottle of lotion.

"He's hanging in there," Sean said, sounding muffled. "Kid's a champ. Lost another tooth. We're hoping the tooth fairy brings him enough tonight to buy a used book at the place by NASA."

He paused, called out, "I'll be back in a minute, buddy."

Devlin heard the scrape of a boat companionway opening. And the scrape of it shutting.

"Okay," Sean continued a moment later, "I'll stroll down the dock with you while we talk. Kid's on the boat reading right now. He's struggling with the tutor lady a little, I think, but I think that's more about stress than anything else."

"What's going to happen to him when his bastard father gets locked up for eight years?" Devlin sniffed and sat up, wadded the tissues up and pitched them toward the wastebasket beside the mirror across the room.

The other end of the line stayed quiet.

"His grandparents are bastards, too," Devlin said. "It would be horrible for a kid like that to have to grow up with them. He's so," she rubbed her teary face, "sensitive. He's a good kid." She dropped back over into the pillows. "And those people are," she groped for a word, as she had groped for the Kleenex, "heartless."

She inhaled with a shudder and rolled into a tight, fetal ball. "If Nils goes away, there'll be no one who can take care of that kid. No one to—"

"To take care of Devlin?" Sean's words washed through the phone ether and crashed over her.

She buried her face in one of Irene's blue-cased pillows, a ball of cotton and down, smelling of soap that likely carried the title Mountain Breeze or Alpen Fresh. The blue pillowcase turned soggy quickly and the odor of moist feathers blended with the fake mountain scent-scape.

"It doesn't matter anyway," she choked out after another sob. "He never took care of me. I loved that motherfucker. I loved him so fucking much. And he left me high and fucking dry. I don't even know why I think about him now . . . why I," she coughed, cleared her throat, "why I care about him." She gasped in a breath. "Why I— I want to touch his fucking hair when I visit him at the jail."

"Are you talking about when he left you before when you were young or how he's left you now by being in jail?" Sean sounded too much like a therapist. "Or both?"

"Both, Dr. Phil. Thanks for the insight." But she pulled her face out of the pillow, sighed. "When we were young, I really thought I loved that fool. Thought we'd get married, have kids, all that jazz. Then he was just gone."

The sloped ceiling, the rafters just overhead, seemed so awfully close to the bed. Devlin reached up, as though to touch the beams, and ran her fingers through the air.

"Honestly, there really was no one after him," she whispered into the phone. "I dated a couple guys in undergrad, a pompous asshole in law school, and a law professor at John Marshall for a New York minute when I was at Sondheim Baker. But I guess, after Nils Bryson, I never saw myself like that . . . like someone who'd get married . . . who'd . . . ," she rolled back over and balled up, "who'd like end up like that . . . like . . . ."

"Like happy?" Even through the phone, Sean sounded large, solid.

"Maybe," she mumbled.

She listened to the silence on his end of the line, listened to her own breath, to the stillness of the dark windows on a cold night.

"Whatever happens this week," Sean finally said, "Grant's going to be all right. I'll bet Viggo Bryson will reach out to make better arrangements for him than with his grandparents. Heck," he seemed to falter, "we could probably take the kid. He's a good kid. You and I could watch him. I like the little man. I don't want him to get ground up by all this."

Devlin heard the kindness, the sincerity.

"Devlin," he said, "I've seen you drive boats. And I know you're even better at lawyering. You're going to kick ass.

You may not win. There's a lot you can't control. But I know you'll fight to the death." Another falter. "And in the end, Devlin, you're going to be happy."

She wanted to believe him, but nothing from the outside world could break through the blackness of the windows and the amber of the lamp on the nightstand. She was all alone in the room tucked under the eaves, her only friend that night, and his comforting words, twelve hundred miles to the south.

Chapter 34
Pajamas

Lillian's decision to change into pajamas after dinner had disconcerted Xavier. He had remained sparing in his consent to dinners at her apartment for obvious reasons, moral gray area that it was for two people courting to be alone like that. But after opening statements today, she had insisted on him joining her for macaroni and cheese and some "downtime," as she put it, and he was just grateful she'd had the foresight to put ample amounts of bacon in the macaroni.

Now she sat watching *The Good, The Bad, and The Ugly*, in pink flannel pajamas, and Xavier sat with Miles Bakker's 302 forms in his lap, reviewing the Blue Tide, L.L.C., client's prior statements made to Lillian and another agent. Greedy fool. Bakker had known exactly what was going on with the Brysons, knew it from the very beginning, knew it when he bought his confounded boat—yacht—from Nils Bryson two years ago, knew it when he named the tasteless thing *Bad Investment*. Bad investment, indeed. In exchange for Bakker agreeing to testify against the Brysons, Xavier had let Bakker off with a hefty restitution order, a $250,000 fine for his company, a bill for the cost of prosecuting him (Xavier relished that provision in section 7201), and five years of probation. Bakker would take the stand after Lillian tomorrow.

"*Mea femina*, wouldn't you like to look over any notes?" Xavier set his papers aside and reached for his glass of water on the cheap, assemble-at-home end table beside Lillian's secondhand couch.

Lillian paused the movie. "Honey, what for? I'm ready to go. I'm literally bursting with Bryson-fraud details. I could tell you anything about those men, Monique Arthurton, Miles Bakker, the other partners Nick Giannakopoulos and Lloyd Roberts, anyone. Try me."

She squeezed a throw pillow to her chest, studied the ceiling.

"Nils Bryson," she told the ceiling plaster, "received a C- at Rollins College in Classics 305: Socrates and Sophistry. Viggo and Monique took out an Illinois marriage license twenty-seven days before she tried to kill herself. They never used it and it expired. Grant Bryson was enrolled in senior kindergarten, whatever that is, at the Latin School of Chicago for four months before Viggo withdrew him and began homeschooling him. Government exhibits 96 through 148 are examples of return-of-premium riders from SK and N, Incorporated, a Federation of St. Christopher and Nevis corporation that returned to the Blue Tide, L.L.C., and Gray Hill, L.L.C., clients the majority of the monies paid in insurance premiums to those companies after those clients made certain tax-deductible donations to SK and N's cause of coral-reef conservation in the Caribbean Basin. The tax-deductible nature of these donations arose through another shell entity organized as SK and N, L.L.C., under the laws of the State of Florida and tax exempt under title 26, section 501(c)(3) of the U.S. Code as an educational entity, its alleged educational mission being that of a focus on marine conservation. SK and N, L.L.C.,'s twenty-eight-page IRS Form 1023 application for recognition of exemption comprises government exhibit 152, exhibit 151 being SK and N, Inc.,'s affidavit of records custodian Monique Arthurton."

She dropped her gaze to meet Xavier's eyes.

"I'm ready," she repeated.

Chapter 35
Captain

Miles Bakker took the witness stand looking like a man who owned a Porsche Cayenne and strip malls from Detroit to Green Bay. He wore a double-breasted navy suit and had a rosy pate with a fringe of blond curls hanging on for dear life. Xavier Charles started out with the basics: an introduction that included Bakker spelling his name for the court reporter and a disclosure of the very favorable plea agreement Bakker had reached with the government in his own case, an agreement that came in exchange for Bakker's testimony against Viggo and Nils.

Devlin glanced at Nils. She had gotten him out of the Armani, thank goodness. He sat to her left in a J.C. Penney's suit she'd picked up for him before trial but which he'd initially set aside in favor of an Armani Viggo had given him. Viggo sat to Nils's left, still in Italian silk. Irene, to her client's left, at the end of the defense table, hadn't had any luck making Viggo more relatable to the jury. Apparently, Viggo had told her Armani *was* dressing down. Devlin pitied her colleague. Irene hadn't met Grant, didn't know personally the one thing that made Viggo worth saving from himself.

Bakker began rattling off the details of the insurance policies he'd purchased from Blue Tide, L.L.C. Charles's questions led the testimony right down the path Special Agent Lillian Carter had just finished blazing through the forest of government exhibits. Carter had served as the government's first witness and had laid the groundwork for the case. Devlin had to admit: the woman knew the evidence. Neither Devlin nor Irene had wasted much time cross-examining her.

Devlin hadn't bothered bringing up the agent's improprieties on St. Kitts or her threats about essentially kidnapping Grant and turning him over to Monique Arthurton if Nils didn't cooperate with the out-of-jurisdiction arrest. Devlin figured it was her legal presence (even if it was still with a suspended license then) that had kept the kid out of the St. Kitts judicial system. Raising any of those issues would have resulted in an angry sidebar conference with Judge Montgomery and a lot of jury speculation. Not worth the risks.

"Now, Mr. Bakker, could you tell us who sold you these insurance products?" Xavier Charles seemed to spend a lot of time making eye contact with individual jurors.

"Initially, I worked with an agent named Jocelyn Kennedy. She sold me each of the policies I bought." Miles Bakker had his hands resting on the wooden lip of the jury box, his arms floating high, making him look stiff, uncomfortable.

I'd be uncomfortable, too, up there.

Devlin thanked herself for the after-lunch espresso she'd had and which was keeping her alert now in the chilly courtroom.

"All right," Charles glanced at the jury box, "Mr. Bakker, but besides Ms. Kennedy, did you work with anyone else at Blue Tide, L.L.C.?"

"Well, yeah." Despite the courtroom's low temperature, Bakker was growing pinker. And moister. "I mean, most of the real business I did with them was with Viggo Bryson."

Xavier Charles let several beats slide by, pretending to shuffle through his notes. Devlin turned her head away from the jury and Judge Montgomery and rolled her eyes.

"So, Mr. Bakker, you had direct contact with defendant Viggo Bryson?" Xavier flipped a page of notepad.

"Viggo and I have known each other for years," Bakker replied. "We've done business together for years."

"And can you identify Viggo Bryson for us here today in the courtroom?" Xavier gestured toward the defense table.

Bakker lifted a hand toward Viggo. "Viggo Bryson is sitting there beside his attorney and his brother. In the gray suit."

"Let the record reflect that Mr. Bakker has identified one of the defendants as Viggo Bryson." Charles set his legal pad down and stepped away from the attorney podium. "Now, Mr. Bakker, you just mentioned Viggo Bryson's brother. Could you give us this brother's name and identify him for us?"

"Um, yeah. Nils Bryson is Viggo's brother. He's sitting there between Viggo and his own attorney, wearing the tan suit." Bakker again gestured toward the defense table.

After announcing what the record should reflect, Charles asked Bakker, "Now, Mr. Bakker, how do you know Nils Bryson?"

"Well, really, I know him through Viggo, but I also know him because I like boats and Nils is a yacht broker."

Devlin cringed inside. The word yacht kept popping up, dripping an uncomfortable unction of wealth, privilege, and entitlement over the Brysons and—Devlin could smell it—alienating these jurors in their discount cardigans and Faded Glory khakis.

"Tell us more about that." Xavier sounded like an evil fox in an animated kid's movie.

"Well," Bakker glanced at the jurors, like he was perhaps getting more comfortable on his perch, "a couple years ago, I bought a Hatteras from Nils."

"Mr. Bakker, I'm going to stop you for a second. Could you tell me what a Hatteras is? I'm afraid I've never had the privilege of being a yachtsman." Xavier managed to look humble in his smugness.

Devlin wanted to spring up, wanted to scream objection, wanted to punch Xavier Charles in that pursed kisser. But she also wanted to make that remark die, not sear it into juror brains by making a scene.

"A Hatteras is a type of boat." Bakker sounded like maybe he realized what he was doing to Nils and Viggo, sounded reluctant now. "It's a brand of boat I bought from Nils Bryson. And when I say bought from him, I mean he was the salesman. It wasn't his boat. I didn't really buy it *from* him." The *from* sprawled out over the room.

"Now," Charles was back at the podium, leaning over it, "did Nils Bryson do anything else for you with regard to this Hatteras yacht?"

"He captained it for me from Fort Lauderdale to Corpus Christi." Bakker paused, like he was remembering. "And I think he brought it from Corpus up to Galveston for me, too."

"All right, so let me make sure I'm clear here. Did you buy the boat using Nils Bryson as a broker? And then he drove the boat from Florida to Texas for you as well?"

"Yes, that's correct. Could I get some water? I feel like I'm going to sound really hoarse in a minute. The air in here is really dry." Bakker fidgeted, drummed fingers on the witness-stand rail, looked from side to side.

"Of course, of course." Charles turned from the podium and pulled a Styrofoam cup from a short stack on the prosecution's table, filled it from a plastic carafe sitting in front of Special Agent Lillian Carter.

The agent smiled at Charles like he was more than her dictatorial boss, a weird combination of admiration and something that made Devlin feel slightly dirty. Were they like *a thing*? Had the couple-act on the dock in St. Kitts been more than an act? Ew.

Bakker accepted the cup and took a long sip. "Thanks," he said, setting the cup down on the edge of the witness stand. "Now?"

"Yes," Charles stepped back around to his podium, "you were telling us how Nils Bryson drove your Hatteras yacht for you. Now, how much did you pay Nils Bryson to drive the yacht for you?"

Objection: asshole. Couldn't asshole be grounds to sustain an objection?

Bakker's eyes flickered.

Devlin inhaled, knowing what was coming and dreading how it was going to feel, going to smell, for the jury.

"I— I didn't pay him." Bakker glanced toward Nils, and Devlin fancied an apology in the quick look.

"Wait, Mr. Bakker, you didn't pay Nils Bryson to drive this Hatteras boat from Fort Lauderdale, Florida, all the way across the Gulf of Mexico to Corpus Christi, Texas? How long a trip is that?"

Bakker faltered. "I'm not sure how long a trip it is. I think it took Nils and the crew a couple weeks. They— they didn't go across the Gulf. They came up the intracoastal waterway."

"So Nils Bryson, out of the kindness of his heart, took a few weeks off work to drive your boat from Florida to Texas?" Charles scratched his head.

You missed your calling, Mr. Theatrics.

Devlin glanced past the brothers to Irene, who'd had her head down for most of the circus and was scratching out likely meaningless notes now.

"Well, he said it was part of the sale," Bakker mustered. "He earns commission on the sale of boats, and when I asked about a captain to bring her—bring the boat—over to Texas, he said he'd take care of it. I guess I figured it was like a perk for buying from him or because we knew each other socially." His eyes danced from Nils to

Viggo to Charles, and even to Judge Montgomery, and then back to Charles. "You know?"

"No, I'm afraid I don't know, Mr. Bakker. I've never gotten to buy a boat," Xavier responded.

Devlin was on her feet. "Objection, Your Honor! I think we can all see what Mr. Charles is doing here, and it's just irrelevant and argumentative."

Judge Montgomery sighed, looked from Devlin to Xavier Charles over the top of her glasses. "Sustained. Mr. Charles?"

Xavier Charles's heavy frame bowed up. "I understand, Your Honor." He returned to Bakker. "Now, Mr. Bakker, are you aware that Viggo Bryson gave Nils Bryson a check shortly after you purchased the boat and then purchased an insurance policy from your Blue Tide agent Jocelyn Kennedy? Could this have been Viggo paying Nils to deliver your boat for you?"

"Objection, Your Honor." Devlin sighed, shook her head. She could do theatrics, too. "Calls for speculation and hearsay."

"Your Honor." Charles shot a dark-eyed look at Devlin. She met it, didn't blink. "Mr. Bakker has testified he has a significant social history with Viggo Bryson. He could certainly know whether Viggo Bryson paid Nils Bryson to bring his boat over from Florida."

"Overruled." Judge Montgomery pushed her glasses up the bridge of her nose.

Devlin couldn't stop herself from sniffing. She descended into her chair, met Nils's eyes. At least they had light in them, giving her a brief sense of relief. His eyes had been so dull for so long.

"Mr. Bakker," Charles returned to his witness, "did Viggo pay Nils to deliver your boat for you?"

Bakker shifted in the witness chair, the look of discomfort having returned. "He may have said something about that."

"Who may have said what?" Charles's tone had an edge, and Devlin wondered if the jurors heard it.

"Um, well, Nils, I think, well, you know, it's been a while, but I think maybe Nils mentioned for me not to worry, that as long as I paid for provisions, we were all set."

"All set?" Charles's eyebrows had risen.

"I guess Viggo was giving him some money to make the trip, so he told me not to worry about anything and to just stock the boat up with provisions." Bakker's eyes had started flitting from face to face again. "I bought a bunch of good cuts of meat and a couple bottles of Blood Oath bourbon. Good stuff, you know?"

"No, again, I'm afraid I'm not a bourbon man."

Devlin stood.

Judge Montgomery leaned forward.

Xavier Charles stepped back, lifted his notepad. "Moving on."

And he did move on, leading Bakker through Bakker's purchase of a Blue Tide insurance policy soon after he had bought the boat, Bakker's donation of $15,000 to SK and N, Inc., through the Florida, L.L.C., and his tax deduction for that, and the return of monies amounting to close to the total of the Blue Tide premiums, a return which came through SK and N, Inc. The only thing Devlin could do on cross-examination was confirm that Bakker did not know the details of Viggo's payment to Nils, and bring up a loan Bakker had made to SK and N, Inc., in the amount of $12,000 for some sort of inflatable rubber boat. Or so Viggo had told Irene, and so Bakker was willing to testify to on cross-examination.

Bakker affirmed that he could not trace the payment of monies from SK and N, Inc., back to his purchase of the Blue Tide insurance policy. And Devlin succeeded in bringing out that Bakker never discussed his donation to SK and N, Inc., or the return of the alleged premium payments, with Viggo or Nils. Bakker explained that the sales agent Jocelyn Kennedy had put him in touch with a woman named Monique Arthurton simply because Mr. Bakker was an avid lover of the ocean, and it was through Ms. Arthurton that he made the donation to the coral-reef clean-up efforts in the Caribbean, and ultimately received a significant amount of money that may have related to his Blue Tide premium payments.

When Devlin sat down and announced "no further questions," she noticed dark, heavy ink lines splashed across Viggo's legal pad. Line after line of GRANT ran across the page. When he caught her eye on the pad, the smile Viggo mustered at his brother's elbow looked sad and his eyes almost teary.

Chapter 36

No Further Questions

Devlin Winters made Xavier think of a female Dean Moriarty: a feckless, likely drunken, ne'er-do-well. She had just enough Moriarty-like charisma to dupe the Illinois Bar into returning her license, and now she wanted to stand against him in his district's courtroom? Xavier had always despised Kerouac's drivel.

This morning, that woman sat at the defense table with her worthless client, and with that paper tiger who was her colleague, and with Viggo the Despicable . . . sat wearing a prosaic suit in a color between tan and something like peach. The best Xavier could say about her was that her skirt went past her knees.

"Counsel, what am I seeing today?" Judge Montgomery still had the jury in its assembly room while she questioned the attorneys about the day's schedule.

"Your Honor," Xavier rose to his feet to reply, "the government will be opening with Ms. Monique Arthurton this morning. She is the CEO of SK and N, Incorporated, if you can refer to a shell corporation as having a CEO."

"Your Honor," Irene Stockton stood and interrupted him, "the government is making some very inappropriate remarks in this case, and while I understand the jury is out, I must still object to these remarks here with you. We still have motions for judgments of acquittal coming, and this poisoning of the waters is troubling."

A motion for a judgment of acquittal? My dear Irene, a remark about a shell corporation is the least of your worries.

"Your Honor," Xavier interjected, "we can move on. I will tame my tongue. My apologies."

Judge Montgomery gave him an indulgent look and a shake of her head. He'd sat next to her at a recent Federal Bar Association luncheon, and while he couldn't say they had had a truly pleasant chat, she'd talked to him about her Persian Longhair named Figaro, and he'd told her about the boys and their preference for tuna-in-oil on their dry food.

The Strumpet Winters made an exasperated sound.

I've gotten to you, have I?

Xavier fought back a smile.

The Brysons smelled of desperation and defeat, quite literally. Even on the prosecution side of the aisle, Xavier could smell the odor of incarceration, perspiration, and inadequate hygiene facilities. Italian silk and wool couldn't civilize an almost-convict. Xavier had to admit: Nils Bryson's decision to tone down his attire had been a disappointment, though no amount of cheap polyester and rayon was going to endear Nils Bryson to honest men and women.

"My case agent Lillian Carter is outside now with the witness, Your Honor. The government is ready to proceed at your leisure." Xavier glanced toward the courtroom doors.

In accordance with a pre-trial order, all the witnesses save the defendants and Special Agent Carter were to be sequestered outside the courtroom, so as to prevent any tainting of their testimony. Xavier had left Lillian in the elevator lobby outside the courtroom to give Niqi one last pep talk and to remind her not to get anywhere near her "history," as Lillian was referring to it, with counsel for the prosecution. That was the only wildcard: Niqi's caprice and that wretched "history."

"Mr. Charles, how long do you anticipate this witness taking?" Judge Montgomery adjusted the sleeves of her robe.

"Your Honor, the government remains quite cognizant of the value of this court's time, and we understand that this trial has already taken up a week. We believe Ms. Arthurton will take the better part of today, but she is the government's final witness, and we do not anticipate direct examination lasting more than the day." Xavier leaned forward over his stack of a Westlaw code book, a copy of the Federal Rules of Evidence, and a laminated sheet of evidentiary objections he anticipated and citations to case law he had ready in answer.

"All right." Judge Montgomery glanced at her case manager. "Then that means we can wrap up cross-examination of Ms. Arthurton tomorrow and immediately move onto the defense's case?"

"Yes, Your Honor." Xavier rested his fingertips on the evidentiary-rules book.

"You Honor," Irene Stockton addressed the bench, "we would still need time for motions after the close of the government's case. Mr. Bryson—my Mr. Bryson, Mr. Viggo Bryson—anticipates moving this court for a judgment of acquittal once the government rests."

Devlin Winters rose. "Your Honor, Mr. Nils Bryson anticipates a similar motion."

Again with the judgments of acquittal, ladies? Please. Menelaus has a better chance of starving to death than your clients have of walking out of here without chains on. Oh, that reminds me: I should get the boys something celebratory for dinner tonight.

"All right. Okay." Judge Montgomery made a note. "I'll bear that in mind. Well, if there's nothing further, let's go ahead and bring in the jury, and Mr. Charles, you may bring in your final witness."

Even amid the flurry of people rising and the jury entering and the judge addressing the room, Monique's presence radiated, dominating the courtroom, filling it. Lillian had talked her into an elegant, long, navy dress with a modest neckline, a string of pearls, and mid-height heels. Her hair sat atop her head in a glossy knot, and from somewhere, a superfluous pair of tortoiseshell glasses had appeared on her nose. She strode through the gallery, through the low, swinging gate, through the sanctuary of counsel tables, and arranged herself on the witness-stand-turned-throne.

"Your Honor, the government calls Monique Arthurton as its final witness." Xavier shuddered. Why did his voice sound that way? Why did his stomach feel that way?

Pull yourself together, man.

Across the aisle, Viggo Bryson stared ahead, some shadow coloring his face, some glint in his eyes Xavier didn't want to name. Viggo was not smiling, but something in the set of his jaw made Xavier set his own.

"Ms. Arthurton, thank you for testifying this morning. Would you introduce yourself and spell your name for the court reporter?"

Monique's smile glowed, her lips crimson. When she'd finished speaking, she sat back, removed the unnecessary glasses, and cast her eyes across the jury box.

Xavier unrolled the preliminaries, led her through an explanation of the immunity agreement and then presented her with the Brysons. "Ms. Arthurton, how do you know the defendants Viggo and Nils Bryson?"

Niqi's eyes felt hard, flinty and sharp, behind the lenses she'd replaced on her face, as they met his own bespectacled gaze. Xavier couldn't stop himself from glancing toward Viggo again. Something didn't feel right. Beneath Xavier's sensible pinstriped suit coat and cotton shirt, the hairs on his forearms rose.

"Mr. Charles, I have known Viggo Bryson since I was seventeen years old. I am the mother of his son and I have a business relationship with him through our companies." Her eyelashes looked a mile long and like black concertina wire as they wound over the tortoiseshell.

He slowed his questioning, wary, but let her explain that she'd met Viggo when Viggo had been traveling and visited St. Kitts. She told the jury about becoming pregnant at age seventeen and following Viggo to the United States because she felt ashamed of her circumstances. She confessed she'd never married the man and admitted she had tried to kill herself by overdosing on pills when she was twenty-one.

"I was young, the mother of a three-year-old boy, living in a foreign country." She blinked several times. "I was overwhelmed." A tear.

Xavier watched himself lift a box of tissues off the prosecution table, watched himself step across the carpet to the witness stand, watched himself hand the box to this woman he'd once adored above all else. The room grew impossibly large and quiet, and filled with that invisible, thick substance that slowed movement.

"You recovered from this attempt to take your own life, of course." He waded through the density back to his lectern.

"I did," she said. "I spent a few weeks at a psychiatric facility outside Chicago. Tried to get my feet back under me. When I returned to the home I'd been sharing with Viggo, he told me he was going to have my parental rights terminated, that I was an unfit mother." She pressed a tissue to her eyes. "He told me that if I did not contest his having sole custody of our son he would set me up in business, give me a charity I could run back in St. Kitts. He told me I could see our son periodically and that he would make sure his wealthy clients donated to my charity. So I— well, I— I accepted his offer and SK and N, Inc., was born. I've run it ever since, and indeed, Viggo has always pushed his clients my way, encouraging them to donate and support our cause of keeping the maritime environment of the Caribbean Basin healthy."

She dabbed at her nose.

Xavier scanned his notes, flipped sheets of paper, tried to inhale in the still-too-heavy atmosphere.

He could feel some devilish energy, smell some corruption, coming from the defense table and turned, against his will, to see Viggo still staring ahead, face impassive but also—

"Now, Ms. Arthurton," he jerked himself back to face the witness stand, "can you tell us a little about SK and N, Inc.?"

"SK and N stands for St. Kitts and Nevis." She turned to the jury and flashed a shy grin. "I know—not very creative."

Two or three jurors offered comforting fake laughter.

"We fight to save our endangered and irreplaceable coral reefs." She shifted away from the jury box and her eyes burrowed into Xavier's, pierced his gaze and penetrated his skull. "And it's all completely legitimate."

Xavier forced himself to cough to avoid something worse, covered his mouth with the back of his right hand. "Of course, Ms. Arthurton, you know you're not on trial here. You know the protections you enjoy with the immunity agreement we've discussed. And we can understand your sincerity in your concern for your island's natural habitat, but let's discuss SK and N's relationship with Blue Tide, L.L.C. What was that relationship?"

"It was a business relationship. You see," she shifted in her seat once again to face the jurors, "after I returned to the island and settled into the charitable work Viggo set me up with, I found I liked life. I loved what I had. Viggo and I cultivated a strong, even caring, working relationship. Blue Tide, L.L.C., sells insurance products to American companies. Many of these companies are owned by people who care about our natural environment, who love the oceans, and who want to support maritime conservation. After these business people purchase insurance from Blue Tide, Blue Tide employees often recommend tax-deductible donations to SK and N."

She stopped, looked up at Judge Montgomery. "Your Honor, do you think I might have a glass of water?"

"Of course." Judge Montgomery's tone betrayed nothing to Xavier.

His gaze swam. He turned from the podium and went through the motions he'd become accustomed to with this trial's thirsty witnesses, reaching for a cup from the prosecution table, but this time, he fumbled to remove one from the stack. Lillian touched his hand, lifted the cup for him, filled it, handed it to him. Her eyes seemed to be trying to say something to him, but he couldn't read them, couldn't hear anything, couldn't stop the room from spinning.

"Is it your testimony today then that SK and N has a business relationship with Blue Tide, L.L.C.?" Xavier gripped the podium's edges, tried to will the thing to stop floating up and away from him.

"Absolutely." Her eyes drove further into him.

He knew no one could see it, but he felt like he should pluck a tissue from the box in front of her and try to wipe away the blood he knew must be running down his face. Wipe away— He brushed at his right eye.

"Now, Ms. Arthurton, isn't it true that you told Special Agent Lillian Carter that Blue Tide, L.L.C., is—"

"Objection!" Devlin Winter's voice broke through the thickness. "Leading and hearsay."

"Sustained." Judge Montgomery sounded so very far away.

"Let me rephrase." Xavier inhaled.

Saints. . . . Saints and angels. . . . St. Thomas Aquinas, please. . . .

"Did you tell Special Agent Carter something different when you met with her last week?" Xavier swiped at his eyes again.

"I did, Mr. Charles. I lied to Agent Carter."

Did everyone in the room gasp or was he imagining that whooshing sound?

Xavier tried to resist the urge, but he failed and turned to look over his shoulder at Agent Carter. Should he continue? Could he salvage anything? Was she shaking her head? Was Lillian shaking her head? Did that mean she wanted him to end this? They still had the documents, didn't they? Didn't they still have the paper to prove it all?

Xavier flipped his notes together and lifted his legal pad from the lectern. "No further questions, Your Honor."

Chapter 37
A Soul Gambled and Lost and Kept

S hit! Did that just happen? Devlin glanced past Nils and Viggo to Irene. Irene was looking back at her. *What do I do with this?*

Devlin shot a look at Judge Montgomery, who wore a grim expression as she glared down at Monique Arthurton in her faux-good-girl dress on the witness stand.

Do I ask for a recess? Should I let Irene take the lead here? We've still got a long paper trail we have to beat. But we have a witness! A real witness! Who can help us!

She tapped her legal pad with the back end of her pen. She didn't dare look at Nils . . . or even Viggo. But she could feel the air vibrating off them. The smell of the men's custody suddenly dissipated and she felt some sort of power shivering over the table.

First things first: the return-of-premium riders. If she's gonna get on the stand and say she lied, she must have an answer for those damned riders.

Devlin caught Irene's eye again. "I've got this," she mouthed.

Irene nodded.

Devlin grabbed her legal pad and stood (pen still in her hand) and marched to the podium, looked straight at Monique Arthurton. "Well, Ms. Arthurton, I'm Devlin Winters. I represent Mr. Nils Bryson in this matter, and

I'm sure you're aware that you have everyone's attention right now."

Nervous laughter from somewhere, maybe from jurors or a marshal.

"I'm sure I do." Monique didn't blink.

"Let's start with your last statement. You just told the court that you lied to the government, correct?" Devlin didn't blink either.

"Correct. I lied to Special Agent Lillian Carter last week, and before that, as well, when she was questioning me about SK and N's relationship with Blue Tide, L.L.C. Contrary to what I told Ms. Carter, the two companies have a legitimate business relationship and many of Blue Tide's clients are also donors and investors for SK and N."

"Why did you lie to Special Agent Carter?" Devlin rubbed a palm on the smooth finish of the lectern's rail.

"Ms. Winters, I tried to kill myself six years ago. I've been in in-patient psychiatric care. I don't always . . . use good judgment." She finally lowered her eyes and seemed to be smoothing her skirt. "I can be . . . overly . . . volatile."

Devlin waited.

"And I still get angry at Viggo sometimes." Monique returned her gaze to Devlin. "And with this trial looming, at times, I'm afraid I have wanted to see Viggo hang. He's done some not-nice things." She inhaled. "But he didn't commit any sort of business or financial fraud, and I can't come in here now and say he did." An exhale and another long inhale.

What are you hiding, Monique Arthurton?

Something glided across the woman's face, something Devlin couldn't place.

"If anyone has committed fraud, it's me." Monique's expression didn't change. Her eyes didn't move. She didn't falter. "I've committed some accounting . . . indiscretions, perhaps . . . over the years."

Despite doubts about the timing, the cadence, of it, Devlin shot a glance at the jury box. Every head sat high and alert and facing Monique.

"Can you elaborate on these financial indiscretions for us?" Behind her, Devlin heard papers shuffling, likely Special Agent Carter and AUSA Charles scrambling for a documentary mop to clean up the mess.

"There are days I regret what I did in giving up my son," Monique replied. "There are days I resent things Viggo did to me. Honestly," she turned to the jury, "there are times I feel he cheated me." She sighed and returned her face to Devlin. "So over the years, I've cheated Blue Tide, L.L.C., a little."

Devlin resisted the urge to push the woman forward.

"I'm guessing," Monique continued on her own, "Xavier Charles has already presented everyone with the return-of-premium riders for some of the Blue Tide, L.L.C., insurance policies? Those are the big pieces to this puzzle, correct? With Blue Tide clients supposedly getting their premium payments back, but not telling the IRS about those refunds, and claiming the premium payments as tax deductions?"

Why are you asking me that? I'm questioning you.

Devlin let a beat pass and received her reward for it.

"I wrote up those riders." Monique lifted her chin. "Mr. Charles, I'm sure, got them from clients I gave them to. Viggo doesn't know about them. Or he didn't. I guess he knows now."

Glancing over at Viggo, at the file-cluttered defense table, Devlin saw something reach across the space between them, between Monique and Viggo, saw a strange energy pass between the pair.

"Look like the innocent flower, but be the serpent under 't."

"A selection of those riders have been admitted into evidence as the government's exhibits 96 through 148," Devlin offered, watching.

"Yes, well, I designed and wrote up those riders . . . with the help of a friend on the island," Monique resumed. "Viggo's parents are very wealthy, and they've helped him get a good start in life, and now he's very wealthy, and his companies do very well. And," she paused, fidgeted with the empty foam water cup on the edge of the witness stand, "I figured I deserved to benefit a little more given what I'd been through with Viggo and given that he had custody of Grant."

"So you wrote up these return-of-premium riders to benefit SK and N, and thus yourself, financially?" Devlin knew she was breaking every rule to be walking out on ice this thin, but everything was rolling in her favor—in Nils's favor.

"Yes, you see, I handle certain accounts between Blue Tide and SK and N. These accounts are in my son's name— Grant Bryson's name—although Viggo and I both have access to them. They were to be for his benefit, my son's benefit, in the event something happened to Viggo . . . or me, I suppose." She turned, foam cup in hand, to face the jurors. "Viggo never checked those accounts." Her eyes returned to Devlin, her nails seeming to scratch into the soft foam in her hands. "And I would return SK and N investor loan monies with funds from these accounts, essentially with Blue Tide funds, so SK and N investors could claim tax deductions for monies they gave me. It made it look like the monies were donations, rather than loans. I didn't repay loans per se. I returned Blue Tide premium payments, even though Blue Tide knew nothing of these refunds. The riders and the payments went directly to clients, who had no reason to question getting money like that back, though I suppose they may have wondered. But they obviously didn't want to look a gift horse in the mouth. So they didn't. And I knew they wouldn't. They aren't people to question money. The whole thing kept my donors happy and it created a benefit for Blue Tide clients, so they would tell others to buy Blue Tide policies and would keep buying those policies themselves. And Blue Tide, in turn, kept recommending people donate to and invest in SK and N, without knowing I was using its money to pay my investors. It required a certain amount of discretion from the clients, but they behaved."

The faintest trace of a smile.

"I had another account in Grant's name, for his true benefit," she mumured.

This doesn't sound right at all.

Devlin wished she could stop the action and get a cup of water like the witnesses had done so many times in this godawful trial. More papers rustled behind her, now likely Charles and his agent-flavor-of-the-day exchanging notes about why Special Agent Ms. Thing had failed to find the accounts in the kid's name. Devlin glanced over at Irene. The other attorney was watching her. Nils was watching her, too. Viggo was watching Monique. With that look on his face . . . like—

Come on, girl, it's reasonable doubt. Keep going. You just need reasonable doubt.

"So, you fabricated these return-of-premium riders and essentially misappropriated Blue Tide funds to pay your SK and N investors, is that correct?" A spot on Devlin's back had started to itch. She desperately wished she could scratch it.

"Exactly," Monique answered. "I have the loan documents from my investors here." She ducked down on the witness stand and popped back up with a stack of papers she must have retrieved from her purse. "I knew if there were any problems I wouldn't need to worry in St. Kitts. It would all be on Blue Tide, and I was," she rolled her eyes upward, "ambivalent? Maybe that's the word I want? Ambivalent? About Viggo getting in trouble. Sometimes, I hated him. Sometimes, I—"

Aw, fuck, stay on track. Do not—

"Sometimes, I still love him." Monique seemed to refocus with an exhale. "Anyway, I couldn't let him go to prison now for something he didn't know about."

Okay, that wasn't so bad.

"Your Honor," Devlin turned her attention to the bench, "might we call a brief recess for the jury and discuss these loan documents? I'd like to question Ms. Arthurton about them, but I think we should determine their admissibility here first."

Judge Montgomery seemed to be hovering over her bench on a thunderhead of upset. "Ms. Winters, that is a sound idea. Ladies and gentlemen of the jury, please make yourselves comfortable in the jury-assembly room. We will be as expeditious as possible. Thank you for your patience."

All rose for the jury to file out. And more than buttocks dropped when Judge Montgomery announced, "Be seated."

"Counsel," she glowered from the bench, "I understand that witnesses can go south. I understand the difficulties of arranging testimony and evidence, but I have to say I am more than disappointed right now. We essentially have a witness up here confessing to any number of crimes, including offenses related to false statements, and some sort of immunity agreement shielding her, and a stack of documents that may or may not be admissible—I see multiple evidentiary and custodial issues related to these records—and a jury whose time I will not waste. What is going on?"

Xavier Charles rose, hand on those suit-coat buttons.

I pity the fool . . . and I hope he won't be able to say that about me in a second.

Behind Devlin, who couldn't figure out how to retreat from the podium gracefully, it sounded like Irene Stockton was searching for something in the sea of defense files.

"Your Honor," Charles started, "I understand that this trial has taken an unorthodox turn, but I don't think we are without options here."

"Of course we have options, Mr. Charles." Judge Montgomery sniffed. "I just want to hear what you think they are."

Was Xavier Charles turning red? His Little Miss Agent certainly was. Why was he looking at Monique Arthurton like that? Like he wanted to cry or something.

"At this time, Your Honor, the government objects to admission of any documents from Ms. Arthurton." Charles dropped his head, but then seemed to get himself back together. "Given Ms. Arthurton's admission of making false statements to Special Agent Carter, the government sees serious issues in terms of the reliability of any of her documents, even business documents, under Rule 803. That rule still requires a showing of trustworthiness," he fumbled through his books and papers, "under subsection," another second of fumbling, "(6)(E) . . . under 803(6)(E) . . . we still need a showing of trustworthiness." He sounded gasp-y or shuddery when he inhaled. "And we just don't have that here."

"I'm inclined to agree with you, Mr. Charles, but what does the defense say?" The judge's glasses had slipped down her nose, as Devlin had come to expect of them. Perhaps the federal government gives all its judges slippery glasses. Devlin had seen so many black robes topped by low-riding lenses.

Devlin blinked, tried to clear her head, inhaled. Finally, she could turn to the defense table without awkwardness. Nils had a hand over his mouth, like he was hiding a smile. His eyes were alive and they caught hers, and she debated grabbing his hand and running from the courtroom to Irene's Jeep in the parking ramp next to the courthouse. They could jump on Interstate 196 and jet south and get back to the boats and untie from the docks and be gone. Gone.

Gone. The one who needed to get gone was Monique Arthurton. Devlin looked over Nils's and Viggo's heads to the gallery. Investigator Mya Reynolds sat in the second row behind the defense, at the ready for Irene in case they needed any last-minute documents, copies, help—help like getting Monique the fuck out of here. Devlin would keep Monique on the stand a bit longer and then that woman needed to get out of the courtroom and over to Gerald R. Ford International and out of the country before Mr. Xavier Charles could exact his revenge with a charge that her immunity agreement could not rebuff. Devlin saw Mya see her, saw Mya give the tiniest nod. Okay, that problem was as taken care of as it was going to get. Mya could get Monique away ASAP.

"Your Honor," Devlin turned back to the bench, "the defense would like to take a look at these documents for a moment before we speak on the issue."

"Please do." Judge Montgomery waved down at Monique and her offending stack of copies.

Irene rose to approach the witness stand with Devlin, and as she did so, Devlin allowed herself another glance at the defense table. Viggo looked impervious and ethereal, a weird mix of too many things, his perfect carved features revealing nothing and everything simultaneously—a man about to cheat the Devil out of getting his soul, the soul he'd gambled and lost fair and square.

At the witness stand, Devlin and Irene pulled papers off Monique's stack. The loan documents memorialized loans to SK and N, Inc., from numerous familiar players: Miles Bakker (including the $12,000 he'd testified about, which allegedly went to buy the rubber boat), Nick Giannakopoulos (a Blue Tide partner who, the document said, had lent SK and N $28,000 for refurbishing a dive boat), and numerous Blue Tide policy purchasers. The loan amounts were not, relatively speaking, large, but the number of loans was extensive, with total amounts adding up quickly, adding up to mean that stealing money from Blue Tide to repay the loans could make sense.

Devlin leaned into Irene. Irene nodded, handed the paper she was reading to Devlin, communicating an assent to let Devlin address the matter.

"Your Honor," Devlin tilted her head up toward Judge Montgomery, "the defense sees these documents as admissible under Rule 803(6). It's clear these are business records. But if the court does not admit them, we would at least ask leave to question Ms. Arthurton about them. We'd argue a due-process right to present a complete defense and that the details of these documents are part of that defense."

Monique Arthurton had picked up the foam water cup again and was now pushing it back and forth along the edge of the witness box, so it made a squeaking sound.

"May I?" The judge leaned down, hand extended.

"Of course." Devlin passed a few copies of the loan documents up.

Then Judge Montgomery was ruling that Devlin could question Monique about the documents, even if the documents themselves couldn't come into evidence, and the jury was coming back in, and Devlin was going through the loans with Monique and discussing Monique's repayment of the monies with misappropriated Blue Tide funds. And Monique was explaining again how she hadn't minded exposing Viggo to the risk of prosecution because of the way he'd treated her at times, and because she thought she might get her son back if he went to prison. And then she was dabbing at her eyes, contrite and apologetic for her insouciance toward him. She was sashaying off the witness stand and into Mya Reynolds's sphere and out of court . . . with Xavier Charles standing and telling the glass top of the prosecution table that the government rested, and Devlin wasn't quite sure why he didn't scramble to get Judge Montgomery to let him pick another last witness to put on the stand, just for appearances' sake. Special Agent Lillian Carter was patting his shoulder blade and whispering in his ear, and Irene was at the podium saying something about motions. And the jury was shuffling out.

"Rule 29 . . . Viggo Bryson . . . moves this Honorable Court for a judgment of acquittal . . . no reasonable juror could . . . insufficient evidence to sustain a conviction. . . ." Irene's words weren't all clear, but Devlin was on her feet.

"Mr. Nils Bryson . . . joins this motion . . . insufficient evidence. . . ."

Judge Montgomery was saying something about a short recess, about ruling on these motions after a short recess.

And Devlin was standing beside Irene and Nils and Viggo at their littered table and watching Assistant U.S. Attorney Xavier Charles and Special Agent Lillian Carter virtually sprint out of the courtroom, the door swinging shut behind them, three pieces of paper falling from the prosecution table in their airy wake.

Chapter 38

Putus: (Noun) Sweetheart; the One Who Has Stood the Test of Time

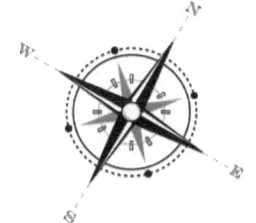

As soon as the courtroom door swung shut behind him, Xavier broke into a run. He sprinted past the elevators, around a corner, and down a colorless hall to a stairwell. He heard Lillian's high heels clicking behind him for several steps, but the stairwell door cut their sound off when the door clanged shut behind him. He took the stairs two and three at a time, his feet pounding, his steps echoing up and down the empty column of stairs and landings, his knees jarred as he launched himself off each step. He burst into the federal building's lobby and sprinted past the court security officers in their glass cage, one of them shouting something like "Hey, Mr. Charles, you okay?" as he charged through the glass doors and into a quiet, chill, ozone-smelling mist devoid of human movement.

They would have headed to the parking garage. That sham investigator, hussy Reynolds woman would have parked in the garage under the city clerk's building. He'd seen her put an arm around Niqi, hustle her out of the courtroom. He turned left and sprinted toward Ottawa

Avenue and the underground garage's entrance, his lungs heaving, his ankles aching now from the pounding in unsupportive Oxfords. Did he want to arrest her? Shake her and demand an explanation? Drop to the concrete and scream?

His glasses misting over and robbing him of clarity, he turned right down the vehicle lane into the garage, running, slipping on the slick oily-wet pavement, and there it was: a line of perhaps half a dozen cars sitting behind a red Accord with a stove-in back door and an elderly man fumbling in the driver's seat in front of the payment booth. Directly behind this obstruction sat an older-model green SUV with two women in the front seats.

Niqi.

"Niqi!" he screamed. Her name echoed off the concrete walls, flung the indignities he'd suffered back in his face. He gasped in oil and exhaust and dark, underground spaces that never receive fresh air, and shouted again. "Niqi!"

He reached the SUV's passenger-side window and pounded a fist against it. "I'm not going to arrest you. Please. Just tell me why. Why, Niqi? Why? Why?"

Now his palm was pounding the window.

The Accord hadn't moved.

Xavier dropped back, bent his trembling legs, rested his hands on his knees and panted like the dog he realized he'd become. A kicked, humiliated, despised dog.

The passenger window descended.

"*Putus*," she cooed. "I'm sorry. I really am." She'd disposed of the fake glasses and her eyes danced limpid and clear.

He lifted his head, but not his body, looked over the top of his wet lenses. "You lied to save him, Niqi? I could arrest you right now. You risked all that for him? Why? Just tell me why."

He dropped his head again, pulled his dripping glasses off, sucked in fumes, shuddered. "Why him, Niqi?"

The Accord pulled forward. Mya Reynolds pointed toward the exit and put the car into gear, coasting ahead. Xavier straightened, slashed his glasses across his damp trousers, replaced the streaked lenses on his face, and limped after the SUV. Reynold's left hand reached out the window with a credit card in it, and the woman in the booth conducted her transaction. Then Reynold's left hand appeared again, taking the card back and waving for Xavier to follow them. He hobbled up the exit ramp behind the vehicle, watched it turn right onto Ottawa Avenue, put on its flashers, and pull over, idling. As he reached Niqi's window again, Xavier pulled a handkerchief from his pocket and wiped mist and cold perspiration from his face, then pulled his glasses off for another futile try at drying them.

Niqi repeated rolling down the window, and met his eyes. "I'm sorry, *putus*, I really am. But I've been in love with Viggo for ten years and I couldn't let you hang him. I just couldn't. I know you don't like him, but he's mine, *putus*. We have an understanding, he and I." She reached an arm out into the damp, dripping air and stroked Xavier's cheek.

The world slowed and he could see things again, even through those droplets on his lenses. The whirling and blurring had ceased. He felt the tingle of his skin beneath her fingers, inhaled long and hard, and jerked back.

"No, Niqi," he whispered.

"Oh, *putus*," she murmured, resetting her hand, placing it atop his on the SUV's windowsill. "So good. Always so good. So much better than Viggo. I know that. I do, *putus*. I know you're the better man."

He shut his eyes, bowed his head, tried to get some damn air into his lungs. His hand remained beneath hers on the car's window sill. "Just tell me this: why didn't you tell the court about us? You could have ruined me."

"Oh, my sweet, good *putus*, I never wanted to ruin you."

With his free hand, he mopped the handkerchief under his frames and over his eyes. "He beat you, Niqi."

"Beat me?" The surprise in her voice startled him, made him open his eyes and study her.

"Yeah," he said, "in Chicago. Lillian got police reports from domestic calls when you lived on the south side."

"In that awful place on Kimbark? Oh, *putus*, he never beat me. I told the police. I explained it all. I like it rough, *putus*, and sometimes, it got out of hand." She patted his hand beneath hers. "This got out of hand, too. We didn't plan for you to be involved. We planned for a prosecution, you know. Just in case. We knew someone would give me immunity to testify, especially if I made a scene on all those recorded calls and writing letters and emails to everybody. People would believe it all and they'd come looking. But we never expected it to be you." She lifted her hand from his and touched his cheek again.

He couldn't have explained why he didn't pull away as he had before.

"I never thought it would be you on the other end," she breathed, paused. "But that just made it easier."

And he could never have explained how her lips felt on his or how it felt to stand eviscerated in mist turning to drizzle, watching taillights recede through beads of fog on glass, with high heels clicking up the sidewalk behind him.

Chapter 39

Monterrey

W e did it, Sean, man! We did it!" Devlin crowed into her phone.

Despite the inhospitable forty-degree drizzle outside Irene's Jeep Grand Cherokee, the world felt champagne-toast warm. Beside her on the backseat, Nils had his head in his hands, his shoulders shuddering softly, almost imperceptibly.

"Honey, I knew you could do it." Sean's voice crackled on the line, the parking garage likely interfering with the cell signal.

"Here, *hamo*, I'll call you in a little bit. Reception's bad and we still gotta figure some things out." Devlin didn't have a chance to end the call before it simply dropped.

Irene was holding a credit card out her window for the woman in the parking garage's payment booth. "So where are we going?" she asked, turning to Viggo beside her in the passenger seat and then to Devlin and Nils in the back. "I mean, besides the airport. You boys are getting out of here before Mr. Charles has a chance to indict you for something else." She and Devlin had just retrieved the men's passports from the U.S. Probation Office with the judgments of acquittal Judge Montgomery had granted. Devlin's own passport lay at the bottom of her purse.

Viggo tapped at his phone. Nils lifted his head, his eyes red and bleary yet also bright. "You saved my ass, D. Winters." He faced her. "That was too fucking close." His voice broke.

"Hey, don't thank me. Thank Judge Montgomery, your crooked-ass brother, and that crazy baby-momma. How long you been planning this, Viggo?" She glanced at Viggo in the rearview mirror. His stare didn't lift from his screen.

She made a show of shrugging. "Well, good job duping old Uncle Sam." She offered three languid, sarcastic, hollow claps of acerbic applause.

"Good to finally get to talk freely to you again, too, Devlin Winters," he snarled.

"Oh, Viggo, you haven't changed." On the other side of the window, the drizzle had firmed itself up into real rain and had proceeded to start soaking downtown Grand Rapids.

"Neither have you."

"Well, on that loving note, book yourselves some tickets, boys," Irene reiterated. "I'm dropping you at the airport in twenty minutes. Seriously." Her gaze reached the backseat through the rearview mirror. "Unless you think it would be better to fly out of O'Hare, in which case I'll turn around and head west."

With the engine warming up, the vehicle's cabin had started to get physically warm, to match the warmth of the relief washing through it. Without any music on, the heater's whir filled the space. Viggo tapped at his phone. Irene braked at a red light. In front of the Jeep's hood, two figures crossed the street: a petite woman in rain-soiled heels held an umbrella over a dark man in a pinstriped suit, who was dragging behind him over the crosswalk a handcart of files in see-through plastic crates. Despite the umbrella, Assistant United States Attorney Xavier Charles's pant legs and the back of his suit coat were soaked. As they passed the Jeep, Special Agent Lillian

Carter placed her free hand on Xavier's upper arm, leaned into him.

The pair reached the far curb, the light turned green, and Irene accelerated. Viggo raised his focus from his phone. "There's a nonstop to Monterrey, Mexico, at 7:30 p.m. out of Detroit. We can make that. And that's close for Grant." His eyes darted to the mirror and hit Devlin. "Devlin, can your friend who has Grant get him on a plane to Monterrey tonight? I'll make it worth his while. I want to see my son. Now."

The only thing that's happening now *is you confirming your status as asshole of the year, Viggo.*

Devlin satisfied herself with an eye roll. "Lemme call him."

She brought Sean up on her display of recent calls. "*Hamo,*" she said after two rings, "can you have Grant on a plane to Monterrey, Mexico, today? Here—" she elbowed Nils, whispering to him, "Pull up flights out of Houston to Monterrey."

She watched Nils bring up a travel app. Tap, tap— "Okay, there's a 6:25 nonstop on United out of IAH tonight," she said into the phone. "Could you get him up there? We'll book it right now. Tell him it's a quick flight. An hour and a half. And he'll get to see his dad tonight. His dad'll be there—"

She looked from Nils to Viggo. "When does Viggo land?"

"Nine," Viggo grumbled.

"His dad will be there an hour after he lands," she said into the line to Sean. "Yeah, I'll miss him, too. He's a cool little soldier. . . . Yeah, you're the best, man. . . . His dad will PayPal you some cash right now. . . . Take it, man. I mean it. If you don't take it, I will. . . . Okay, thanks, man. I'll see you soon. Yeah, I'll tell him. Peace." She tapped the phone, turned to Nils. "Sean says congrats."

Slipping the phone into her purse, she leaned forward toward Viggo. "You can PayPal twenty grand to Sean dot

Tofilau at Southern Coast Yachts dot com right now. For his troubles. That's S-E-A-N dot T-O-F-I-L-A-U."

Viggo's head jerked up.

"He's had your kid for how many months now? That's cheap." She shook her head when Viggo narrowed his eyes. "Nope. You just weaseled your way out of eight years in Club Fed. You don't get to say no." She sat back.

"I'll get whatever you guys have at the jail," Irene broke in. "I'll send it to wherever you want whenever you want it." She shot a look at Devlin in the mirror. "Sister, if you want to take off now, you might as well, too. I can ship your stuff from my place. Hey, in case this craziness doesn't let up, I'll thank you now. I'll try a case with you again any time you want."

Devlin snorted. "Yeah . . . no. Thanks, but I'm not trying any more cases any time soon." She hadn't told Irene more than had been necessary in the circumstances, but she figured the other attorney had mobilized the google elves and likely knew at least some of the sordid details of her implosion at Sondheim Baker.

Irene must have liked peaches. Devlin inhaled, slid her shoulders away from her ears where they'd glued themselves, and drew in a deep breath of synthetic peach and the reasserted scent of unwashed Brysons.

"You need a shower." She poked Nils.

"Don't I know it." He dropped his head back on the rest.

"Okay, last call for Gerald R. Ford International," Irene announced, changing lanes to pass a laboring truck.

"No, I've bought the Monterrey tickets already," Viggo said. "I booked mine and Grant's." He didn't bother glancing in the mirror or turning. "Devlin, I sent your friend the money and the flight details."

"Nice job, Viggo." She shut her eyes.

"What about Nils?" Irene's voice had risen an octave.

"Where do you want to go?" Nils whispered, sliding his hand over Devlin's.

She opened her eyes and considered the sullen rain. "Viggo's treat? Someplace warm and expensive." She squeezed Nils's hand.

"Fuck that." Viggo whipped around. "I'm not paying for her. I'll pay for you, brother," the word came out more than angry, "but I am not paying for her."

"Viggo," Nils sat up, glared, "you just about got me convicted of a federal crime and sentenced to prison. To fucking federal prison, Viggo! You are paying for me to get the fuck out of here. And you're paying for her to come with me. It is very truly the least you can do."

Viggo untwisted, faced the windshield wipers.

Yeah, and if you don't, I'm sure I can set up a nice proffer meeting between Nils and Mr. AUSA Charles to arrange a madness-ending plea to probation for Nils and some new charges for you, jackass.

"So where do you want to go, beautiful?" Nils suddenly looked just as he had fifteen years ago: eager, sincere, adoring.

Devlin doodled in the condensation on the window. "Someplace warm," she repeated.

"I've got a six o'clock nonstop to Paris," Nils said a moment later. "It's not tropical, but. . . . What do you think, Irene? Can we make that?"

Irene seemed to glance at the dashboard's clock. "Yeah, we can make it. It'll be close, but you don't have any bags to check." She chuckled. "Devlin, honey, if you dig around in the back, there's a bag of emergency tire-changing clothes, some jeans and a pair of sneakers. There's also a bag of books I was going to donate. Help yourself. You'll at least have flat shoes and something to read."

"Thanks, you really are a good person." Devlin unlatched her seatbelt and twisted onto her knees to rifle through the Jeep's cargo space behind the seat.

"Well, if you're going to make me pay for all that," Viggo started, "why don't you stay at my place on Lake Zurich once you've had enough of France? I'll ship Grant over to you. He loves Switzerland. He can show you around. He'll get a real kick out of that. And that'll give me a chance to go over to St. Kitts and—" He paused.

Devlin unwound herself, dragging a duffle bag over the back of the seat.

Viggo's tone and what she could see of his face when she looked up gave Devlin a weird impression of derision, affection, and school-boy giddiness. "And thank Monique," he finished. "I don't take Grant over there. To the island."

Nils caught Devlin's eye. She looked away.

Fucking Viggo.

***

Irene was right. She got them to DFW in time to make the Paris flight. Devlin had slipped into the tennis shoes, and she made it through the airport without any complaints from her feet. Nils had insisted on first-class tickets, and now as Devlin sat with a glass of in-flight champagne in her hand—real champagne, not some sparkling knock off—everything inside her broke loose: the self-doubt, the anxiety, the fear, the loneliness, the demons. She set her wine on the seat's table and rolled to the side, burying her face in Nils's J.C. Penney-suited arm. Tears. Tears and gasps and letting go and getting back.

She had him back.

She had him back and Grant was safe and Sean had made almost half a year's brokering commissions and she was secure on a plane bound for Europe. With him.

They'd lay low for a while. Xavier Charles would get a nice hot shower and a hearty dinner and move on. Heck, maybe he could end up happily-ever-after with Little Miss Agent. The two of them would find new fish for their fryer.

She and Nils would stay out of Dodge for a while, and when things had blown over, they would go home.

Home.

To the boats. To the water and the quiet. Home. With him.

Yes, she had him back.

After all these years.

She had Nils Bryson back.

"Your brother's an asshole." She raised her head from his sleeve. How many times had she told him that?

"I'm not arguing with you there." Nils rubbed his other hand across his face. "And for the record, I really had no idea. Maybe I didn't ask enough questions, but I wasn't into his shit."

Devlin scooted up, laid her head on his shoulder. "Doesn't matter now."

Charcoal sky filled the plane's window and the thrill of something new on the horizon swept away courtrooms and jail meetings and immunity agreements and even old wooden boats in need of deck caulking. The venturi tube had released them and the world was slowing down again . . . finally. Devlin smiled up at Nils. He slipped a hand beneath her chin, tilted her lips up toward his.

"It's good to have you back, Devlin Winters."

Sneak Peek
The Cult of Mammon

Devlin Winters, Xavier Charles, and the Bryson brothers return in 2021 in *The Cult of Mammon*. Enjoy a first-look peek here.

Chapter 1
Plumeria

The perfume of plumeria blossoms drifted in the window slits of the bunker-cum-chapel. The blooms outside the windows gave off the scent of sunrise on the Big Island, of Hawaii's paradise . . . an odor of hope for a new day in which to honor the Creator. Sister Esther had long ago come to associate Bishop Timothy with the smell of the pink and white and yellow flowers that covered the trees lining the walk to the chapel and which helped turn her thoughts to heaven as she came and went for prayer.

At the altar, Bishop Timothy called for his brothers and sisters to bow their heads and sit silent. Esther studied his steady, unemotional features as he shut his eyes and dropped his chin. On the two occasions he had come to her, things had not gone well. Perhaps it had been her nervousness, the anxiety of it all. But one of the evenings had given her Daniel and for that she was grateful to God. She lowered her eyes, shut them. She would express her gratitude now. Bishop Timothy had told the congregation to tell God their hearts. She would tell Jesus about her babies, about how Ruth was learning to fish and Micah had started to sleep all night, about how happy her three darlings made her when she got to be with them.

Jesus already knew all these things, of course, but there was still value in telling him herself. Bishop Timothy said that often: There's value in telling omniscient God the good things and the trials in our lives. Esther wrapped an index finger in a white organdy bonnet tie. Jesus knew of her disobedience, too. Sister Martha had told her just yesterday that her two dozen years of life ought to have given her more wisdom and forbearance. Jesus knew she lacked these things. She smoothed her calico dress over her lap. Esther never meant to be disobedient. It was just that the things Bishop Timothy and Brother Amos told her to say on the phone and over email didn't always seem like things Jesus would want her saying to people, especially to people like those she had to call.

Lord, I'm ever so grateful for all the children, but especially for those I've borne, for Daniel and Ruth and Micah. Daniel brought me three moana kali *and a* kahala *to cook up after the brothers all went over to Punalu`u on Thursday. He loves spearfishing, Lord. He really does. And he's gotten so good at it, and the goatfish tasted so nice, and I couldn't believe he got that big jack, too! Brother Isaiah told me my Daniel had to have help getting it out of the water. It was huge, Lord! Huge!*

I'm sorry for what I said to Sister Martha about feeling ashamed of making the calls and sending all the emails. I'm sorry I felt so disobedient toward our mission, Lord. I know Bishop Timothy is a very smart man and I know he's leading us closer to Thee, Lord. I know that the calls and the messages make it possible for us to serve Thee as we do.

She paused, casting about in her mind for exactly what she wanted to say.

But I do pray for all those poor souls, Lord. The souls that will suffer eternal damnation, the souls that don't know Thy Truth, Lord. It makes me sad, Lord, that some are old and sick and so many are so lonely, but Thy will be done, Lord. Thy will be done.

The flower scent had strengthened in the warmth of the morning. With a deep inhale, she resolved to be less willful, to be more obedient in the coming week, to make the calls cheerfully, faithfully, and to work for the ark of the colony. As she lifted her eyes to Bishop Timothy, his head still bowed in prayer, she felt a fresh dedication to her purpose to serve her brethren and her Lord and to be a mother to all the children of the colony. Tomorrow, she would make twelve calls, secure eight promises of contributions, and win over two personal apostolic supporters. She could do all that. She would do all that. God willing, of course.

Chapter 2
Rule 35

Yes, yes. Let's move this along.

Devlin Winters tapped the top of her desk with an impatient index finger, sighed.

"This call is from a federal correctional institution," the recorded voice on the other end of the line droned.

Devlin wished she could fast forward through the preliminary announcements of the incoming prison call, and despite the recorded message, one could argue the call hadn't originated from a true federal correctional institution. The call was from FCI Oxford's satellite camp. Viggo Bryson had gotten convicted of wire fraud, not slinging eight balls. A little crack, a little heroin—then he might have ended up at the actual FCI.

Wonder if he ever did dabble in the old rock candy? Devlin picked up a pen and drummed the desk with it.

"Hello?" Viggo's voice finally flowed through the phone ether.

Even at his sentencing hearing, staring down Judge Hadley Elizabeth Montgomery, whom he'd had the extreme misfortune to draw as his presiding judge (and who very definitely remembered granting Viggo a motion for a judgment of acquittal in a tax-fraud case a year earlier), Viggo Bryson had maintained an appearance of equanimity, his perfect Nordic features and mesmerizing eyes floating above the Italian silk of a bespoke suit. Till the end, he had remained, in Devlin's informed opinion, a demon stalking souls. She wondered if prison jumpsuits and the strain of trying to protect commissary purchases from theft had changed him.

"Good morning, Viggo Bryson." Devlin set the pen aside and pulled a legal pad from a drawer. "And how is FCI Oxford's satellite camp? Are they treating you well?"

"It's delightful. It's all fucking delightful. How's Grant?"

In the thirty-ish years Devlin had known Viggo, he hadn't changed much. And at thirty-six years old, Devlin had given up on the thought of being a mom . . . until Grant Bryson had come into her life and shown her the wonders of a world seen through eleven-year-old eyes.

"He's good," she replied. "He likes his tutor. His test scores are fantastic. He's learning to sail dinghies on his own." She smiled to herself. "But he complains about putting on sunblock now."

Viggo sighed into the phone. Devlin could hear in the breath the brokenness of a dad who missed his only son. That was the one redeeming thing about Viggo: He truly did love his kid.

"I need a Rule 35, so I can get the fuck out of here and get back to him," Viggo said.

Devlin wrote RULE 35 in large letters across the top of her yellow pad's first page. Oh, that would be fun—calling up Assistant United States Attorney Xavier Charles and asking him to file a motion with the court to reduce Viggo's sentence under Rule 35 of the federal criminal rules because Viggo was now eager to switch sides and wanted to give the government information to prosecute new bad guys. Yep, that would be a real joy.

"What've you got?" Devlin paused, putting thoughts of Grant out of her mind and settling into business. "Do I need to come visit you?" She didn't want to talk on the recorded prison line about anything that could earn Viggo a royal ass kicking inside. Although she wouldn't have minded seeing Viggo get an ass kicking, she didn't want him to get a prison-level one.

"Yes. I'd love to see you. And Wisconsin is lovely this time of year. Why, it hasn't been above twenty-five degrees since Christmas. Come on up."

On Devlin's list of things to do in January, visiting a federal prison camp in the middle of Wisconsin did not appear. "Call your folks for money?" she asked. Viggo's parents, parents her boyfriend Nils Bryson shared, had doled out funds to support Viggo's intermittent legal needs since Viggo's conviction, and they'd sent Nils money to support Grant's homeschooling and hobbies since Nils had become Grant's guardian.

"Have Nils call them," Viggo replied.

"Will do. How does your schedule look in two weeks?" Devlin couldn't resist baiting Viggo.

"I think I can squeeze your visit in." Viggo sounded unamused.

Devlin discussed a few more things with her client-slash-childhood-nemesis, urged him, sincerely, to stay safe, and then signed off. She swiveled in her chair and gazed out her office window to the South Shore Harbor Marina across the parking lot from her building, to Clear Lake, and toward the Kemah bridge under which flowed the channel from Clear Lake to Galveston Bay. Even in January, the Gulf Coast could be warm, and today the temperature had hit sixty-five by lunch. It had probably gotten even warmer up the highway in Houston. Being right on the coast helped with keeping things temperate.

Somewhere out of sight on the bay, Nils had a 2006-model Nordhavn forty-foot trawler out on a sea trial. If the old girl handled well and behaved, Nils would basically have the massive boat sold by the end of the day, and he'd have the yacht brokerage's paperwork for the deal wrapped up completely in less than a week. Devlin hoped she and Nils would be celebrating on their own trawler tonight, perhaps enjoying something special for dinner on the thirty-six-foot-long mahogany Grand Banks they called home with Grant.

Pho maybe? I could stop and pick up some pho.

She started thinking about spring rolls.

"How's it going out there?" she texted into her cell phone. "Feel like pho tonight?" She hadn't heard from Nils in a couple hours. Hopefully, that was a good sign. Hopefully, he was engrossed with his boat-buying clients and they were all enjoying their ride on that beautiful Nordhavn.

Nils wasn't going to welcome the task of calling his parents to tap them for Viggo-defense money, but so be it. Devlin still didn't understand her significant other's loyalty to a cheating brother who'd managed to get himself indicted on multiple occasions and convicted once—and who'd left a now eleven-year-old son parentless. Nor could she quite understand how she'd come to be playing mother to the kid . . . and maybe even, once in a while, enjoying that role.

Yeah, pho for sure. Grant loved pho. The kid'd be psyched to have a big old bowl of pork and noodles.

Her phone vibrated.

"Pho sounds good. Everything with this boat is going good. We should be heading in soon." Nils's text ended in a little pink heart.

She'd explain to him later the issue of calling his folks. Viggo wouldn't have reached out or suggested trying to get a sentence reduction through his efforts to snitch unless he had good, solid info. Even without a lengthy criminal history, Viggo now knew how the game was played, knew that the only hope of a sentence reduction would be detailed (and plentiful) information against someone the government could prosecute. He wasn't going to waste his parents' money (and limited feelings of support) or risk someone inside figuring out his desire to snitch, and administering penance, unless he had something of value to say to the government.

Devlin darkened the screen with its pink heart and turned back to her computer to find a ticket to Milwaukee and a rental car to get her to FCI Oxford's camp.

Acknowledgments

When the manuscript for *The Venturi Effect* pulled out of the harbor and started on a course toward publication, it did so with a stellar crew aboard, including Robyn Kelly, Katelin Cummins, a few special ITW members, and a couple lawyers (they know who they are) who've fought losing battles at counsel table with the utmost valor. This book needed these middies and mates on her deck to get where she is. So thank you all for your tricks at the helm. To SLM, "here's to going places . . . slowly . . . always." And to Elizabeth Sterling and Karen Jennings, you both rock.

About Sage Webb

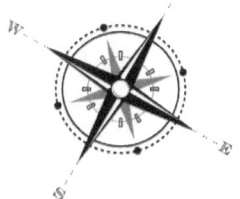

Sage Webb practiced criminal defense for over a decade before turning to fiction. She is the author of two novels (*The Unremarkable Circumstances of Inmate 17656-090*, released by Martin Brown in 2018, and *The Venturi Effect*, launched by Stoneman House Press in 2020) and a short-story collection (*Love & Other Misunderstandings*, from Stoneman House Press in 2020). Her literary awards include second place in the 2017 Hackney Literary Awards and Red City Review's 2018 Best Debut Novel Prize. In 2020, Michigan's Mackinac State Historic Parks named her an artist in residence. She belongs to International Thriller Writers and PEN America, and lives with her husband, a ship's cat, and a boat dog on a sailboat in Galveston Bay.

You can find her at www.sagewebb.com.

If you enjoy her work, she always appreciates a review on your favorite book-purchasing platform.

Stoneman House Press

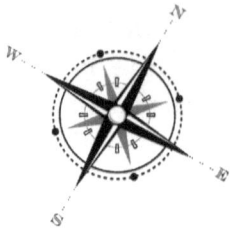

Stoneman House Press, L.L.C., prides itself on publishing books that blur boundaries, raise questions, and keep readers up late into the night: intelligent, original, and unexpected. Find your next favorite read at www.stonemanhouse.com.

Read Local

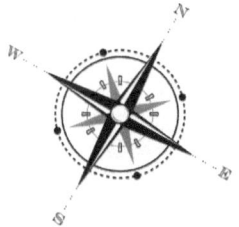

Read Local® offers an online community dedicated to the works of independent presses, with book reviews and thoughts on things literary, local, small, and funky. Join the discussion at www.readlocalbooks.org.